'Here…' Jake offered her a hand. "Take it easy, though. That foot won't want much weight on it.'

He held out his other hand as Ellie started to rise, and a heartbeat later she found herself on her feet, holding both Jake's hands.

And he wasn't letting go.

She couldn't even look away from his face. From a gaze that was holding hers with a look that made the rest of the world cease to exist. Everything seemed to coalesce. Surviving the rescue, finding their way to shelter, being rescued herself and the bond that had grown and grown today, thanks to Jake's heroism. So many powerful emotions.

His face was so close. She only had to lean a little and tilt her face up and her lips would meet his.

And, dear Lord… She could feel it happening, and no alarm bells were going to halt the process, no matter how loudly they tried to sound.

She was so close now, she could feel his breath on her lips, and her eyes were drifting shut in anticipation of a kiss she wanted more than anything she could remember wanting in her life.

The sharp crackle of static from behind made her jump.

'Medic One, do you read? Ellie…are you there?"

THE LOGAN TWINS

Twin brothers Ben and Jake Logan have each become wildly successful in their own way, and yet they're still getting into trouble together. This time it's when they're sailing off the coast of New Zealand and a massive storm hits, tearing their boat apart…

But the Logan brothers aren't beaten easily. And when they find themselves on very different shores neither of them knows just how much the storm—and the strong, irresistible women they meet in the heart of it—will change their lives for ever!

Read both books in this amazing duet!

NINE MONTHS TO CHANGE HIS LIFE
by Marion Lennox, June 2014

THE MAVERICK MILLIONAIRE
by Alison Roberts, July 2014

THE MAVERICK MILLIONAIRE

BY
ALISON ROBERTS

Published in Great Britain 2014
by Mills & Boon, an imprint of Harlequin (UK) Limited,
Eton House, 18-24 Paradise Road, Richmond, Surrey, TW9 1SR

© 2014 Alison Roberts

ISBN: 978-0-263-91298-2

23-0714

Harlequin (UK) Limited's policy is to use papers that are natural, renewable and recyclable products and made from wood grown in sustainable forests. The logging and manufacturing processes conform to the legal environmental regulations of the country of origin.

Printed and bound in Spain
by Blackprint CPI, Barcelona

Alison Roberts lives in Christchurch, New Zealand, and has written over sixty novels for Mills & Boon® Medical Romance™. This is her debut for the Cherish™ line. As a qualified paramedic she has personal experience of the drama and emotion to be found in the world of medical professionals, and loves to weave stories with this rich background—especially when they can have a happy ending.

When Alison is not writing you'll find her indulging her passion for dancing or spending time with her friends (including Molly the dog) and her daughter Becky, who has grown up to become a brilliant artist. She also loves to travel, hates housework, and considers it a triumph when the flowers outnumber the weeds in her garden.

CHAPTER ONE

No. NOT THIS TIME.

Jacob Logan was not going to let his older brother assume responsibility for sorting out the mess they were in. Not again. Not when he was still living with the scars from the last time.

Ben was only the elder by twenty minutes and their parents were long gone. Why was it so incredibly hard to break free of the beliefs that had got embedded in childhood?

But this time it was *his* turn to take charge. Yet again, it had been his bright idea that had got them into this mess and it was a doozy. So bad that it might be the only chance he ever got to look out for Ben for once.

This was more terrifying than the aftermath of their father's wrath for any childhood scrape they'd got themselves into. Worse than being in the thick of it in Afghanistan after they'd both escaped by running off to join the army. This was a life or death battle and the odds were getting higher that they weren't going to win.

There'd been warnings of possible gale-force winds yesterday and they'd known they could be in for a rough day, but nothing like this. Cyclone Lila had changed course unexpectedly overnight and dawn had broken to mountainous seas, vicious winds and driving rain that almost obliterated

visibility. The strong currents made the waves unpredictable, and the fleet of yachts in this Ultraswift-Round-the-
World Challenge had been caught, isolated and exposed in
the open seas east of New Zealand's north island.

They'd caught some of the stats on the radio before the
yacht had finally been crushed under a mountain of water
and they'd had to battle to get into their bubble of a life
raft. Winds of sixty-five knots and gusts up to two hundred miles per hour. Waves that towered up to fifty feet,
dwarfing even the biggest boats. Competitors were retir-
ing from the race in droves and turning to flee, but not
fast enough. Boats had overturned. Masts had snapped
like matchsticks. Mayday calls had gone out for men over-
board. Bodies had already been recovered. There were
search aircrafts out all over the place, but the only thing
the Logan brothers had heard over the sound of an angry
sea had been the deep drone of an air force Orion and that
had been a long way away.

The Southern Ocean was a big place when you were
in trouble.

They'd been drifting for hours now. Being tossed like
a cork in the huge seas.

By some miracle, they'd finally been spotted. A helicopter was overhead and a crewman was being lowered
on a winch. Jake could see the spare harness dangling.

One harness.

No way could more than one person get winched up
at a time.

And he wasn't going to go first. This weather was getting worse by the minute. What if the chopper *couldn't*
get back?

'You're going first,' he yelled over the noise of the sea
and the chopper.

'Like hell I am. You're going first.'

'No way. You're hurt. I can wait.'

The guy on the end of the winch had disappeared behind the crest of a wave. Caught by the water, he was dragged through and suddenly swinging dangerously closer. Someone was putting their life on the line here to rescue them.

'Look—it was my stupid idea to do this. I get to decide who goes first.'

He didn't have to say it out loud. It was his fault. Things that turned to custard had always been his fault.

Desperation had him yelling loud enough to be really heard as the rescuer got close enough to shove a harness into his hands. He pushed it towards Ben. Tried to wrestle him into it.

'Just do it, Ben. Put the harness on. You're going first.'

But Ben pushed it back. Tried to force Jake's arm into a loop.

'Someone's got to look out for you,' he yelled.

'I'll be okay. I can wait.'

'This isn't make-believe, Jake. It's not some blockbuster *movie.*'

'You think I don't know that?'

'I know you don't. You wouldn't know reality if it bit you. You're just like Mom.'

And now it was their rescuer yelling. Helping Ben to shove the harness onto Jake.

'There's no time for this.' Good grief…was this person risking life and limb to rescue them *female?*

Jake was still resisting. Still focused on his brother. 'What the hell is that supposed to mean?'

'She couldn't face reality. Why do you think she killed herself?'

That did it. The shock took the fight out of Jake. The harness was snapped into place.

'The chopper's full,' the rescuer yelled at Ben. 'We'll

come back for you as soon as we can.' She was clipping heavy-duty carabiners together and she put her face close to Jake's. 'Put your arms around me and hang on. Just hang on.'

He had no choice. A dip into icy water and then they were being dragged into the air. Spinning. He could see the bright orange life raft getting smaller and smaller, but he could still see his twin brother's face looking up at him. The shock of his words was morphing into something even worse. Maybe he'd never find out the truth even if he wanted to go there.

Dear God… *Ben*…

This shouldn't be happening. Would he ever see his brother again?

CHAPTER TWO

THE WAVE WAS the last straw.

As though the adrenaline rush of the last few hours was simply being washed away as Eleanor Sutton faced the immediate prospect of drowning.

How much adrenaline could one person produce, anyway? She'd been burning it as fuel for hours as the rescue helicopter crew she was a part of had played a pivotal role in dealing with the stricken yachts caught up in this approaching storm. They'd pulled two people from a life raft and found another victim who'd had nothing more than his life jacket as protection as he rode the enormous swells of this angry sea.

Then they'd plucked a badly injured seaman from the deck of a yacht that was limping out of trouble with the broken mast that had been responsible for the crewman's head injuries. The chopper was full. Overfull, in fact, which was why Ellie had been left dangling on the winch line until they could either juggle space or get to a spot on land.

With her vantage point of being so much closer to the water as the chopper had bucketed through the menacing shark-gray sky, she'd been the one to spot the bright orange bubble of a life raft as it had crested one of the giant swells and then disappeared again. In the eerie light of a day that was far darker than it should be for the time, it had been all too easy to spot the two pale faces peering up at the potential rescue the helicopter advertised.

The helmet Ellie wore had built in headphones and a microphone that sat almost against her lips. Even in the howl of driving wind and rain and helicopter rotors, it was easy to communicate with both her pilot, Dave, and fellow paramedic, Mike.

'Life raft at nine o'clock. At least two people on board.'

'We can't take any more.' It was Dave who responded. 'We'd be over limit in weight and this wind is picking up.'

There was a warning tone in those casual last words. Dave was a brilliant pilot, but he was already finding it a challenge to fly in these conditions. Some extra weight with the approaching cyclone getting ever closer might be enough to tip the balance and put everybody in even more danger.

But they couldn't leave them behind. The full force of Cyclone Lila wouldn't be felt for a good few hours yet, but they shouldn't still be in the air as it was. All aircraft would be grounded by the time they reached land again. It was highly unlikely that this life raft would be spotted by any other boats and, even if it was, it would be impossible to effect a rescue.

If they didn't do something, they were signing the death warrants of another two people. There had already been too much carnage in this disastrous leg of the Ultraswift-Round-the-World yacht race. At least one death had been confirmed, a lot of serious injuries and there were still people unaccounted for.

'We can get one,' Ellie said desperately. 'He can ride with me on the end of the line. We're so close to land. We can drop him and try going back for the other one.'

There was a moment's silence from above. It was Mike who spoke this time.

'You really want to try that, Ellie?'

Did she? Despite the skin-tight rescue suit she was wearing under her flight suit, Ellie knew she was close to becoming hypothermic. Would her fingers work well enough to manipulate the harness and carabiner clips to attach another person to the winch safely? She was beyond exhaustion now, too, and that old back injury was aching abominably. What if the victim was terrified by this form of transport and struggled? Made them swing dangerously on the end of the line and make a safe landing virtually impossible?

But they all knew there was no choice.

'Let's give it a try, at least,' Ellie said. 'We can do that, can't we?'

And so they did, but Dave was having trouble keeping the chopper level in the buffeting winds, and the mountainous swells of the sea below were impossible to judge. Just as they got close enough to hover near the life raft, the foaming top of a wave reached over Ellie's head and she was suddenly underwater, being dragged through the icy sea like a fish on a line.

And that did it.

She wasn't under the water for very long at all, but it was one of those moments where time seemed to stand still. Where a million thoughts could coalesce into surprising clarity.

Eleanor Sutton was totally over this. She was thirty-two years old and she had a dodgy back. Three years ago this hadn't been the plan of how her life would be. She would be happily married. At home with a gorgeous baby. Working part time, teaching one of the subjects she was so good at. Aeromedical transport or emergency management maybe.

The fact that she could actually remember this so clearly was a death knell. This kind of adrenaline rush had been what had got her through the last three years when that life plan had been blown out of the water so devastatingly. Losing personal priorities due to living for the ultimate challenge of risking her life for others had been the way to move forward.

And it wasn't working any more.

If she could see all this so clearly as she was dragged through the wave and then swinging in clear air again over the life raft, Ellie knew it would never work again. She shouldn't be capable of thinking about anything other than how she was going to harness another body to her own in the teeth of the approaching cyclone and then get them both safely onto land somewhere.

This was it.

The last time she would be doing this.

She might as well make it count.

Unbelievably, the men in the life raft weren't ready to cooperate. Ellie had the harness in her hands. She shoved it towards one of them, holding it up to show where the arm loops were. The harness was taken by one of the men, but he immediately tried to pass it to the other.

'Just do it, Ben. Put the harness on. You're going first.'

But he pushed it back and there was a brief struggle as he tried to force the other man's arm into one of the loops. Too caught up arguing over who got to go first, they were getting nowhere.

'I'll be okay,' one of them was yelling. 'I can wait.'

'This isn't make-believe,' the other yelled back.

Static in her ears made Ellie wince.

'You still on the air?' Dave's voice crackled. 'That radio still working after getting wet?'

'Seems to be.' Ellie put her hand out to stop the life raft

bumping her away. It was dipping into another swell. And the men were still arguing. Good grief—had one just accused the other of being just like his *mother?*

She thought the terrifying dunk into that wave had been the final straw, but this was just too much. Ellie was going a lot further than the extra mile here, making her potentially last job as a rescue helicopter paramedic really count. She shouldn't be doing this and this lack of cooperation was putting them in a lot more danger. Suddenly Ellie was angry.

Angry with herself for endangering everybody involved in the helicopter hovering overhead.

Angry with these men who wanted to save each other instead of themselves.

Angry knowing that she had to face the future without the escape from reality that this job had provided so well for so long.

She was close enough to help shove the harness onto one of the men. To shout at them with all the energy her anger bestowed.

'There's no time for this.'

But they were ignoring her. 'What the hell is that supposed to mean?' one yelled.

There was another painful crackle of static in Ellie's headphones. 'What's going on?' Dave asked in her ear.

'Stand by,' Ellie snapped. She was still angry. Ready to knock some sense into these men, but whatever had been said while Dave had been making contact had changed something. The man she'd been helping to force the harness onto had gone completely still. Thankfully, Ellie's hands were working well enough to snap the clips into place and check that he was safely anchored to the winch line.

'The chopper's full,' she shouted at the other man.

'We'll come back for you as soon as we can.' She clipped the last carabiners together and put her face close to her patient's. 'Put your arms around me and hang on,' she instructed him grimly. 'Just hang on.' She knew they would have been listening to every word from above. Hopefully, they'd think the lack of reassurance she was providing was due to the tension of the situation, not the anger that was still bubbling in her veins like liquid lava.

'Take us up, Dave. Let's get out of here.'

'Ben...'

The despairing howl was whipped from Jacob Logan's lips by the force of the wind as he felt himself pulled both upwards and forwards in a violent swinging movement. It was also drowned by the stinging deluge of a combination of rain and sea spray, made all the more powerful by the increasing speed of the helicopter rotors above.

It was too painful to try and keep his eyes open. Jake squeezed them shut and kept them like that. He tightened his grip around the body attached to his by what he hoped was the super-strong webbing of the harnesses and solid metal clips. There was nothing he could do. However alien it felt, he had no choice but to put his faith in his rescuers and the fact that they knew what they were doing.

Shutting off any glimpse of the outside world confined his impressions more to what was happening internally, but it was impossible to identify a single emotion there.

Fear was certainly there in spades. Terror, more like, especially as they were spinning in sickening circles as the direction of movement changed from going up to going forward, interrupted by drops and jerks that were probably due to the turbulence the aircraft was having to deal with.

There was anger there as well. Not just because he'd

lost the fight over who got rescued first. Jake was angry at everything right now. At whoever had come up with the stupid idea of encouraging people to take their expensive luxury yachts out into dangerous seas and make the prize prestigious enough to make them risk their lives.

At the universe for dropping a cyclone onto precisely this part of the planet at exactly this time.

At fate for ripping him apart from his twin brother. The other half of himself.

But maybe that anger was directed *at* Ben, too. Why had he said such a dreadful thing about their mother? Something so unbelievable—so *huge*—it threatened to rip the brothers apart, not just physically but at a much deeper level. If what he'd said was true and he'd never told *him,* it had the potential to shatter the bond that had been between the men since they'd arrived in this world only twenty minutes apart.

Was life as he knew it about to end, whether or not he survived this dreadful day?

And there was something else in his head. Or his heart. No…this was soul-deep.

Something that echoed from childhood and had to be silenced.

Dealing with it was automatic now. Honed to a talent that had made him an international star as an adult. The ability to imagine the way a different person would handle the situation so that it would all be okay in the end.

To *become* that person for as long as he needed to.

This was a scene from a movie, then. Reality could be distorted. He was a paratrooper. This wasn't a dreadful accident. He was supposed to be here. It wasn't him being rescued, it was a girl. A very beautiful girl.

It was helpful that he knew that this stranger he had his arms wrapped around so firmly was female. Not that she felt exactly small and feminine, but he could work around that.

He'd never had this much trouble throwing the mental switches to step sideways out of reality. A big part of his brain was determined to remind him that this horrible situation was too real to avoid. That even if it was a movie, there'd be a stuntman to do this part because his insurance wouldn't cover taking this kind of a risk. But Jake fought back. If he could believe—and make countless others believe, the way he had done so far in his stellar career— didn't that make it at least a kind of reality?

He was out to save the world. The chopper would land them somewhere and he'd unclip his burden. He'd want to stay with the girl, of course, because he was desperately in love with her, but he'd have to go back into the storm. To risk his life to rescue…not his twin brother, that would be too corny. This was the black moment of the movie and he was the ultimate hero so maybe he was going back to rescue his enemy.

And, suddenly, the escape route that had worked since he'd been old enough to remember threw up a barrier so solid Jake could actually feel himself crashing against it.

Maybe Ben *was* the enemy now.

Even if it hadn't been a success, the effort of trying to catch something in the maelstrom of thoughts and emotions and turn it into something he could cope with had distracted him for however long this nightmare ride had been taking. Time was doing strange things, but it couldn't have been more than a few minutes.

Close to his head, he could hear his rescuer trying to talk to the helicopter pilot. The wind was howling like a wild animal around them and she was having to shout, even though she had a microphone against her lips. As close as he was, Jake couldn't catch every word.

Something about a light. A moon.

Was she kidding?

In even more of a fantasyland than he'd been trying to get into?

'The lighthouse,' Ellie told Dave, her words urgent. 'At five o'clock. It's Half Moon Island.'

'Roger that.' Dave's voice in her ears sounded strained. 'We're heading southeast.'

'No. The beach…'

'What beach?'

'Straight across from Half Moon Island. The end of the spit. Put us down there.'

'What? It's the middle of nowhere.'

'I know it. There's a house…'

It was hard enough to communicate through the external noise and the internal static without trying to explain. This area was Ellie's childhood stamping ground. Her grandfather had been the last lighthouse-keeper on Half Moon Island and the family's beach house was on an isolated part of the coast that looked directly out at the crescent of land they'd all loved.

The history didn't matter. It was the closest part of the mainland they could put her down and she knew they could find shelter. It was close enough, even, for them to drop their first victim and try to go back for the other one.

He still had her in a grip that made it an effort to breathe. An embrace that would have been unacceptably intimate from a stranger in any other situation. His face was close enough to her own to defy any concept of personal space but, curiously, Ellie didn't have any clear idea of what he looked like.

The hair plastered to his head looked like it would be very dark even if it was dry and it was too long for her taste for a man. The jaw was hidden beneath a growth of beard that had to be weeks old and his eyes were screwed shut so tightly they created wrinkles that probably made him look a lot older than he was.

He was big, that much she could tell. Big enough to make Ellie feel small and that was weird. At five feet ten, she had always towered over other women and many men. She'd envied the fragility and femininity of tiny women— until she'd needed to be stronger than ever. That had been when she'd finally appreciated the warrior blood that ran in her veins from generations past.

No man was ever going to make Eleanor Sutton feel small or insignificant again.

She put her mouth close enough to the man's ear to feel the icy touch of his skin.

'We're going to land on the beach. Keep your legs tucked up and let me control the impact.'

Dave did his best to bring them down slowly and Ellie did her best to try and judge the distance between them and the solid ground, but it had never been so difficult. The crashing rolls of surf kept distorting her line of sight and the wind was sending swirls of sand in both horizontal and vertical directions.

'Minus twenty…no…twenty-five…*fifteen*…' This descent was crazy. They were both going to end up with badly broken legs or worse. 'Ten… Slow it down, Dave.'

He must have done his absolute best, but the landing was hard and a stab of pain told Ellie that her ankle had turned despite the protection of her heavy boots. There was no time to do more than register a potentially serious fracture, however. She fell backwards with her patient on top of her and for a split second she was again aware of just how big and solid this man was.

And that she couldn't breathe.

But then they were flipped over and dragged a short distance in the sand. Ellie could feel it scraping the skin on her face like sandpaper. Filling her mouth as her microphone snapped off. The headphones inside her helmet were still working, but she didn't need Dave's urgent orders to know how vital it was that she unhook them both from the winch line before they were dragged any further towards the trees that edged the beach.

Before they both got killed or—worse—the line got tangled and brought the helicopter down.

Somehow she managed it. She threw the hook clear so that it didn't hit her patient as it was retracted and the helicopter gained height. Once she'd unclipped herself from this man, she could get into a clear position and they could lower the line to her again.

But it was taking too much time to unclip him. Her hands were so cold and she was shaking violently from a combination of the cold, pain and the sheer determination to get back and save the other man as quickly as possible.

He was trying to help.

'No,' Ellie shouted, spitting sand. 'Let me do it. You're making it harder.'

His hands fisted beside his face. 'You're going back, aren't you? To get Ben?'

'Yes. Just let me…' Finally, she unclipped the last carabiner and they were separated. Ellie almost fell the instant she tried to put weight on her injured ankle but somehow managed to lurch far enough away from her patient to wave both arms above her head to signal Dave. There was no point in shouting with the microphone long gone, but she did it anyway.

'Bring the line down. I'm ready.' She wouldn't need to worry about her ankle once she was airborne again. It shouldn't make it impossible to get the other man from the life raft.

'Sorry, El. Can't do it.' Dave's voice was clear in her ears. 'Wind's picking up and we've got a status one patient on board under ventilation.'

The helicopter was getting smaller rapidly. Gaining some height and heading down the coast.

'*No...*' Ellie yelled, waving her arms frantically. '*No-o-o...*'

The man was beside her. 'What's going on?' he shouted. 'Where's he going?' He grabbed Ellie's shoulders and it felt like he was making an effort not to shake her until her teeth rattled. 'You've got to go back. For Ben.'

His face was twisted in desperation and Ellie knew her own expression was probably close to a mirror image of it.

'They won't let us. It's too dangerous.'

The man had let her go in order to wave *his* arms now. 'Come *back,*' he yelled. 'I *trusted* you, dammit...'

But the bright red helicopter was vanishing into the darkening skies. Ellie could still hear Dave.

'We've got your GPS coordinates. Someone will come as soon as this weather lifts. Get to some shelter. Your other radio should still work. We'll be in touch.' She could hear in his voice that he was hating leaving her like this. It broke all the unspoken rules that cemented a crew like this together. 'Stay safe, Ellie.'

The helicopter disappeared from view.

For what seemed a long, long time, Ellie and the rescued man simply stood on this isolated, totally deserted stretch of coastline and stared at the menacing cloud cover, dark enough to make the ocean beside them appear black. The foam of the crashing breakers was eerily white.

The man took several steps towards the wild surf. And

then he stopped and let out a howl of despair that made Ellie's spine tingle. He knew he'd lost his friend. The lump in her throat was big enough to be painful.

'I would have gone back,' she yelled above the roar of the wind and surf. 'If they'd let me.'

He came closer in two swift strides. 'I would have *stayed*,' he shouted back at her.

He was angry at *her*? For saving his life?

His words were a little muffled. Maybe she'd heard wrong. Dave was too far away for radio contact now and the communication had been one-sided anyway, thanks to the broken microphone. Ellie undid the chin strap of her helmet and pulled it off. The man was still shouting at her.

'Who gave *you* the right to decide who got rescued first?'

Ellie spat out some more sand. '*You're* lucky to be alive,' she informed him furiously. 'And if we don't find any shelter soon we'll probably both die of hypothermia and then all this would have been for nothing.' He wasn't the only one who could be unreasonably angry. 'Who gave *you* the right to put *my* life in danger?'

She didn't wait to see what effect her words might have had. Ellie turned and tried to pick out a landmark. She had to turn back and try to catch a glimpse of Half Moon Island to get any idea of which direction they needed to go. The lighthouse was well to her left so they had to go north. The beach house was in a direct line with the point of the island where the lighthouse was.

Confident now, Ellie set off up the beach. She didn't look to see whether he was following her. He could have his autonomy back as far as she was concerned. If he wanted to stay out here and die because she hadn't been able to rescue his friend then maybe that was *his* choice. She was going to survive if she could, thank you very much.

Except that she didn't get more than two steps away. Her ankle collapsed beneath her and she went down with a shout of anguish.

'What's the matter?' The man was crouched over her in an instant. 'What's happened?'

'It's my ankle. I… It might be broken.'

If he was swearing, the words were quiet enough for the wind to censor them. Ellie felt herself being picked up as if she weighed no more than one of those tiny women she'd once mistakenly envied. Now she was cradled in the arms of this big man as if she was a helpless child.

'Which way?' The words were as grim as the face of the man who uttered them.

'North.' Ellie pointed. 'About a mile.'

A gust of wind, vicious enough to make this solid man stagger, reminded her that this was only the beginning of this cyclone. Things were going to get a whole lot worse before they got any better.

The stabs of pain coming up her leg from her ankle were bad enough to make her feel sick. On top of her exhaustion and the knowledge that they were in real trouble here, it was enough to make her head spin. She couldn't faint. If she did, how would he know how to find the beach house, which was probably their only hope of surviving?

'There's a river,' she added. 'We turn inland there.'

She could feel his arms tighten around her. It had to be incredibly hard, carrying somebody as tall as she was in the face of this wind and on soft sand, and they had a long way to go.

Could he do it?

Ellie had no choice but to put her faith in him, however hard that was to do. With a groan that came more from defeat than pain, she screwed her eyes shut and buried her face against his chest as he staggered along the beach.

It had been a very long time since she had felt a man's arms around her like this.

At least she wouldn't die alone.

CHAPTER THREE

SHE WAS NO lightweight, this woman in his arms.

Jake had to lean forward into the fierce wind and his feet were dragging in the soft sand that was no match for these conditions. It swirled around enough to obscure his feet completely and it would have reached his nose and eyes if the rain hadn't been heavy enough to drive it down again.

Another blast of wind made Jake stagger and almost fall. He gritted his teeth and battled on. They had to find shelter. She'd been right. He might wish it was Ben instead of him, but he *was* lucky to still be alive and he owed it to her to try and make sure the heroic actions of his rescuers weren't wasted to the extent that one of them lost her life.

A river, she'd said. Good grief. He didn't even know the name of the woman he was carrying. A person who had risked her life for his and he'd been ungrateful enough to practically tell her he wished she hadn't. That he would have stayed with Ben if he'd been given a choice.

His left leg was dragging more than the right and a familiar ache was tightening like a vice in his thigh.

Another vice was tightening around his heart as his thoughts were dragged back to Ben, who would still be being tossed around in the ocean in that pathetically small life raft.

The combination of his sore leg and thoughts of his brother inevitably dragged his mind back to Afghanistan. They'd only been nineteen when they'd joined the army. Sixteen years ago now but the memories were as fresh as ever. Had it been his idea first that it was the ideal way to escape their father?

Charles Logan's voice had the ability to echo in his head with all the force of the gunfire from a war zone.

You moronic imbeciles, you're your mother's children, you've inherited nothing from me. Stupid, stupid, stupid...

No. They'd both wanted to run. Both had needed the brutal reality of the army to find out what life was like outside an overprivileged upbringing. To find out who *they* really were.

But *he* had been more excited about it, hadn't he? In the movies, the soldiers were heroes and it always came out all right for them in the end.

They weren't supposed to get shipped home with a shattered leg as the aftermath of being collateral damage from a bus full of school kids that had been targeted by a roadside bomb.

His brother's last words still echoed in his head.

Why do you think she killed herself?

It *had* been Ben who'd found her, all those years ago, when the boys had been only fourteen.

Did he know something he'd never told *him?* Had he found evidence that it hadn't been an accidental overdose of prescription meds washed down with alcohol?

A *note,* even?

No. It couldn't be true. She wouldn't have deserted her children with such finality. She'd *loved* them, even if she hadn't been around often enough to show them how much.

A cry was ripped from Jake's lips. An anguished denial of accepting such a premeditated abandonment.

Denial, too, of what was happening right now? That his brother was out there somewhere in that merciless ocean? Too cold to hang on any longer?

Drowned already, even?

No. Surely he'd know. He'd feel it if his other half was being ripped away for eternity.

The cry of pain was enough to pull Ellie from the mental haze she'd been clinging to as she kept her face buried from the outside world, thinking of nothing more than the comfort of being held in strong arms and, hopefully, being carried to safety.

What had she been thinking? Eleanor Sutton wasn't some swooning heroine from medieval times. She didn't depend on anyone else. She could look after herself.

'Put me down,' Ellie ordered.

But he kept lurching forward into the biting wind and rain.

'No. We're not at the river.'

'I need to see where we are, then.' She twisted in his arms to look towards the sea.

Taking her helmet off had probably been a bad idea. The wind was pulling long strands from the braid that hung down over Jake's arm. They were plastered against her face the moment they came free and she had to drag them away repeatedly to try and see properly.

'I can't see it. The waves are too high.'

'See what?'

'The light from the lighthouse. The bach is in a direct line with the light, just before the river mouth.'

'The *what?*'

'The bach. A holiday house.' Ellie had finally picked up the drawl in the man's voice. 'Are you American?'

'Yep.'

'A cabin, then. Like you'd have by a lake or in the woods. Only this one's near the beach and it's the only one for a hundred miles.'

'How do you know it's even there?'

'Because I own it.' Maybe it wasn't dark enough for the automatic light to be triggered, but she'd seen it earlier, hadn't she? When she'd told Dave where to drop them?

Maybe she'd only seen the lighthouse itself and it had been childhood memories that had supplied the flash of light. The flash she'd watched for in the night since that first time she'd stayed on the island with her grandfather. A comforting presence that had assured a small girl she was safe even if she was on a tiny island in the middle of a very big sea.

'We'll have to keep going till we get to the river. I can find the way from there.'

How long did he keep struggling against the wind before they finally reached the river mouth? Long enough for Ellie to know she'd never felt this cold in her life. At least they had the wind behind them as they turned inland, but there was a new danger when they reached the forest of native bush that came to meet the coastline in this deserted area. The massive pohutukawa trees were hundreds of years old and there were any number of dead branches coming loose in the vicious wind to crash down around them. Live bits were breaking off, too, leafy enough to make it impossible to see the old track that led to the bach.

Ellie had to rely on instinct. Her fear was growing. Had she made a terrible mistake, telling Dave they could find shelter here? The little house that Grandpa and her father had built had seemed so solid, wedged into the bush that had provided the wood to make it. A part of the forest that would always be here even if she had never come back. A touchstone for her life that was a part of her soul.

But how many storms had there been in the years that had passed? Had the tiny dwelling disintegrated—like all the hugely important things in her life seemed to have a habit of doing?

No.

They almost missed it. They were off to one side of the patch of land she owned. She might have let herself get carried right past if she hadn't spotted the tiny hut that sat discreetly tucked against the twisted trunk of one of the huge pohutukawas.

'We're here,' she shouted.

The man looked at the hut. If he went inside the bleached wood of its walls, he would have to bend his head and he wouldn't be able to stretch out his arms. 'Are you *kidding* me? *That's* your cabin?'

Ellie actually laughed aloud.

'No. That's the dunny.'

'The *what?*'

'The long drop. Toilet.' Oh, yeah…he was American. 'It's the *bathroom.*'

She didn't wait to see a look of disgust about how primitive the facilities were. The track from the outhouse to the real house was overgrown, but Ellie knew exactly where she was now. And if the outhouse had survived, maybe everything else was exactly as it should be. Within a few steps they could both see the back porch of the beach house, with its neatly stacked pile of firewood. The relief of seeing it look just like it always had brought a huge lump to Ellie's throat.

She felt herself being tipped as he leaned down to grasp the battered iron knob of the door. He turned and pushed. The door rattled but didn't open.

'It's *locked.*'

She couldn't blame him for sounding shocked. It wasn't

as if another living soul was likely to come here when the only access was by boat so why would anybody bother locking it?

Another childhood memory surfaced. The door that had been purchased in a city junkyard had been roped to the deck of the yacht, along with an old couch and a pot-belly stove.

'The door's even got a lock and a key.' Her father had laughed. *'That'll keep the possums out.'*

A family joke that had become a tradition. Unlocking the bach meant they were in residence in their tiny patch of paradise. Locking it meant a return to reality.

'I know where the key is. Put me down.'

This time he complied and it was Ellie's turn to be shocked as she felt the loss of those secure arms around her, along with the chill of losing his body warmth that she hadn't been aware of until now. She staggered a little, but her ankle wasn't as bad as it had been. Hellishly painful but it didn't collapse completely when she tested it with a bit of weight. Maybe it was a bad sprain rather than a fracture.

'Can you walk?'

'I only need to get to the meat safe. The key's in there.'

The wire netting walls of the meat safe were mangled, probably by possums, and the box frame was hanging by only one corner, but the big, wrought-iron key was still on its rusty nail. Getting it inside the lock was a mission for her frozen hands, though, and turning it seemed impossible.

'It must be rusty.' Ellie groaned with the effort of trying to turn the key.

'Let me try.' His hands covered hers and pushed her fingers away so that he could find the end of the key. She was still wearing her rescue gloves and his hands had to be a lot colder than hers were, but the pressure of the contact felt like it was skin to skin. Warm.

Maybe it was the reassurance that she wasn't alone that was so comforting?

He was shivering badly, Ellie noticed, but when he jiggled the key and then turned it, she could hear the clunk of the old lock opening.

And then they were inside and the sound of the storm was suddenly muffled.

Safety.

They might be frozen to the bone and in the middle of nowhere, but they had shelter.

Jake was safe, thanks to this woman. Thanks to her astonishing courage. She'd not only risked her life to get him out of that life raft, she'd battled the elements, despite being injured, to lead him here. To a place where they had four walls and a roof and they could survive until the storm was over.

She seemed as stunned as he was. They both stood there, staring at each other, saying nothing. It couldn't be nighttime yet, but it was dark enough in here to make it difficult to see very clearly. She was tall, Jake noted, but still a good few inches shorter than his six feet two. Eyes dark enough to look black in this light and her lips were deathly pale but still couldn't hide the lines of a generous mouth. A rope of wet hair hung over one shoulder almost as far as her waist.

'What's your name?' He'd been so used to shouting to be heard outside that his voice came out loudly enough to make her jump.

'Eleanor Sutton. Ellie.'

'I'm Jacob Logan. Jake.'

'Hi, Jake.' She was trying to smile but loosening

her facial muscles only made her shiver uncontrollably. 'P-pleased to m-meet you.'

'Likewise, Ellie.' Jake nodded instead of smiling.

His name clearly didn't mean anything to her and it was a weird feeling not to be instantly recognised. He didn't look much like himself, of course. Even his own mother probably wouldn't have recognised him in this dim light with the heavy growth of beard and the long hair he'd had to adopt for his latest movie role. But instant demotion from a megastar to a...a *nobody* was very strange.

Jake wasn't sure he liked it.

And yet it was oddly comforting. It took him back to a time when he had only been known for being 'one of those wild Logan boys.' Closer to Ben, somehow.

Should he tell her? Was it being dishonest not to? Would Ben consider this a form of play-acting as well?

Keeping silent didn't feel like acting a part. Just being the person he used to be. And there would be no reason for this Ellie to present herself as anything other than who she really was and, in Jake's experience, that wasn't something he could ever trust. This might be the only time in his life that he got to see how a stranger reacted to him as a person without the trappings of extreme wealth or fame. He was curious enough to find this almost a distraction from his desperate worry about Ben.

'We need to get warm.' She wasn't even looking at him now. 'There should be enough dry wood to get the fire and the stove going. Hopefully the possums won't have been inside. There'll be plenty of blankets on the beds. And there's kerosene lamps if the fuel hasn't evaporated or something. It's been a fair few years since I was here.'

Beds? For the first time, Jake took a good look around himself.

The dwelling was made of rustic, rough-hewn boards

that had aged to a silvery-gray that made it look like drift-wood. An antique glass-and-metal lamp hung from a butcher's hook in the ceiling and there was a collection of big shells lined with iridescent shades of blue and purple attached to the wall in a curly pattern. Beside that was a poster of a lighthouse, its beam lighting up a stormy sky while massive waves thundered onto rocks below. There was a kitchen of sorts in one corner of the square space, with a bench and a sink beside the potbelly stove close to a small wooden table and spindle-back chairs.

The other half of the space was taken up with an ancient-looking couch and an armchair, positioned in front of an open fireplace. Two doorless openings in the walls on either side of the fireplace led to dark spaces beyond. The bedrooms?

'Don't just stand there.' The authority in her voice made Jake feel like he was back at school. Or under the charge of one of the many nannies the Logan boys had terrorised. Incredibly, he had to hide a wry smile. No woman had ever spoken to him like this in his adult life. And then he remembered being shouted at on the beach. Being told that no one would be going back to rescue his brother.

What did it matter whether Ellie knew who he was? Or what she thought of him?

Nothing would ever matter if he'd lost Ben.

Ellie was opening a cupboard in the kitchen. She pulled out a big tin. 'Do something useful. You'll get even colder if you don't move. You can get some wood in from the porch.' She prised open the lid of the tin. '*Yes*…we have matches.'

A fire. Warmth. This basic survival need drove any other thoughts from Jake's head as he obeyed the order. He took an armful of small sticks in first to act as kindling and then went back for the more solid lumps of wood. His brain felt as frozen as his fingers. Worry about Ben was still there along with the anger of no attempt being made to rescue him, but he couldn't even harness the energy of that anger to help him move faster. And then something scuttled away as he lifted a piece of wood. Did New Zealand have poisonous spiders, like Australia did? Or snakes?

Man, he was going to have some story to tell Ben when he saw him again.

If he saw him again.

There was a puddle of water on the floor where Ellie was crouching to light the fire and he could see how badly her hands were shaking, but she'd managed to arrange small sticks on a nest of paper and while the first two matches spluttered and died, the third grew into a small flame.

She looked up as he walked towards her with the wood. He saw the way her eyes widened with shock.

'You're limping.' Her tone was accusing. 'You're hurt. And I let you carry me all that way. Why didn't you *tell* me?'

'I'm not hurt.' He dumped the wood on the floor beside her. His old injury was hardly a state secret, but it wasn't something he mentioned if he could avoid it.

'I'm a paramedic, Jake. I've got eyes. I can *see*—'

'Drop it,' he growled. 'I told you. I haven't been injured. Not in the last ten years anyway.'

'Oh…' She caught her bottom lip between her teeth. Maybe she was attempting a smile. 'Old war wound, huh?'

He glared at her. 'First time anyone's found it funny.'

Her face changed. Was she embarrassed? Not that she was about to apologise. There was an awkward silence as she turned her attention back to the fire and then she must have decided that it was best ignored.

* * *

'Some rats or mice had shredded the paper for me,' Ellie said. 'Good thing, too, because my fingers are still too cold to work properly.' Her tone was deliberately lighter. Impersonal, even. 'Don't think we'll use the beds, but the blankets might be okay.'

The wood sizzled a little, but the flame was still growing. The glow caught Ellie's face as she leaned in to blow gently on the fire. Water dripped from her long braid to add to the puddle at her feet. Smoke puffed out and made her cough.

'There could well be a bird's nest or two in the chimney, but they should burn away soon. We'll get the potbelly going, too, if we can, and that should get things toasty in no time.'

Jake had to forgive the dismissal of his old injury as some kind of joke. She didn't know the truth and, if he wasn't prepared to enlighten her, it would be unfair to hold a grudge. And he had to admire her. She was capable, this Eleanor Sutton, but that was hardly surprising given what she did for a job. Jake was given the task of feeding larger sticks into the fire as it grew while Ellie limped over to the kitchen to get the stove going. His hands began aching unbearably as heat finally penetrated the frozen layer of skin and, when he looked up, he saw Ellie's pained expression as she shook her hands.

'Hurts, doesn't it?'

'It's good. Means there's some circulation happening and nerves are waking up.' She nodded in satisfaction at the fire Jake was tending. 'I'll see if I can find us some dry clothes. My dad kept a trunk of stuff under the bed and it's a tin trunk so it should have kept the rats out.'

'Do you get snakes, too?'

'No snakes in New Zealand. Have you never been here before?'

'No.'

'I guess you were just passing by with the yacht race. Wasn't there a stop planned in Auckland?'

'Yeah. I was getting off then. I'm here for a job. That was why I talked Ben into giving me a lift on his yacht.'

'Ben? That's your friend who was on the life raft with you?'

'He's my brother. Twin brother.'

'Oh…'

The enormity of having to leave Ben behind and not trying to go back and get him was clearly registering.

'I…I'm sorry, Jake.'

'Yeah… Me, too.'

'It was a good life raft. There's still hope that he'll make it.'

Jake found himself staring at Ellie. It felt very odd—his gaze clinging to hers like this. As if he was pleading…

Desperately wanting to believe.

Begging her to prove herself trustworthy?

She was in the business of rescuing people who found themselves in dire situations so she should know what she was talking about.

'We weren't the only rescue team out there,' she told him quietly. 'There were other choppers. Planes. And there's other boats. Container ships as well as the coast-guard. There's plenty of daylight left and…'

There was such compassion in her eyes and her body language. The way she was leaning towards him. Holding out one hand. If she'd been close enough, she'd be touching him right now.

He wished she was that close.

'And there are literally hundreds of islands on this part

of the coastline. All it needs is for a current to get him close to land and he'll be able to find shelter until the worst of the storm is over.'

Maybe it was the compassion he could see that did it. Or the comfort of the reassurance she was offering. Or maybe it was because of that longing that she had been close enough to underpin her words with human touch.

Whatever it was, Jake could pull back. Yes, she was offering him what he wanted more than anything in this moment. And the invitation to believe her was so sincere, but they were all like that, weren't they? Especially women.

He knew better than to trust.

'Yeah…right…' He wrenched his gaze free, turning back towards the fire and using a stick to poke at it. He didn't want to talk about Ben. He didn't want to show this stranger how he was really feeling. How *afraid* he was. Who knew what contacts she might have? What could turn up as a headline on some celebrity website?

The warmth Ellie had been getting from the stove seemed to have been shut off and the cold in her gut turned into a lead weight.

No wonder they'd been arguing about who got to be rescued first. Or that Jake had said he would have stayed if he'd been given the choice. She didn't even have a sibling and these men were twin brothers. She could imagine how close they were. As close as she'd dreamed of being with another living soul. Loving—and being loved—enough for one's own safety to not be the priority.

She would have gone back for Ben if it had been possible, but it hadn't been. At least she'd brought Jake to safety, but maybe, in the end, he wouldn't thank her for that. He obviously didn't want to talk about it. He was hunched over in front of the fire, looking very grim as he poked at the burning sticks, sending sparks flying and creating a new cloud of smoke. Fiercely shutting her out.

Was it the smoke in his eyes that made him rub at them with the heel of his hand? Even hunched up, she was aware again of what a big man he was. Intimidatingly big. She knew that trying to offer any further comfort would be unwelcome. She'd probably put her foot in it, too, the way she had when she'd tried to make some kind of joke about his obvious limp.

It had been the way Grandpa had brushed off any concern about his physical wellbeing.

It's nothing, chicken. Just the old war wound playing up.

But Jake was an American. Had she made a joke about some horrible injury he'd suffered in somewhere like Afghanistan? She'd been too flustered to think of a way to apologise without it seeming insincere. Or prying. There was something about this man that suggested he valued his privacy a lot more than most people.

So, once again, she simply avoided anything personal.

'I'll go and see if I can find us those dry clothes.'

By the time Ellie returned with an armload of clothes from the old tin trunk, the living area of the small house was already feeling a lot warmer.

'The trousers are pretty horrible, but we've scored with a couple of Swanndris.'

Jake looked up from where he was still crouched in front of the fire. He was shivering uncontrollably despite being so close to the heat. 'S-swan—what?'

'They're shirts. I'm wearing one.' Ellie dumped the pile she was holding onto the sofa, extracting a black-and-red-checked garment to hold out to Jake. 'New Zealand icon. A hundred percent wool. Farmers have relied on them for decades over here and they're the best thing for warmth. Even better, these ones are huge. Should fit you a treat.'

Neither her father or grandfather had been small men by any means. The shirt Ellie was wearing came well down over the baggy track pants she'd struggled into in the bedroom, but it was just as well they were so loose because they'd gone right over the sodden boots that had laces she couldn't manage to undo yet. And maybe it was better to leave them on. At least her ankle was splinted by the heavy leather and padding of her socks.

He took the shirt and nodded. 'Thanks.'

'Don't just stare at it. Put it on. No, hang on…' Ellie dived back into the pile. 'Here's a singlet that can go on first so it's not itchy.'

Getting changed into dry clothes was easier said than done. Ellie had found it enough of a struggle getting out of her wet clothes in the bedroom and she'd been wearing state-of-the-art gloves to protect her hands up until now. Jake's hands had been bare ever since he'd been plucked from the life raft and were still so cold there was no way he could manage the zipper of the heavy anorak he was wearing.

He fumbled several times, cursed softly and then stopped trying. Ellie dragged her gaze up from his fingers to his face and, for a long moment, they simply stared at each other.

The fire was crackling with some enthusiasm now. Adding enough light to the dark, stormy afternoon for her to get a good look at this man. He was big, broad shouldered and…and *wild* looking, with that long hair and the beard. His face was fierce looking anyway, with a nose that commanded attention and accentuated the shadowed eyes that had an almost hawk-like intensity.

The pull of something—an awareness that was deep

enough to be disturbing—made Ellie's mouth go dry. She tore her gaze away from those compelling eyes. They both knew she had no choice here.

'I'll help you,' she said.

Her voice sounded weird so she pressed her lips together and said nothing else as she started to help him undress. The scrape of the metal zip sounded curiously loud. He had layers underneath. A sodden woollen pullover and thermal gear beneath that.

And then there was skin. Rather a lot of skin covering the kind of torso that spoke of a great deal of physical effort.

Ripped. That was the only word for it.

Dark discs of nipples hardened by the cold decorated an almost hairless chest that seemed at odds with the amount of hair Jake favoured on his head and face.

And…dear Lord, there was a tattoo in the strangest place. A line of what looked like Chinese characters ran from his armpit to disappear into the waistband of his jeans.

It was discreet body art and it must have significance, but Ellie wasn't about to ask. She shouldn't even be looking. Just as well it got covered up as Jake pulled on the black singlet and then the thick woollen shirt. He managed to pop the button on his jeans but, again, the zipper was beyond the motor skills that had returned to his hands so far.

Ellie had undressed countless patients in her career. She'd cut through and removed clothing and exposed every inch of skin of people without the slightest personal reaction. Why did it have to be now that she was so aware of touching someone in such an intimate area? Why did she feel so uncomfortable she had to swallow hard and actually close her eyes for a heartbeat?

Like remembering her past when it should have been

totally obliterated by the adrenaline of being in real danger, maybe this was a sign that she was no longer fit for active service as a paramedic. Something like grief washed through Ellie at the thought and it was easy to turn that into a kind of anger. Impatience, anyway, to get the job over with.

'I'll do the zip,' she snapped. 'You should be able to manage the rest.'

She tried not to think of what her fingers were brushing. The zipper got stuck halfway down and she had to pull it back up and try again. A warmth that had nothing to do with the fire crept into her cheeks. As soon as she got the zipper down past where it had stuck, she dropped her hands as though the metal was red hot and she turned away as Jake hooked his thumbs into the waistband and started peeling the wet fabric from his skin.

She'd seen enough.

Too much.

Nobody had undressed Jake Logan without his invitation since he'd been about two years old and had kicked his nanny to demonstrate his desire for independence.

Except for when he'd been in the care of the army medics, of course, and then of the nurses in the military hospital back home. He'd flirted wickedly with those nurses, making a joke of the humiliation of being helpless.

He couldn't have flirted to save his life when Ellie had been struggling with that zipper. He'd been looking down at her bent head. The rope of black hair was still dripping wet, but the fronds that the wind had whipped free were starting to dry and they were softening the outlines of her face. Or they would have been if it wasn't set in such grim lines of determination.

She *really* didn't want to be touching him, did she? This

was an ordeal she was forcing herself to get through because she had no choice.

Like being unrecognised, this was an alien experience for a man almost bored by the way women threw
themselves at him. Not a pleasant experience either, but
it wasn't humiliation or even embarrassment that was so
overwhelming. He couldn't begin to identify *what* it was
he was feeling. He just knew that it was powerful enough
to be disturbing.

Very disturbing.

The choice of trousers *was* embarrassing with the only
pair he had any hope of fitting being shapeless track pants
that didn't cover his ankles. At least the socks looked long
and he could be grateful there were no paparazzi around.

'What will we do with the wet gear?'

Ellie had taken the lamp down from the hook on the
ceiling and was pouring something from a plastic bottle
into its base.

'We'll hang them over the chairs. They might be dry
enough to get back into by the time we get rescued from
here.'

'How long do you reckon that'll be?'

Ellie had the glass cover off the lamp now. She struck a
match and held it to a wick. 'We had a lot of info coming in
about the cyclone while we were in the air. The worst of it
won't hit until early tomorrow, but it should blow through
within about twelve hours.'

The flame caught and Ellie eased the glass cover back
into place. She fiddled with an attachment to the base,
pumping it gently, and suddenly the light increased to a
glow that seemed like a spotlight focused on her. As she
looked up and caught his gaze, a hint of a smile made her
lips curve. 'It's going to get worse before it gets better, I'm
afraid.'

Jake's mouth felt suddenly dry.

Even the hint of a smile transformed Ellie's face. Made it come alive.

She was an extraordinarily beautiful woman. He could actually feel something slamming shut in his chest. Or his head maybe.

Don't go there. Don't get sucked in. Even if she doesn't know who you are, it's not worth the risk.

Remember what happened last time.

But Ellie stretched to hang the lamp from its hook and the unbuttoned sleeves of her oversize shirt fell back to expose slim, olive-brown arms. Long, clever fingers made another adjustment to the base of the lamp.

Jake couldn't drag his gaze free.

Yeah…it probably *was* going to get worse before it got better.

But he could deal with it.

He *had* to.

CHAPTER FOUR

THE KEROSENE LAMP hissed and swayed gently in the draughts that were a soft echo of the fierce storm outside. The glow of light strengthened as day became night and shadows danced in the corners of the room as the light moved—a dark partner to the bright flicker of the flames in the open fireplace.

The room was warm enough for the wet clothing draped over the spindle-back chairs to be steaming gently and one end of the table was covered with a collection of items that had come from the pockets of Ellie's flight suit, like a bunch of keys, ruined ballpoint pens and an equally wet and useless mobile phone. Most importantly, there was a two-way radio that had been securely enclosed in a waterproof pouch.

Jake had been disappointed that they couldn't use it to listen and hear updates on the weather, but Ellie was more concerned about whether it was in working order. It didn't seem to be transmitting.

'Medic One to base—do you receive?'

A crackle of static and a beeping noise came from the device, but there was no answering voice. Ellie gave up after a few tries.

'We may be out of range or it could be atmospheric conditions. I'll turn it on in the morning and we might get communication about our rescue.'

The radio sat on the edge of the table now—a symbol of surviving this ordeal.

Except, for the moment, it didn't seem to be that much of an ordeal. They were safe and finally warm. And Ellie had discovered a store of tinned food in the bottom of a cupboard.

'Chilli baked beans, cheesy spaghetti, Irish stew, peas or tomatoes.' She held up each can to show Jake. 'As my guest, you get to choose. What do you fancy?'

'They all sound good. I don't think I've ever been this hungry in my life.'

'Hmm…' Ellie had almost forgotten what it felt like to really smile. 'That's not a bad idea. I'll see if I've got a pot that's big enough.'

The result of mixing the contents of all the chosen cans together was remarkably tasty. Or maybe she was just as hungry as Jake. Whatever the reason, sitting cross-legged in front of the fire, spooning the food from a bowl, Ellie decided that it was probably one of the most memorable meals she would ever eat.

'There's more in the pot if you're still hungry,' she told Jake.

'Maybe we should save it for tomorrow.'

'There's still more cans. My mother must have stocked up big time on their last trip.'

'When was that?'

'Six years ago. I didn't come on that trip because I was in the middle of my helicopter training.' Ellie stared into the fire. 'Who knew it would save my life?'

'How d'you mean?'

'Their yacht ran into trouble on the way home. Both my parents drowned.'

'Oh…I'm sorry.'

Ellie could see Jake put his plate down suddenly, as if his appetite had deserted him. She kicked herself mentally.

'No, *I'm* sorry. I didn't mean to remind you of...' Her voice trailed into silence. He didn't want to talk about Ben, did he? She didn't need to glance sideways at his bent head to remind her of that walled-off private area. It was none of her business, anyway.

But she heard Jake take a deep breath a moment later. And then he shook his head as he got to his feet. He shoved his hair behind his ears.

'You wouldn't have a rubber band or a piece of string or something, would you? My hair's going to drive me nuts if I don't tie it back.'

Ellie blinked. 'I can find something.' She couldn't help a personal question. 'Why do you wear it so long if it annoys you?'

'Not my choice. It's temporary. You could say it's a—a work thing.'

'Ohh...' Ellie was bemused. 'What are you—a male model?'

Jake's breath came out in a snort. 'Something like that.'

Ellie could well believe it. She'd seen that body. The dark wavy hair that almost brushed his shoulders would probably be wildly exciting for a lot of women, too, but the beard? No...it wouldn't do it for her.

She almost changed her mind as Jake used his fingers to rake his hair back properly from his face. Even with the beard hiding half his face, she had trouble dragging her gaze away from him.

'What? Have I got spaghetti on my face or something?'

'No...you just look...I don't know...different.'

Different but oddly familiar. Or was that simply a warning signal that something unconscious was recognising the magnetic pull this man seemed to have? Ellie turned away with a decisive enough head movement to make her aware of the heavy weight of her own hair. The loose bits had long since dried, but the braid was still wet.

'Here. Have this…' She pulled the elastic band from the end of her braid. 'I need to get my hair dry and it'll take all night if I leave it tied up.'

So Jake bound his hair back in a ponytail and Ellie unravelled hers and let it fall over her back with the ends brushing the wooden boards of the floor. Now it was Jake's turn to stare, apparently. She could feel the intensity of his gaze from where he was sitting on the sofa behind her.

Was it the hissing of the lamp or the crackle of the fire or was there some kind of other current in the air that Ellie could actually *feel* instead of hear? It had all the intensity of a bright light and the heat of a flame and something warned Ellie not to turn her head.

The current was coming from Jake.

She heard him clear his throat. As though he thought his speech might be hoarse if he didn't?

'Must have been tough, losing your parents like that. Have you got any brothers or sisters?'

'Nope.'

'Husband? Boyfriend? Significant other?'

'Nope.' Ellie felt her hackles rise. It was none of his business. He wasn't about to let her into personal areas. Why would he think she was willing to share?

'Sorry. Didn't mean to pry.' Jake's voice was flat. 'I just thought…it's going to be a long night and it might be kind of nice to get to know each other.'

Did that mean that if she was prepared to share, he might too? That she might even find out the significance of that intriguing tattoo, even?

'Fair enough.' But Ellie got to her feet. 'Let me find us some blankets and pillows first, if they're useable. And

I'll boil some water. We don't have milk, but there's probably a tin of cocoa or something around. We need a drink.'

It was some time before Ellie was satisfied they had all they needed for a while. The fire was well banked up with wood. They both had a blanket and a pillow and, by tacit consent, Jake would have the couch to try and sleep on while Ellie curled up in the armchair. Neither of them wanted to move any further away from the fire.

Exhaustion was taking over now. Her body ached all over and her injured ankle was throbbing badly despite the hastily applied strapping with a damp bandage that she'd found in one of her suit pockets when changing her clothes.

It had been one of the longest days of Ellie's life and the physical exertion had been draining enough without the added stress of the emotional side of it all. Not only the fear for her own safety but also the grief of knowing that the job was no longer enough to shield her from what she had run from.

Maybe part of it was renewed grief for the family she'd lost. Impossible for that not to be surfacing now that she'd finally come back to a place she'd been avoiding for that very reason.

And maybe that was what made her prepared to talk about it. About things she'd never had anyone to talk to about.

'I haven't been here since my parents died,' she told Jake. 'It was bad enough when we all came here after Grandpa died and I didn't want to come back knowing that I had no family left.' She sighed softly. 'I didn't have a boat anyway. I wasn't sure I wanted anything more to do with the sea.'

'Hard to get away from, I would think, when you live on an island.'

'Well—it's a big island, but you're right. The home I

grew up in is in Devonport in Auckland and it's right on the beach. I still live there. There's salt water in my family's blood, I reckon. That's why Grandpa took the job as the lighthouse-keeper on Half Moon Island.'

'The moon… Yeah, I heard you say something about that on the radio.'

'I recognised it from the air. I spent so much time there when I was little that it's like part of the family. That's a picture of it over there, on the wall.'

'I thought most lighthouses were automatic now.'

'They are. And Half Moon was automated long before I was born, but Grandpa couldn't bear to leave it behind. That's why he bought this patch of land and virtually lived here from when my dad was a teenager. I sailed up with them every school holiday until he died when I was seventeen. And then Mum, Dad and I still came at least a couple of times a year. Having Christmas here when all the pohutukawa trees are in full bloom is quite something. And we could still go over to Half Moon and explore. It's got an amazing amount of birdlife. It should be a national reserve.'

'Why isn't it?'

Ellie shrugged. 'Too remote, I guess. And it would be too expensive to run a pest eradication programme.'

She was so tired now, her eyes were drooping shut. That was enough of a foray into personal space, wasn't it?

Apparently not.

'I don't get it.' Jake's words broke a silence in which Ellie had been drifting closer to sleep.

'What?'

'Why someone like you is all alone.'

'Someone like me?' Ellie opened heavy lids and turned her head far enough to find Jake staring at her again.

'Yeah… Someone talented, incredibly brave…gorgeous…'

His words were doing something to her stomach. It felt like she'd swallowed one of the flames from the fireplace and it was tickling her with tendrils hot enough to be uncomfortable.

It made a response easy to find. 'Once burned, twice shy, you know?'

'Oh, I do know.' The words were laced with bitterness. 'What happened?'

'Same old story. Fell in love. Got betrayed. I won't bore you with the details, but it would have made a pretty good story line for a soap opera.'

The huff of sound that came from Jake managed to encompass both disgust and empathy. 'Good way to look at it, anyway.'

'How's that?'

'Like it's a movie and you can see the whole disaster up there on the big screen.'

A strangled sound of mirth escaped Ellie. 'And what would the humiliated, heartbroken heroine do in this movie?'

Jake's voice was soft. 'Pretty much what you've done. Got on with her life and turned herself into a real-life heroine.'

Ellie didn't want to hear any more of his praise. 'Life's not a movie,' she muttered.

'Helps to look at it like that sometimes, though.'

That woke Ellie up a little. Annoyed her, in fact. 'How does avoiding reality help exactly?'

'Because you see your life up on the screen and you're part of the audience. How would you feel if you were watching yourself giving up? Pulling the blankets over your head or crying in a corner? You wouldn't think it was worth watching any more, would you? Isn't it better to be cheering yourself on as you face the obstacles and overcome them?'

'Is that what you do?'

'Kind of, I suppose.' Ellie got the impression she was hearing something very personal here. 'Gets you through the tough bits.'

'The "fake it till you make it" school of thought?'

'Uh-uh.' The negative sound was very American. 'It's not fake. You're not pretending to be someone *else*. You're practising being the best person you can be, even if it feels like the skin doesn't quite fit yet.'

Had she annoyed him this time? The lapse into another silence suggested she had.

'So…' Ellie tried to keep her tone light. 'I'm guessing you're not married either?'

'Not anymore.'

It shouldn't make any difference to know he was single so why did her heart rate pick up a little?

'Used and abused, too, huh?'

'You said it.'

This time the silence felt like a door slamming. There was no point waiting for Jake to say anything else and his guard was up so firmly that Ellie wondered if she'd imagined that she'd been allowed briefly into a personal space. Instinct told her that if she pushed, that barrier would only get bigger.

She backed away. 'What's the happy ending going to be in the movie of my life, then? Do I get swept off my feet by the love of my life? Some gorgeous guy that I have no trouble trusting absolutely?'

'Of course.' There was a smile in Jake's voice that almost felt like praise. For not prying, perhaps?

She had to dismiss the fairy tale, though. 'That's why I don't watch movies. What's the point in escaping into fiction instead of facing reality?'

'If we couldn't hope for something better, life could be a pretty miserable business sometimes for a lot of folks.'

'I suppose.' Ellie snuggled deeper into her blanket and let her head sink into the pillow. 'Can't see it happening for me.'

'Me neither.'

The agreement felt like a connection. They were on the same page. And maybe what he'd said about playing a role had some merit. She could try faking it a bit herself.

'I'm happy with my reality,' she said. 'Why would I risk that happiness by hanging it on someone else? When it really boils down, the only person you can trust is yourself. Unless...' The words were sleepy now. Almost a murmur. 'Unless you've got a twin. That would be like having two of yourself.'

Jake said nothing and Ellie drifted closer to sleep, happy that they had got to know each other a little better. Had found a connection of sorts, albeit a negative one, in that relationships were currently a no-go area for both of them. Did that open the door, perhaps, to a friendship without the hidden agenda that always seemed to become a problem?

No. In those last moments before losing consciousness, Ellie's mind—and her body—insisted on remembering how it had felt to be so close to Jake's bare skin. To touch him. And just the thought of it meant she could still actually feel that sizzle that had been in the air when she'd felt him staring at her back.

There would be an agenda there all right, even if she didn't want it.

And it might not be just Jake's agenda.

It was a sudden change of temperature that woke Jake from a fitful, nightmare-plagued slumber. A slap of cold air on his face.

Sitting up to see over the back of the sofa, he found Ellie struggling to open the outside door.

'What's happened? What's *wrong?*'

'Nothing.' Ellie was wearing a heavy, oilskin coat. Her hair was still loose, but she had a woollen hat pulled down over her ears. 'I just need to go to the bathroom.'

'Are you crazy?' Now fully awake, Jake realised that all hell seemed to have broken out beyond the walls of their small shelter. The howling shriek of the wind was as unearthly as the weird half-light of the new day. Rain hammered at the tin roof and there was an ominous banging noise that suggested a piece of the roofing was coming loose.

Ignoring painfully stiff muscles and joints, he got to his feet and close to the window in time to see the meat safe give up any attempt to stay attached to the porch wall and the wind pick it up and send it bouncing into the trees.

'Wow…' Ellie sounded impressed by the force of the wind.

And she was planning to go out there? 'It's dangerous,' Jake growled.

'It's urgent,' Ellie said calmly. 'It's only a few steps. It's not as if I'm in danger of getting blown over a cliff or something.'

'There's branches flying everywhere. You could get hurt.' It was the sheer stupidity of what she was intending to do that was making Jake sound fierce. Or was it a sudden urge to protect this woman?

'You can get hurt crossing the road.'

She wasn't about to listen to him and who was he to tell her about assessing risk anyway? This woman dangled on thin wires underneath helicopters for a living, for goodness' sake.

'There's a pot of water on the stove,' Ellie told him. 'I'll be back by the time you've made us some cocoa.'

He could do that. He should do that instead of standing here by the window watching as Ellie bent almost double to force herself forward against the wind. It looked like she wasn't going to get the narrow door of the outhouse open against the wind, but he saw her wedge her boot inside a crack and then use her shoulder to force it open further.

Man…her strength was impressive, but her determination was downright intimidating.

Jake rubbed his eyes as he turned back to the stove. Not that he needed to be any more awake but there were still fragments of his nightmares that were swirling in his head.

Ellie—looking like a warrior princess with her long hair flowing in the wind behind her—pointing a finger at him and shouting.

Fake…fake…fake…

And Ben had been standing beside her. Equally accusing.

Play-acting… Just like Mom… You can't face reality.

But you're another me. I'm another you.

No. Jake prised the lid off the cocoa tin with the edge of a spoon. Ellie had been way off the mark with that sleepy observation. He and Ben had always been a unit, for sure—united against the outside world—but there were two distinct parts of that unit. They weren't the same person—not by a long shot.

Not even two halves of a whole. More like yin and yang. Very different but a perfect fit together.

And he'd never feel the same shape if Ben was gone.

But she hadn't been so far off the mark in suggesting that using a movie mode was sidestepping reality. Or Ben had been when he'd said pretty much the same thing in the life raft. Wasn't that pretty much how it had all started, even though he'd been far too young to realise what he was doing?

The water in the pot was boiling now. Ellie had been gone quite long enough so any second now she would burst back in through the door. Jake tipped water into the mugs, grateful for the need to focus and the distraction of the rich smell of chocolate. He could get on with surviving another day and banish the last of those disturbing dreams.

Especially the one where he hadn't been able to tell himself apart from his brother. When it was him who was lost on that unforgiving ocean. Tossed out of the life raft and dragged deeper and deeper under the weight of icy water. *Drowning…*

The explosive cracking noise from outside was more than enough to send that dream fragment into oblivion. It was enough to drain the blood from Jake's face. The whole house seemed to be shaking and the noise just got louder. One of the mugs toppled over and steaming liquid poured onto the floor, but Jake didn't notice. The light was changing. Getting darker. And then there was an impact that had all the force of an earthquake. The second mug crashed to the floor and shattered. A chair toppled. The kerosene lamp swung so violently the flame was extinguished.

The sound of any wind or rain felt like silence after that.

A very ominous silence.

Jake was already at the door, wrenching it open. He'd never shouted so loudly in his life.

'Ellie…'

CHAPTER FIVE

SHE FELT THE first shudders of the ground just as she tried to open the door of the outhouse again.

She heard the terrible cracking that could only mean one thing. A tree was coming down. A very large tree.

Was she about to get crushed? Trapped in what was little more than a wooden box?

This was more terrifying than being dragged through that wave like a fish on a line yesterday. At least she'd had a crew looking out for her and elements of the situation she could control herself. As she felt the outhouse being picked up with her still inside it and thrown through the air, Ellie was convinced she was about to die.

Did she imagine hearing someone calling her name?

A split second of sheer longing overwhelmed her. She wanted to be inside the beach house. With Jake's arms around her. Holding her tight. Keeping her safe.

The impact of hitting the ground shattered the old wooden boards around her, but instead of seeing daylight, Ellie found she was inside a layer of branches and the stiff leaves of a pohutukawa tree. A layer so thick it was hard to breathe. Miraculously, she didn't seem to be injured. Curling onto her knees, she started snapping small branches around her face and pushing them away to clear a space.

'Ellie...'

She definitely hadn't imagined it this time.

'I'm here, Jake.'

'I can't see you.'

'I'm under branches. I… *Ahh*…' Ellie groaned with the effort of trying to snap a bigger branch.

'Oh, God…are you *hurt?*'

The concern in his voice was enough to bring a lump to Ellie's throat. She might not have the backing of an experienced rescue team right now, but there *was* someone there who seemed to care whether or not she was okay.

She had to swallow hard before she could shout back. 'I don't think so. I'm just…stuck.'

'I'll get you out. Keep shouting so I know where you are.'

Ellie did keep shouting. She kept trying to find a way through herself, too, squeezing herself through smaller gaps and turning away from branches so big they would need a chainsaw to break them. She could hear the snapping of wood as Jake tried to create a path from the other side of the massive tree canopy.

It was dirty work and exhausting and Ellie could feel the scratches and bruises she was accumulating on her bare face and hands. Her hair kept getting caught and having to be painfully wrenched free. She was going to get it cut off when she got out of here, she decided.

If she got out of here.

The next desperate attempt to wriggle through a gap was badly judged. Ellie's leg got caught and trying to get free only wedged her foot further into a fork of thick branches. It was her injured foot that was caught, too, and even trying to pull it clear brought a sob of both frustration and pain from deep in her chest.

'I *knew* you were hurt.' After what had seemed an interminable amount of time, there was Jake's face only inches from her own. 'How bad is it?'

'It's just my ankle. From yesterday. But…it's wedged… I can't…'

'I can.' Jake crawled further into the mess of tangled tree and took hold of her foot. 'Sorry—this might hurt a bit.' He held onto her ankle and eased it out of the boot with a seesawing motion. Without her foot inside, it was easy enough to pull the boot free.

And then he was showing her which way to crawl after him.

'We'll go around the roots. The path's not so blocked that way.'

It was so wrong, seeing the massive trunk horizontal to the ground, with half the roots snapped off and taller than Jake's head. He had his arm around Ellie, taking most of her weight as he helped her move forward against wind that felt like a wall that kept shoving them viciously, but Ellie's cry, as they stumbled on the uneven, disrupted earth that had been beneath the tree, halted their progress. They were on the edge of a large hole and the earth was crumbling.

'I'll carry you.'

'No—it's not that. *Look*…' She had to shout to make herself heard. This was worse than it had been on the beach but not simply because of the weather.

Jake pulled strands of hair away from his eyes as he turned his head to where she was pointing.

'What *is* it? A rat?'

'It's a kiwi. A brown kiwi.' He wasn't to know how rare and precious this native bird was, but Ellie was too close to tears.

'Nothing we can do. It's been squashed. We've got to get inside or it'll be us next.'

But Ellie shook her head. 'There might be a nest. We've got to check.'

Jake was looking at her as if she was crazy. Could he see the tears that were now escaping? How important this was to her?

He stared at her for just a heartbeat longer. 'You stay here. What am I looking for?'

'A burrow. An egg…or a baby…'

Jake slipped as he stepped down into the hole and there he was on his hands and knees, with a cyclone raging around them, looking to rescue a small creature that could be in danger because it was important to Ellie.

He didn't even know what a kiwi was, so it couldn't matter to him.

He was doing this for *her*.

A piece of her heart felt like it was breaking away. Ready to offer to Jake? And then he was coming back— streaked with dirt and a trickle of blood on his forehead— with a huge, creamy egg in his hands. The wind was even louder now and Jake didn't bother trying to say anything.

He put the egg inside the boot that had come off Ellie's foot, shoved it into her hands and then kept one arm firmly around her body as he pulled them forward for the short distance back to the house.

'Let me look at that ankle.'

'No. I have to look at the egg first.'

What was it with this egg?

Okay, he'd heard of kiwis. It was what New Zealanders called themselves, wasn't it? Weird enough that they identified so strongly with some flightless bird, but was it that big a deal?

Had he really kept them both out there in such danger-

ous conditions because she was so worried that there might
be an orphaned chick or egg?

Yeah... But he'd seen the tears, hadn't he? And coming from the bravest woman he'd ever met, they had been
shocking.

Now the whole episode felt ridiculous. Jake ignored
Ellie as she eased the egg out of the boot and examined it.
He picked up a toppled chair and unhooked the lamp so
that she could show him how to light it again. As the room
brightened, however, her exclamation made him stop and
join her at the table.

'Look at this.'

It was a hole at one end of the egg. Something was pok-
ing out of it.

'Must have got damaged when the tree came down.
Shame.' Was Ellie going to start crying again and, if so,
what would he do about it this time? Hold her in his arms?

But she was smiling. 'It's called an external pip. It's
hatching.'

'No way...'

Even more astonishing was the way Ellie picked up the
egg and sniffed at the hole.

'What *are* you doing?'

'I want to know how far along it is. Sometimes you
can tell by the smell whether the chick's all sweaty and
in trouble.'

'How on earth do you know that?'

'My granddad was passionate about birds. We looked
after a lot of them on the island. And I volunteer, these
days, at a captive rearing centre that's trying to save endangered kiwi. It's run by one of my best friends, Jillian.
We look after eggs and chicks and then release them back
into the wild.'

Okay. It was official now. Eleanor Sutton was the most

extraordinary woman Jake had ever met. He knew he was staring and probably looking vaguely starstruck.

Ellie simply shrugged. 'I've got a thing for nature, that's all. Enough Maori blood in me to revere the land. And our *taonga*. The treasure.'

Something fell into place. That gorgeous, olive skin and the impressive mane of black hair. The fighting spirit. It wasn't surprising in the least that Ellie was in some part descended from a warrior race.

But he had to stop staring at her so he stared at the egg instead. 'How long does it take to hatch?'

'Can be days but there's no way of knowing how long it's been already... Oh, look...'

The bump that had been protruding from the egg suddenly got longer. A piece of shell broke free and then he could see the head attached to the strange-looking beak. A tiny eye amongst wet-looking feathers.

In fascinated silence, they both perched on the edge of the spindle-backed chairs and watched as the chick struggled free.

It took a while and every so often they both raised their heads to make eye contact with each other. They were both witnesses to what seemed like a small miracle in the face of such destruction going on in the outside world. The shriek of the wind and the sound of the driving rain on the tin roof punctuated by the occasional bang of a branch hitting it was no more than a background at the moment. They were sharing the birth of something new and amazing.

Jake knew that whatever else happened in his life he would remember this. Ellie and the kiwi chick. New life. This was important. Momentous, even.

It was the strangest baby bird Jake had ever seen—totally out of proportion with a small head, long beak, distended belly and huge feet.

But Ellie was rapt. Her eyes were glowing. 'Congratulations, Dad.'

Jake snorted. If he'd felt ridiculous risking his life to save an egg, it was nothing compared to feeling parental pride over its hatching. And if he was the surrogate father, that made Ellie the mother. An almost wife scenario.

He glared at Ellie and she looked away quickly.

'We need to let it rest for fifteen minutes or so and then I can pick off any bits of shell and stuff. Then we need to keep it warm.'

'We need to check your ankle. And your face is a mess.'

Ellie's eyes widened, but she reached up and touched her face and then looked at her blood-streaked fingers.

'Soon. I need...' She twisted to look at what was draped over the back of the chair she was sitting on. 'Can you spare your thermal?'

'Sure.'

Ellie twisted the dry garment into a thick rope and then curled it into a circle, leaving a hollow in the centre. Very gently, she picked up the baby kiwi and placed it carefully into the hollow.

'They have a distended abdomen because of internalised yolk. It needs support so that it doesn't end up with splayed legs.' With a touch on the tip of its beak, so light it was no more than a thought, Ellie smiled. 'It needs a name, too.'

'I don't do baby names.' Jake turned away. 'I'll heat up some water so you can wash those scratches.'

'Pēpe,' he heard Ellie say softly behind him. 'It's Maori for baby.'

With Pēpe safely on his doughnut nest inside an old plastic container and close enough to the fire to keep warm, Ellie finally hobbled to the couch to check out the extent of her own injuries. Not that it mattered how bad her ankle felt or how awful her face must look. The miracle of the egg not only being viable but hatching was enough to make this whole ordeal worthwhile.

Her ankle certainly looked impressive, though. Her foot was so swollen her toes looked ridiculously small and the bruising down her ankle and along the sides of her foot was black and purple now.

Jake was horrified. Kneeling beside the sofa, he reached out to touch her foot.

'How bad does it feel?'

Ellie simply shrugged because right then she wasn't aware of any pain. All she could focus on was the feel of Jake's hands on her skin and how gentle they were as he traced the swelling and touched the tips of her toes.

'Can you feel that?'

Oh, yeah…

'Mmm. I've still got circulation.'

'Can you wriggle your toes?'

Yes. Ellie could.

'Can you press down against my hand?' He was cradling her foot on his fingers now.

Ellie actually grinned. 'Yes, Doctor. Oh… *Ouch*.' But she was still smiling. 'I'm sure it's only a sprain. I just need to strap it up again and rest it for a bit.'

'I'll strap it up.' Jake was rolling the dirty bandage he had helped her remove. 'Don't suppose you've got a dry one of these somewhere?'

'Hang it by the fire for a while. I won't try and walk until I've got my ankle wrapped up again.'

'I'll get the water. You can wash those scratches.'

Ellie nodded, but she was finally noticing how scratched Jake was himself, especially his hands. How hard had he worked to rescue her? And then she'd made him do more by sending him under the tree roots to look for the dead kiwi's nest.

How magic had it been, seeing the wonder of the chick hatching reflected in Jake's eyes every time she'd been able to look away from what they'd been watching?

And how gentle had he been in checking out her injuries?

Not that she was ready to put her trust in a man, but imagine if you *could* trust someone like Jake? So strong. Protective. Caring. Gentle…

So incredibly *male*…

She reached out to touch his arm as he got to his feet. 'I…I couldn't have got out of there by myself. And Pēpe would have died. Thank you…'

Was it intentional, the way he kept moving…escaping her touch? He looked down at her again and his mouth was twisted into a crooked smile.

A very endearing smile.

'Guess that makes us even, then,' he said gruffly. 'Equal partners?'

'Yeah…' Ellie was still caught by that smile. By the intensity of those dark eyes. Beneath all that hair, Jake Logan was an extraordinarily good-looking man.

He looked away first. 'So maybe next time you'll listen to me when I say something's dangerous.'

'Maybe…'

Outside, the storm still raged, but Ellie felt safe again.

More than safe. She felt cared for. By someone who had as much to give as she did. An ideal partner. There weren't many men who could match Ellie Sutton in terms of courage and resourcefulness. They had a lot in common, didn't they? Not only a spirit of adventure and the fortitude to deal with adversity but they'd both been burned by love. Not that Jake had shared any personal details about the marriage that didn't exist any longer, but that didn't break a sense of connection that only strengthened as the long day wore on.

Frequent checking of the baby bird created a shared pleasure that he seemed to be doing well.

'He's so fluffy now that he's dry,' Jake commented, crouched beside the container and staring into it intently.

'They're unusual feathers,' Ellie told him. 'Kiwis don't need to fly so they're more for warmth. More like hair than feathers.'

'How long until he can go back to the wild?'

'I'll take him to the centre back in Auckland. Jillian will want to put him in a brooder unit for a few weeks and, if he's healthy enough, he'll only need a few more weeks in a quarantine period. They can put a transponder on him and hopefully I can bring him back here. Or, even better, I might be able to release him on Half Moon Island. Grandpa would have been thrilled by that.'

'I'd love to see that. If I'm still in the country.'

Ellie wasn't sure how to respond to that. Give him her phone number? Ask him for his? Admit that she'd be keen to see him again? The ramifications were alarming.

'I'll have to see if it's even possible,' she said cautiously. 'There's lots of regulations.'

'Of course.'

Jake's expert bandaging of her ankle was something else that bound them into more of a team.

'I couldn't have done that better myself. You're not actually a doctor, are you? Or a medic?'

'I've learned a bit of first aid in my time. What with the army and stuff.'

So she'd been right. The limp was probably a legacy of being a soldier.

'Afghanistan?'

'Yep. A long time ago.'

And his tone told her that he still didn't want to talk about anything personal. Ellie got that. What was harder to get her head around was the intense curiosity she was developing. She had so many questions she wanted to ask. So much she wanted to know about this man. And it was more than mere curiosity, if she was honest with herself. This felt more like longing.

A longing to let go?

To trust again?

Maybe he wouldn't have to warn her about something dangerous.

Perhaps he *was* that something.

They slept for a while in the afternoon and by the time they woke it was obvious that the storm had eased considerably. There wasn't much daylight left, though, so perhaps they would be here for another night.

Ellie eased her legs off the couch as Jake stood up. They needed some more firewood if they had a second night to get through and it was past time to check on Pēpe again. Her first attempt to get to her feet failed, however, and she sat back down with a rush.

'Here…' Jake offered her a hand. 'Take it easy, though. That foot won't want much weight on it.'

He held out his other hand as Ellie started to rise and, a heartbeat later, she found herself on her feet, holding both Jake's hands.

And he wasn't letting go.

Ellie certainly couldn't let go first. For one thing her hands were encased by his and for another her body simply wouldn't cooperate. She couldn't even look away from his face. From a gaze that was holding hers with a look that made the rest the world cease to exist. Everything seemed to coalesce. Surviving the rescue, finding their way to shelter, being rescued herself and the bond that had grown and grown today, thanks to Jake's heroism in saving the egg. So many, powerful emotions.

His face was so close. She only had to lean a little and tilt her face up and her lips would meet his.

And, dear Lord…she could feel it happening and no alarm bells were going to halt the process, no matter how loudly they tried to sound.

She was so close now she could feel his breath on her lips and her eyes were drifting shut in anticipation of a kiss she wanted more than anything she could remember wanting in her life.

The sharp crackle of static from behind made her jump.

'Medic One, do you read? Ellie…are you there?'

CHAPTER SIX

A MOMENT HAD never been broken so decisively.

Jake froze. Ellie dived for the radio.

'Medic One receiving. Mike, is that you?'

Another crackle of static and Ellie's heart sank. Maybe she could receive but not transmit.

'…on our way. Can you…on the beach in twenty…?'

Ellie was used to filling in gaps in broken messages. *'Yes.'* Radio protocol was forgotten. 'We'll be there.' Aware of the intense focus of Jake, who was still standing as still as a stone, Ellie pushed the transmitting button again and held it down. 'Mike? Any news on…on the other man in the life raft?'

She held her breath through another burst of static. What if there was no news or—worse—bad news? Jake would be devastated and she would be the one who'd been the bearer of the news. He might shoot the messenger and she would never get as close to him again as she had a moment ago.

A curious wash of something like grief came from nowhere. Ellie could actually feel the sting of tears behind her eyes.

'…fine…' The unexpected word burst through the static. 'Washed onto island…taken to… Be in Auckland by the time you… Ellie, have you any idea who…?'

It didn't matter that the rest of the message was lost. Or

that Ellie still had tears in her eyes as she turned to Jake. He wouldn't notice anyway. She could see that he was shaking and he had a hand shielding his eyes as though he didn't want anyone to see whatever overwhelming emotion he was experiencing.

If she went to him and put her arms around him he would probably kiss her, Ellie realised. But would it be only because he needed an outlet for the joyous relief he was struggling to control?

But when he dropped his hand, his face looked haggard. 'I can't believe it,' he said hoarsely. 'I *won't* believe it...not until I see Ben again.'

'Let's move, then.' The switch of professionalism was easy to flick. Could still provide protection, even. Ellie didn't have time to indulge in any personal reactions. 'We need to change our clothes, put the fire out and get ourselves—and Pēpe—down to the beach. There's not enough daylight left to muck the crew around.'

The media were waiting.

No surprises there. It was enough of a story to have an elite yacht race decimated by the worst storm in decades and they had probably been earning their keep for the last couple of days editing and broadcasting film of dramatic rescues, interviews with survivors and heart-wrenching intrusions on the families of those killed or missing.

What a bonus to have an A-list celebrity as one of the survivors. The paparazzi would be fighting for the best spot to get a photograph that would earn big money. Any one of his favoured charities could be in for an enormous windfall when he chose the best offer for magazine coverage. And not only was Jake a survivor, there was a juicy glimpse into his family life thrown in. Coverage of the twin brother who'd successfully evaded any media spotlight until now because he hated the whole industry so much, thanks to what it had done to their mother. Their childhood.

The story would just keep growing legs, wouldn't it? A savvy journalist could delve into their background and rake over their father's reputation as an utterly ruthless businessman. Their mother's degeneration into reliance on prescription medication and alcohol, which had been her ultimate downfall.

Or had it?

He had to get to Ben. To talk to him.

The shouting from the gathered crowd as the helicopter landed took over from the noise of the slowing rotors as the doors were opened.

'Jake...'

'Mr Logan... This way...'

'Dr Jon... Code One...'

Good grief. Did someone think he would respond to the name of a character he played instead of his real name? It wasn't so stupid, though, was it? He almost turned towards the incessant flash of camera lights in that direction. Instead, he looked back to where Ellie was being helped from the helicopter. She was still clutching the container that held the baby kiwi and seemed to be arguing with her colleague over whether she was fit to walk on that ankle. Jake felt his lips twitching and suppressed a smile. Good luck to someone who wanted to make Ellie do something she didn't want to do.

But then she looked up and saw the media. She had to be hearing all the yelling of his name. She really hadn't had any idea of who he was, had she? No wonder she was looking so bewildered. The man beside her was grinning. He raised an arm to wave at the photographers and television crews. And then he was saying something to Ellie and she turned her head to stare at *him*.

She looked horrified.

Betrayed, even.

There was nothing he could do about it. People from his film production crew were here, too. The director and his PR manager were coming towards him and there was a black limousine with tinted windows waiting with its doors open on this side of the fence that was keeping the media at a respectable distance. An ambulance, with its back doors also open, was parked near the limousine.

'Jake… *Mate*…I can't tell you how good it is to see you. Let's get you to hospital for a check-up.'

'Don't need it,' Jake said.

'We do,' the director insisted. 'Insurance protocol.'

'Do you know where my brother is?'

'No. We do know he's okay, though. You can see him as soon as you've been given the all-clear.'

Ellie and her fellow paramedic were close now. The man had his arm around Ellie, supporting her as she limped. He couldn't hold her gaze. She seemed to lean into her companion, looking up as he spoke to them.

'Survivors have all been taken to The Cloud. Big building down at the Viaduct on the waterfront,' he told Jake. 'There's a medical team there and it's not far from the hospital if they decide you need attention. That's where we're taking Ellie—to the hospital.'

He kept moving, steering Ellie towards the ambulance. For a crazy moment Jake almost followed them—just to stay close to Ellie for a little longer. Who knew when or even if they would ever see each other again? He wanted…

He didn't know what he wanted. To try and explain why he hadn't told her who he was? To try and figure out if this guy she worked with was more than a colleague?

No. He did know what he wanted. What he had to do first.

'Take me to this cloud building,' he ordered his director. 'I'll do whatever I have to but not until I've seen Ben.'

'The media will be all over you.'

'I'll cope.'

'We've got a film crew tailing us.' Mike peered through the small windows at the back of the ambulance. 'You're famous, El.'

'I was just doing my job.' Ellie sat back on the stretcher, letting her head rest on the pillows. She closed her eyes, her breath escaping in a ragged sigh. 'I hope Dave's being careful, taking Pēpe to the centre.'

'He will be. He loves a challenge that's a bit different. You want some pain relief?'

'No. I'm fine.' Apart from feeling gutted without having any reasonable grounds.

The only sound for a moment was the rumble of the truck's engine.

'Did you really have no idea who he was?'

Her eyes snapped open. 'How could I? He didn't *tell* me.'

'Not even his name?'

'Well...yeah. He told me his name. It was just a name.'

Mike snorted. 'You've just spent more than twenty-four hours holed up with one of the most eligible males in the universe. Most girls would kill for an opportunity like that.

It was Ellie's turn to snort.

'*ER* used to be your favourite TV show. You must remember that French surgeon. What was his name? Pierre or something. And then the *Stitch in Time* series? Where that modern doctor keeps going through that portal and saving lives that change the course of history?'

Ellie shook her head. She hadn't seen it. And it had been

years since *ER* had been her entertainment fix. Jake would have been ten years younger and wouldn't have been disguised by far too much hair. She never knew the real names of actors anyway—she had enough trouble remembering the names of the characters they portrayed. But it made a horrible kind of sense.

No wonder Jake could act like a doctor. Gentle and caring and skillful. He'd learned how to pretend to *be* one, hadn't he?

'That's what he was coming to New Zealand for. To film the last bits of the movie they're making from the series. You wouldn't believe the coverage the E channel's been giving this disaster thanks to him being in it. And did you know that the other guy in the life raft was his brother? Not just a brother but his *twin?*'

'Yes. I did know that.'

Everybody would know that. Was that why Jake had revealed that much? And was the reason he'd been so shuttered about anything else personal because he knew it would be gold for the waiting media and he didn't trust her not to go and spill the beans?

The television crew had beaten the ambulance to the hospital. They were waiting for Ellie to come out of the back. A couple of photographers were there as well.

'Ms Sutton…how are you feeling?'

'What can you tell us about Jake Logan? Is he coming here as well?'

'You saved his life… How does he feel about that?'

'Ellie—over here. Slow down… We just need one shot.'

Ellie ducked her head behind Mike's arm. 'For heaven's sake,' she muttered. 'Just get me inside.'

The Cloud was an extraordinary building right on the waterfront of Auckland's harbour. Designed to accommodate up to five thousand people, it was long and low with an undulating white roof that had given it the unusual name. A perfect space to be catering for the huge numbers of people.

The Ultraswift-Round-the-World yacht race had come to a temporary halt due to Cyclone Lila. The boats that had made it safely to Auckland were all moored nearby and their crews were using The Cloud as their base as they had repairs done on their yachts and waited for the weather to settle. Families of those injured or still missing were here as well, and there were almost as many reporters as the race officials, crews and their supporters.

Jake was hustled through the crowd and allowed to ignore the press of attention. He was taken to a mezzanine level at the far end of the building that had been roped off to allow only authorised personnel. Up the stairs and in a private area of a large bar, Ben was waiting.

He had apparently refused to allow their reunion to be anything other than completely private and, as the two men held each other in a grip powerful enough to prevent a breath being taken and Jake felt the trickle of tears on his face, he had never been more thankful that the moment wasn't going to be shared with the world.

It was a long time before they broke apart enough to stare intently at each other.

'I thought I'd lost you.'

'Me, too.'

'I couldn't believe it. I *didn't* believe it until now. Are you okay?'

'Pretty good. Got a bit banged up and dislocated my knee. I'll be on crutches for a week or two. And I wouldn't mind sitting down again.'

There were comfortable chairs here. A small table had been provided with a cushion on it for Ben to keep his leg supported. A pair of elbow crutches lay on the floor beside the table. Apart from the splint on his knee, though, Ben didn't seem to have suffered a major injury.

'How did you do it? What happened after I got rescued? It felt like the worst moment in my life when I found out that the weather had got so bad they couldn't even *try* to get back to rescue you.'

Ben looked about as haggard as Jake was feeling. He was nodding and it looked as if he was swallowing hard before he could answer. 'And the worst moment of mine was thinking I'd never see you again.'

'So what happened?'

'Bit of a blur. Didn't think I was going to make it. Thought I was dead until I found myself being dragged up a beach.'

'Someone *found* you?'

'Wouldn't be here if they hadn't. And it wasn't just someone. It was a nurse who goes by the name of Smash 'em Mary.'

Jake had to grin. 'Sounds formidable.'

Something flickered in Ben's eyes but was gone before Jake could analyse it. 'She saved my life,' was all he said. 'And she was a nurse. If she hadn't put my knee back I'd be a lot worse off than I am now.'

'You got saved by a nurse.' Jake shook his head. 'And I got saved by a paramedic. A *girl* paramedic.'

Except that 'girl' was totally the wrong word. Courageous, determined...beautiful...Eleanor Sutton was a powerful woman. Compelling. And Jake was already...*missing* her? Not that he could begin to explain to Ben what had happened in the hours they'd been apart. It would have to wait until they had more time. Until Jake had had a chance to get his own head around what may well have been a life-changing incident. Best to ignore it for the moment.

'What happens now?'

'Guess I'll get the first flight I can back to the States. You?'

'I'll get on with what I was coming here for in the first place. There's a deadline on getting this film into the can.'

Ben nodded. 'We both need to get back into it. Put this disaster behind us.'

'Any word on *Rita*?'

'Doubt they'll even find any wreckage. She's gone.'

Just like her namesake. Rita Marlene. Their mother.

Jake closed his eyes and took a deep breath. 'What you said, Ben…it's not true. Mom didn't kill herself. It was an accident. That was the coroner's verdict.'

Ben was silent.

'It's *not* true,' Jake insisted. '*Is* it?'

'I wouldn't have said it if it wasn't true.'

'How do you know? Did you hide something? Like a *note?*'

Ben shook his head.

'So how do you know?' Jake's voice rose. 'You have to tell me. I've got a right to know.'

'I can't.'

'Can't…or *won't?*'

'Jake…' Ben held up his hands—a pleading gesture. 'Let it go. Please. It's so long ago it doesn't make any difference now.'

'Are you *kidding?* You can't say something like that and just leave it. If you've got some evidence and you've been hiding it all these years, you've been *lying* to me.'

'I haven't got any evidence. I just…*know.*'

'Jake?' It was his PR manager, Kirsty, who approached the men in their corner of this big space. 'Sorry to break in on the family reunion but we've got all the major TV networks queued up downstairs to talk to you. Adam's getting an ulcer, waiting for you to get a proper medical clearance. How long do you think you'll be?'

Jake glared at Ben. The joy of seeing his brother safe was being undermined by anger at not getting the answers he needed.

And there was fear there, too. Ben was the only person in the world he'd ever had complete faith in. Absolute trust.

He was looking completely shattered now. Instead of celebrating their joint survival, Jake had turned it into a confrontation that was something he'd never anticipated between them. Was he even ready to hear the truth?

And now they were being interrupted by the lifestyle that Ben deplored. The pursuit of fame that had always seemed more important to their mother than they had been. Play-acting. Sidestepping reality.

He could hear an echo of Ellie's voice in his head.

How does avoiding reality help exactly?

Maybe it didn't help but it was the only protection Jake knew.

Ben seemed to sense his train of thought. The softening in his eyes suggested that he understood. He gripped his brother's shoulder.

'Go, Jake. It's what you do. Your public needs you. *You* need them. We'll talk soon.' He even summoned a cheeky grin. 'And, hey…no amount of money could buy this kind of PR for the movie. You may as well milk it.'

'Amen,' said Kirsty. 'Come on, Jake. Pretty please… We'll set up a press conference so you only have to do it once. And while we're doing that, you can let the doctors check you out properly.'

X-rays had revealed no broken bones, but the ligament damage to Ellie's ankle meant that she needed a plaster cast for a couple of weeks at least. And complete rest. She was off active duty on the helicopter crew for the foreseeable future.

'I'm going to be bored out of my skull,' Ellie informed Mike, who had come back to hear the verdict and take her home.

'They'll find some light duties for you on base for a while.'

'Mmm.' Maybe fate was stepping in here, forcing her to take some time out and think about her future. Did she really want to give up on the part of her career that had meant so much to her for so long?

Right now, all Ellie wanted to do was to get home and eat something that hadn't come out of an ancient can. To call Jillian at the bird centre and get more information than Dave had passed on to Mike about the condition of the rescued baby kiwi. To sink into her own bed and sleep. A week or so should do the trick.

There was a slight problem with the plan, however.

'Where's my other boot?'

'You can't wear it with your foot in a cast.'

'No, but it had all the loose stuff from my pockets in it. I had to find a way to carry it all in a bit of a rush. My keys are in there.'

'You can't drive either.'

'My house key is on the same ring.'

'Haven't you got a spare?'

Ellie was too tired to be reasonable. 'I want my boot.'

'I'll ring the base. It might still be in the chopper.'

He ended his phone call a short time later. 'Dave reckons it went with some other clothing—to The Cloud.'

Ellie sighed. There had been a bundle of clothing. Jake had changed out of the horrendous trackpants and put his jeans back on, but either he'd run out of time or had become attached to his black-and-red-checked shirt because he had only put his coat on top and bundled his other belongings under an arm.

'Fine. That's on the way home, if you don't mind a quick detour.'

Mike's face lit up. 'And get a chance to rub shoulders with the rich and famous again? See you become world famous as the woman who rescued Jake Logan? I don't mind at all.'

'There'll be no rubbing shoulders,' Ellie warned. 'We get my boot and get out. I'm not in any mood to get interviewed.'

She had no intention of talking to Jake if she could avoid it. The shock of learning who he really was had more than one aspect that was making her cringe.

She'd made a joke about his limp. Ordered him to make himself useful. And had she really dismissed his whole career by suggesting that he might be a male *model?*

He hadn't enlightened her, though, had he?

And you didn't have to lie outright to be dishonest. You could lie by omission.

Arriving at their destination wearing their bright red flight-suits and with Ellie hopping on crutches should have attracted attention, but instead they slipped in virtually unnoticed. Everybody was crowded around an area that had been set up with a long table in front of a big screen.

Images of yachts and rescue scenes were providing a backdrop to a press conference. Jake sat centre stage, flanked by the man who'd met him at the helipad and others who were wearing lanyards and looked like race officials. Just under the mezzanine level of the building, there were people leaning over the balcony to watch as well and Ellie noticed she wasn't the only person on crutches here.

Jake's voice was clear and loud, not only because of the

lapel mike he was wearing but due to the rapt silence of an audience that was hanging on every word.

'…we thought that was it. And then we saw the chopper with the crewman on the end of the winch. Or should I say crewwoman?' Jake's headshake was slow and incredulous. 'I can't speak highly enough of the courage and skill of the New Zealand helicopter rescue service. You guys should be very, very proud of yourselves.'

Mike nudged Ellie, but she was heading purposefully towards someone on the edge of the crowd at the very front. A woman with blond hair and high heels, who was holding a clipboard. She'd been at the helipad with the other people who'd been waiting to whisk Jake off in that ridiculous limousine. Maybe she'd know where her boot was.

'Oh…you must be Ellie.' The woman's smile was very wide. 'I'm Kirsty. This is great. Can we get a shot of you and Jake together after this interview? I understand it was you that rescued Jake? That it was *your* beach house you used as shelter? And did you guys really watch a kiwi hatching? That's so *awesome…*'

Someone from the floor was asking a question about whether the race organisers were at fault for not postponing this leg of the race. One of the officials started explaining the cyclone's erratic path. A video clip of a weather map was now playing on the big screen.

Ellie looked at Kirsty's perfect hair and makeup. She might have been able to brush out the tangled mess of her own hair at the hospital and rebraid it but it was still filthy. And while the scratches and bruises on her face had been well cleaned, she didn't have a scrap of any makeup on to soften the effect.

'No,' she told Kirsty firmly. 'I look like I've been dragged through a hedge backwards.' It wasn't far from the truth, was it? If Jake had told people about Pēpe, maybe he'd also told them about saving her life by getting her out from under that tree? Wouldn't the media love that—to find that a movie star had morphed into a real live hero? But it felt like something private was being exploited.

'And I'm exhausted,' she added. 'I just want to find my boot and get home.'

'I had it sent to the front reception desk. I didn't know that you'd be coming to collect it in person. Are you sure I can't change your mind about a photo? Or a quick interview? There's a lot of people here who are super-keen to talk to you.'

The need for officials to deflect blame for the disaster the yacht race had become was still going on. Not needing to answer any questions for the moment, Jake was looking around the room. Ellie watched, using it as an excuse to ignore Kirsty's request even though she knew that she had to be very obvious, standing here on the edge of the crowd, not far from the end of the long table. Wearing bright red.

She was prepared for him to notice her.

What she wasn't prepared for was the effect of the eye contact.

For just a heartbeat, he held her gaze. Clung to it as though seeing her again was a huge relief. As if he'd been afraid of never seeing her again?

For just that infinitesimal fraction of time it felt like that moment when Ellie had known they were going to kiss. That the connection was far too strong to resist.

But then it was gone. So fast she could believe she had imagined it.

And Jake was interrupting the race official.

'There's no point in trying to blame anyone,' he said smoothly. 'It happened. Yacht racing is a risky business. I'd like to take this opportunity to say how devastated we all are that lives have been lost. And how incredibly grateful both my brother and myself are for being rescued. There's one person in particular that I will be grateful to for the rest of my life.'

'Who's that?' someone yelled.

Jake was smiling now. He stretched out a hand. 'Paramedic Eleanor Sutton. My real life heroine.'

Kirsty beamed, stepping aside slightly to allow Ellie to be seen more clearly.

Ellie cringed as cameras swung in her direction.

'They want you to join them.' Kirsty sounded excited now. 'Do you need some help?'

'No.' The word came out through gritted teeth. Jake had caught her gaze again as he'd stretched out that hand as an invitation to share his fame.

She must have imagined that connection she'd felt because it certainly wasn't there this time. This was Jake Logan the movie star looking at her and he wasn't the man she had rescued or shared the miracle of watching new life emerge with.

Couldn't anyone else see that he was only showing what he wanted the world to see?

That that warm smile and the over-the-top praise wasn't *real?*

She didn't know this man.

And she didn't want to. She had personal experience of a man who could make others believe whatever he wanted. An experience she would never repeat, thank you very much.

With nothing more than a dismissive shake of her head for Kirsty's benefit, Ellie turned and started moving.

She had to get out of there.

CHAPTER SEVEN

In the end, it was the rescue base manager, Gavin Smith, who gave the media at least some of what they wanted, providing details of the horrific day from the viewpoint of the emergency services and fielding some awkward questions from journalists.

'Is it normal practice to keep a victim on the end of a winch line like that? Isn't it incredibly dangerous?'

'The pros and cons of any emergency situation are something our crews are trained to weigh up. The chopper was already fully loaded. The only way to get the men out of the life raft was to try and transfer them to the closest land.'

'So why didn't they go back for Jacob Logan's brother?'

'Not only had weather conditions worsened, the condition of a patient on board was also critical. The risk to everybody involved was simply too great.'

'So they just got abandoned?'

'They weren't abandoned.' The base manager stayed perfectly calm. 'By a stroke of luck, the paramedic who was on the winch knew the area well. She knew that they could find shelter.'

'Why won't Eleanor Sutton talk to the media? Has she been told not to? What went on that needs to be kept so private?'

Gavin's bland expression made the question lose any

significance. 'As far as I'm concerned, there's nothing to tell. Our crew did their job under exceptionally trying circumstances. Successfully, I might add. If one of them chooses not to be in the public eye for doing that job, I'm more than happy to respect that. Perhaps you should too.'

It didn't appear that they were going to.

The phone had been ringing from the moment Ellie had got home. The offers to buy her story were starting to get ridiculous. Thousands of dollars turned into tens of thousands as the days passed and she continued to refuse an interview or photographs.

Maybe Jake had had good reason to keep so much personal information to himself. He wasn't to know that she was financially secure in a mortgage-free house she had inherited from her parents. Or that she'd been earning good money for years with no dependants to share it with. How many people would be tempted by an offer of such a windfall?

And wouldn't the gossip magazines love an account of what now seemed like a personal revelation about how Jake Logan saw movies as a means of coping with adverse life events?

About how he didn't see role-playing as being fake but as a chance to practise being the best version of himself he could be?

A tiny insight into how his mind worked, maybe, but it would be gold for these hungry journalists.

It was gold for Ellie, too. A small nugget that she had every intention of keeping entirely to herself, although she wasn't sure why it seemed so important. She'd probably never see him again so why should it matter what he thought of her?

Ellie had always been too trusting, and she had always

been utterly trustworthy herself. Deception was anathema to her. Okay, she'd been burnt too badly to ever be as trusting again, but she'd never sink to that level.

She was trustworthy.

If Jake had inadvertently trusted her with even the tiniest piece of something personal and she kept that information safe, at least he would know that her integrity was intact. That she could be trusted.

And that gave her the moral high ground, didn't it? Jake might wrap it up in words that made it sound almost acceptable, but acting was a form of deception. Fine for movies when people knew that the people on screen were only characters, but he'd proved he could do it in real life, too, with that polished performance for the media.

You'd never know whether he was being honest or acting.

Did he even know himself?

In the absence of any new material, magazines were using what they could find, and to her horror the picture that appeared all over the internet, newspapers and magazines was one that had been taken just after they'd landed. When she'd seen the media falling all over Jake and Mike had been telling her who he actually was. There was no mistaking the confusion and sense of betrayal on her face. Others were passing it off as no more than a bad photo and her expression was probably due to the pain of her injured ankle, but Ellie knew the truth. She now had a permanent reminder of exactly how she'd felt in learning Jake's real identity.

She had been deceived.

Again.

It shouldn't have come as such a surprise. Given her experience, it should be a lot easier to deal with than last time but, somehow, this was harder. Because she'd got to a point where she'd *wanted* to trust Jake?

For the first time since the devastating betrayal of a man she'd been about to marry, Ellie had been able to see that it might be possible to fall in love again.

To trust.

Such a hard-won step forward and she'd been shoved backwards again with what felt like a cruel blow.

Whatever. She had no choice but to deal with it and get on with her life.

The extent of the battering her body had taken and the exhaustion of both the rescue and its aftermath cushioned Ellie for several days, but then she began to feel like a prisoner in her own home.

In solitary confinement.

She was totally used to living on her own. Why did she suddenly feel so lonely?

The big windows of her living area had a stunning view of the beach and the distinctive shape of Rangitoto Island—an ancient volcano. Her father's telescope still had its position at one side of the French doors that led out to the balcony and Ellie had spent a lot of time watching the activity on the stretch of water that divided Auckland harbour from the open sea. It seemed like a good way to reconnect to her own life.

To forget about Jake Logan?

Except that the bleak landscape of Rangitoto made her think about the lush rainforest cover of Half Moon Island and long to see it again. The barrier that had been there ever since her parents had been tragically killed had been forced open. It wasn't just memories of her time with Jake that were haunting Ellie now. They were competing with memories of her parents and her beloved grandfather. Happy times in a place that was a part of her soul. People that were missing from her life and had taken such big pieces of her along with them.

Everyone knew that nothing was for ever but why had she had to lose every person she had ever truly loved?

No wonder she was feeling lonely.

The usual traffic of container ships, naval vessels and ferries had been noticeably interrupted by the fleet of racing yachts when the Ultraswift-Round-the-World race was started again a few days after the cyclone and by then Ellie had to accept that it was not going to be so easy to get Jake out of her head.

It was bad enough getting reports of the way he was still touching her real life.

The helicopter rescue trust had received an impressive donation that was labelled as anonymous but it was obvious it had come from one—or both—of the Logan brothers.

Jillian, at the bird-rearing centre, was almost speechless at the size of the donation the kiwi trust had received within days of Pēpe's arrival.

'I know it's anonymous,' she told Ellie, 'but it's a bit of coincidence, wouldn't you say?'

'Lots of people care about saving kiwis. Pēpe's famous now. He was on the news.'

'Not many people can afford to care to the tune of hundreds of thousands of dollars.'

'*That* much? Phew…' Ellie closed her eyes but it didn't shut out the pictures appearing in her head. If anything, it made them clearer. The way Jake had looked as they'd watched the baby bird hatching. The way he'd looked at *her* as they'd shared that unforgettable experience.

'I did an internet search on him,' Jillian confessed. 'He's seriously hot, isn't he?'

'Bit hairy for me.'

'Have a look at some of the older photos, then, where he's clean shaven. Like back in the day when he was on *ER*. Oh, *my*…'

Ellie had to laugh. It sounded like Jillian, who was in her early sixties and had several grandchildren, was busy fanning herself.

'Amazing he's still single,' Jillian continued. 'Or maybe not. That wife of his really did a number on him, didn't she?'

'I wouldn't know. I don't read that stuff and we didn't talk about anything personal.'

They'd come close, though, hadn't they? She could still hear the bitterness in Jake's voice when he'd answered her query about him being married.

Not anymore.

And she'd wanted to find out. It had been a personal challenge not to search the internet and devour every piece of information she could find. The curiosity was over-powering now.

'What did she do?'

'Only went and got herself up the duff by the leading man on her first movie. A part she only got because of her connection to Jake.'

'Oh…' Ellie was stunned.

How could any woman be that *stupid*? If she'd wanted a baby she couldn't have picked a better father than Jake. Impossible not to remember how protective he'd been in trying to stop her going out into that storm. The strength he'd shown in rescuing her. How gentle he'd been in that impressive examination of her injured ankle.

'And then she dropped the bombshell online so that the whole world knew before he did.'

'That's horrible,' Ellie said, but she was backing away fast from the onslaught of emotions she didn't want to try and handle. 'Jill—I've got to go, but it's great to know how well Pēpe's doing. I'll call you again soon.'

'Okay. Speaking of calling, has *he* called you?'

'No. Why would he?' To thank her again, perhaps? With the kind of polished speech he'd given the media? What if he offered *her* money as a gesture of gratitude—or apology?

'Someone from the film company rang to ask after Pēpe the other day. A woman called Kristy or something.'

'Kirsty?'

'That's it. She asked for your phone number. Said they'd tried to get it from your work, but they wouldn't hand out personal information. Anyway, I gave her your mobile number. Hope you don't mind.'

'My phone got wrecked. I haven't got around to replacing it yet.'

'Maybe you should get a new one. And talk to him if he rings. You've got a lot in common when you come to think about it.'

'Oh…right. Like he's a famous movie star and I'm a very ordinary mortal?'

'You're on the same page as far as your love lives go.'

Ellie's snort of laughter was not amused. 'Hardly. Guess I can be grateful that it was only my friends who found out how narrowly I escaped a bigamous marriage. Far more humiliating to have the whole world devouring every detail of your betrayal.'

She didn't want to talk about Michael and, this time, she was more successful in pleading a need to end the call. Having made a note to remind herself to sort out a new phone the next day, Ellie stared at the piece of paper and then screwed it up.

What would happen if her number worked again? Would she be waiting for it to ring? Be picking it up every five minutes to see if she'd received a message? Be disappointed if it rang and it wasn't Jake on the other end?

It would be better not to risk it. In fact, when she got a new phone she'd ask for a new number as well. It would be best to forget about Jacob Logan and the way he'd managed to stir up feelings that she'd thought she was immune to. Jake needed to be tucked into the past and largely forgotten. As Michael had been.

But everything conspired to remind her, even in the seclusion of her own home. Trying to put any weight on her foot would create a throb of pain that took her back to that awful moment of finding she had been unable to walk on the beach when they'd desperately needed to find the beach house. When Jake had scooped her up into his arms and carried her to safety.

Opening her pantry to look for something to eat, the sight of canned food would take her back to that extraordinary meal by the fire.

Just needing to go to the bathroom would remind her of that terrifying moment of the tree coming down. Of Jake screaming her name as if it would be the worst thing in the world if something bad had happened to her.

The nights were even worse. There was no protection to be found from the moments that she was forced to relive in her dreams. Helping Jake take his clothes off or that almost-kiss just before that radio message had come in was always the catalyst but her unconscious mind wouldn't leave it alone. The fantasy of what could have happened if they hadn't been so uncomfortable with the situation or interrupted was played out in glorious Technicolor with the added dimension of sensations Ellie had never realised could be so powerful. More than once, she woke to find her body still pulsing with a release that left...a kind of shame in its wake.

Here she was, a thirty-two-year-old woman, mooning after a celebrity like some starstruck teenager.

It had to end.

Ellie rang her boss. 'Smithie? I'm going nuts here. I might be stuck on the ground but I really need some work to do. Can we talk?'

Jake thought he looked more like a pirate than a nine-teenth-century deckhand but that was okay. Fun, even. The baggy trousers weren't as bad as those old trackpants Ellie had given him to wear and they were tucked neatly into black leather boots that folded down at the top. The white shirt with its wide collar, laced opening and gener-ous sleeves was a bit girlie but the waistcoat hid part of it and with some artfully applied smudges of grime and a rip or two it was quite acceptable.

He eyed himself in the mirror as the makeup techni-cian started on his hair. Ellie certainly wouldn't think he was wearing his hair like this for a photo shoot as a male model, would she?

'What is that stuff?'

'Basically grease. We need that nice, dirty, dreadlocked vibe.'

'At least the bandanna hides most of it. Have to say I can't wait to get a proper haircut again.'

The makeup girl smiled at his reflection. 'I dunno… it kinda suits you. And I'm getting so used to it I almost didn't recognise you in that new article that's out.'

'Another article?' There'd been so many of them in the last few weeks that Jake didn't bother to look unless Kirsty insisted. He should be delighted that Ellie wasn't prepared to reveal anything about herself or her time with him, but perversely it was like a hurt silence that told him he'd done something wrong.

Because he hadn't trusted her?

'One of the local women's magazines. It's over there, by the wigs.'

He shouldn't have opened it. Why did they keep using that dreadful photograph of Ellie? The one where she'd clearly been told who it was that she'd rescued. When she'd realised that he had been less than honest with her. Where she looked not only as if she was in pain and exhausted but that she'd been betrayed somehow.

He'd wanted to try and explain. Of course he had. But she'd publicly turned her back on his invitation to share that press conference and she'd been unreachable ever since. Not that he'd been able to visit the rescue base where she worked in person. Or the bird sanctuary place that the baby kiwi had been taken to, but Kirsty had managed to find a phone number and he'd tried that repeatedly, only to get the message that the phone was either out of range or turned off.

How much clearer did Ellie have to make it that she didn't want anything more to do with him?

He should be over it by now. Well into the full-on work that was his career on set. They were on deadline here, with a release timed for the summer holiday season in the United States and a lot of editing, as well as special effects, that would have to be done before then. With practised focus, Jake dropped the magazine and stepped into the dark of predawn outside the caravan to begin his new day.

A good percentage of the movie was already in the can. The opening scenes with him being a surgeon with a tension-racked relationship in a high-paced American hospital before he stepped into the portal, and the ending when he was back there and trying to get to grips with normal life and able to repair the relationship thanks to what he'd faced centuries ago. There'd been scenes shot in London, too, where he'd started to grow his hair and beard to look the part as he got swept into employment on an immigrant ship.

They'd had to come to New Zealand to film the guts of the story, though, with the premise being that his medical knowledge would save the life of a woman who would go on to raise a child who would change history. A square-rigged sailing ship that was going to be wrecked just off the coast of the north island. A life-and-death struggle for survival in the wild land of a new colony. A love story that could never be consummated because that would have altered history, but the lessons learned meant that the real-time love story would come right.

Too ironic, really, given the experience Jake had been through before arriving on set. The media had jumped on that.

'How does it feel, having to be on a ship, given your recent brush with death?'

'Safe,' Jake had told them smoothly. 'Everything that happens here is carefully controlled. I doubt that we'll be doing any scenes at sea if there's another cyclone forecast.'

There was medical cover, too, in case anything untoward happened. An ambulance was always parked nearby, manned by volunteer officers from the nearest local town of Whitianga on the Coromandel Peninsula. One of them was a young woman, but thankfully she looked nothing like Ellie. It was bad enough having the emergency vehicle on site, reminding him every time of the unfortunate way they'd parted.

It was just as well the female lead didn't look anything like Ellie either. Amber was petite and redheaded, with skin so pale it was almost transparent. And her eyes were green, not that dark, chocolaty brown.

One of today's scenes was the first meeting of the deckhand and the immigrant girl during the arduous voyage in an overcrowded ship infested with lice, cockroaches and rats. He would be coming from a confrontation with a drunk and incompetent ship's-surgeon. She was out of the cramped, working-class cabins below deck to attend the funeral of a friend's baby who'd succumbed to typhoid fever.

That was an emotionally wrenching scene he was witness to, but being out on the water in the beautiful replica ship being used for filming was a pleasure. The sea was calm, the sunrise spectacular and the first scene of the day only needed one take.

The scene with the ship's surgeon didn't go so well. It was supposed to be a busy time for the crew, with sails being shifted to catch the wind while the argument was happening. Getting enough activity to ramp up the tension was difficult and by the third take people were tiring. During the filming, one of the extras managed to get tangled up in a rope as one of the huge sails was being lowered and he dislocated his shoulder.

It was Jake who helped carry the man to shore once the ship got back to the jetty, but the paramedic on duty wasn't qualified to administer IV pain relief. When she rang for backup, the only other ambulance in the area was out on a job.

'He'll have to be transported,' she informed the director.

He was already stressed about the hold-up in the day's filming. 'Call for a helicopter, then.'

But the closest rescue helicopter was attending a serious accident well north of Auckland and it would be over an hour before it would be available.

'I'll have to transport him myself,' the paramedic decided. 'At least I've got Entonox available.'

'How long will that take?'

'The closest hospital is in Thames. The round trip will

be at least two hours. Probably more like three, what with handing him over and roadworks and things.'

'Who's going to cover the set, then?' The director shook his head at the paramedic's expression. 'Nobody, obviously. That means we can't film.'

'Maybe one of the local doctors could come out for a bit.'

'We've got weeks of filming ahead of us. We can't afford this kind of hassle.' He looked over his shoulder towards the unfortunate extra, who was sitting on a stretcher in the back of the ambulance, Kirsty beside him, offering comfort. 'Go,' he ordered wearily. 'Get that poor guy sorted. I'm not going to make him wait.' He raised his voice. 'Kirsty? Can you come over here, please?'

'We'll have to hire independent medical cover,' was Kirsty's suggestion when she heard the tale of woe. 'Someone who's qualified to deal with any situation and give whatever treatment is needed until ground or air transport can get here. Someone who could live on site in the camping grounds with us and be available twenty-four seven.'

'How on earth are we going to find someone like that?'

'I don't know,' Kirsty admitted. 'But we do, at least, have a personal contact with the ambulance service, thanks to Jake.'

'I don't have contact, exactly,' Jake said. 'I haven't even spoken to Ellie since the rescue. The only contact was when I rang the base to see how she was a couple of weeks ago.'

It had been a last attempt to make some personal contact given that the mobile number had been such a failure. Had she really been unavailable or were her colleagues protecting her from a call from someone she didn't want to speak to?

'And how was she?'

'Getting over the ankle injury, apparently, but only on light duties. Her boss said something about her preparing teaching material. She wasn't on the base and she wouldn't be back on active duty for some time but she was fine.'

It had been a relief to know she hadn't been left with any lasting disability caused by the rescue of himself. Oddly disappointing to know that he'd have no more excuses to ask after her, though.

'Sounds perfect,' the director said. 'She's certainly qualified and not afraid of doing something different or challenging. Still got the number of her boss?'

'I have,' Kirsty said helpfully. 'His name's Smith.'

'Get him on the blower. We need to talk.'

Jake watched them walk away. It was highly unlikely that Ellie would want to take such an unusual job, even if it could be arranged, but the flare of something curiously like excitement told him that he hoped she would.

That he would get the chance to see her again.

To talk to her.

The feeling intensified as the day ticked on. Because they couldn't film without medical cover, there was too much time to think.

To feel bad that he had been less than honest with her about who he was. Had he really been worried that she might sell her story to the media? She hadn't breathed a word. She hadn't even taken the opportunity to bask in any glory associated with the dramatic rescue.

To feel frustrated, too, that he had never had the chance to try and explain anything. To apologise?

She hadn't believed him when he'd told her how acting could help you deal with real life. Maybe if she saw what really went on, she would see that it wasn't fake—not on an emotional level, anyway.

She might understand what he'd been trying to say when he'd told her something that he'd never told anybody else.

He had to admit that there was a longing there to have somebody who really understood. Ben understood his need for his career, but he still saw it all as play-acting. An escape from reality. He wasn't ever going to get close enough to the action to really get it because he hated the whole industry with such a passion.

And yet Ben had reaped the benefits of his twin's ability to act and make others believe in their early years. How often had he instigated a game that would take them away from what was happening around them?

Their lifestyle had had a veneer that was a dream to most people, but they didn't know what it was really like. A father rich enough to seemingly own half of Manhattan. A heartbreakingly beautiful mother who was loved by millions but desperately unhappy in her marriage to a bully who resented her fame.

Play-acting had been a way to escape the fights and misery and lingering bitterness. If he and Ben were pirates and they were being forced to walk the plank, the screaming row their parents were having could seem like nothing more than seagulls overhead and circling sharks below and the two small boys could poke them in the eyes and swim to safety.

All Ben could see in the industry of play-acting was the damage it had done to their mother. Their family. No wonder he hated it. And no wonder he was sticking to his unspoken vow of never repeating history. Had he ever got even as close to a woman as *he* was currently feeling about Ellie?

Ellie would probably agree wholeheartedly with Ben about the negative side of the movie industry, but…what if he could change her mind?

If someone like her could understand and maybe even approve of what he did, it could validate what he did for a living. Make him feel like he was contributing to making the world a better place.

Like Ellie did?

'That's a crazy idea.'

'A few weeks on the Coromandel Peninsula? In a nice little cabin in the camping grounds? Gorgeous weather. Probably still warm enough to swim and that would be as good for your ankle as the physiotherapy.'

'There's lots of people who'd jump at the opportunity. Why me?'

Gavin Smith grinned. 'I guess you proved yourself by saving the star of the movie once already. Maybe he asked for *you* personally.'

Why did her heart skip a beat like that? Her mouth suddenly feel unaccountably dry? Could that be true? More importantly, did she want it to be true?

Had she proved her trustworthiness by not saying anything to reporters? Did Jake realise, without knowing why, how hurt she was at having been deceived?

'I can't believe they can just click their fingers and get someone from the service who's that qualified just to sit around in case something happens.'

'New Zealand's getting a reputation as a great place to make movies. The government's keen to support the industry. The word's come from on high to provide the best we can.' Gavin raised his eyebrows encouragingly. 'That's you, Ellie.'

It was impossible not to imagine what it would be like to see Jake again. Their time together was too tangled in emotions that were partly due to the traumatic situation they'd been in. Maybe she'd get there and find that it had been nothing more than a reaction to the circumstances and that there wasn't any real attraction on either side.

And, if that was the case, maybe she could finally put the whole, disturbing episode behind her and get on with the rest of her life. It wouldn't be nibbling away at her peace of mind as it had done ever since she'd had that time with Jake.

Gavin was saying something about her being able to carry on with her current project of writing lectures about aeromedical transportation. About providing her with an extensive enough kit that she would be able to cope with any emergency with ease. That by the time she got back she'd be fully recovered and they could decide about what she wanted to do next in her career.

But all Ellie could think about was being close to Jake again. Would he look at her again the way he had in that moment before they'd almost kissed?

'Okay…' Her voice came out in a whisper. 'I'll do it.'

CHAPTER EIGHT

THE DRIVE FROM Auckland to the Coromandel township of Whitianga only took two and half hours, but it was enough time for Ellie to have a good think about how she was going to handle the moment when she and Jake met again.

It was ironic that she was joining a film crew and would be on set while a movie was being filmed because the only way she was going to be able to cope with this was to become something of an actress herself.

Well…she could hardly reveal to the world that she—an ordinary Kiwi girl—had some kind of mixed-up crush on a famous movie star, could she? How humiliating would that be?

And she had been humiliated before. She wasn't going there again.

Funny how Jake's words kept echoing in her head during that drive. And it was definitely motivating to imagine watching herself on the big screen here. Cheering herself on. Facing obstacles and overcoming them.

Practising being the best person she could be, even if it felt like the skin didn't fit yet.

She would be pleased to see him—as she would be to catch up on any of the patients she'd rescued during her career. Keen to do something so different. Excited, even, to be part of a totally new world.

She would realise that the crush was no more than the aftermath of an overly emotional situation and that there was nothing real to hang any fantasies on. She would re-affirm her faith that dealing with reality was preferable to trying to escape and then she would go back to her own life, with her head held high, to do exactly that.

The autumn weather was stunning as she wound her way through over the mountain range and through the small township of Tairua. Beneath a cloudless blue sky, the lush native forest looked cool and green and the glimpses of ocean a bottomless blue. The main holiday season was well over so Whitianga was quiet, but there was a buzz of excitement in the air that Ellie noticed when she stopped for a few supplies and directions to the camping grounds. That, and her uniform, earned her a curious glance from the shopkeeper.

'Someone been hurt again?'

'Again?' The pang of concern that it could be Jake came from nowhere and the way Ellie could feel her eyes widening was disturbing. She'd never make an actress if she couldn't keep her reactions under better control.

'Someone broke their arm a couple of days ago. Or was it their shoulder? Anyway…they had to stop filming for a day. Did you know they're doing a movie here? Have you seen the boat at the marina?'

'I did. It's beautiful.'

'They're going to do a shipwreck scene round at Cathedral Cove in the next week or two. There's places that people are allowed to go and watch.'

'Sounds fun.'

Her items were being slotted into a carrier bag. 'So no one else has been hurt, then?'

'Not that I know of.'

'But that's why you're here?'

'I'm here to give some first-aid cover.' Ellie practised the kind of smile she would use for a reporter, perhaps, who wanted information. 'Hopefully just as an insurance policy. Can you tell me where the local ambulance station is, too? I'll drop in and say hi on my way.'

She was here.

The SUV painted in ambulance insignia, with the beacon strip on its roof, stood out as clearly as if the lights had been flashing, when Jake emerged from the makeup caravan. The director, Steve, was obviously showing her around the camping ground, along with Kirsty and the camp manager.

Jake could feel his heart rate pick up. The kind of warmth in his chest that he'd only ever noticed when he saw his brother after a longer than usual period apart.

Relief, that's what it was. Mixed with joy. And…hope?

She looked very professional in a crisp, white shirt that had epaulettes and patches on the sleeves. Dark trousers and a belt that had things clipped to it, like a pair of shears and some sort of radio or phone. Her black boots were shining. So was the rope of neatly plaited hair that hung down her back.

Another image flashed into his head. Ellie, sitting in front of the fire, in shapeless trackpants and a checkered woollen shirt, her hair loose and tumbling as she raked her fingers through it.

He preferred that image…

He wished he wasn't in full costume and makeup himself because he was going to look as different to Ellie as she did to him and it felt…wrong.

She didn't even seem to recognise him as her gaze swept around and past where he was standing motionless. But then Steve spotted him.

'Here's someone you'll remember,' he heard the director say. 'Not that there's much time for a catch-up. I'm sorry. We're due to head down to the ship in a couple of minutes.'

'Jake…' Ellie's smile was wide and friendly. She was holding out her hand and when he caught it, the handshake was firm and brief. 'It's so good to see you again.' The smile was directed at the others in the group now. 'It's a bonus you don't often get in my job—catching up with the patients that get rescued.'

Jake blinked. He was a *patient?* Just one of the dozens—or possibly hundreds—that Ellie had rescued in her career?

'Great that you could come,' he heard himself saying. 'I didn't think we'd be lucky enough to get our first choice.' He was smiling, too. He wanted Ellie to know that he'd wanted it to be her. Had wanted to see her again.

'How could I say no?' The smile hadn't dimmed. In fact, it got wider. 'This is a once-in-a-lifetime opportunity for me. How many people get the chance to be part of what's no doubt going to be a blockbuster movie? I'm hoping you're all going to stay nice and safe and it'll work out as a holiday treat for me.'

'Hear! Hear!' Steve muttered.

'Not that I'm not fully equipped to deal with any emergency,' Ellie added hastily. 'My car is full to the brim with everything from sticky plasters to a portable ventilator.'

'And with your connection to the helicopter service, I'm sure we'd get priority treatment.' Kirsty nodded.

Ellie's smile faded only a notch. 'Doesn't work like that, I'm afraid. No preferential treatment because of who you are.'

Jake couldn't read the glance flicked in his direction, but it had been impersonal and there was something about the inflection in her words that struck a cool enough note to send a tiny shiver down his spine.

And then it hit him.

This wasn't Ellie talking. Not the *real* Ellie.

She was...*acting,* dammit. Saying the things that were presenting the image she'd chosen to present.

The way *he* had the last time they'd been breathing the same air, at that media conference in The Cloud? When he'd been putting all that warmth and gratitude into his pretty little speech about how good the New Zealand rescue services were and about one paramedic in particular? Had he really gushed on about his 'real-life heroine'?

This felt like a slap in the face. Payback.

But that wasn't Ellie either. Not the Ellie he remembered, anyway.

'Come on, Jake. Time to get to work.' Steve thumped him on the shoulder as he headed off. 'Kirsty will bring Ellie down to the set once she's had a look at her cabin and got herself sorted.'

With a nod at the women, Jake was happy to comply. Maybe it had been a mistake, getting Ellie here.

He certainly wasn't feeling any of that warmth or joy or hope of special moments to come anymore. The emotion he was left with after that little reunion was more like wariness. Dread, even, that Ellie might have more planned as some kind of revenge.

No. Someone as open and honest and caring as Ellie wouldn't even think like that. He knew her better than that.

Didn't he?

He'd seen straight through her.

And Ellie felt ashamed of herself.

The warmth in Jake's eyes when he'd seen her had been genuine, but Ellie had already been locked into her role as the caring and professional medic who just happened to have rescued one of the stars of this movie and she had been unable to find any middle ground between that image and the stupid, starstruck teenager with a crush she'd been scared of revealing.

She'd seen the moment he'd twigged that she was acting. Had seen his surprise and then the flash of something that had looked remarkably like hurt.

So now she felt bad.

It didn't take long for the camp manager to show her the tiny cabin that would be hers for the duration of her stay. Or to give her a bag of coins and explain about the showers.

'You get five minutes of hot water for one dollar. Just put another coin in if you need longer. The company's paying all those costs so I've got lots of coins available.'

Ellie nodded.

'The caterers have taken over the main kitchen areas and they've been putting on some amazing barbecues. You'll get well fed.'

'Excellent.' Ellie managed another smile but the churning sensation in her gut made her think she might never feel hungry again.

'Well, I won't hold you up. You probably can't wait to get down to the set and see what's going on. I'd kill for a chance to spend my day watching Jake Logan.' The middle-aged woman grinned at Ellie. 'If I was twenty years younger, he wouldn't stand a chance. Okay…make that thirty years. But you know what I'm saying?'

Ellie nodded politely.

'I'd be in a long queue, mind you. And it's not as if anything lasts in Tinseltown, but it would sure be fun for a while, wouldn't it?'

'Mmm.' Ellie couldn't manage to sound remotely enthusiastic. Of course Jake would have a queue of women happy to take their turn, even knowing how temporary that would be.

She wouldn't be joining any queue.

The camp manager gave up on having a girlie chat. 'Just knock on the office door, love, if you need anything.'

'Okay. Thank you.'

She wasn't in as much of a hurry to get to the set as the camp manager had assumed, however. She wasn't even sure if she wanted to be near Jake again so soon. She'd snuffed out the warmth she'd seen in his face in that reunion.

There was no use dressing it up as self-protection. The truth was she'd snubbed him and he'd known. Someone like Jake Logan didn't have to bother with people who snubbed him. He could just pick one of those willing women in the queue. If she never saw even a hint of that warmth again, she only had herself to blame.

That she'd made a bad mistake and that things could have gone very differently haunted Ellie for the rest of that first day.

Her nose was rubbed in it, in fact, by being allowed on the ship during the early evening to watch a sunset scene being filmed on the gentle roll of the open sea just outside the harbour.

A kiss scene between Jake and his stunningly beautiful leading lady, Amber.

Bad enough to have to watch it once but, for some reason, the director made them do it over and over again. And Ellie was forced to watch. Not only was she trapped on a ship but she couldn't even slip out of sight because the area of the deck not being used for the scene was so small that she and the other people watching were hemmed into a corner.

The clapboards came down again and again as another take began.

Ellie had to grit her teeth. She had no hope of controlling the stirring of feelings like longing. Envy, possibly. Just as well nothing had really happened between her and Jake. Imagine having to watch this if you were in a real relationship with one of them?

'Couldn't see what was wrong with the last one,' someone close to Ellie muttered.

A snort of mirth came from someone else. 'Maybe they're enjoying it too much.'

Jealousy was such a destructive emotion. She had no right to be edging dangerously close to feeling that herself. No right at all and she would be wise to remember that.

The director went in to talk to them at this point. He waved his arm, indicating the last of the glorious sunset gilding the water behind them and throwing the slopes of tree-covered land in the distance into soft silhouette. Maybe he said something about time being money and it was running out because Jake turned and took a couple of paces as if suppressing frustration.

'Places, please,' came the call for a new take. 'Picture is up.'

Jake turned back and it felt as if he'd known all along exactly where Ellie was standing.

For a long, long, moment he simply stared at her, his face completely expressionless.

And then the assistant director called for quiet, the sound crew confirmed they were ready and a now-familiar bark of 'Action!' was heard. The new take started and it felt to Ellie like she, along with the rest of the world, had been completely shut out.

Amber was his sole focus. Kissing her was something Jake couldn't avoid any more than taking his next breath. It was inevitable. As necessary to life as the oxygen around him.

The cameras were gliding in for a close-up, but Ellie felt like she was too close already. She could feel the intensity of every moment of that long, long kiss. Could feel Jake looking at Amber in exactly the way he'd looked at her in the moments before that radio message had interrupted them. She could actually *feel* his lips getting closer. Touching…

Dear Lord… How far did they go in a movie kiss? Were their tongues touching?

Desire was still there. She could feel it curling—almost exploding—deep in her own belly. Ellie didn't dare look at anyone near her in case they could see what she was feeling in her face. Not that she could look away from the kissing couple, anyway.

Until, finally, it was over.

'That's the one,' the director shouted. 'Thanks, guys. It was *perfect*.'

The caterers, once again, had done an impressive job with the barbecue dinner laid on for cast and crew when the day's filming was over. The array of meat and fish was complemented by numerous salads and fresh, crusty bread. Wine and beer were freely available at the table set up as a bar and clusters of people were enjoying the alfresco meal as stars glittered in an inky sky above.

Jake had used a handful of coins with the time it took to get rid of his makeup and hair product. Dressed in black jeans and a matching sweater, he set out to look for food.

And Ellie.

Time was a luxury because the meeting to watch the dailies of today's footage would be on before long and he needed to collect the next day's shooting schedule, but if he didn't do something about this, it was going to do his head in. For the first time in his life he'd felt self-conscious on set this evening. It was no wonder they'd had to do that kiss scene so many times. It had been impossible to get in the zone with Ellie standing there, *watching* him.

Either they needed to clear the air between them or he'd have to ask for her to be kept off set and he could imagine the awkward questions that might result from that request. It would, no doubt, get back to Ellie too, and that would only exacerbate any ill feeling that was there.

He spotted her, standing to one side of the large group of people, looking a little uncertain. She had changed out of her uniform and, like him, was wearing jeans. She might find that camisole top wasn't enough for the chill the evenings could offer later, but even as Jake had the thought he saw Ellie push her arms into the sleeves of an oversized cardigan that draped gracefully, like a kind of shawl. She might be feeling out of place here, but she still held herself tall, confident in her independence.

The cast and crew were predominantly male. Actors, stuntpeople, camera crews, sound technicians, the grip crew, the continuity guys and others. Yeah… There were a lot of men here and Ellie was a very beautiful young woman. She wouldn't be standing alone for long, that was for sure.

Snagging a bottle of lager and a glass of wine, Jake headed in her direction. He held the glass up as he got closer as if it could pass as a peace offering.

But Ellie shook her head. 'I might be out of uniform for the night but I'm on duty twenty-four seven,' she told him.

No chance that a drink might ease the atmosphere, then.

'Doesn't sound like much fun.'

Ellie's smile was bright. Too bright. 'I'm loving it so far,' she said. 'I've never been on a movie set before. Can't believe how lucky I am to score this gig. Guess I have you to thank for that?'

Jake said nothing. He was staring at her, but Ellie was looking around. At everyone except him.

'I didn't think you'd want to come,' he said quietly.

'Hey...' Her gaze brushed past his fleetingly. 'This is my chance. Who knows—the fame might rub off on me. Someone will spot me doing my job and Hollywood might be calling with a role for a paramedic in some upcoming movie.'

That did it. Jake's voice was quiet but cool. 'If you'd wanted fame, you could have had it in spades by now. You must have had any number of chances to get your picture in magazines and all over the internet by now. Why didn't you take them?'

That threw her. He managed to catch her gaze this time. And hold it. He could actually see the way she was searching for a new line. A plausible way of covering the real reason.

He almost smiled. She'd never make an actress, the way her feelings played out over her face like that. Unless she could tap into them, of course, and use them when she needed to. Like he did.

When he saw the softening in her eyes he knew that the real reason she hadn't acceded to the media's demands was because of...what was it...loyalty? To *him?*

What had he done to deserve that? Now was the time to thank her for respecting his privacy. To apologise. Explain and put things right. But even as he took a breath he could see Ellie's expression changing again. Getting distant. She had found something to hide behind.

'That would have been more like *shame* than fame,' she said. 'D'you think I wanted the whole world knowing what an idiot I was for not recognising you?'

Jake raised an eyebrow. 'I was in disguise.'

'You told me your *name.*'

'So? It's just a name. Have you ever done an internet search on yourself and found how many people in the world have the same name as you?'

'Fine.' But Ellie wasn't going to accept an excuse. 'Maybe I didn't want to come across as some uncultured slob who never watches movies.'

It was nowhere near the truth and Jake wasn't getting anywhere. Moving so fast Ellie had no time to prepare a defence, he discarded the drinks he was holding and grabbed her hand. Never mind if he missed seeing the dailies. He could catch up later. This was more important.

'Come with me,' he ordered.

She had no choice. It was lucky she'd been standing where she was, not only on the outskirts of the group but almost beside a track that Jake knew led to the beach. Intent on their meals and downtime, no one saw them slip away.

'What the—?' Ellie was resisting the firm grip on her hand and the way Jake was pulling her forward. 'Where are you taking me?'

'The beach.'

'Why?'

'We need to talk.' The words were clipped. 'Somewhere private.'

He felt her resistance ebb. By the time they reached the beach it almost felt like Ellie was happy to hold his hand, but it was harder going in the soft sand. When they got to the firmer sand close to where the gentle waves were slowly curling onto land, she gave a tug that made Jake let go.

'My shoes are full of sand.' She pulled off the canvas sneakers and emptied them but didn't put them back on. Instead, she rolled up her jeans as far as her knees and walked out far enough to let the foamy water cover her feet and ankles.

'Bit of sea water's just as good as a session of physio,' she said.

Jake closed his eyes and groaned. 'I didn't think. I'm sorry. There I was pulling you along that rough track and I didn't even ask how your ankle was.'

'It's fine. And this is nice. The water's delicious. You should try it.'

There was something different about Ellie's voice. She sounded more like the Ellie who Jake remembered.

And the suggestion sounded more like a peace offering than he'd managed with that unwanted glass of wine. Jake toed off his shoes, but he couldn't get his jeans any further than the swell of his calves. He walked into the water, anyway, uncaring when the first tiny wave soaked the denim.

For a while they simply walked together, listening to the wash of the sea. Smelling the fresh air and looking up at the deepening blanket of stars. The moon was rising now, but the pale light didn't dim the night sky.

And it was perfect. Even alone with his brother, Jake had never felt this…peaceful…in the company of another person. Able to be exactly who he was and know he would be accepted for that.

Liked, even?

Maybe. He had a bit of work to do first.

It was Jake who finally broke the silence. 'The sky never looked like this in New York. I grew up not even realising how many stars there are out there. I grew up without the chance to realise a lot of other important things, too.'

He waited out the hesitation in Ellie's response. 'Such as?'

'That who you are doesn't mean as much as *what* you are.'

Ellie stopped walking. Jake could feel her puzzled look behind him. He stopped too, and turned back.

'I grew up as Rita Marlene's kid,' he told her. 'That won't mean much to you but—'

'I know who she is,' Ellie interrupted him. 'Everybody knows who she is...*was*. She's up there with Brigitte Bardot and Marilyn Monroe. One of the world's most beautiful women.'

'And she was married to my father. Charles Logan. One of New York's most powerful men. There wasn't anybody who didn't want to get close to one or both of my parents. Getting their kids to get friendly with the Logan kids was a goldmine.'

Ellie said nothing but he could tell she was listening.

'I didn't mean to get into acting as a career,' he continued. 'I just sort of fell into it when Ben and I got back from Afghanistan. Well...after I got rehabilitated, that is. The opening was always there, thanks to who my mother was, and it seemed like a fun thing to try for a while. More fun than Ben was having, being responsible and getting into the family business anyway. So I took that part in *ER* and then it just snowballed.'

'Mmm...' Ellie was still standing there, letting the waves soak her ankles.

'What I'm trying to say, in a roundabout way, is that I didn't tell you who I was because I had the chance to be someone nobody else ever sees. *Myself*.'

The moon was bright enough for Jake to see Ellie's face so clearly he could swear her eyes were shining with unshed tears. He allowed his gaze to travel over her features. That glorious hair. The proud way she held her head. She was *such* a beautiful woman.

'I thought...I thought it was because you didn't trust me.'

'We were complete strangers,' he pointed out. 'Thrown together by extraordinary circumstances. We were trying to survive in what felt like the middle of nowhere and I was worried sick about Ben. Did *you* trust me?'

The hesitation was there again. 'Y-yes,' Ellie finally said. 'After you carried me along the beach like that? And after you rescued me from under that tree?' Her lips wobbled slightly. 'I…trusted you.'

'Past tense?' Maybe they were clearing the air here, but could they get back to what it had been like between them? It was only now that Jake realised how much he wanted that.

'I…' He could see the muscles in Ellie's throat working as she swallowed. 'I don't really let myself trust anyone these days.'

'Why not?'

The silence went on too long this time and Jake had no right to push. He could respect her need for privacy. It didn't need to stop him being honest.

'Not trusting you *was* part of it, I guess,' he admitted. 'But that was something I *did* learn as I grew up. A lesson that's only been hammered in a lot deeper in recent years. The only person I've ever been able to trust completely is my brother Ben.' Jake flinched as a higher wave splashed the back of his legs. Or was it because of the thought he couldn't repress? 'And I can't even trust Ben now.'

'Why not?'

He could have followed Ellie's lead and simply stayed silent, but he chose not to. 'Because he lied to me.'

'What about?'

Jake couldn't help looking around but they were alone on the beach. Two dark figures, late at night. They were probably virtually invisible.

'If I tell you,' he said softly, 'you'll know I'm trusting you. *Really* trusting you.'

And maybe this was the most sincere apology he could

offer. He saw Ellie nod, but he also saw her slight shiver. Anticipation? Or was she cold?

He held out his hand and this time she took it willingly. He led her up towards the softer sand that still held the warmth of the day's sun and, although he let go of her hand when they sat down, they were still sitting close enough to touch.

For a long time he couldn't find the words to start. It was too big and by telling it to someone else it was going to make it real. But Jake had forgotten how he'd met Ellie, hadn't he?

'I heard him yelling at you,' Ellie said quietly. 'When you were both arguing about who got to get rescued first. I heard him say "Why do you think she killed herself?" Is that what this is about?'

Jake's nod was jerky. 'I didn't know. I've always believed it was an accidental overdose.'

'Who was he talking about?'

'Our mother.'

'Oh…*Jake*…' This time it was Ellie who reached for *his* hand. 'That's horrible.'

'It's believable, though.' Jake's voice was raw. 'Looking back, I can see she was an alcoholic, but who wouldn't be, married to my father? He was a bully. A complete bastard, if I'm honest. And she was dependent on prescription meds. The media used to describe her as being "beautiful but fragile" and that hit the nail on the head. But…I thought she loved us. That she wouldn't choose to leave us alone with our father.'

'Of course she loved you.' Ellie's tone was fierce. 'But sometimes that's not enough. And sometimes people convince themselves that the ones they love will be better off without them, however wrong that is. How…how old were you?'

'Fourteen.'

'Young enough to still think it was somehow your fault.'

'Except I didn't. Because I didn't know it was suicide.' Ben kept that to himself.'

'He loves you, too. He was protecting you.'

The words were simple.

And Jake could feel the truth of them. There was only a twenty-minute difference in age but Ben had always had the mindset of an older brother. The more responsible one. The more protective one.

Ben had been the one to spend a night in jail after one of their worst teenage pranks, hot-wiring the Lamborghini belonging to one of their father's guests and then crashing it. He himself had been safely out of the way, admitted to hospital overnight thanks to the concussion he'd suffered.

They'd never talked about that night either. Because it had been the next morning that their mother had been found dead?

And, while Jake had been the one with the more visible injury after that dreadful incident in Afghanistan, it had been Ben who'd really been traumatised. *He* had been unconscious after the bomb blast. He had no memory of it. Ben was the one who'd been in the midst of the carnage. Trying to keep his brother alive amidst the screams of dying children.

His brother had retreated into being even more responsible after that, finally—reluctantly—picking up the reins of their father's empire when the old man had been felled by a stroke, whereas *he* had just kept having fun. With easy access to the first rungs of a Hollywood career thanks to the legacy of their famous actress mother, his own talent at making others believe combined with what the glossy magazines called his raw sex appeal had ensured a meteoric rise to stardom.

The brothers had drifted apart in the intervening years and maybe he had been harbouring resentment about the way Ben viewed the movie industry. In the light of what he'd said about their mother, though, it was far more understandable.

Was there a way back?

It had taken Ellie to point out what should have been obvious all along. Maybe she was wise enough to have some other answers.

'Why can't he tell me that himself? *Talk* to me?'

'You'll have to ask him that yourself. But he's a bloke.' Ellie slanted him a look that was pure woman. 'You lot have trouble talking about feelings.'

'Yeah…'

'And speaking of feelings, I'm kind of hungry.'

'Me, too.'

'Shall we go back and see if there's any food left?'

'Sure.' Jake got to his feet and offered Ellie his hand to help her up. He held onto it for a moment longer. 'Friends again?' he asked softly. 'Am I forgiven?'

'Of course. And thank you for trusting me. I won't let you down.'

'I know that.'

He did. And the knowledge gave him the feeling of finding something very rare and precious.

Trust was a good foundation for friendship. Better than good. The fizzing sensation of unexpected happiness was magic. A bit like being drunk. Maybe that was why he opened his mouth and kept talking as they entered the darkness of the bush track that led back to the camping ground.

'I hope tomorrow's not such a long day. I couldn't believe how many times I stuffed up that last scene.'

Ellie's voice was a little tight. 'I heard the director say that it was perfect in the end, though.'

'You want to know why?'

They were almost back at the barbecue area. They could hear the sound of voices and laughter. Their private time was almost over.

And Ellie was looking up at him, her eyes wary.

'Why?'

'Because I stopped being aware that you were watching me.'

'I was putting you off?' Ellie sounded horrified. 'Maybe I shouldn't be on set, then.'

'No. It was good that you were there. That's how I got it right in the end.'

She was puzzled again now. Jake felt like he might be stepping over a precipice right now, but he'd gone this far. He couldn't stop now.

And maybe it was a cheesy thing to say and Ellie would think it was some kind of line, but Jake realised he'd been needing to do more than apologise. He needed to let Ellie know that the time they'd had together had been special. That he wished he *had* kissed her back in that beach house. Before she'd known who he was. When he'd just been being himself.

'I just had to take myself back in time a bit,' he said softly. 'I imagined that we'd never heard that radio message. And that Amber was you.'

Once again, Ellie had been stopped in her tracks by something Jake had said.

She didn't have the wash of sea water around her ankles this time and she wasn't at all puzzled by these words. There was no mistaking the meaning this time.

Jake was telling her that he'd wanted to kiss her when

he'd had the opportunity. As much as she had wanted him to?

He hadn't forgotten the moment anyway. Any more than she had.

Beyond Jake, she could see the lights and movement of the large group of people they were about to rejoin. She could smell the tantalising aroma of roasted meat, but her hunger for food had evaporated. Here, on this unlit track through the trees, she and Jake were still alone. Unseen.

On her first day on this job, Ellie had achieved what she'd hoped she might. Time with Jake Logan that had eliminated any sense of being deceived or betrayed.

Was she just being gullible, falling for that idea that she'd given him some kind of precious gift by allowing him to be simply himself and not a household name or the son of famous people?

How could she not believe it? Especially when he'd gone on to share what had gone wrong in his relationship with his brother. That was the kind of story a journalist would kill for and Jake had *trusted* her with that information.

That was enough to give her the closure she'd wanted, wasn't it? To turn that experience into something positive that she could remember with pleasure in years to come.

But…Jake was looking at her now, the way he had in all those secret fantasies she'd indulged in during some of the long nights in the last few weeks. As if every word he'd uttered this evening had come straight from the heart and she was special to him.

Special enough to want to be more than friends.

And, heaven help her, Ellie knew without a shadow of doubt in that moment that she was in love with Jake. She had been, ever since that moment he'd gone into the hole beneath the tree roots to rescue a kiwi egg for her. She might have buried the realisation because of what had come next, but she had nothing to bury it with now.

There it was. Newly hatched and exposed. Making Ellie feel vulnerable in a way she'd sworn never to let herself feel again. So vulnerable she could actually feel herself trembling. Had she really told him that she'd trusted him?

And meant it?

Yes… She'd not only reclaimed that step forward in her life, there was a part of her doing a victory dance on the new patch of ground.

Even if nothing was showing on her face, it was going to be a mission to try and disguise that trembling. Unless she said something about how cold it was getting?

She had to say something. She couldn't stand here all night staring at Jake as though the world had stopped spinning.

But it was Jake who moved. Stepping closer without breaking the eye contact that was holding Ellie prisoner.

That on-screen kiss must have been merely a practice session because this one was a thousand percent better. The way he touched her face with reverent fingers, still holding her gaze as if reading something printed on her soul. The infinite slowness with which he lowered his head. The sweet torture of his lips hovering so close to her own she could feel the warmth of them and a buzz of sensation that went through every cell of her body.

And then his fingers slid into her hair and cradled the back of her head as the whisper of touch danced and then settled. As her lips parted beneath his and she felt the first, intimate touch of his tongue, Ellie knew she was lost.

The world really had stopped spinning.

CHAPTER NINE

BY TACIT AGREEMENT, no direct mention was made about whatever was growing between Ellie and Jake. They both knew it was there and it was getting bigger every day. Perhaps trying to confine it to words would put it at risk of being caged and stunt its growth. Or maybe, by acknowledging it, it would somehow make it visible to others. This was theirs alone and it was too fragile and precious to put at risk.

Keeping it secret became a game that only added excitement to the stakes as they went about the jobs they were paid to do. Jake had to spend hours in makeup and costume, learning his lines and filming scene after scene as the movie inched towards the major finale of the shipwreck. Ellie treated people for minor and sometimes moderate injuries and illnesses. A cameraman needed a night in hospital to check that his chest pain wasn't cardiac related. One of the catering crew got a nasty burn and someone else had an asthma attack that kept her busy for some time.

She'd never known that an ignition point of sexual tension could be stretched *so* far. One day led to another and then another where nothing happened other than an apparently innocent conversation over a meal, a lingering glance during the hours of a working day or, at best, a stolen moment of physical contact that was unlikely to arouse anyone's suspicion—like the brush of hands as Jake passed her a plate of food or a drink.

The movie's star didn't really need the skills of a highly qualified paramedic to tend to the small scratch he received after a fight scene. It wasn't very professional of Ellie either to spend quite so much time assessing and cleaning the insignificant wound but the time in the caravan set aside as an on-set clinic was as private as they'd been since that walk on the beach and that seemed so long ago it was getting shrouded in the same mists of fantasy that Ellie's dreams were.

As she used a piece of gauze to dry the skin on Jake's neck that she'd cleaned so thoroughly, the swiftness of his movement when he caught her wrist startled her.

'I'm going mad,' he said softly. 'I need some time with you. Away from this crowd. Or any of those nosy reporters.'

Oh…my… Ellie knew exactly what would happen if they were really alone again. Like they had been in the beach house.

Did she want that, too?

Oh…yeah… With every fibre of her being.

Even if a part of her knew perfectly well it couldn't last? That her world was so different from Jake's she knew she could never fit in and that, if she allowed herself to go any further down this alluring path, it had to end in tears?

Her tears?

But it was so easy to blot out the future and live in the moment. To view this interlude in her life as a one-off and that, if this was the only time she would ever have to be with Jake, it would be worth it. Yes. If the invitation was there, she could no more stop herself going down that path than stop breathing for a week.

The time it had taken to reach that conclusion had been

no more than the time it had taken Ellie to suck in a long breath, but it was enough for wariness to cloud Jake's eyes. He kept his voice low enough for no one to overhear, even if they were right outside the slightly open door of the caravan.

'Do you want that, too, Ellie? Is it only me that's going crazy, here? Would you rather—?'

Ellie stilled his words with her finger on his lips. She looked over her shoulder to ensure they were alone and then she used the tip of her finger to trace the outline of Jake's lips. When she felt the touch of his tongue against her fingertip she had to close her eyes. Stifle the tiny cry that escaped her own lips.

It was the only answer Jake needed.

'I'm overdue for a bit of down time. A day off. We could go somewhere. I've got a chopper available. We could go anywhere we liked.'

'Wouldn't it be rather obvious what we were doing?'

The media had been trying to link Jake romantically with Amber and it hadn't stuck. They'd have a field day if he took off to an unknown destination with the on-set paramedic, who just happened to be the mysterious woman he'd been confined in a remote cabin with for two days. Unless…

'What if we went to visit Pēpe? That would be a legitimate reason to go somewhere together. A photo op for you, even. I'm sure Jillian would love the publicity that it would give the bird-rearing centre.'

'And then…?' Jake was smiling. He loved the idea. Excitement had Ellie's blood fizzing like champagne and a million butterflies were dancing in her stomach.

'If we've got the use of a chopper we could go anywhere.' She was on a roll here. 'We could buy some cans of spaghetti and restock the pantry at the beach house.'

You couldn't get more private than that. Especially if they sent the chopper away for an hour or three.

'You…' Jake was still holding the wrist he'd caught. He pulled Ellie's hand to his lips and pressed a kiss to the palm of her hand. '…are brilliant. I'll talk to Steve today. We're going to make this happen. Soon.'

'You almost done in there, Jake?' A crew member didn't bother knocking as he stuck his head in the door. 'Make-up's waiting to make you beautiful again.'

'All good.' Jake dropped Ellie's hand as if it was red hot. 'On my way.'

She hid her face by dropping to pick up the piece of gauze that had fallen, unnoticed, to the floor but looked up as Jake reached the door. The glance he sent over his shoulder said it all.

'Soon' couldn't be soon enough.

It was Kirsty who persuaded Steve that the publicity the visit would engender would make it more than worthwhile to give Jake a day off.

Unfortunately, she also insisted that she go too.

'I'm organising the coverage,' she told him. 'Setting up the interviews. I *have* to be there.'

'Look…' Jake tried to keep a note of desperation out of his voice. 'I was planning a little surprise for Ellie. The place we were when she rescued me is close to an island where her grandfather used to be the lighthouse keeper. I wanted to use the chopper to take her there to see it again. As a…a thank-you, I guess, for what she did for me. I hadn't planned on having a…a…'

'Chaperone?' Kirsty's glance was amused. And knowing.

'It's not like that.' Good grief… He was good at this acting lark. He could channel his frustration into injecting just the right note of irritation here to put Kirsty off the track. 'Would you want to swap your stilettos for trainers so you could go tramping around on an uninhabited island for a few hours, looking for native birds?'

'Heavens, no.' Kirsty was horrified. 'But I do need to do the media wrangling.' She raised an eyebrow. 'And wouldn't that make it seem more like what it is? Just a visit to somewhere that you both happen to have an interest in visiting?'

She was right. The more official it was, the less likely it would be that Ellie would start getting hounded by reporters or chased by the paparazzi. He had to protect her from that at all costs because, if anything was going to kill what was happening between them, it would be the relentless intrusion of the media and the way they could blow things up out of all proportion and offer their own twisted motivations for whatever was happening in a relationship. Ellie would hate that even more than Ben did and it would undoubtedly be a deal-breaker.

Maybe it could still work. He just had to come up with a way of making sure it did.

It was hard to tell whether Jillian was more thrilled by the attention the centre was receiving or by meeting Jake Logan. Everybody, including Kirsty, was delighted with how the morning went.

Jillian got to talk about the centre.

'Captive rearing centres like this are vital to the survival of our iconic native kiwis. Especially the endangered ones like Pēpe, who's a rare brown kiwi. Out in the wild, a chick has about a five percent chance of making it to adulthood. The ones we hatch and rear here have more like a sixty-five percent chance. We need support to do our work, though. We rely on public contributions as much as government funding.'

The small army of photographers and television crews loved the shots of Jake holding Pēpe. Having been told what a rare privilege it was, Jake was loving it too. His smile had camera shutters clicking madly and the reporter interviewing him couldn't help the occasional coo of appreciation.

'So he's due to be released soon? Will you want to be a part of that occasion, too?'

'If it's possible, I would consider it an honour.'

Ellie was more than happy to stay in the background. She was the link between the film star and the new poster bird for the centre and that was enough.

Having coached Jake on how to hold the bird by the legs with one hand so he wasn't in danger of being scratched and cradling the bird's body in the crook of his other arm, Jillian stood aside with her friend as they watched Jake being interviewed.

'You're right,' Jillian whispered. 'Too much hair.'

'He gets to cut it all off after they do the big shipwreck scene. He says he can't wait.'

'Does he, now?' Jillian's voice was a murmur. 'And what's with this threesome business on your day off? Did he have anything to say about that?'

'Apparently he has a plan.'

Something in her tone must have revealed more than Ellie had intended because Jillian's eyes widened.

'Oh…*my*…' she whispered. Then a shadow dimmed her smile. 'Be careful, won't you, hon?'

'Maybe I need to stop being so careful,' Ellie whispered back. 'This is too good to lose and…and I think I can trust him.'

'I hope so.' But there was concern in Jillian's eyes now. 'I don't want you getting hurt again.'

* * *

Ellie didn't know what Jake's plan was, any more than she knew what was in the basket that the caterers had given Jake to store in the helicopter. When they took off and headed north of Auckland after the visit to Pēpe, her heart sank. She assumed the basket was full of tinned food for the beach house and it looked as if Kirsty was coming with them. But as they got close the helicopter veered away from the shore and began to lose altitude.

'Oh, look…' Kirsty said. 'It's the lighthouse. And there's another house, too. Is that where we're going to land?'

Nobody answered her. Ellie was still too astonished to speak when the chopper touched down on the long grass of a small clearing between the lighthouse and the keeper's cottage. She didn't need the instruction to keep her head down as Jake helped her out but she did wonder why the engine wasn't being shut down. Jake followed her, carrying the basket and then he raised an arm and the helicopter took off again.

With Kirsty still inside it.

'He'll be back by four p.m.,' Jake told her. 'He's going to drop Kirsty off and refuel and have some lunch.' He raised the basket. 'This is our lunch. I hope the champagne's still cold.'

Ellie's jaw dropped. 'I thought it was full of cans of spaghetti.'

'Spaghetti's strictly for emergencies,' Jake told her. 'This was carefully planned.' His smile faded and he looked solemn. 'This is just for us, Ellie. Kirsty's job would be on the line if she said anything and the pilot's too well paid not to be trusted. We can restock the beach house another time.'

He was already planning another time? Ellie's joy—and her smile—expanded another notch. 'I can't believe I'm here. Standing on Half Moon Island. I haven't been here since…for ever. Are you sure it's okay? Did you check with the owners?'

'Owners? I thought it was government property.'

'I'm not sure now. It was put up for sale a few years ago, but I never heard whether anyone bought it.'

'It was for sale?'

Ellie smiled. 'A snip at only a few million. Pretty pricey for a holiday house with no amenities, don't you think?'

'And you didn't find out whether someone bought it?'

'I didn't want to know.'

'Why not?'

'I just didn't.' But, as her gaze was drawn back to her beloved lighthouse, she knew that wasn't enough of an answer. She'd never really thought about her reason herself but standing here was like being on a bridge to the past.

Old ground on one side. New ground on the other because Jake was there. The past and the future? For whatever reason, it felt important to say more.

'I guess it felt like it was ours. When Grandpa was the lighthouse keeper we knew the government owned it, but you couldn't put a face to anyone and they weren't going to change things and make it into a tourist resort or clear the bush for farming or something. It was ours. Part of our family. Where our roots were. If I knew it had been sold or—worse—the name of the person or people, it would stop being ours and I'd lose something precious. A part of my family when I'd already lost too much.'

Jake was nodding as if he understood, but he didn't say anything for a long time. He stood close beside her, looking up at the impressive height of the lighthouse. 'There's something magic about them, isn't there? Steeped in legends and with the history of dramatic shipwrecks swirling around the rocks they're guarding. Symbols of danger and safety at the same time.'

'Mmm…' A bit like Jake, then. How could she feel so safe in his company when she knew how dangerous it was to her heart?

The imaginary bridge beneath her feet was evaporating and the lines between her past and her future blurring, as if the magic of the lighthouse was drifting over her.

'Come with me.' She held out her hand. 'If the track hasn't disappeared, I can show you what used to be my favourite place.'

The track led down to the only point on the island where a boat could land, but they didn't need to go as far down as the dilapidated jetty. Halfway down the cliff you could still turn off and scramble to where massive boulders had shifted to form a kind of basin shape and pohutukawa trees grew almost sideways to provide shelter from the brisk sea breeze and dappled shade from a surprisingly hot autumn afternoon.

Directly under the lighthouse, they could see its shape through the canopy of leaves. Directly below them, waves crashed over more of the huge, volcanic boulders but the sound was muted, like the view of the lighthouse. This was a private spot in an already completely isolated place.

'This was where I always came when I was a kid,' Ellie said. 'When I wanted to be by myself.'

'You're not by yourself now.' Jake's eyes held a question.

'I'm where I want to be,' she said simply. Her heart was beating a tattoo inside her chest. 'With you.'

Jake dropped the basket and took a step closer to Ellie. Without taking his gaze from hers, he lifted his hand to touch her cheek and then cradled her chin as he tilted his head and brought his lips to hers.

Hints of the cool sea breeze kissed Ellie's skin as Jake

helped her out of her clothes. She could even taste the salt of it on Jake's skin as she got to kiss places she had only stolen a glimpse of before. She could still hear the sound of the waves below, but that sense faded, along with sight as her eyes drifted shut. Touch and taste were all that existed.

The touch of Jake's hands as he shaped her body as if imprinting it as quickly as possible on his memory cells. Learning the feel of her breasts and the silky skin of her inner thighs. She was doing the same thing. Too overwhelmed to do anything more than skate over what she wanted to learn so badly. The delicious dimples of his hardened nipples. The pulsing heat of his arousal. There would be time later for retracing these steps with the attention they deserved. Right now, a release from tension that had been building for far too long was what they both desperately needed.

And it was over too soon but they both knew it was only a beginning.

'Now we can take our time.' Jake smiled. 'We've got hours before our transport comes back.' His hand was still resting on her breast and the tiny circles he made with the tip of his little finger were enough to make her nipple hard again.

But Ellie wanted to touch, too. Turning on the blanket of the woollen Swanndri shirt Jake had insisted on wearing for the visit to Pēpe, she ran a fingertip down the intriguing tattoo.

'What does it say?'

'He who dares wins.'

Ellie liked that. She could use the mantra herself. And, in this moment, it seemed like a truth. She was daring here, allowing herself to fall in love again. To dream of a future. It even seemed possible that she could win Jake.

'And this?' Her fingertip had reached the end of the tattoo, just past the jut of hipbone. 'It's yin and yang, isn't it?'

'That's for being a twin. Ben has one too. He didn't go with the Chinese characters, though. Thought it was tacky thing to do.'

'I think it's beautiful.' Yin and yang. Two shapes that curved together to make a perfect circle. Two parts of a whole. Was that discordant jangle a hint of jealousy that it was his twin brother who was that close to Jake?

When *she* wanted to be?

Did something show on her face? Jake traced the outline of her cheek and jaw before pressing a soft kiss to her lips.

'You were wrong, you know.'

'What about?'

'About it being like having two of yourself, having a twin. We're very different. I don't think he even understands me. I'm not sure anyone does.'

Ellie's whisper felt like a promise. '*I'd* like to.'

His smile was a reward all by itself. 'I'd like you to.'

Ellie's fingers drifted sideways from where they'd been touching the symbol. She didn't want to talk about Jake's brother any more. This was *their* time. Hers and Jake's. Who knew when—or even if—they would ever get another time like this?

She felt Jake stir and harden beneath her hand and heard the way he caught his breath.

She was smiling as his mouth claimed hers again. Nobody else existed and this…this was paradise.

It was no surprise that there were reporters waiting to cover Jake's return to the camping ground, but he wasn't really prepared for it either. His heart sank as he saw the cameras. This wasn't good.

Maybe it had been a mistake to crack that bottle of champagne on the flight back from Half Moon Island.

More likely, it had been too hard to hide the glow that

their time together in the privacy of the island had left shining in their faces and the loose-limbed relaxation of their bodies. Laughter came too easily and it seemed physically impossible not to hold eye contact for a heartbeat longer than was socially acceptable if they were just friends. And he was still holding the hand he had taken to help Ellie alight from the helicopter.

He dropped it hastily. 'I'll deal with this,' he said. 'Just head off to your own cabin as though this afternoon never happened.'

Ellie managed a very creditable casual wave as she turned away before they got too close to the waiting photographers and she raised her voice so that her words could be clearly heard.

'Thanks, Jake. It's been fun. And I'll keep in touch about how Pēpe's doing.'

Nice try but Jake could sense the expectation ahead of him. These guys knew they were onto something.

'Had a nice afternoon, Jake?'

'Where did you take Ms Sutton?'

'You're looking happy, mate. You're not going to deny that there's something going on between you two, are you?'

Jake considered trying to silence the barrage of questions with a filthy look but he knew that would be tantamount to admitting he had something he wanted to hide. So, instead, he grinned at the cameras.

'No story here, sorry. I've been bird watching, that's all. And soaking up some of the stunning scenery this country's got to offer.'

'*With* Ellie Sutton.'

Jake's head shake was amused. Dismissive. 'Of course. She's got just as much of a vested interest in how our baby kiwi is doing as I have.'

'She's very different from your ex-wife, isn't she? Couldn't be more different.'

'Exactly.' Fear about Ellie running because of media interference in their lives was getting harder to contain. He had to put them off. 'Not my type, as you've so kindly pointed out. Yes, we visited the bird-rearing centre together. And, yes, we had lunch, but you're all wasting your time. It means absolutely nothing.'

His smile became more relaxed as he saw two reporters exchange disappointed looks. One had to have a last try.

'You were holding her hand.'

'As any gentleman would, helping a lady alight from a helicopter. Now, if you'll excuse me, I've got things to do. I'm sure you do, too. There's a lot that's going to be happening in the next day or two.'

'It's weather-dependent, isn't it? Shooting the shipwreck scene?'

'Yes. But I believe the forecast isn't too bad. Check the press release. Or talk to Kirsty. I'll talk to you again soon, yeah?'

Jake walked away, confident that he'd put them off the scent.

That he'd protected Ellie, at least for now.

But it wouldn't last, would it? At some point, if he wanted to keep Ellie in his life, it would have to be made public.

Jake had no idea what would happen then.

What he did have a very clear idea of, however, was that he *did* absolutely want to keep Ellie in his life.

And it was looking more and more like he might want that for ever.

The weather wasn't as good as expected over the next couple of days and the sea swell was too big to make filming close to shore safe. Camera crews were dispatched to get some good footage of the wild surf at Cathedral Cove that could be used later and there was some editing work, production meetings and rehearsals going on that Jake was involved with, but there wasn't much for Ellie to do.

She tried to use her time productively and got out her laptop to work on some of the lecture material she was writing on aeromedical transportation, but the world of academia and even front-line rescue work seemed very distant. It wasn't long before she was checking in with the local meteorological website for both the short-and long-range weather forecasts. She almost hoped the weather would stay uncooperative because when the final scenes had been done, this interlude in her life would be over, and what would happen then between her and Jake?

He'd go back to the United States. Move on to his next movie project.

Email for a while, perhaps. Talk on the phone occasionally?

And then the contact would fade and all she'd have left would be memories of time spent with the most remarkable man she'd ever met.

Finding herself doodling a yin and yang design in her notebook made Ellie sigh and drop her pen. She clicked out of the page of weather charts and found herself on the home page of the news service she favoured. The pop-up box of hot topics was one she never normally took any notice of, but Jake's name jumped out, along with the words '…denies new romance…'

It only took a tiny movement of her hand to click on the link and there it was—a photograph of her and Jake with their hands linked, laughing as they ducked and ran from the private helicopter.

Looking, for all the world, like a couple in love.

*Jacob Logan categorically denies any love interest
with the mysterious paramedic who's not dishing on
the time she shared with the star recently in the wake
of rescuing him so dramatically. Could it be that he's
protesting too much? Judge for yourself.*

The triangular 'play' button on the video clip was also
only a click away. And there was Jake, smiling confidently.
    *'...not my type, as you've so kindly pointed out. Yes,
we visited the bird-rearing centre together. And, yes, we
had lunch, but you're all wasting your time. It means absolutely nothing.'*
How believable was that dismissive tone? That amused
smile that said they were all barking up a totally ridiculous tree?
It wasn't true. He was just saying that to protect her
from the media. To keep what they had private. But, even
knowing that, it was still so...convincing. And weren't the
best lies the ones that were a version of the truth?
Echoes of things that had unwillingly embedded themselves in her brain floated to the surface. Like what the
camp manager had said. *It's not as if anything lasts in
Tinseltown...*
And Jill—her most trusted friend—had had her doubts,
hadn't she? *Be careful...I don't want you getting hurt again...*
The echoes became a chant until a new thought rocked
Ellie. They'd been so careful to keep things secret, but was
that really because it was something special and private?
Or was it because it actually wasn't important? Because
it meant absolutely *nothing?*
Stunned, Ellie slowly closed the lid of her laptop. She
sat there, in her cabin, for a long, long time, trying to make
sense of the emotional roller-coaster she'd been on ever
since she'd met Jake.

She'd believed in the connection they'd made at the start, only to have it dismissed with the distant way Jake had treated her at that first press conference.

She'd totally believed him during that heartfelt conversation on the beach and…yes, she'd been insanely flattered that he'd pretended he'd been kissing her instead of Amber when he'd filmed that *perfect* scene.

Jake could never know how much it had meant to tell him that she trusted him, and that *had* been the truth.

Or had she been acting herself without realising it? Trying on that new skin that would allow her to be the best person she could be? It had felt so good, too.

She'd willingly gone along with the game of ramping up the sexual tension, but now she'd swooped down to a new low on the roller-coaster and the skin was too tight.

It felt like it was ripping in places.

Bleeding.

What if this was all just a game to someone who could make people believe whatever he wanted to make them believe?

And she was just as gullible as she'd always been?

CHAPTER TEN

HE HADN'T SEEN Ellie for hours.

When the afternoon wore on into the evening, everybody gathered for a meal. Standing beside Steve as they joined the queue to help themselves to steak and salad, Jake took another look around.

'Seen Ellie today?'

Steve shook his head. 'Things were quiet. She said she needed some time to work on lecture notes or something. She's probably in her cabin.'

'Might let her know it's time for dinner.' Jake abandoned his empty plate and slipped away.

Something about how quiet this part of the camping ground was made Jake frown. Or maybe it was the closed look of the cabin he knew was Ellie's. The door was shut. The curtains on the small window were drawn. He knocked on the door with a sense of foreboding that only increased sharply when he saw her face.

'What's wrong?'

'Nothing.' Her voice was tight. '*Absolutely* nothing, in fact.'

Good grief…had she been *crying*?

'Ellie…' Jake gave the door a push, but Ellie was pushing back, keeping it only slightly ajar.

She was clearly upset about something. Her words, and

their tone, repeated themselves in his head. *Absolutely* nothing.

Oh, no… Had someone printed what he'd said in dismissing any suspicion of their relationship? Had she *believed* it? How could she? It was too ridiculous for words.

'Let me in.' It was a command, not a request, and Jake emphasised his intent by a shove at the door that Ellie couldn't prevent.

'Someone might see you.'

'I couldn't give a damn.' Jake pushed the door shut behind him with his foot. 'We need to talk. This is about what I said to those reporters about our day together, isn't it?'

She didn't say anything. She didn't need to.

'You *believed* it?'

That hurt, dammit.

'I didn't want to believe it.' The rawness in Ellie's voice only added to his own hurt. 'It was the *last* thing I wanted to believe but you're *so* good at lying.'

'Acting.' The word was a defensive snap. 'For both our sakes. You should have known that's what I was doing. I thought—*hoped*—you knew me better than that. That you would know I was trying to protect you.'

'By *lying?*'

He couldn't win, could he? The pain of being labelled a liar and untrustworthy was gathering heat and morphing into anger.

'What did you want me to say, Ellie? That I'd just had the most incredible afternoon of my life, making love to the woman I'm head over heels in love with?'

Her jaw dropped and she went a shade paler. No wonder. He was almost shouting, which wasn't exactly a romantic way to tell someone how you felt about them, but he had to try and make her understand.

'Can you imagine what that would have unleashed?

Do you want the whole world pointing out how different our lives are? What the odds are that it could never work? Dredging up all the sordid drama of my last marriage? Finding people they could pay to reveal details of your past?'

Yes. She was beginning to understand. He could see the flicker of fear in her eyes. His voice softened.

'I know you have things you'd rather keep hidden and I respect that. I'm not going to ask you what they are because I know you'll tell me when you're ready to. When you trust me enough.'

'I *want* to trust you, Jake. I do…but…'

Her voice trailed into silence but she wanted to believe him and maybe that was enough. All he needed to do was chase the last of that uncertainty from her eyes. What he said next might be the most important lines of his life.

'I want that day to have a chance to get here,' he said slowly. 'I want…'

What did he want?

So much. A future that included Ellie. The longing was so fierce that it made the prospect of failure terrifying.

Words deserted Jake. This was too big to try and put into words because he might get it wrong. What could he say that might help Ellie see the same future he could?

Future…

Suddenly the words were there. Jake swallowed hard and stepped closer to Ellie without breaking their eye contact by so much as a blink.

'I can see the future in your eyes,' he said softly. '*My* future. Without you, it's not going to happen and…and you can't begin to know how much that scares me…'

There was more he should say but the words vanished as swiftly as they had come. He'd hit a kind of verbal wall and it felt jarring. Had he said the wrong thing?

No. From the way Ellie's gaze was softening, his words had hit the right note. He could close the gap between them now and kiss her and everything would be okay.

Except that Ellie shifted her head back a fraction. Enough to stop his movement.

'You don't need to lie to protect me, Jake,' she said. 'I can look after myself. And—if this *is* real, it can't stay hidden for ever, can it?'

'No.' Jake touched her lips softly with his own. 'And I don't want it to. But let's just get through the next few days and get this filming finished before the world goes crazy.'

The next kiss made it feel like it should. Made Jake feel like they were back on Half Moon Island and the whole world was right there in his arms.

'Does anyone know where you are?'

'Only Steve. He won't say anything.'

'So you could stay for a while?'

'Oh, yeah…' It was becoming such a familiar pleasure, scooping Ellie into his arms and taking her somewhere.

And taking her to bed was the best possible place.

Cathedral Cove was a perfect location for what would be the most dramatic scenes of this movie. The marine reserve area was only accessible by boat or on foot, which led to some major logistical issues for the huge crew, but the setting was a jewel in a country already renowned for its unbeatable scenery. With a backdrop of sheer limestone cliffs topped with ancient pohutukawa trees, the cove was named for the spectacular archway rock formation that linked its two beaches.

The frame of the archway, with the sinking ship in the sea beyond would be used for the scene in which Jake saved Amber's life and ensured that history would stay the same. First he had to persuade her to jump off the ship, keep her afloat in the waves despite the dead weight of her long dress and petticoats and then carry her through the surf and onto the safety of the beach.

Everybody was hoping a single take would be enough, especially Ellie, who'd had to carry all the gear she might need to the scene in a backpack. There were rescue boats available and she had lots of foil blankets in case of hypothermia but it was going to be a long and tense day.

No amount of anxiety or tension could undermine how happy she felt, though. Jake had told her he was in love with her—albeit in a roundabout way—with what he could have told those reporters. The time he'd spent with her last night had told her more than any words could anyway, and soon—when these final scenes were in the can—he would stop trying to hide anything and then she could really trust that this was, in fact, *real*. That she and Jake had a future together.

Her heart was in her mouth as she watched Jake jump from the tilted ship. Why wasn't he using a stunt double, like Amber was? Boats stayed near enough to help if needed during the difficult swim and then they had to reposition everyone to do the bit where an exhausted Jake staggered through the shallower surf to carry the heroine to safety.

Just like he'd carried her when they'd still been strangers.

She could remember the comfort of being encircled by those strong arms and being carried to safety. She'd thought later how amazing it would be to be able to trust someone as protective and caring as Jake.

And she was so nearly there. As scary as it was, she was ready to trust him completely with her heart. With her life. To banish for ever those warning whispers in the back of her mind.

She was close enough to hear every word of the final beach scene to be filmed. To be so proud of Jake as he played his role to perfection—using modern medical resuscitation procedures to save the life of someone who would have died if this had really been back in the eighteenth century.

The portal that would take him back to the present day was within the ancient stone archway and the heart-wrenching scene where Jake had to leave the woman he thought he loved but could never be with was gripping.

Especially that last kiss.

Was he still pretending that Amber was *her?* Ellie was having trouble hiding a tender smile as she watched. And listened. She could certainly pretend that she was the one being kissed and, yes…it did make her feel uncomfortable, watching Jake kiss another woman, but she'd have to get used to this, wouldn't she? She had to remind herself that he was only acting here. When he was with her, it was *real*.

Jake was holding Amber in his arms now. The cameras moved in for a close-up.

'I can see the future in your eyes,' he said softly. '*My* future. Without you, it's not going to happen and…and you can't begin to know how much that scares me…'

The smile on Ellie's lips died. Those words he'd said to her that had finally won her fragile trust had been nothing more than lines in a script, written by someone else. A rehearsal for an upcoming scene.

She felt faint. Dizzy and sick.

A huge cheer went up from cast and crew as the director signalled that this was a wrap and filming was over. Even if she'd wanted to, she couldn't have got near Jake in the midst of the congratulatory buzz and the chaos of moving all the people and gear from this location.

But that was fine.

Because she *didn't* want to get near him. Not before she'd got her head around this. Before she knew how on earth she was going to handle what felt like a kind of death.

There was nothing like the buzz of a wrap party.

The hard work was over, at least for the cast and crew. There was still a lot to do, of course, and Jake would be very busy for the next few weeks because he wanted to be involved with the post-production work. Thank goodness Steve had contracted some brilliant New Zealand musicians to write and record the score, and this country was beginning to lead the world in special effects. It gave him a reason to stay here for some time. Enough time, hopefully, for he and Ellie to figure out how they were going to make things work. To nurture their newborn love and make it strong enough to withstand the pressures that would inevitably come.

Jake's heart sank when he saw Ellie finally arrive but stay on the outskirts of the exuberant gathering. She looked tired and less than happy despite the smiles with which she was greeting the people she'd come to know. She wasn't enjoying being with them and that was a worry. These people were his colleagues. The faces might change from movie to movie, but the feeling of camaraderie was always the same. By the time they got to the end of a big production like this, having coped with all the hassles and hiccups, there was a real sense of being comrades-in-arms. A family.

It took a while for him for fight his way to where Ellie was standing.

'It's over, babe. Real life can resume.' He couldn't wipe the grin off his face. 'As soon as we're back in Auckland, I'm heading straight for the barber shop. You won't know me.'

'Yeah…' Ellie's smile looked brittle. 'It *is* over.'

Someone thumped Jake on the shoulder as they went past. 'Well done, Doctor.' They laughed. 'Another life saved.'

Jake ignored them. He was staring at Ellie, trying to make the connection that should automatically be there when he looked into her eyes.

But it wasn't. It was like shutters were down and there was no way he could see past them.

'I'm all packed,' Ellie said. 'I'm heading home as soon as I've said goodbye to everyone.'

Jake simply stared. Bewildered. Demanding an explanation for the inexplicable. Why was Ellie raining on his parade like this? Okay, they'd hit a speed bump yesterday but they'd sorted all that last night, hadn't they?

More than sorted it, as far as he'd been aware.

'I thought you'd been honest with me last night.' Ellie's voice was dangerously quiet. 'I actually believed what you said about the future, but you were just practising your lines, weren't you? "*I can see the future in your eyes.*"' The mimicking of his voice was painful. '"*My future.*"'

Oh…*God*… He *had* used those lines. Because he'd been lost for words and that bit of his script in the back of his head had happened to be just what he'd wanted to say. No wonder the words had come so easily. Why hadn't he realised why they'd suddenly jarred?

He must have looked as horrified as he was feeling. The look Ellie gave him dripped with pity.

'You didn't even notice, did you? I don't think you even know the difference between reality and fiction. It's all fake, isn't it?'

'*No*…' But Jake could hear echoes of the accusations Ben had levelled at him so many times.

'Do *you* even know who *you* really are, Jake Logan?'

'Of course I do. And so do you. You know me better than anyone, Ellie. You know more about who I am now than even Ben does.'

His tone was fierce enough for someone approaching them to take a second glance and turn away hurriedly.

'But I can't *trust* you.' The words were clearly being torn from a painful place.

'Don't do this.' Jake cast a desperate look over his shoulder. How could the party be still going in full swing when the bottom was falling out of his world? He had no idea how he could fix this.

If he could fix it.

And a tiny voice in the back of his head was asking him if he even wanted to if it was going to be this difficult.

'You said I'd tell you what I'd been hiding when I was ready to. Well…I'm ready.'

'When you trusted me enough, I said.'

'What comes first, do you think? Trust…or love?' Ellie didn't wait for an answer. 'I grew up with my parents and my grandfather—people I loved with all my heart and trusted without ever having to question it.'

He could see the muscles move in her throat as she swallowed hard. 'When you lose someone you love that much you lose a part of your soul and I…I lost everyone I had.'

He wanted to touch Ellie. To try and comfort her. To let her know that she still had someone. *Him*. But Jake knew that she wouldn't welcome the touch. She had more she wanted to say.

'It took a long, long time before I was ready to risk that kind of pain again. To love again. But I finally did. I met Michael and I fell in love. We dated for about two years and when he asked me to marry him, I was happy to say yes.'

Her tone was almost conversational. 'I already had the house with the picket fence but I was so ready for the husband who would be the father of my babies. The wedding was all planned. He travelled a lot with his consultancy work, but he promised me that we'd make it work. I just had to trust him.'

Jake knew this story was not going to end well. The sinking feeling he'd had when he'd first seen Ellie this evening was getting rapidly stronger.

She had an odd smile curling her lips now. There was no hint of genuine amusement in it.

'I guess I'm lucky that his wife and three kids didn't turn up at the church in that bit where they ask if anyone knows any reason why someone can't be lawfully wed. He left his phone behind one day when he went out to the shops to get some milk and for some reason I picked it up and answered it when it rang. His wife thought I was a colleague who was attending some conference with him. She asked me to pass on the message that he needed to remember to pick up the birthday cake for their daughter on his way home.'

Jake was stunned. 'He wasn't really going to go through with a bigamous marriage, was he?'

Ellie shrugged. 'That's not the point, is it, Jake? The point is that I trusted him. Believed everything he told me. I'm willing to bet that his wife believed everything he told her, too—all the lies that covered the time he spent with me.' She turned her head enough to break their eye contact. 'I loved him and I trusted him and when I lost him I realised I'd lost another part of me. On top of all the other parts I'd already lost. And I knew there wasn't enough of me left to risk that again because if I lost any more there might be nothing left.'

He could see the slow tears tracing the side of her nose and the tremble in her voice was heartbreaking. 'I knew I'd never be able to trust another man like that, but then

I went and fell in love with you. Of all the people in the world, I had to pick an award-winning actor.'

She looked back and Jake had never seen so much pain in anyone's eyes. He couldn't hope to make this better. It was too big.

But he had to try.

'So you're going to throw away what we've found together? Because I made the stupid mistake of saying something that was in my head thanks to a script? Because I couldn't think of a better way to say it myself?'

That tiny voice in his head was there again. Man, she's got issues, it said, but it's not your job to try and fix her. Maybe nobody can. And if she's prepared to throw it away this easily it can't mean that much to her anyway.

'What we had wasn't real. Any more than my "engagement" was real. It's all a fantasy. You're watching yourself on a big screen all the time, Jake—whether you're aware of it or not. It's the way you live your life, but I can't live like that. I don't have a script and I don't want one.'

Not being able to help soothe the pain of someone he cared about this much felt like an epic failure. Jake wasn't up to the task and it made him feel inadequate. As useless at keeping a woman happy as—God help him—his father had been?

What had he done that was *so* wrong? All he'd tried to do was love Ellie. And keep her safe. She wasn't the only one with trust issues and wasn't she doing pretty much what she thought he'd done to her? Offering something precious, only to snatch it away again?

This wasn't fair, but it *was* happening and now fear kicked in. He was going to lose Ellie and there was no way this scene could end well.

Fear and frustration were easy to twist into anger, but was he going to harness that anger to fight for this? For *them?*

'I can never, ever know whether you're for real or whether you're acting because I've been there before. Michael may not have been a famous actor, but he was as good at pretending as you are.' She seemed to get taller as she straightened her spine. 'I can't ever trust you and without trust there's nothing. Nothing worth fighting for anyway.'

She wasn't going to fight, then. So why should he?

'You're right,' she said softly. 'It's over. *Really* over.'

This time, when she turned her head, she began to walk away as well. But she had one last parting shot to send over her shoulder.

'Reality isn't that bad, Jake. Maybe you could try it one day.'

CHAPTER ELEVEN

NOTHING WORTH FIGHTING FOR.

The words were a mantra now. Part of him agreed wholeheartedly. The part that wanted to argue just needed to be reminded that it took two to tango and if one of them didn't think it was worth fighting for, it was pointless for the other to batter themselves to bits in the name of a hopeless cause.

There were elements of drama queen in it as well that reminded Jake disturbingly of his mother's reaction to life. Blowing things out of proportion. Overreacting. Making grand gestures. Did her suicide have anything to do with trying to turn real life into a scripted drama? A grand gesture gone wrong?

Maybe he'd finally find out.

Ben was unexpectedly in the country and they'd arranged to meet in Auckland after Jake's busy day of setting up the post-production work he was really looking forward to.

Had been looking forward to, anyway.

The creativity that came with the editing and sound and special effects were more satisfying than acting in many ways. Jake had been seeing his future moving in this direction for a while now and he'd viewed the next few weeks as the highlight of this whole project.

Even more so, given that it would have provided extra time with Ellie.

But Ellie was gone and her cutting last words had fuelled an anger that he was trying to hang onto because it made her disappearance from his life easier to handle.

Or not.

He couldn't keep her out of his head. No matter how hard he tried to concentrate, it seemed like every few minutes something would sift through a tiny gap in the barrier. Images of her face—the way it changed and softened with that special smile that he knew was only for him. The tone of her voice—and her laughter. The way the connection between them had made him feel…like that moment they'd looked at each other when Pēpe had been hatching.

Even Steve noticed that he wasn't entirely present in some of those meetings.

'You don't like the music?'

'I love it.'

'Could've fooled me. And the workshop for special effects? It's going to be fantastic, don't you think?'

'Absolutely.'

Steve just gave him a look. Shook his head and moved off to talk with the crowd of technical wizards they were pulling together.

No wonder he wasn't in the best of moods when he walked down to the bar he'd heard of near the Viaduct to meet Ben. It was late. He was tired.

Tired of the silent battle going on in his head.

And his heart.

He missed Ellie…

She was no drama queen like his mother. You couldn't get more real than Ellie. She didn't have a script and she didn't want one.

She thought he was fake. And here he was about to spend time with his brother, who also thought he was fake.

It was important to see him, though. If there was some way they could resolve the lingering tension between them, at least he'd have someone back in his life who meant the world to him.

He wouldn't continue feeling so…so *lonely*.

It had been weeks since the brothers had seen each other and initially it was too much like a rerun of their reunion after the rescue. Huge relief at seeing the other was okay but there was an undercurrent that was swirling over rocks that weren't very far below the surface. Weird to feel nervous about talking to Ben but Jake felt his heart skip a beat as the small talk faded. Jake needed to find a way to steer the conversation towards what really mattered.

'I gather you're not here just to see me?'

'That's why I'm here in Auckland.'

'That's not what I meant. Why come to New Zealand?'

'I brought Mary home.'

'Mary?'

'The girl who saved my life. She came to New York, but she was ill so I brought her home.'

The words were stark. The sentences bald enough for Jake to know there was a lot being left unsaid. But they were still too far apart. He needed to tread carefully if he wanted to get as close as they had once been. Close enough to really talk about the biggest rock in that undercurrent?

'So, now you're heading back?'

'Yes. Tomorrow.'

'How ill is she?'

'She's okay now.'

'And you're not getting involved any further?'

'I brought her home. In the company jet.'

Jake couldn't suppress a soft snort. He knew what was happening here. The control Ben was trying to exert over himself. That he was trying to protect himself. Surely it was enough that one of them was dealing with the dark side of emotional involvement with a woman right now. Maybe Ben needed a push to wake up and smell the roses before it was too late for both of them.

'That's involvement?' The words came out more harshly than he'd intended.

'Cut it with the snide, Jake.'

'I'm not snide,' he said, on an inward sigh. 'I'm worried.'

'She'll be fine.'

'I'm worried about you.'

'Why on earth…?' He could see the way Ben's eyes widened. *He* was the big brother. He was the one who got to be worried.

'I've met a woman, too, Ben,' he said. 'Same as you, it's the woman who plucked me out of the sea. Only, unlike you, I'm in it up to my neck and…well, it's not going so well right about now.'

Talk about an understatement. Why had he said that anyway? It wasn't 'not going so well'. It was *over*. And he didn't even want to try and fight that decision.

Or maybe he did. Maybe even sorting things out with his brother wasn't going to make that lonely place disappear. Man…this was confusing. And how could he begin to try and explain that to Ben when his brother's expression suggested that he couldn't be bothered with another one of Jake's dramas. He even held up a hand as if to ward off any more information.

'You don't need to tell me. Of course it's not going well. But there's no need to talk about it—I'll be reading about it in the glossies soon enough. Maybe it's time you grew up, Jake. Marriages and happy endings belong in one of your movies. They're not the real world. Not for us, that's for sure. You've already tried and failed. You play-acted the perfect husband last time. Wasn't that enough?'

Ben was angry. Fed up with him, or was there something else bothering him even more? Jake was pretty sure there was more to this reaction than the embarrassing publicity that had come in the wake of his failed celebrity marriage. Had he really believed he was in love then? Had Ben been able to see something he hadn't?

'You think I was acting?'

'You've acted all your life—just like our mother. You don't know what's real and what's not.'

And there was Ellie's voice in his head yet again.

You're watching yourself on a big screen all the time, Jake—whether you're aware of it or not.

It wasn't true.

'I wasn't acting the first time round,' he told Ben. It was the truth. He'd believed he'd been in love, but he hadn't really known the meaning of the word, had he? 'Believe it or not, I thought it was real. But now…I'm sure not acting this time. Ellie's different. She's one in a million. This is a million miles from one failed marriage.'

Ben looked really angry now. He jerked himself to his feet. 'Then you're even more of a fool than I thought. One in a million—just like the last one. And the next one and the one after that?'

The sarcasm in his brother's tone was enough to push Jake's buttons. He didn't know Ellie. He had no idea that he was dismissing the most amazing woman on the planet. He pushed himself to his feet, his fists clenched.

'Will you cut it out?' They were getting noticed. The bar might be empty of punters but the barman was watching them carefully. 'Ellie *is* different, Ben. And we're not... we're not our parents, Ben.'

'What's that supposed to mean?'

'Just that. We're our own people.' Jake took a deep breath. 'You finally let it out, didn't you? In the life raft when you said I wouldn't know reality if it bit me. That I was just like Mom. You told me she'd killed herself and you think I'm on the same path. Heading for self-destruction because I can't pick what's real or deal with it.'

'I don't...' Ben's face was agonised. He couldn't find the words.

'Yeah, you do. It's gutted me knowing that Mom's death was suicide, but it's gutted me even more that you've kept it to yourself all these years. You've been protecting me, but you didn't have to. You've been protecting yourself and that's even worse.'

Ben shook his head. 'This isn't making any sense.'

'Maybe it's not.' Jake wasn't sure of what he was trying to say either, but the words kept spilling out. 'But this girl you brought all the way to New Zealand. Mary. She went all the way to the States to see *you?*'

'So...what?'

'I'm not even beginning to guess what that was all about,' Jake continued, 'but I don't have to guess because it doesn't make any difference. No matter who she is, no matter what she's done, no matter what she means to you, you'll never open yourself up. Because if you do, you'll have to open yourself up to the whole mess that was our mom. Our family. And Mom killed herself. Finally, I'm seeing why you're so damned afraid.'

'I'm not afraid.' A knee-jerk response. Defensive.

'If you're not afraid of relationships, then why assume that whatever I have going on with Ellie will inevitably be another disaster for the glossies to gloat over?' He turned away. 'Well, maybe it is a disaster, but at least I'm involved. I know I'm capable of loving. I'm not running away, like you.'

'Oh, for...' Ben was barely controlling his anger now. 'I'm not *running away* from anything.'

'It looks that way to me. You run. You hide. Just like you've been hiding from me all these years by not telling me the truth. Shall we go there, Ben? Talk about it properly? Or do you want to run away from that, too?'

Despair and anger were a curdled mess in his gut. Things were going so wrong here and he couldn't stop it. They were standing here in this deserted bar and staring at each other. If they'd still been ten years old one of them would have thrown a punch by now. Or twenty years old.

Maybe they still would.

The moment could have gone either way, but Jake could see so many things in Ben's face. Fear that what he was saying might be true? Sadness that they were so far apart? A willingness to try and put things right?

It wasn't going to happen, though. Not yet.

'I need to go.' Ben's tone was final.

'Of course you do.' Jake's anger was draining away, leaving a horrible empty feeling in his gut. 'People talk about emotions, you run. You've spent our lives accusing me of being like Mom every time I showed emotion. Play-acting. Yeah, okay...maybe some of it was, but not all of it. I'm trying to figure it out at last. Maybe the real is worth fighting for. The real is even worth hurting for.'

It sounded good to say it out loud.

Right.

'Yeah, well, good luck with that.' It was Ben who was being snide this time. 'What did you say—that things aren't going well between you and this new woman? Amazing. I stand amazed.'

'Get out of here before I slug you,' Jake snapped. He didn't need Ben echoing the other voice in his head. The one that was trying to persuade him to let it go. To let Ellie go. That it *wasn't* worth fighting for.

As if on cue, Ben's phone started ringing.

Someone wanted to talk to Ben. Mary?

What if it had been Ellie ringing *him* right now? Would he want to answer it?

The strength of his affirmation went a long way towards sorting his current confusion.

'Maybe you should get that,' he growled. 'Maybe it's Mary.'

'It's work.' But Ben clearly wanted to answer the call.

'There you go, then.' Jake turned away. 'I don't know why you're not taking it. Work's always been your place to hide, hasn't it, big brother? Why should anything I say make it any different?'

Well…

That had gone well.

Not.

He'd had a few beers with Ben in the bar, but that was a long time ago now. Needing to burn off some of the anger and frustration, Jake had taken a long route back to his hotel to try to walk it off.

All he'd succeeded in burning off had been any mellowing effect the beers might have had. Maybe he needed something stronger. Just as well the minibar in his room was well stocked.

The first Scotch didn't even touch sides. He could, at least, taste the second. The third ended up sitting in its glass on the coffee table in front of him as Jake tipped his head back with a groan of frustration. He went to push his hair back but the barber had dealt with the long locks today and there were no tangles to provide the welcome distraction of pain. He rubbed at his chin. Clean shaven now. He'd been looking forward to getting rid of that beard.

Looking forward to finding out what it would feel like to kiss Ellie without it. Hoping she'd love the change and be attracted to him all over again with that same passion they'd discovered between them.

Maybe he did need that third Scotch after all.

What was going so wrong in his life?

He'd lost Ellie.

It felt like he might have really lost Ben this time, too.

Sleep wasn't an option but sitting here for hour after hour, trying to make sense of the downward spiral his personal life was taking, wasn't either. By 2:00 a.m. he'd had enough. He punched in the number of Ben's phone, only to get an engaged signal. Who was he talking to at 2:00 a.m.?

This Mary maybe?

More likely to be someone in New York.

Whatever. Jake dropped the phone and closed his eyes. If he didn't catch at least a few hours' sleep, he'd have trouble keeping up with the hectic schedule tomorrow would bring. And if he couldn't keep up with the play, he might as well kiss goodbye any ambitions he had to move into a directing and editing role in the near future.

Things were bad enough already. He really couldn't afford to let his life spin any more out of control right now.

'I wish I could help, hon. I hate seeing you so sad.'

'It's helping being here, Jill. I love this place.'

Ellie was spending the afternoon at the bird-rearing centre. There was always plenty for a knowledgeable volunteer to do. The brooder pens needed to be wiped down and the peat moss dug over and checked for moisture content. Food for the older chicks needed preparation by mincing the beef heart to mix with shredded fruit and vegetables. If she was lucky, she would get to help weigh chicks or to sit quietly to observe and record their behaviour. A real treat would be helping to feed a chick, but there weren't any that needed that kind of assistance today. Maybe next time.

It *was* helping. Being here and being with one of her closest friends.

'How's the lecture writing going?'

'Okay, I guess.' Ellie put gloves on to push raw meat through the mincer. 'I've just finished one on the physiological effects of altitude. Tomorrow I'll get stuck into the biodynamics of flight. And I'm spending some time on base, getting images of aeromedical equipment. I'm keeping busy.'

'Are you enjoying it?'

'Honestly?' Ellie looked up as she moved to get a set of scales to start weighing portions of the minced beef. 'I don't think I'm cut out for an academic life. It's kind of lonely…and boring.'

'It'll be better when you're actually teaching it instead of writing about it.'

'Maybe.' Ellie was really trying hard to be optimistic but being less than honest with someone she trusted felt wrong. 'I'm not sure I'm cut out for being in a classroom, day in, day out, either. You know what they say? Those that can—do, those that can't—teach…'

'Nonsense.' Jillian emphasised her contradiction by turning on the food processor to shred some carrots. She threw Ellie a speculative glance when she turned it off again.

'Can you really not go back to active duty? Your ankle's fine now, isn't it?'

'My back isn't. That injury I had years ago was always going to limit my time on the choppers. It's time to be careful if I want to be walking properly when I'm old and gray.'

'You miss it, don't you?'

'Yeah…' But active duty as a paramedic wasn't the only thing Ellie was missing. Not by a long shot.

'You could go back on the road, then.'

Ellie shook her head. 'If I want to stay in the ambulance service, I'll either have to teach or I'll get put behind a desk as some kind of manager.' The dismal prospect made her throat feel tight. Or maybe that was due to the never-ending ache of what else she was missing.

Jake…

She tried to smile at Jillian. 'Maybe I'll just come and work for you instead.'

'Cool. We won't be able to pay you, but you'd be most welcome.'

Turning on the taps to wash some feeding bowls, Ellie had to blink hard. She needed to get over herself. There must be dozens of people who'd love the chance to do the kind of work she had the skills to do now. Like teach… or manage.

The problem was, she'd had a taste of things that were so much more exciting. Even if she knew she was lucky to have had that taste and there was no way to have it again, there was no easy way back to reality.

In her working life *or* her love life.

Jillian handed her one of the feed bowls when everything had been weighed and charted. 'That's Pēpe's. You get to feed him. He's your baby.'

The squeeze around Ellie's heart was a physical pain. He wasn't just hers, he was Jake's too. She'd never again be able to look at as much as a picture of a kiwi without thinking of him. Without the pain of knowing that she'd lost something precious. Not really fair when she lived in a country that had made the bird its national icon.

Except she hadn't lost it, had she?

It had never really been there. Just an illusion on her part and play-acting on Jake's.

If it had been real, she would have heard from him by now. How many days would it take before she gave up and started getting over him?

Right now it felt like there wouldn't be enough days in the rest of her life for that to happen.

She needed to try harder.

'Have you had any luck getting through the red tape for Pēpe's release? Did you find out who owns Half Moon Island now?'

'I'm working on it.' Jillian tapped the side of her nose. 'I have contacts. Give me a bit more time and I'll get it sorted.'

Ellie nodded. She managed a genuine smile this time.

A bit more time. Perhaps that *was* all that was needed. For Pēpe's release and for her own return to happiness.

The headache Jake had the next morning was entirely self-inflicted. The weariness was bone deep, but at least the combination of physical and emotional suffering made him feel like he might have finally hit rock bottom.

Did that mean the only way might be up?

It was during a meeting with sound technology experts that a moment of clarity hit. He wasn't the only person present who was dubious about what was being planned to emphasise the crashing of surf against rocks during the shipwreck scene and the music that would accompany it.

Steve was frowning. 'Isn't it a bit over the top?'

'It'll work,' the sound guy said. 'Trust us.'

And there was Ellie's voice in his head yet again.

Without trust there's nothing.

The echo stayed with Jake for the rest of the day. It got louder when he didn't have to focus on work and was try-

ing to kill the last of his headache and fatigue with a brutal workout in the hotel gymnasium.

Lack of trust was what had blown them apart.

It was what was still wrong between himself and Ben.

With a towel knotted loosely around his hips, Jake
caught his reflection in the locker-room mirrors as he
walked back from the showers. His tattoo was such a part
of his body these days he barely registered its presence
unless it had to be masked for a scene. Or when someone
asked about it. Like Ellie had.

It was actually possible to still feel the light touch of
her fingers as she'd traced the characters. To hear his own
voice as he'd explained their meaning.

He who dares wins.

Jake's step slowed. His gaze lifted to stare into his own
eyes.

Did he dare?

Could he win what he wanted most?

The answer was suddenly crystal clear. He had no other
choice but to try his best, because if he didn't, he would
be haunted by what-ifs for the rest of his life.

But how?

Again, the answer seemed obvious. He would ask someone who might know. Someone whose advice he could
trust.

This time, Ben answered his phone straight away.
'Jake... Hey, man! I'm glad you rang. I—'

'I need help,' Jake interrupted. He couldn't afford the
distraction of any small talk. This was too important. 'I've
done something and I don't know how to fix it. How to get
Ellie to trust me again.'

She had every reason not to trust him. He'd proclaimed
publicly that their relationship meant absolutely nothing
and then he'd compounded the situation by using lines that

had meant nothing because they were no more than part of a rehearsed script.

The silence on the other end of the line was startled. Jake rushed to fill it.

'I lied, Ben. I told the media that Ellie meant nothing to me.'

'Well…of course you did. They would have destroyed any privacy you could have had for the foreseeable future. You were protecting her.'

'That's what I thought. But what it's really done is destroy the trust that was there. And that's what matters most, isn't it? It's what's gone wrong between us, too.'

The silence was heavier this time. He could imagine Ben closing his eyes or starting to pace as he tried to figure out what to say to that.

'I understand that's why you lied about Mom,' Jake said quietly. 'To protect *me*. And it's okay. I *get* that and…and I still love you, man. It's why I knew you'd understand. Why you can help me out here.'

'It's not that simple.' The words were almost a sigh. 'I wasn't lying to protect you. I was trying to protect myself, I guess. I was…hiding—like you accused me of doing—and…I can't do that any more. I've…' He sounded choked now. 'I've learned something today. Something *huge*… and—'

Again Jake interrupted his brother. 'I don't understand. How were you trying to protect yourself?'

He didn't try and fill the silence this time. He simply waited it out.

'It was my fault.'

The incredulous huff came out almost like a snort of laughter. 'Are you *kidding* me?'

'You weren't there, Jake. You were in hospital, remember? And I was in jail for the night.'

'The car conversion incident. Of course I remember.' Jake couldn't help a wry smile. 'A highlight in the disreputable adolescence of the wild Logan boys.'

'Things were bad at home when I got out. Mom had a black eye and she was hysterical. She kept crying. Telling me how sorry she was. Telling me I had to look after you.'

'Sounds like Mom.' That sadness was never going to go away completely. Jake sighed. 'Was Dad responsible for the black eye or did she get drunk and fall over?'

'I'm pretty sure it was Dad.'

'Bastard.'

'You said it.'

'Even so, Mom was being a drama queen. That's the way she always reacted to stuff.'

'No. She was telling me she was going to kill herself. I could have done something, Jake, and I didn't. And I was too ashamed to tell anyone. That's why the coroner ruled it had been an accidental overdose. Because I was hiding and not telling the truth.

The expletive Jake used dismissed any credence the statement had.

'You were *fourteen*. A kid. Even if it *was* a cry for help, she couldn't have expected you to recognise it, let alone know what to do about it.'

'You don't…blame me, then?'

'The only thing I'd blame you for is hiding it from me. Not telling me right from the start.'

'You were so gutted. I couldn't make it worse. I…love you, too, bro.'

Jake wished he was close enough to give Ben a hug. 'And let's agree to leave the bad stuff behind, okay? No more thinking the past is going to shape the future. We might be Charles Logan's sons but we're *nothing* like him.

You were wrong when you said that happy endings only belong in one of my movies. They can happen for real.'

'I know.' Ben sounded choked up. Good grief...was that a *sniffle* Jake heard?

'No more hiding,' he ordered, trying to keep his tone light. 'Put the truth out there and live with it. The people who love you will understand.'

'You're right.' Yep. Ben certainly sounded more emotional than Jake had ever heard him sound. 'I've done that, Jake. With Mary—the woman I'll love till the day I die. You're not going to believe this but...I'm getting married. Not only getting married but I'm going to be a father.'

'Holy heck...'

'I *can* do it. Love. Family. The whole shebang. So can you. Get the truth out there and see what happens. *Trust.*'

The truth?

The truth was that Jake loved Ellie and didn't want to spend another minute without her in his life if it could be helped.

There was still the small problem of finding a way to tell her.

Of even getting her to agree to see him. He might not be responsible for the way her trust in men had been shattered in the past but he'd still have to pick up those pieces as well as the contribution he'd made.

The route from the hotel gymnasium to his room took Jake past the reception desk and a souvenir shop, the window of which had a display of cute, fluffy, soft toy kiwis.

Jake stopped in his tracks, staring through the window.

Then he pulled out his phone and hit a number on his speed dial.

'Kirsty? How's it going in Queenstown? You having

a good break?' He listened for only a moment. 'Can you do me a big favour? As soon as you hang up, text me the number for the woman who runs the bird-rearing centre we took the baby kiwi to. Jillian? I need to talk to her.'

CHAPTER TWELVE

FOR A MOMENT Jillian hesitated before dialling the number she needed.

Was she doing the right thing—interfering in her friend's life like this? Jake had been very convincing, of course, but wasn't that part of why Ellie didn't believe she could trust him anymore—because he was capable of making people believe whatever he wanted them to believe?

No. It wasn't just that she was prepared to believe the best of people. Or that she didn't have the kind of tragedies and disappointments that Ellie had had in her life that made it harder for her to trust. This was a time when the wisdom of years counted. When you could see the big picture and more than a glimmer of hope that someone you loved so much might be able to find the happiness she deserved.

Waiting for the call to be answered, Jillian deliberately put a big smile on her face so that her voice wouldn't give away the secret she'd been keeping for days now. She'd be able to sound no more than excited.

'Ellie…I've got news.'

'Hi, Jill. Is it good news?'

'Sure is.' Jillian's smile widened. 'I've managed to track down the new owners of Half Moon Island. And we've got permission to release Pēpe there.'

'Oh…that's *fantastic* news. When?'

'As soon as it can be arranged. I'm onto it...but...' Jillian took a deep breath. 'Hang onto your hat, hon. That's not all.'

'Oh?'

'The new owners are really excited by the idea. So excited they're planning to turn Half Moon into an official bird sanctuary.'

She could hear Ellie's gasp. 'Have they got any idea how much that would *cost?*'

'I get the impression they're not short of funds. What they *are* short of, though, is expertise. They need to find someone who could set it up and keep it running. I said I might know someone who could be interested.'

There was a stunned silence on the other end of the line. And then Ellie's voice was no more than a whisper.

'You mean *me*...? Oh, Jill...That might be exactly what I need in my life right now.' Her voice grew stronger. 'Have you met the owners? Who are they? What are they like?'

'You can find out for yourself. I suggested that we meet for a drink. They're pretty busy, but are you free late on Thursday night? Say nine p.m.? I'm thinking somewhere local for you. One of those gorgeous little café bars in Devonport?'

'I'm free. Of course I'm free. Oh...I can't believe this is happening. Am I dreaming?'

Jillian laughed. 'No. You're not dreaming and neither am I but— I've got to go, hon. I think we've got a new arrival coming in. See you Thursday.'

Ending the call, Jillian looked through the window of her quiet office into an equally quiet area outside. Nobody was arriving, but she hadn't been sure how much longer she could keep the lid on her secret.

She closed her eyes. Her part was over.

It was up to Jake now.

And Ellie could still make her own choices. It wasn't really interfering, was it?

Just helping.

The timing was perfect.

Ellie had been dreading Thursday night ever since that invitation had arrived in the mail a few days ago.

An invitation to a private screening of the first cut of Jake's movie. There was still a lot of work to do, but the production crew was ready to get a feel for the whole movie and not just sections, and they wanted a big screen so they'd hired a small theatre. The venue was top secret so that there was no chance of anyone from the media sneaking in or someone trying to pirate the footage. Anyone who wanted to attend would have to ring Kirsty on the day to find out the location and time.

Ellie had been circling the problem, torn between a longing to see Jake again—even if it was only on a big screen—and not wanting to take such a huge step backwards in the programme of 'getting over Jake.'

Now she didn't have to fight the battle. Meeting the new owners of Half Moon Island and discussing what could be an entirely new future for herself was not only the sensible thing to do—it was the first time since things had ended with Jake that Ellie was feeling hopeful that life could still be good.

What did you wear to a meeting that might be such a huge turning point in life? Someone who was serious about bird conservation and was prepared to live in isolation on a tiny island wouldn't be interested in dressing up to the nines and they were only meeting in a casual bar, but Ellie still wanted to present herself well.

She'd lost weight recently so her jeans looked pretty good, especially since it was cool enough in the evenings

now to tuck them into long boots. Something for warmth
was needed over her pretty top but when Ellie pulled out
her favourite long shawl cardigan, she had to fight back
sudden tears.

This was the cardigan she'd worn on that first night on
set. When she'd gone for that walk on the beach with Jake
and he'd shared secrets with her because he trusted her.

The night he'd kissed her and she'd known there was
no point in trying to deny that she was in love with him.

The soft wool felt warm and comforting as she buried
her face in it. Could she bear to wear it again? This might
be the real test. If she could wear an item of clothing that
almost had the smell of Jake on it and still step forward
into a new future she would know that everything would
be all right. That she could survive.

By the time she'd stepped off this particular ride on her
emotional roller-coaster, Ellie was running late. With no
time to braid her hair, she simply brushed it, grabbed her
bag and headed out to meet Jillian. At least the meeting
point was within easy walking distance.

'Which bar are we going to?' she asked, having greeted
her friend.

'Come with me. It's not far.'

Ellie knew this area like the back of her hand, but she
had no idea where they were going as Jillian ducked down
a side street, into a driveway and past a row of rubbish bins
to a very unassuming wooden doorway. Oddly, a man who
looked like a bouncer was standing outside. Even more
oddly, he gave Jillian a nod and opened the door that led
into a long, narrow and very dark corridor.

'Where on *earth* are you taking me?'

'*Shhh...*' Jillian held a warning finger against her lips
and Ellie was startled enough to fall silent.

And then she heard them. Voices. And one of those

voices was someone she knew so well that the sound entered every cell in her body and took her breath away.

Jake's voice. So loud and clear it could only be a recording.

She would have stopped in her tracks. Turned around and fled even, but Jillian was blocking any escape route. Urging her forward. And suddenly Ellie found herself in the back of the small theatre, having come through a curtain screening one of the emergency exits.

And now she couldn't have moved even if Jillian had tried to force her. The screen was huge and it was filled with Jake's face. The room was resonating to the sound of his voice. It was the first time Ellie had seen him on a big screen and the effect was totally overwhelming. She shrank back into the folds of the curtain, trying desperately to get a grip on such a larger-than-life experience. To cope with the wash of such an overwhelming rush of emotion.

The comfortable, plush seats of the theatre were full of people, but they were all riveted by what was happening on screen. Apparently nobody had seen Jillian and Ellie sneak in and while she was appalled at how her evening had been hijacked, there was nothing she could do for the moment. And they were standing near the back. It would be possible to slip out before the lights came back on and nobody would even have to know she'd been here. It wouldn't be for very long either, because they'd come in quite close to the end.

Jake was busy saving Amber. How had they managed to get such good close-up footage of him making the dangerous jump off the ship into the sea with Amber in his arms, without revealing that it was a stunt double he was carrying?

Watching him walk out of the surf with those wet clothes clinging to his body was almost too much. Ellie's hands clutched a fold of the velvet curtain beside her and crushed it into her palm.

The cardigan wasn't the real test of her resolve, was it? Not even close. *This* was going to be the real test. Having to listen to Jake say those lines again. The lines he'd deceived her with. Ellie steeled herself and willed them to happen because they would hurt all over again and they'd make her angry and get rid of any doubts she might be harbouring that she'd done the right thing in walking away.

And it was so much clearer. Not just bigger. The cameras had gone in for a very close shot as Jake was speaking and it was a perspective that she couldn't possibly have had, seeing it in real life.

Dear Lord…she actually got to see the very pores of his skin and every minute twitch of muscles as he spoke the lines. To see right into his eyes. Those beautiful, dark gray eyes.

Except…something felt wrong.

Ellie had the curious sensation that her body was simply vanishing as she concentrated so hard on the screen, trying to figure out what was so discordant between what she was registering on screen and what was happening in her head. It was almost as if she was floating…getting closer and closer to the screen and those enormous eyes.

And then, with a blinding thump, well after the lines had finished and the scene was racing forward as Jake stepped through the portal and back to real time, she realised exactly what it was.

What was missing.

Jake's eyes hadn't looked anything like that when he'd said those words to her. They'd been so much more…alive.

Genuine?

Ellie was gripping the curtain again, but this time it

was to help her stay on her feet because the realisation was enough to make her feel dizzy.

Okay…the lines *were* part of a script and Jake had rehearsed them enough to have them well tucked into his memory so that he could produce them perfectly on screen.

But he had been acting when he'd used those lines in the movie.

He *hadn't* been acting when he'd said them to her. He'd meant every single word.

He *could* see his future in her eyes.

And he *had* been scared.

And what had she done when he'd made himself so vulnerable? She'd hit back and thrown everything away.

Any thoughts of escaping before Jake could see that she was here drained away. This might be the last chance she ever had to say something to the man she had loved and lost.

Still loved.

The very least she could try and do was to apologise. She owed it to Jake to let him know that he hadn't deserved the way she had treated him. Not that she would expect a mere apology to put things right but surely it would be better for both of them to make at least a kind of peace with which to move forward?

She was here.

He'd seen the two women slip in through the emergency exit because he'd been watching for it. He'd barely focused on the majority of the movie until then. It was even harder to try now.

Despite the darkness of the theatre, there had been more than enough light coming from the screen to reveal that Ellie's hair was flowing loose and Jake's hands itched to bury themselves in that cascade of silk again. And she was wearing *that* cardigan. The one she'd worn that evening when they'd paddled in the sea. When he'd known he was with someone he felt totally safe with.

But if focusing on the movie was hard then, he knew it would be nothing compared to having to watch *that* scene. He would never be able to watch that without cringing. It was all too easy to put himself in Ellie's place and imagine how she must have felt, learning that his apparently heartfelt declaration had been nothing more than rehearsed lines.

It was so hard not to turn his head again, but if Ellie knew that he knew she was here, she might simply vanish again and he wouldn't have the chance to say what he wanted to say so much. He could only hope that she wouldn't see all this as being stage-managed. Fake. That maybe she would understand that desperate times called for desperate measures.

The clapping and cheering of all the people still involved with the movie, or staying on in New Zealand to have a holiday, faded as the massive curtains settled back into place in front of the screen and Steve stepped up onto the stage to say how happy he was with the way the movie had come together and thank everyone for all their hard work.

'Drinks and supper will be served in a few minutes,' he finished, 'but I know you're all waiting to hear a few words from the star of the show. So here's Jake...'

He'd never been this nervous giving a speech in public. His heart had never thumped this hard or his mouth been this dry. Jake didn't dare look to see if Ellie was still there, shrouded by the curtain. Not yet anyway.

'Obviously, I want to echo Steve's thanks to you all,' he began. 'It's not only a great movie but I've had the best time of my life making it. Acting's the best job in the world because—for a while—you get to play—to live the fantasies that most people can only dream about.'

He swallowed hard. 'Maybe the lines between reality and fantasy get a bit blurred now and then, but I want you to know that *I* know what's real.' He took a deep breath and allowed his head to turn slowly until he was looking straight at Ellie.

'What's worth fighting for.'

Her gasp was involuntary.

He had to have known she was there all along for his gaze to find her so unerringly as he said those words. She hadn't been able to take her eyes off him. He looked so different, with his hair short and only a dark shadowing on his jaw as a faded echo of that beard. She wanted to bury her fingers in his hair. Stroke the outline of that strong jaw and then leave kisses in the trail her fingers had made.

Shocked out of where her thoughts had been drifting, Ellie tried to cling to that gaze but Jake looked away. Let his gaze rove over everybody present.

'It's been a real privilege to spend time in New Zealand and I have to say I've fallen in love with kiwis. One in particular anyway.'

Ellie's head was spinning. Was he talking about Pēpe? Or *her*? And why on earth was he doing this in public?

A somewhat panicked scan of the theatre reassured Ellie that she knew most of the people here and that she could feel safe as part of the family that the cast and crew of the movie represented, but this was still a huge step into a space between something private and something that would be on display for the whole world. Jake couldn't know that what he was saying wasn't going to be leaked to the media.

And this was…*real*.

With her new-found ability to see the difference, Ellie could read Jake's body language and hear it in the tone of his voice. It felt like she had suddenly become fluent in a new language.

She could speak Jake.

And fear had been replaced by trust.

He might be an amazing actor but Ellie could see the difference between the acting and reality now. So clearly, even a tiny flashback to the lines he'd given the media about their relationship meaning nothing made her cringe inwardly. How could she have believed—even for an instant—in something that was such obvious acting?

Did other people ever find a connection like this? On a level so deep that it felt like something vital in her very soul could see its own reflection in Jake's?

To love someone this much was terrifying.

Especially when she couldn't know where this was going or what Jake was going to say next.

Those words only confused her even more.

'I have a new project,' Jake said. 'I want to give this kiwi a home. Security for the rest of her life. Love.'

Jillian nudged Ellie and leaned close to whisper. 'Did I tell you that the feather test results came through? Pēpe's a girl.'

No. She hadn't passed on the news. He was talking about the baby bird, then. So why was her heart thumping so hard and so fast that Ellie thought she might pass out?

'This special kiwi has given me a new direction,' Jake continued. 'As some of you know, I've been looking at taking my career in a new direction. The Logan brothers' company funds wildlife projects and I intend to start filming and fronting documentaries about them. To try and do my bit, I guess, to make the world a slightly better place.'

The clapping was appreciative and encouraging, but

Ellie couldn't join in. Her hands wouldn't move. Her body was frozen. She had that odd, floaty feeling again.

'Acting has taught me a great deal,' Jake told everybody then. 'And maybe I've learned that the most important lesson is the value of *not* acting. Of being able to be myself.'

He was looking at Ellie again. So intently that other heads began to turn as well, but it didn't matter. The only thing that mattered was the next thing that Jake was going to say.

'And I've heard tell that you don't go looking for the person you want to live with for the rest of your life.' His voice was soft but it still carried in a silence that felt as if everybody in the theatre was holding their breath. 'You go looking for the person you can't live without.'

Everybody was staring at Ellie now.

What had she said to him that time? That if this was real then other people would have to find out some time?

This was that time. She couldn't be the only person here who could feel the electricity in this room. A current that was adding a delicious kind of buzz to that floating sensation.

'I've found that person,' Jake said, raw emotion making his voice a little hoarse. 'My kiwi.'

The trust being put on public display was breathtaking. From a man who'd been humiliated in public by a woman before, it was courageous to say the least. He couldn't know whether he was safe. He'd put his vulnerability into her hands once before and she'd trampled on it. Not only was he prepared to trust her again—in front of all these people and potentially in front of the whole world—he was trusting what they had found between them.

That connection. And a love that was strong enough to last the distance.

The rest of their lives.

Was Jake the person *she* couldn't live without?

Oh…there was absolutely no doubt about that.

Suddenly Ellie's body could move again, although her legs felt distinctly wobbly. She didn't have to think about where to move because there was only one direction she could possibly go.

Judging by the crescendo of applause and cheering as she floated towards the stage to join Jake, everybody else thought exactly the same thing.

They belonged together.

It was surprisingly easy to escape the champagne supper after the first wave of congratulations had been made.

Using the same emergency exit that Jillian had tricked Ellie into entering the theatre by, Jake took her out into the night to walk down to a tiny beach near the marina where the moonlight filled the sea with flashing diamonds of light.

Not that they could compete with the flash of the diamond Jake produced from his pocket.

'You can change it if you don't like it.' He smiled. 'But I couldn't ask you to marry me without having something to put on your finger.'

'I love it,' Ellie said. 'I love *you*. I think I have, ever since you carried me along that beach into the teeth of a cyclone.'

'And I think I started to fall in love with you when you gave me your hair tie.'

Ellie made a face. 'Wasn't much of a gift.'

'But I already knew how brave and amazing you were. When I saw you sitting there in front of the fire with that glorious hair all free—like it is now…' Jake's fingers wove themselves into her hair. 'That was when I realised you were incredibly beautiful as well. I might not have known it then, but I was already lost.'

'And I should have known I was lost when you went down into the hole to rescue Pēpe just for me.'

There was no more talking for some time then. They sat, side by side on the top of a rock wall, sharing magically tender kisses under the moonlight.

'I've missed you so much,' Jake whispered. 'It's only been days but I feel like I've wasted half my life.'

'Me, too.'

'We'll never let that happen again. Wherever we need to go, let's do it together. Even if we have to drag half a dozen kids with us to a hut in a wildlife park in Africa or a lighthouse in a bird sanctuary on Half Moon Island.'

Ellie's jaw dropped. 'Oh…*no*. I totally forgot. I was supposed to be meeting the new owners of Half Moon Island tonight. Or was that just a trick of Jill's to get me to the theatre?'

'It wasn't and you have.'

Ellie laughed. 'Fire that scriptwriter,' she said. 'I didn't understand a word of that.'

The flash in Jake's eyes was fierce. 'It's not a script,' he said. 'And it never will be, between us. Even if the words happen to be the same. This…this is as *real* as it gets. The truth and nothing but the truth, okay?'

Ellie could only nod. Her heart was so full it hurt.

'Always.' Her smile wobbled. 'But I still didn't understand.'

'Jill's been a rock,' Jake told her. 'She knew how I felt about you and she gave me hope. She also put me in touch with some other people. The paperwork's not through yet, but you've met the new owner of Half Moon Island. It's me. Us.'

The gift was priceless. Because of the memories. Because it was already a part of her soul.

'And…and you're serious about turning it into a sanctuary?'

'Couldn't be more serious. And not just a sanctuary for birds. I'm hoping it will be a sanctuary for us, too. We could do up the cottage, couldn't we? Put in a proper helipad and boat ramp and go there whenever we need time just for ourselves? A place that couldn't be more private?'

To always be able to go back to the first place they'd made love? Blessed by the memories of the other people in her life that she had loved and been loved by? Ellie couldn't stop the tears filling her eyes and her chest being too tight to speak, but it didn't matter. She could simply kiss Jake until she found her voice again.

'That would be…just perfect.'

'You know what else would be perfect?'

'What?'

'If we could get married there.'

EPILOGUE

It *WAS* THE perfect place for a wedding.

Okay, the logistics had been a bit challenging, but they were getting used to that now, after months of ferrying tradesmen and materials to the tiny island. But given that it was a ceremony half the world seemed to want to watch and that the stars of this particular scene wanted to keep it as private as possible, the isolated venue couldn't have been better.

They weren't shutting the world out completely. The important people in their lives were here. An off-duty rescue helicopter, which had brought Dave and Mike and Smithie and their partners, was sharing the helipad with the sleek black machine that Ellie intended to learn to fly herself because Jake had claimed the captain's duties for their yacht.

There was company for that yacht down at the new jetty, too. Steve and Kirsty and others from the movie crowd had come by boat and Ben and his new wife, Mary, had been excited to try out their new yacht—a gorgeous replacement for the one wrecked in that long-ago storm.

As she took a last peep through the window of the cottage, Ellie could see the brothers standing side by side outside the white, open-sided marquee that had been erected on the newly mown grass beneath the lighthouse. They weren't identical twins, but they were equally tall and gorgeous-looking and they were wearing the same elegant gray suits with the flash of red from the posy of pohutu-kawa flowers in their buttonholes.

She saw them exchange a glance and smile at each other. She saw Ben squeeze his brother's shoulder as Jake cast a hopeful look towards the doorway through which his bride would emerge. He had to shade his eyes against the glare of the summer sunshine. The marquee had been an insurance policy against helicopters and cameras with telephoto lenses, but the shade it provided was going to be a bonus on this stunning day with its clear blue sky and calm seas.

The conditions couldn't be more different from when Ellie had first met Jake. And Ben, come to think of it, when the brothers had been fighting over who was going to be rescued first.

Who could have dreamed that that storm would have changed the futures of both the Logan brothers? Not only because they'd both found new happiness and life partners but because, in the end, the rift between them had been healed and they were now closer than ever.

She saw the brothers turn and enter the shade beneath the marquee. They would all be waiting for the bride and matron of honour to arrive now.

'You look gorgeous. I don't think I've ever seen you wearing a dress, but that is absolutely perfect on you.'

'Thanks, Jill.' Ellie smoothed the raw silk of the sheath dress that fitted like a glove until it flared out from knee level. How long would it take Jake to see the private message in the beadwork on the bodice and cap sleeves? Subtle shades of white and cream in the tiny pearl beads had lent themselves to a discreet repeating pattern.

Yin and yang. Two halves creating a whole.

Not just for twins.

For herself and Jake now.

She picked up her bouquet. The main flush of red blooms from New Zealand's native Christmas tree was well over, but they flowered a little later out here on Half Moon Island and it hadn't been hard to find enough to accompany the white roses. More of the feathery red flowers were clipped into the twist of hair that was supposed to make Ellie's loose hair behave in the sea breeze.

Jillian's youngest granddaughter, Charlotte, was holding a basket of red and white rose petals.

'Can we go now?' she begged. 'I want to throw the petals.'

Jillian smiled at Ellie. 'You ready, hon?'

'I can't wait. I'll be right behind you.'

Jillian took Charlotte's hand and moved towards the door. 'Don't start throwing until we're under the tent. We don't want to run out of petals, do we?'

Stepping outside, Ellie looked up at the lighthouse.

Tears blurred her eyes for a heartbeat as she gathered the memories of her family around her.

'I so wish you were all here,' she whispered. 'Grandpa and Mum and Dad—I hope you know how happy I am. And how much we love this place. We're going to take such good care of it, I promise.'

Jake had seen this lighthouse as a symbol of both danger and safety.

Ellie could only see the safety. A strong, silent sentinel that was always going to be there to help bring people home safely.

Gathering her skirt in her hands, Ellie moved towards the marquee.

She was going home.

Because that was where the heart was, wasn't it?

It wouldn't matter where in the world she and Jake were, she would always be home because she would be with the man she would love for the rest of her life.

She paused again before she stepped onto the trail of rose petals Charlotte had created to lead her through the centre of the intimate gathering.

Just for a moment.

So that she could bask in the expression on Jake's face when he saw her. The admiration. The love. The promise…

And then she walked forward. Past smiling faces and murmurs of appreciation. Past where Mary was sitting with the cocoons that held her and Ben's newborn twins.

Tears threatened to blur her vision again then. She would never forget the look in Jake's eyes when he'd met his tiny niece and nephew for the first time a couple of days ago.

He'd caught her gaze and held it and she'd seen the same kind of wonder she'd seen when they'd been watching Pēpe hatch. And more…she'd seen his hopes and dreams for their own future family. She'd seen the love that would be there for all of them.

For ever.

That look was there again as she reached his side, handing her bouquet to Jillian so that she could link hands with Jake in front of the celebrant.

For a long, long moment, however, they could only look at each other.

Sharing vows in public was merely a formality. Those vows had already been made and were locked in place for ever. Their hopes and dreams were the same.

And it would happen.

Sooner than Jake might expect.

Later, when everyone had gone, they could go back to their secret place. Even more special now because it was where the burrow had been made for Pēpe's new home, it had been used more than once to share their love.

It would be the perfect place to tell him that he was going to become a father.

* * * * *

Careful, Larson, don't let her beauty mess with your head.

How many times today had he admired her light bronze complexion, the sprinkling of freckles across her nose and those rich dark eyes? Not to mention the lush lips begging to be— He shook his head. *Think straight. She lives hand to mouth, picks up jobs here and there, doesn't stick with any particular thing for long. She's spent her life traveling the country, never settling down. She's just passing through.*

His fists opened and closed as he did battle with the two strongest organs in his body. His brain knew without a doubt she'd break Steven's heart. More than anything Kent wanted to protect his son, but he knew life had a way of playing out in the least expected ways. Why deprive the kid of the dazzling Ms Desi?

Why deprive himself?

A DOCTOR FOR KEEPS

BY
LYNNE MARSHALL

MILLS & BOON

Published in Great Britain 2014
by Mills & Boon, an imprint of Harlequin (UK) Limited,
Eton House, 18-24 Paradise Road, Richmond, Surrey, TW9 1SR

© 2014 Janet Maarschalk

ISBN: 978-0-263-91298-2

23-0714

Printed and bound in Spain
by Blackprint CPI, Barcelona

Lynne Marshall used to worry that she had a serious problem with daydreaming—then she discovered she was supposed to write those stories! A late bloomer, Lynne came to fiction writing after her children were nearly grown. Now she battles the empty nest by writing stories that always include a romance, sometimes medicine, a dose of mirth, or both, but always stories from her heart. She is a Southern California native, a dog lover, a cat admirer, a power walker and an avid reader.

Sincerest thanks to Tara Gavin for giving me
the opportunity to write this book and series.

Special thanks to my friend Sylvie Fox
for her input in a key scene.

As always, thanks to
my steady-as-a-rock critique partner, Dee J. Adams.

Chapter One

Desi wished she had a flashlight as she crept around the side of the ancient house in the dark. A thorn from an equally old and gnarly bush snagged her T-shirt, puncturing her skin.

"Ouch!" She immediately regretted her outburst since it was almost midnight. *Where did Gerda say that painted rock is?*

Her grandmother, a woman Desi had met only a few times in her twenty-eight years, had earlier instructed over the phone where the extra house key was hidden. Determined not to wake up Grandma Gerda, she tramped through the overgrown grass and shrubbery along the side of the house, searching for the mark.

Success! A brightly patterned rock nestled against the wooden gate stood out under the moonlight like fluorescent paint under black light. As she'd been told, she searched along the bottom for the small stick-on box holding the house key, hoping there weren't any nighttime creepy crawlers around. Just as she retrieved the box and opened it, the assaulting aroma of night-blooming jasmine tickled her nose. Sneezing with gusto, she dropped the key and got on her hands and knees to search for it, grateful there was a full moon.

A few seconds later, with key in hand, she emerged out of the thick overgrowth between two houses, heading for the huge wraparound porch belonging to her maternal grandmother. But not before tripping on a brick along the walkway. She lurched forward, swatting at the night for nonexistent support and letting fly a few choice words.

A bright light blinded her just as she stopped teetering and regained her balance.

"Who's there?" A distinctly deep and masculine voice came from the vicinity of the light.

She shielded her eyes with her forearms. "I'm Mrs. Rask's granddaughter. Who're you?"

The light lowered, allowing Desi to see a huge shadow, making her wish she'd kept up those kickboxing classes... just in case.

"I'm Kent, Gerda's next-door neighbor." The man stepped closer, studying her, as though he didn't believe her story. "I've never heard about a granddaughter."

Why would she expect otherwise? Wasn't she supposed to be the secret granddaughter? Especially since a Scandinavian stronghold like Heartlandia along the Columbia River in Oregon probably wasn't used to people like her.

"Are you saying you're Ester's daughter?" His voice, a moment ago deep and intriguing, had jumped an oc-

tave higher. He must have known who her mother was…
or had been.

"Yes. Could you please turn off that light and not
talk so loud? I don't want to wake my grandmother. I
had no idea how long the drive from Portland to Heartlandia would be." On a whim, and for future reference,
she'd taken a detour through the big city just to see it,
suspecting her father might still live there. Determined
not to spend extra money for a motel, she'd made a decision to drive straight through tonight. "Took me two
and a half hours. And what's Oregon got against street-
lights, anyway?" she said in a raspy whisper. "Thought
I'd driven into a black hole on Highway 30 for a while
there." She fussed with the leaves that had stuck to her
shirt and her hair, and brushed off the dirt from her
hands, then reached out. "I'm Desi Rask, by the way."

Stepping closer, with her eyes having adjusted to the
dark again, she realized how tall the man was. At five
foot nine it was hard to find many men to look up to.
He had to be at least six foot three. And blond. As in
Nordic-god blond. "Kent Larson." He accepted her hand
and shook it; hers felt incredibly petite inside his grasp.
"Your mother used to babysit me before—"

He stopped without completing the sentence. *Before
she ran away from home.* Yeah, Desi knew the story.
Her mother, the piano-bar queen of the Midwest, had
finally cleared up most of the missing pieces before
she'd passed.

"Desdemona? Is that you?" a reedy voice called out.
"Kent?"

Succeeding at doing what she'd hoped to avoid—
waking up her grandmother—Desi turned toward the

porch to face her for the first time since her mother's last days in the hospital.

"It's me. Your greeting committee from next door decided to interrogate me before I could let myself in."

"That's not it," Kent the Viking said. "With Mrs. Rask being the mayor, I look out for her is all."

She'd seen the doubt on his face and the hesitation to swallow her story when she'd told him who she was. But being half-black, why should she expect otherwise when she didn't look anything like the Norseman or her equally pale grandmother, the mayor of Heartlandia?

Kent worked quickly to put two and two together. Ester Rask had been a teenager when she'd run away from home. Being only eight at the time, the same age as his son Steven now, he'd never heard the whole story. He remembered the town searching high and low for Ester without success. He also remembered that Ester had never been declared dead, just missing, and eventually, his parents had quit talking about her disappearance altogether and he'd had a new babysitter. That had to be twenty-eight years ago. Hard to believe.

Now, having run into Desdemona in the dark of night, he understood why Ester had run away—she must have been pregnant.

Gerda flipped on the porch light, and Kent got his first good look at the dark and enchanting one named Desdemona. Or Desi, as she'd introduced herself. Tall, sturdy in build, coffee-with-cream-colored skin with an extra dollop of milk, wide-set rich brown eyes, a smoothed out variation on the pointy Rask family nose, full lips and straight teeth. It had been a long time since he'd seen such an exotically beautiful woman in person and it threw him off-balance.

She wore a bright yellow top that hung off one shoulder, with the straps of a black tank top playing peekaboo from beneath. The midnight-blue jeans fit like second skin, and black flats countered her height. Wow, her outfit didn't leave a whole lot to the imagination, and right now his was running wild. Loads of thick dark hair danced around her shoulders, long and full-bodied like how he'd remembered Ester's, except Ester's hair had been blond, nearly white-blond. Kent's hands grew suddenly restless, his fingers itching and his mind wondering what it would be like to dig into those gorgeous waves and curls.

Even at eight he'd had a crush on his babysitter, and tonight a fresh rush of infatuation was springing up for another brand of Rask woman.

She'd introduced herself as Desi Rask, so Ester had probably never married. For some reason, maybe his general mood about marriage lately, that knowledge landed like a sad clunk in his chest.

"Are you going to come inside?" Mayor Rask asked, drawing him out of his rambling thoughts.

"Oh, no. Steven's sleeping. I should be getting back."

Desi didn't hug her grandmother when she approached the porch. Instead they stood with a good three feet between them, offering polite smiles, seeming more like mere acquaintances than relatives. It didn't feel right by a long shot, but who was he to figure out the way life should go?

"Let me get my stuff first," Desi said, rushing back down the six porch steps toward the Ford Taurus station wagon from at least two decades back. That car had definitely seen better days.

"I'll help you," he said on impulse, waiting for her to open the back liftgate. There were two suitcases, a few boxes and assorted household items, including a potted plant or two. Was she moving in?

"All I need is my overnight case for now."

Maybe she was just passing through.

"I can get whatever else I need in the morning," she said, her alto voice already beginning to grow on him. Would she still be there by the time he got off work tomorrow?

"May as well bring this one inside, too." Ignoring her wish, he grabbed both suitcases and carried them up the porch and inside his neighbor's house. This one gave the impression of being flighty, and he wanted to make sure for Gerda's sake that her long-lost grand-daughter stuck around for more than one stinking night. Surreptitiously catching Gerda's gaze on his way inside the dimly lit house, he inquired with a raised brow, "Everything okay?"

She nodded in her usual stiff-upper-lip way, clutching the thick blue bathrobe to her throat. "She'll have Ester's old room, upstairs and down the hall." Gerda's robe was the exact shade of blue as Desi's painted-on jeans, and he wondered if either woman noticed their similar taste in color.

Kent carried the bags around the grand piano in the center of the living room—the piano he'd once taken lessons on and now Steven also took lessons on—and headed up the stairs. The third door on the left was the room where Ester had taught him how to play Go Fish. He knew this house like it was his own, having lived next door nearly his entire thirty-six years. Being so deeply rooted in Heartlandia when his parents moved to a retirement village in Bend, he'd bought their house.

As a doctor and part owner of the Heartlandia Urgent Care, he had an early shift tomorrow, so he excused himself. "Welcome to Heartlandia, Desdemona, but I've got to go."

Desi sent a hesitant but thoughtful glance his way just before he headed for the door, her eyes filled with questions and suspicion. He nodded good-night, recognizing the mistrustful look, since he saw the same expression each morning when he shaved. When had he lost his natural trust in women? Oh, right, when his wife walked out.

"Gerda, I'll check in tomorrow."

"Tell Steven to be sure and practice," Gerda said, reminding Kent that his son could come up with a hundred excuses when it came time to take his piano lesson.

A few minutes later, lying on his bed, hands behind his head on the pillow, Kent stared at the ceiling, wrenching his memory all the way back to when he'd been eight. Ester Rask had run away and had never come back. So much of the story had eluded him all these years. Now he understood it was because she was pregnant. He'd never known that part of the equation before. He'd heard she'd died last year, seen how distraught Gerda had been when she'd come home from her mysterious trip to California just before she'd been appointed mayor pro tem. Yet she'd barely spoken about it, just moped around for months. At least Gerda had been able to see her daughter one last time—a sad consolation to a lost life together.

Now, like a prodigal granddaughter, the woman named Desdemona had shown up.

The downright sadness of all the lost family years hit him where it hurt most—in the gaping wound his wife had ripped open when she'd left him. As he clearly didn't need to be reminded, Gerda wasn't the only one moping around for months on end.

He shook off the negative memories, choosing to focus on the stars outside his window instead of the ache in his heart.

The strangest thing of all was, tonight he'd immediately reacted to Desi's exotic beauty when he saw her under the soft glow of the porch lamp. But that was such a shallow response. He should ignore it. Yet, in the still of the night, under the gentle beams of moonlight, he couldn't get her or those questioning, mistrustful brown eyes out of his mind.

Tall and well proportioned, with extra-fine hips, she was a woman who'd fit with his big, overgrown frame. He grimaced. Why torture himself and think about women? After seven years of marriage, he couldn't make his wife stick around. Not even for Steven's sake. Why fall for their beauty when their motives cut like blades? He ground his teeth and rolled over, willing the young mysterious woman out of his thoughts and demanding his mind go blank so he could finally fall asleep.

The next morning, Desi threw on an old sweatshirt and baggy jeans and made her way down the creaky staircase of the ancient house. Gerda was already up and reading the newspaper, and jumped up from the table the moment Desi set foot inside the kitchen. They tipped their heads to each other in a silent greeting. Like strangers.

"I don't drink coffee, but I've got some if you'd like," Gerda said, sounding eager to please.

"Thanks, but if you show me where you keep it, I'll be glad to make it myself. Sit down."

The thin and almost ghost-white woman pointed to the cupboards near the back door before sitting again. "Your mother always loved coffee, even when she was young. I used to worry it would stunt her growth, and she was only five foot three when she left." Silence dropped like a forgotten net. But Gerda quickly recovered. "I know it's silly, but I've always kept her favorite brand on hand, even now when I know she'll never come—" The sentence broke in half as Gerda lost her voice.

Desi rushed to her grandmother and put her hands on those bony shoulders, her own throat thickening with loss and memories of a family she'd never gotten to know.

Gerda reached up and tentatively patted one of Desi's hands with icy-cold knobby fingers. "I'd asked your mother to come home so many times."

"I know you did. Mom finally told me." Mom had felt fragile like Gerda the last few months of her life. Desi could only imagine how hard it must have been for a mother to lose her daughter when they'd been estranged all those years. As for why her mother had never returned, well, that mystery wasn't likely to be resolved.

"Well, you don't have to worry about coffee stunting *my* growth," Desi said, deciding to change the subject. "I'm five foot nine."

Gerda offered a wan smile and Desi waited for her

face to brighten, even if only a little, then she went
back to making the coffee. Gerda sipped hot tea and
ate a piece of toast with marmalade, putting the taste
for toast and jam in her mind. *Mom loved orange marmalade, too.*

Since Gerda seemed engrossed in the morning paper,
and Desi wasn't sure what to talk about anyway, she
filled her coffee cup and wandered into the living room,
to the gorgeous grand piano in the center of the room.
She took a sip of coffee and carefully placed the cup on
an adjacent TV tray containing a bowl of candy and a
pile of colorful stickers.

Lifting the keyboard cover, she explored the keys,
enjoying the feel of the cool ivory beneath her fingers.
She'd had to sell her mom's piano when she'd sold the
house in L.A. to pay for the medical costs. She'd put
the remaining contents of that house of memories into
storage, the piano and everything it represented in their
lives being the biggest memory of all. Music, and her
mother's talent, had been their bread and butter, keeping them afloat through all the tough times. And there
had been many.

When Desi became old enough to work and was able
to contribute toward house payments, they'd finally
settled into their own home. Though she'd never been
sure where the large down payment had come from,
Desi had a sneaking suspicion her grandmother had
something to do with it. Then her mother got sick. All
those years in smoke-filled lounges had finally caught
up with her. Four years of lung-cancer treatment and
suffering for naught. Even after Mom had died, Desi
was hit with huge medical bills.

As she so often did when she felt sad or moody,

like right now, Desi turned to music. Soon her fingers danced along the keys, as if having memories in their tips. Beethoven's "Für Elise" filled the room with the rich tone of the grand piano. When she'd finished, she moved on to a Chopin nocturne. On and on she played, forgetting all her worries, losses and fears, until her fingers and hands were tired. She hadn't played perfectly, far from it, but what could she expect for not having touched a piano in months, since she'd sold theirs? Still, it felt good. Invigorating.

Desi sipped her tepid coffee then smiled, her mood elevated. She glanced up and found Gerda leaning against the kitchen door, tears brimming in her pale eyes.

"Your mother taught you well," Gerda said.

Desi nodded. "She did. She loved music. All kinds. But you probably knew that."

"I taught her how to play, you know." Gerda stood straighter. "She was such a natural."

The questions swimming in Desi's head almost poured out of her mouth: *Why did mom need to run away? Why did she rarely talk about you? Why did Mom insist it was just the two of us? What could have been so horrible for her mother to run away and sever all ties?* But seeing her grandmother's fragile state, the emotion she wore on the shabby midnight-blue bathrobe sleeve, Desi kept her questions silent.

"Do you still play?" Desi asked.

Gerda's eyes brightened, and she proudly walked toward the piano. "I'll have you know, besides being mayor pro tem of Heartlandia, I'm also the most sought-after piano teacher in town." A mischievous smile stretched her sallow and lined cheeks as she sat on the other half of the bench. "For anyone under the age of twelve, that is." That explained the candy and stickers.

Gerda chuckled and it sent a chill down Desi's center. Her mother had laughed exactly like that. Up close, though Gerda's eyes were milky blue, they were shaped like her mother's, and though Gerda's hair was all white now, she could tell that it used to be blond, also like her mother's. The two women fit together like misplaced puzzle pieces, and why wouldn't they, since they were mother and daughter?

Yet Mom had said very little about her family over the years. That was until her last days. All Desi knew growing up was the road and hotels and Mom. No strings. Just the two of them. Deep down Desi had always suspected it was because she was of mixed race that they'd kept to themselves. Though her mother had not once hinted at that being the reason. Being constantly on the road, with her mother working for a big Midwest hotel chain as the lounge entertainment, playing one month here, six weeks there, made it impossible to make friends or, evidently, keep in touch with relatives. Only on her mother's deathbed had she asked for Gerda to come. And Desi had finally learned about the man named Victor Brown, the father she never knew.

Gerda had started playing a song meant as a duet. Desi had been taught the same song by her mother when she was a kid. Without being asked, she jumped in and played her part in the higher octaves, and if that sparkle in Gerda's glance meant anything, Grandma was pleased.

They smiled tentatively at each other, then sat companionably for several minutes playing the piano together, and Desi was grateful that at least through music, they had a way to open up their communication. Otherwise, she felt like a stranger in a strange land in this place called Heartlandia.

"So you're the mayor?" she asked at the end of the piano piece.

Gerda nodded. "Not by my choice, but the town likes to choose its mayor from people long invested in Heartlandia." She looked straight ahead as she spoke. "I can trace my people almost back to the beginning. The only problem with that method is we get stuck in history, and these days we have a lot of new residents moving in because we have so much to offer families."

"Not keeping up with the times?"

Gerda glanced at her. "Something like that. I'm only temporary, though, and we'll have our general election next year. They promised the job wouldn't be hard, but I'm clearly in over my head."

"And then I show up."

Gerda hung her head. "Desdemona, I wish we could have one huge do-over where you are concerned. Your mother ran away because she was ashamed of being pregnant. We found her when you were born, and I am deeply sorry to say Edvard and I were surprised when we saw you. Ester was such a touchy one. Always had been. I didn't mean her to think what she did… You were my granddaughter. I loved you. But Edvard—"

"—couldn't accept that I was half-black?"

"It's not that simple, Desdemona. Please don't think that."

What was she supposed to think?

"I wanted to bring Ester and you home. She insisted she could take care of herself. I admit, I didn't fight hard enough and gave in to Edvard." Now Gerda connected head-on with Desi's eyes. "I kept watch over the two of you as best I could, though from a long distance. And I sent money whenever Ester was especially hard up."

Her mom must have kept those times to herself because in Desi's memory they lived hand to mouth most of their years on the road. But then, out of the blue five years ago when Ester first got sick, they were able to buy a small house. The home they'd always dreamed and talked about. The timing was perfect, since her mother couldn't keep up with traveling and chemo. Had her mom been saving Gerda's money, or had Gerda helped out, as she'd previously suspected?

There was a reprieve from the cancer and Ester was able to take a few playing jobs here and there, but the cancer came back. Even then, Ester stayed away from Heartlandia.

"Why didn't we ever visit?" Desi asked. It was an honest question that her mom had always evaded.

"It wasn't because I didn't invite you. Please know that. Your mother—" Gerda hung her head again. "She just didn't want anything more to do with her home, I guess."

Desi's heart tightened. It must have been hard for Gerda to be rejected time and again by her daughter. Deciding they'd shared enough heartache for one morning, she went back to playing another simple song and soon Gerda, accepting the quiet reprieve, joined her.

After a few more duets and small talk, they went their separate ways, Gerda to spend some time at city hall and Desi to shower and dress.

She did some laundry and took a walk around the backyard, trying to figure out why her mother had been so stubborn, insisting on keeping her to herself despite the invitations to come home.

An abundance of rosebushes in assorted colors filled the air with a strong fragrance. A huge white hibiscus bush in the far corner seemed no less than twelve feet high. The Victorian-style house hadn't looked nearly as bright yellow in the dark of night. Trimmed in green, with a pitched roof and a third-story dormer with a fan-light window, the house looked like something out of an old movie. Desi circled the perimeter of the house and noticed a partially covered balcony at the front and a second balcony on the side. What a gorgeous place… the home her mother had run away from.

Returning to the scene of the crime of last night—the gated side yard with overgrown bushes and shrubs— she glanced next door at another Victorian. It was painted completely white with a small bay window at the front, the only color in sight an aqua-blue door at the side entrance. Kent's house almost looked medicinal. Churchlike. She wandered toward his house, noticing the artful subtleties of the architecture. But white? Really? It seemed such a waste.

Soon growing bored with trying to figure out why the big guy had the blandest house on the block, Desi's gaze drifted to the imposing Columbia River several blocks away, down by the railroad tracks and the docks. The water twinkled beneath the strengthening sun. In the distance, the longest bridge she'd ever seen arched from this side of Oregon far across to what she assumed must be Washington State.

Though June, the brisk air brought gooseflesh to her arms even through her light sweater. She turned to go back inside. On the hillsides behind her stood dozens and dozens of more modest but brightly painted Victorians overlooking the jagged riverbank. Scattered among the Victorians were dwellings of half timber wood–half brick foundations with tall sloping roofs, reminding her of her Scandinavian heritage.

Her surname, Rask, was Danish, but according to her mother, she'd come from a place filled with Norwegians, Swedes, Finns and Icelanders along with the original Chinook peoples. When Ester rarely did talk about "home," to Desi's ears it sounded like a mythical place, perhaps a figment of her mother's dreams, someplace she embellished to feed the imagination of her young daughter. This vista seemed to prove the point. It did almost look mythical.

Her mother had run away from an idyllic, lost-in-time town called Heartlandia. Or Hjartalanda, as the welcome sign at the edge of town said. She'd scoffed when she'd read the slogan beneath: Find Your Home in Heartlandia.

Was it possible? Could a quaint town fill up that huge hole inside her?

She headed up the stairs to her room. Seeing her grandmother again was only half of the reason for this trip to Oregon. The other half was her father.

A couple of hours later, after doing research on her laptop, Desi's stomach growled. She wandered down to the kitchen, searching for food, but instead found Gerda home and fumbling with a rubber opener and a stubborn jar.

"Let me get that for you," she said.

With a look of defeat in her eyes, Gerda handed over the jar. "My arthritis is giving me fits today." She rubbed her hands and grimaced. "Guess I better start making phone calls and cancel tomorrow's piano lessons."

"How many students do you have lined up?"

"Four. I give lessons from two to six on Tuesdays and Thursdays since I do the part-time mayoral work on Mondays, Wednesdays and Fridays."

"All kids?"

Gerda nodded while searching the cupboard, looking at medicine bottles one by one until she found what she wanted.

"Any advanced students?"

"Oh, heavens, no. They're all beginners in book one or two." She shook out a couple of pills into the palm of her hand. "The next generation of great talent, as I tell their parents."

"Why don't you let me take over for you?"

"I couldn't ask you to do that," she said, filling a small glass with water and popping the pills into her mouth.

"I'm offering. It's the least I can do since you're letting me stay here as long as I want."

Gerda folded her arms, her eyes nearly twinkling. "That would be wonderful."

At five o'clock the next afternoon, a timid tap at the front door let Desi know the last student had shown up. Gerda had been so impressed with Desi's teaching style, she'd dropped out of sight after the beginning of the four-o'clock lesson. Desi suspected it was to take a nap, as she'd been yawning throughout most of the last lesson.

Desi opened the door and found a towheaded boy

with bright blue eyes, who was a little chunky around the middle. "Hi! Are you Steven?"

He nodded hesitantly. "Is Mrs. Rask here? It's time for my lesson." He waved three piano primer books like a fan.

"I'm substituting for Mrs. Rask today. She's my grandmother."

His eyes grew to the size of quarters. "You are? Wow. You don't look like her. You're pretty."

She laughed. The boy was already a charmer. Looked as though that Kent guy needed to take a few lessons from his son.

Last night Gerda had filled in Desi on all of the students. Steven was eight and showed potential, but he didn't put in enough effort to make much progress. Her job would be to light a fire in him for the joy of music. Tall order for a substitute.

The boy seemed tall for his age, and remembering his gigantic father, she understood why. Soon, when the growth spurts started, Steven would probably outgrow his chubbiness as she had when she was around that age.

Desi walked Steven to the piano, pulled out the bench and placed one candy where the boy could see it. "That's for after you show me your written theory homework."

He gulped. "Uh." He screwed up his face, making a bundle of tiny lines crisscross over his tiny nose. "I think I forgot to do it."

She bit back her smile, not wanting to let his cuteness get him off the hook. She subtly moved the candy back to the bowl and opened his book. "Well, then we'll work on it together, okay?"

The fill-in questions for note names and the staffs to practice making treble and bass clefs went by quickly with her guidance, and he brightened up. She put two shiny stickers on the pages, and he grinned.

Desi took the same piece of candy from the bowl and returned it to the prior spot. "Are you ready to play for me?"

He nodded, opened his book and dug right in. Clunky and uneven, he banged out the simple notes, but Desi could tell he'd put a lot of effort into his playing. Even to the point of grunting and muttering "uh-oh" or "dang it, I keep messing up."

She loved looking down at his silky white-blond hair and thought for a boy he smelled pretty good, too. Gerda had been right—Steven showed potential, but he just needed to be nudged. She patiently worked with him, curving his fingers just so, straightening his wrists and gently prodding his spine so he'd sit straighter. When he repeated his slouched posture over and over again, Desi realized he must have liked the way it felt when she walked her fingertips up his spine to get him to sit straight.

"That tickles," he said after the third reminder, smiling up at her, and her strict teacher persona melted around the edges.

When she explained some of the tricky parts of the song and showed him how to play it, she noticed his head had come to rest on her upper arm. The sweetie liked this attention. Maybe she could use that to make a piano player out of him.

"Would you like to learn a different kind of song?"

"Yeah, this one seems kinda dorky."

She played a simple basic blues song that used the bottom notes to make it sound snazzy. Steven sat right up, immediately interested in the piece. She found the page in the book so he could see the notes and showed him how to play the first few bars. He obviously liked the rhythm and soon his shoulders moved to the beat. She'd found it—his kind of song.

"I tell you what," she said. "You live next door, right?"

He nodded, making a serious face, exaggerating his already-deep dimples.

"If you want to come over here after school a couple days during the week, I'll let you practice on this piano, okay?"

"Will you be here?"

"Sure. I'll even help you practice if you want."

"Okay!"

The moment she'd finished carefully writing out his homework, the doorbell rang, and she jumped up to open it. The Norseman stood on the other side, overbearing in stature, first drilling a glance through her then peering inside the house. She'd forgotten how big Kent was. In daylight, his finely carved features and cutting blue eyes almost took her breath away. Too bad he chose to look so serious all the time. He wore a navy blue polo shirt, but the sleeves barely fit around his arms. The standard jeans fit very, very well, indeed.

She smiled a simple superficial greeting, while odd tingles threaded along her skin. "Come in," she said. "We just finished."

"Hi, Dad!"

"Hey, son."

Steven gathered his piano books and rushed toward his father. "Ms. Desi is a really cool teacher!" They hugged, and Desi could see the honest-to-goodness love they shared. It was the same kind of *you and me against the world* love that she and her mom used to have, and the display touched her deep inside. Maybe she'd cut the big guy some slack.

"That's great," he said to his son, then looked at Desi with near alarm in his glance. "Are you taking over for Mrs. Rask?"

"Just today. Her arthritis is flaring up."

"Won't you be my teacher next week?" Disappointment poured out of Steven's voice.

"We'll see how Gerda feels, okay?" She walked back to the piano and picked up the wrapped candy, then came back to Steven and handed it to him. "I promised to help you practice, remember?"

He took the treat as if he'd gotten the biggest present in the world. "Gee, thanks!" Throwing his arms around her hips, he hugged her and squeezed, his cheek flat against her stomach. Such a sweet boy. She couldn't say he was attention starved, not by the way his dad watched over him, but Steven sure liked being around her. It made her wonder where his mother was.

Midhug, she glanced up at Kent, her grin quickly shifting to a more serious expression. Though he tried to hide it, caution and warning flashed in his azure eyes, and the hair on the back of her neck alerted her to let go of Steven and back off.

She'd reacted instinctively to the boy and must have crossed over a deeply engraved line. She didn't have a clue why she'd tripped the alarm, but she'd respect Kent's nonverbal message. He watched steadily as she stepped away, and when they'd said their necessary goodbyes, all she could do was wonder what she'd done wrong.

Chapter Two

"Dad. Dad!" Steven pulled Kent's arm as he unlocked
the front door, drawing him out of his thoughts. "Ms.
Desi's the coolest piano teacher ever!"

"Mayor Rask is your piano teacher. Ms. Desi is just
filling in." He wanted to set that straight, right off.

Steven charged for the electric keyboard in the corner
of the dining room the second they'd hit the front door.
As he turned it on, the excitement in his bright blue
eyes was almost contagious. Kent held firm, refusing
to get swept up in his son's enthusiasm. It wouldn't be
a good idea to let Steven get attached to every woman
who was kind to him. And that had been his pattern
since his mother had left.

No one could fill the void his son must feel.

Steven had his music book opened and seemed raring
to go before the keyboard was even warmed up. Transformed before Kent's eyes, the boy was the embodiment

of eagerness—this from the kid who normally had to be dragged to piano lessons and who forced Kent's patience to get him to practice. Steven pounded out a simple song that had definite blues overtones, and it wasn't half-bad. The infectious smile on his face forced Kent to grin as he leaned against the wall, arms folded, listening. He loved seeing his son happy, especially after the rough couple of years they'd been through.

Blast it. The last thing he needed was for his son to have a crush on his substitute piano teacher—the woman who showed up in the dead of night and who might take off the same way. He couldn't bear to see any more disappointment in Steven's eyes.

How in hell was a child supposed to get over the heartbreak of his mother walking out at such a tender age, with not so much as a phone call on his eighth birthday?

If Kent had his way, Steven would have a couple of siblings by now, but that was the last thing Diana had wanted. Born and raised in Heartlandia, just like him, she wanted to move to a big city where she could spread her cosmopolitan wings and play wife to a doctor who made a staggering salary. She wanted parties and designer shopping sprees. She did not want to be married to a guy running his own urgent-care facility and having to be both businessman and doctor rolled into one. A guy who couldn't predict which side of the red line they'd land on at the end of each month.

She'd thought being married to a doctor meant she'd be home free, rolling in dough. What with staff salaries to pay, the never-ending need for supplies or new equipment, liability insurance up to his ears and the lease on that overgrown building, some months he had to take a rain check on his own salary. Good thing he lived in the same house he grew up in, the one his parents practically gave away when they sold it to him and moved to Bend, Oregon, to enjoy their retirement.

Bottom line, Diana had wanted out. She'd wanted to be far away. She'd wanted San Francisco, not Heartlandia. She'd wanted to be single again. Single without a child hampering her whims.

"See, Dad? I can almost play all the notes."

"That's great." He applauded. "If you practice every day, maybe you'll have it memorized by next week."

"Yeah! That would be the coolest. I could surprise her."

"Now don't go getting ahead of yourself. She's only substituting for Mayor Rask. She may not even be here next week." Kent went into the kitchen to throw some food together for dinner. Steven tagged along, practically on his heels.

"Can we invite Ms. Desi to the festival this weekend, huh?"

Kent didn't want to speak for someone else, but he was quite sure Desi would be bored senseless at their hokey small-town Scandinavian festival. Wasn't that what Diana used to call it? "I don't know."

"I could buy her some *aebleskiver* with my allowance. I just know she'd love them."

Kent wanted to wrap his arms around the boy and hold him close, tell him to be careful about getting his hopes up where women were concerned. Instead, he pulled open the cupboard and rustled around the canned foods for some baked beans. He hoped to change the subject with food, one of Steven's favorite topics. He'd grill some chicken and steam some broccoli, and pretend he didn't hear Steven tell him "for the gazillion-millionth time" that he hated broccoli.

"Dad? Dad! Can we?"

Kent quit opening the can, inhaled and closed his eyes. "We'll see."

"Please, please, please?"

"I'll think about it. Okay?" Feeling a major cave coming on, Kent went the diversion route. "Now go wash your hands."

Already having his father pegged, Steven triumphantly pumped the air with his fist. "Yes!"

The never-say-die kid sure knew how to work his old man. Kent quietly smiled and went back to cooking.

After dinner and a lopsided conversation with Steven talking about life on the school playground and one quick confession that he thought Ms. Desi smelled like his favorite candy—tropical-flavored SweeTarts—Kent mentally relented. Why allow his lousy attitude about women to get in the way of his son enjoying himself? Besides, when Kent was a kid he had a new crush every week. Steven would soon forget "Ms. Desi" and all would be back to normal.

After he cleaned up the kitchen he'd take a walk next door and ask Desi if she'd like to come along on Saturday. He wouldn't say a word to Steven, though, so the kid wouldn't feel the sting if she said thanks but no.

An hour later, Steven was showered and in his pajamas and planted in front of the TV in the family room.

Kent stared at himself in the bathroom mirror, wondering why in hell he felt compelled to brush his teeth and gargle before heading next door. He cursed under his breath as he headed downstairs toward the door. If

he didn't watch it, next he'd be picking posies from the
yard for the substitute teacher.

Nothing made sense about asking the new lady in
town along just because his son wanted her to come.
One thing was painfully clear, though. He'd been hanging out with eight-year-old boys too much lately. Then
one last thought wafted up as he crossed his lawn, heading for Gerda's place—even an eight-year-old could see
Desi was easy on the eyes.

Desi sat on a wicker glider on the large front porch
behind the second arch, the huge living room window
behind her. She'd thrown one of Gerda's warm shawls
over her shoulders to ward off the chill from the night
air. Under the dim porch light she was barely able to
make out the print in the *Music Today* magazine she'd
surprisingly found on her grandmother's coffee table.

Soon she'd have to switch to her eReader and that
novel she'd started before she'd left home if she wanted
to stay outside. And she did want to stay outdoors to
give herself and Gerda some space. There'd been too
many extended silences, too many bitten back questions from Desi and started but abruptly ended sentences from Gerda. So much to ask. So much to say.
So hard to begin.

Tonight her grandmother seemed preoccupied with
mayoral work, and Desi felt out of place. She stared
at her scuffed brown boots, wishing she knew how to
broach the subject of her mother. What was she like as
a kid? Did she always love chili cheeseburgers? What
made her think she had to run away when she got pregnant instead of telling her parents and working things
out? But people were tricky. You couldn't always get

right to the heart of the matter without first building trust, and her grandmother was obviously holding back the details.

She looked around the large, homey porch and inhaled the night air, even detected a hint of that jasmine from the side of the house. She twitched her nose. Something about this old house calmed her down, as if it had reached inside and said, *Hey, you might just belong here. This is where your mother grew up; these rooms, scents, colors, textures and sounds are your roots.*

Soles scuffing up the walkway averted her attention from her thoughts. Her gaze darted to the tall blond man from the bland house next door—the overprotective father with some sort of grudge—Kent.

An unnatural expression smacking of chagrin eclipsed his handsome face. It lowered his brows and projected caution from those heavy-lidded eyes. The sight of him set off a pop of tension in her palms.

He cleared his throat, and she closed the magazine. "Nice night, huh?"

One corner of her mouth twitched with amusement over his awkward opening. "Seems kind of cold to me."

"That's Oregon for you."

She smiled, deciding to toss the poor man a lifeline. "Is it?" When was the last time he'd talked socially with a woman?

"Yup. Unpredictable, except for rain." He came closer to the porch but not all the way up, one foot two steps higher than the other. He put his palms on his knee and leaned on them, an earnest expression humbling his drop-dead looks. "Listen, I want to apologize in case I came off cranky this afternoon."

She sputtered a laugh. "Cranky? My grandmother

might get cranky, but you, well, you seemed bothered. Yeah, that's the word—*bothered*."

He scratched one of those lowered brows. "Sorry."

"I was just being nice to your son, not planning on snatching him. Making him feel good about his progress, that's all."

"Yeah, and he couldn't stop talking about what a great teacher you are when we got home, too."

She smiled and magnanimously nodded her head. *Yes, I am a good piano teacher, thank you very much.* "Is that a bad thing?"

"Not hardly."

As he got closer, the tension in her palms spread to her shoulders, and she needed to stretch. Couldn't help it.

He watched with interest. "So anyway," he said, "this time every June we have this thing called the Summer Solstice Scandinavian Festival. Maybe your grandmother already told you about it?"

She shook her head.

"But as mayor pro tem she starts off the parade," he said.

"She hasn't said a word about it to me."

Gerda hadn't been feeling well tonight, and she'd seemed distracted after a hushed phone conversation. During dinner, Desi had talked about the piano students, even though a big question loomed in her mind. *Why couldn't you and Mom ever patch things up?*

"Really?" He seemed surprised.

During dinner, Desi couldn't bring herself to broach the subject about how bad their mother-daughter relationship must have been. Still, every indication—from the way her grandmother had opened the home to her to the way Desi caught her sneaking loving looks at her—suggested she was wanted. Yet that feeling of not belonging prevailed, along with the thought that Gerda was simply doing her duty out of guilt.

She shook her head at Kent. "The subject of an annual festival never came up."

"Well, the thing is, Steven would really like you to go with us to the parade and festival on Saturday."

Desi liked seeing the big man so completely out of his comfort zone and sat straighter. "So he sent you over to ask me out?"

Finally, a smile. Well, half of a smile. "Not exactly."

"He doesn't know you're asking, and you'd rather die than ask a tall, dark stranger to come along, so you snuck over behind his back to ask me to say no?"

The look he shot her seemed to ask, *Are you a mind reader?* Or she could be reading into it, just a wee bit.

"Not it at all. And, man, you've got quite an imagination." So much for her theory. He shook his head with slow intent. "I was thinking more that you'd rather pull weeds than be stuck with me for an afternoon. But Steven… He's a kick. He wants to spend his allowance on you."

She tilted her head, charmed by her young absentee suitor. "Not every day a male wants to spend his allowance on me. How can I refuse?"

Kent scratched the corner of his mouth. "You were right—I didn't tell him I was asking you in case you didn't want to come with us."

"How thoughtful of you, protecting Steven." Maybe he wasn't as bad as the vibes he gave off. "And thanks for giving me an out…but I'd like to go." *Sorry to disappoint.*

Surprise opened his eyes wide. His *sexy bedroom*

eyes—there were no other words for them. The sight of them did something deep in her belly, making her sit up and take notice. "I'm starting to feel a little cooped up in this big old house already, and I'd like to see the rest of the town." *See what my mother ran away from.*

His quick smile died before it reached his cheeks. "Before you take off again?"

"That's not what I meant." She didn't have time to analyze what stick had been surgically implanted into Kent Larson's spine, or why he was giving her such a hard time about coming and going as she pleased, so she ignored him. She'd stay in Heartlandia as long as she wanted or needed, and she didn't need his permission to leave when she was ready. "I meant, I'm looking forward to spending more time with Steven and seeing more of Heartlandia. And you can tell him I said yes."

"Good. That's good." He sounded hesitant. "Steven will be excited."

And what about you? She'd been around the country a few dozen times, but she wasn't bold enough to ask. Was her crazy physical reaction every time he came around by any chance mutual?

Did this Viking from the bland house next door have any soul? Any passion? He seemed to be bound by courtesy and what was expected of him. She couldn't put her finger on it, but something must have happened to make those invisible walls so high. Yet Steven was as lovable and huggable as a soft teddy bear.

At least Kent hadn't spoiled the boy with his stand-offish attitude. Yet.

With his mission accomplished, and without further words, Kent had already turned to leave.

"Tell Steven I'm really looking forward to going, okay?"

He tossed a thoughtful gaze back at her, took her in with a leisurely tour of her entire body. It was the first sign of life she'd seen in him since the night they'd met in the dark, giving her the inkling that maybe her physical response to him was reciprocated.

A subtle shiver rolled through her, and she clutched the shawl tighter and closer to her neck.

"I'll do that," he said. "We'll pick you up on Saturday morning around ten." And off he went, almost smiling, down the steps and toward the dark path home.

"Got it," she said softly, grateful the boy would be along to ward off the unexplainable reaction she had to the big guy with the aloof attitude.

Saturday morning was cool and damp, and Desi pulled her hair tightly back into a bun and covered it with a knit cap, careful not to catch her huge hoop earrings. She zipped her thin hoodie to the neck and did the final *is my butt too big in these jeans?* check via the full-length mirror. The doorbell rang and she stopped obsessing over what nature had given her and hustled out the bedroom door.

Gerda had answered the door already, and Steven and Kent hung back just outside on the porch, talking quietly.

"Oh, good, you're ready," Gerda said when Desi appeared at the top of the stairs. "I've got to go. Need to be there a half hour before the parade starts."

Desi rushed down the steps. "Don't let me hold you up."

Gerda was already on the porch and halfway toward her car in the driveway. "See you there!"

"We'll be by your booth for some *aebleskiver* later," Kent said.

Gerda's smile widened, setting off a network of wrinkles. "I'll make some fresh just for you," she said, looking at Steven.

She'd be manning the Daughters of Denmark bakery booth all afternoon after playing grand marshal. Somehow the old woman had become a figurehead for Heartlandia, and it was another duty she'd hesitantly accepted.

Pride broke into Desi's chest and she waved to her grandmother. "I'll be cheering for you!"

The car door closed and Gerda continued to smile as she backed out. It always caught Desi off guard how much of her mother she saw in her grandmother's face. So far they hadn't talked nearly enough about her mother, maybe because it was still too painful, but little by little they'd begun to forge their own cautious relationship.

After Gerda had gone, Desi looked at Kent. "Do I need an umbrella?"

"I've got it covered," Kent said, obviously enjoying his first glance at Desi, shaking her up with his sharp blue eyes. "You look like a Scandinavian flag."

Stopped in her tracks, Desi did a mental inventory of her choice of colors. A bright blue knit cap and red sweatshirt. "Gee, thanks. Just what every girl longs to hear."

"You look cool, Ms. Desi," Steven said, beaming at her.

Maybe she'd ignore the father and hang out with the son all morning. "Thanks, Steven." She stopped herself from messing his shaggy, nearly white-blond hair, knowing he wouldn't appreciate it—especially if he was planning to spend his allowance on her. And she had every intention of paying him back with the money she earned from her part-time calligraphy jobs.

"We better get going." Kent nudged Steven along with a hand to his neck. Steven halfheartedly tried to kick his dad's leg. Kent played along, kicking back, missing by a mile. The boy giggled.

Feeling a bit like a third wheel, Desi followed them off the porch toward the curb.

They rode over in a white—why was she not surprised—pickup truck, sitting three across with Steven between them. After a brief silence, Steven spoke up.

"The sons and daughters of Heartlandia first came together to start this festival fifty years ago," Steven recited like a tour guide for the city. "The early summer festival celebrates our Norwegian, Icelandic, Finnish, Swedish and Danish heritage—" he stumbled over some of the words, but managed to spit them out pretty well for an eight-year-old "—from the early fishermen settlers first stranded on our coast." He stopped long enough to swallow. "Our first peoples, the Chinook, saved and nursed our shipwrecked forefathers to health and taught them the secrets of hunting and fishing the waters of the great Columbia River." A quick picture of Linus explaining the meaning of Christmas to Charlie Brown came to mind with the quiet yet capable way Steven told his city's history.

"Okay, Steven, you don't need to repeat your entire class presentation for Ms. Desi."

"I liked it. Thank you, Steven."

"As you can tell," Kent interjected, "Hjartalanda is proud of both the Scandinavian and Chinook heritage."

"We have a special celebration for the Chinook peoples in—" Steven screwed up his face, eyes up and to the right. "What's that month, Dad?"

"October."

"Yeah, October. Then we have a beer barn, too, so that gets the old farts to come."

Desi sputtered a laugh before she could stop herself.

"Watch the language," Kent warned benevolently. "And, Steven, that's not *exactly* why we have the beer barn. It's—"

"That's what you said to Officer Gunnar that time."

Kent flashed a sparkling look at Desi over Steven's head. He enjoyed his son as much as she did. She lifted her brows. *You get yourself out of this one.*

"That was just an observation between him and me, and for your information, I said 'geezers,' not 'farts.'"

Steven giggled. "*Fart* is a funny word. I like it better. Fart, fart, fart." He dissolved into a fit of giggles.

"That's enough of that." Kent tried to sound stern, but the twitch at the corner of his mouth told a different tale.

Desi grinned at the father and son's candid conversation during the drive over. Maybe, if she kept quiet, she'd learn a heck of a lot more about Heartlandia—or Hjartalanda, as Kent had called it—than she'd found out from her grandmother so far.

Steven taught her a hand game for the rest of the short drive over, where one person would place their palms on top of the other, and the bottom person had to try to slap the upper person's hands. Something about his earnest approach to everything he did made her warm inside. He was easy to giggle, too, and she joined right in, even as she nearly got slapped silly from his quick reflexes.

They parked outside the central section of town and hiked up toward the main street called Heritage. Desi glanced far off at one end to see what looked like an official building, maybe city hall, with a totem-pole-type monument in front. She turned and gazed down to the other end, noticing storefronts, restaurants and other businesses in what seemed like a time warp to the 1950s architecture and style with evidence of 1970s expansion. One large building, six stories high, sat apart from the other mostly single- or two-story frames. It smacked of the Art Deco era of the twenties and thirties with geometric domes and lavish ornamental copper accents, which had turned green. Desi wondered if there was an ordinance about not building tall after The Heritage Hotel and Performance Center went up.

She'd slowed her pace to take it all in, and Steven grabbed her hand, pulling her along. Clusters of people grouped around the street corners and more lined the curbs with chairs and blankets to sit on. It seemed as if every person in the city had shown up for the parade.

"Move back, folks. Make way for the parade." A sturdy, broad-shouldered police officer spoke to the thickening group on one particular corner. The guy was built as if he could make a living on the side as a cage fighter.

"Quit harassing the locals. Cut us some slack, Sergeant, would you?" Kent's outburst made Desi tense. This wasn't the kind of guy anyone in their right mind should want to challenge.

The intense-eyed, equally handsome and obviously Scandinavian male turned to Kent. The grim expression on his face broke apart into a wide grin. "You give me a hard time and I'll haul your—" he glanced at Steven then back to Kent "—backside in."

The men shook hands, and Desi knew immediately they were friends. Respect shone through Kent's and the officer's eyes, and something else, too—something that looked a lot like brotherly love.

The policeman with light brown hair and flashing green eyes bent to greet Steven. "How'd you talk your old man into bringing you to the parade this year?"

"I asked my piano teacher along," Steven said, pointing to Desi.

Feeling suddenly on display, she made a closed-lip smile, stuffing her hands into the back pockets of her jeans. The officer looked her way and tipped his head, obvious interest in his gaze. She gave a single nod back.

"This is Mayor Rask's granddaughter, Desdemona," Kent said, reaching for her arm and encouraging her forward. "And this is Gunnar Norling, my best friend since grammar school."

"Hey. Nice to meet you," he said, casting a quick sideways glance at Kent, ensuring he'd get the lowdown later, before smiling at her.

"Call me Desi."

"Okay." He reached for her hand.

A drum-and-bugle corps rent the air, alerting the crowd the parade was about to begin, and Gunnar's attention immediately went elsewhere.

"Enjoy the parade, guys. I'm on duty." Off he went, looking attractive and official in the dark blue uniform.

The next thing Desi saw was the flag corps consisting of six teenage boys proudly displaying the five Scandinavian banners plus the U.S. pennant in the center. Each young man wore a vest in the traditional color of their country as they walked to the rhythm of three snare drummers directly behind them. Then came her grandmother sitting in the cab of an open horse-drawn carriage, waving demurely as she progressed down the street.

Desi waved wildly along with Steven and Kent, and Gerda's eyes brightened, stretching her Mona Lisa smile into a toothy grin.

As the procession continued, individual countries paraded their famous costumes and music while walking beside simple floats and automobiles.

The women and girls wore ankle-length dresses covered with colorful aprons and shawls or capes. Some wore white scarves on their heads, which made them look like flashy nuns, or little hats trimmed in red or blue. All the women wore thick stockings and what looked like homemade leather shoes. Large beaded necklaces seemed to be in vogue with many of the women in costume.

The men's outfits reminded Desi of a famous TV commercial for cough drops. She especially liked the bright vests and little turbans or knit caps with tassels some of the men wore.

The intense colors on all of the apparel impressed Desi—mostly reds and blues with some yellow—along with the pride and joy that poured out of every participant as they strolled by. She glanced at Steven and Kent and saw the same pride and joy on their faces.

"That's Viking," Kent said, pointing to one group.

Steven saw one of his friends walking with the adults and gave a holler. Kent grabbed him and gave him a noogie as they watched the group pass. The father and son touched affectionately a lot, she realized, and seemed to get along great. Mother or not.

"That's Swedish, my people," Kent said, as the next float approached.

The subtle differences between the groups were hard for her to see, yet everyone else seemed to know exactly who was who. What must it be like to belong so deeply to something, to have a heritage you could trace back thousands of years and know like the back of your hand? "Here come the Danes." Kent smiled and glanced at her. In the front row of participants was a young girl of mixed race, like herself, and she led the way. What was he trying to communicate, that she wasn't the only biracial person in town?

Heck, half of her family tree was cut off at the very first fork, a blunt and wide cut that ended with a single name—Victor Brown.

"Here come the Fins." Kent continued his parade coverage, his hands on Steven's shoulders and the boy's head resting against him, just above his belt.

Desi couldn't tear her attention away from the genealogy marching before her. She was made up of just as much of this as the other mysterious side, and today she deeply felt the Scandinavian connection.

"Here's my favorite, the Icelanders!" Steven jumped in, pointing ahead. "They always wear the funnest hats."

Besides the um-pa-pa sounds coming from some of the floats, there were others with fiddles that sounded so similar to what Desi knew as Celtic tunes. There was maypole-type dancing between some floats and livelier, showier footwork, knee and shoe slapping, among the boys and men between other floats. Her cheeks soon grew tired from all of the grinning.

As the parade went on, more modern versions of Scandinavian clothing came through. The easily spotted knit sweaters and caps, and stylish sheep-fur-lined boots sported by preschoolers and kindergartners grabbed her attention. A group of teens showed off what could only be described as *Scandinavian grunge,* complete with famous storybook red braids and raccoon-styled makeup, while doing gymnastics and a little street dancing.

Something was brewing and bubbling in Desi's chest. Could she see herself in the light faces of these people? Her mother's Nordic beauty was hard to detect when Desi looked in the mirror, yet it was there—her high cheekbones, the shape of her brows, the expressive eyes. Her mother was inside her—in every cell and in half of her DNA.

Her mother had run away and given up her entire life for Desi. She owed it to her to keep her mind and heart open to this town and all that it was and could offer. She needed to stick around long enough to learn who she was before she took off searching for the other half.

An hour after it had started, the parade came to a close with a final um-pa-pa group, and a small, sweaty hand on hers brought her back to the moment.

"Let's get over to the booths before the lines get too long," Steven said, tugging her down the street. So far the weather had cooperated, the earlier gray clouds parting, revealing bright blue sky above.

Kent walked a few feet away from them like a tall, benevolent chaperone giving them space.

"Is this where everything happens in town?" she asked over her shoulder.

"Pretty much. We've got a lot of touristy shops for the cruise-line visitors down toward the docks, but most of the travelers like to come up here to eat. We've got some great restaurants."

One redbrick restaurant and bar had a few tables out front and a black-and-white canopy under which an older African-American man sat drinking coffee as they passed. He wore a starched white chef's shirt and hat placed at a jaunty angle on his head. Their eyes met, as two standouts might, and he tipped his head at her without a hint of a smile. She smiled and repeated the gesture, noticing the name of the restaurant and promising to find her way back at some point. Lincoln's Place. "Good food since 1984. Live music and Happy Hour specials daily at the bar," the sign said.

Kent waved and the man lifted his palm in return.

Down the street was a small white restaurant, with a blue-and-yellow canopy out front, called Husmanskost.

"What's that?"

"They specialize in Swedish cuisine. I'll bring you some samples from the booths."

Desi kept walking, but her gaze stayed on the cute little restaurant, wondering what unusual tastes and dishes she'd find inside.

At the food section, the wait at Gerda's Danish Bakery booth was nominal. Gerda was already there working, and she smiled her greeting, then turned and picked up some already-packaged treats.

"I thought you were going to make the *aebleskiver* fresh for us," Kent said with a teasing tone.

"Even an old coot like me knows how to read phone messages. Steven texted you were on your way over as soon as the parade ended."

Desi shook her head and smiled over Steven's resourcefulness. Behind the counter on another surface

were several grills with small round grooves filled
with pancakelike batter. The other cook on hand used
a toothpick to move the pastry ball around to cook it
on all sides. It looked like a tedious job, and Desi knew
she'd wind up with burned pastry if she were in charge.

"I gave you a mixture, Steven," her grandmother
said. "Some have apples inside, others raspberry. Be
sure to put extra powdered sugar on them. Oh, and I
gave you different sauces to dip them in."

The fresh apple and cinnamon aroma of the small
doughnut-hole-type baked goods made Desi's mouth
water. "I'd like to try one with just the powdered sugar,
if you don't mind."

Steven's face lit up. "That's my favorite, too!"

When they perched at a small table, Steven opened
the box. Kent made a quick, stealthy reach right after
Steven powdered them and popped one into his mouth.

"Hey, buy your own, Dad. These are for me and Ms.
Desi."

Kent's brows shot up and, combined with the cheeks
full of bakery goods, the vision made Desi laugh. He
shrugged and said something completely unintelligible
through his full mouth. A crazy urge to lick away some
of the powdered sugar from his lips and chin gave Desi
pause. What the heck was going on?

Of course she understood that Kent was an amazingly attractive man. It was apparent most of the women
in Heartlandia—at least those at the parade who made
obvious eyes at him—thought so, too. Besides, she was
a healthy young woman who hadn't had a date in a long
time. Of course she'd notice a guy like Kent. But this
slow-heat in her lower parts whenever he was around
still took her by surprise.

Step away from the merchandise. The last thing she needed was to complicate her circumstances by developing a crush on her grandmother's neighbor.

Kent slipped away as she and Steven gobbled down the delights. After they knocked off what was left of the dozen, grinning and smacking their lips all the way, Kent reappeared with a couple of containers. "Here you go."

"What's this?"

"I brought you some fish balls."

She didn't think she could eat another bite.

"Just a taste. Come on."

He fed her a nibble of the fish ball, and even though it was a stinky fish ball, all the while she thought this encounter was too intimate for a public place. "Mmm, that's delish."

"There's plenty more you'll have to sample." She glanced at his mouth and thought she'd like to sample that, too. "You haven't lived until you've had a midnight supper."

That sent her mind to a completely inappropriate place and her cheeks heated up. "I need something to drink."

"Steven, get Desdemona some water, will you, please?"

Her name seemed to simmer on his lips. Sheesh, he'd better make that ice water. "Thanks."

"If you'd like, I'll take you for a proper Swedish dinner sometime."

"Thanks, but I'm sure you're too busy with your clinic and all to do that."

"You know about the Urgent Care?"

"My grandmother couldn't be prouder of you if you were her own son."

"Did someone say my name?"

As more helpers arrived, Gerda had taken a break from her booth, coming around the corner and taking Desi by the elbow. "Steven, Kent, may I borrow Desi for a few minutes?"

Kent's police-sergeant friend showed up with a coffee in one hand and a huge Danish in the other. After delivering the water, Steven had waved to a few of the local boys, yet he still looked disappointed at the prospect of Desi leaving.

"I'll be back in a few minutes, okay?"

"We're going to do some boring booth shopping," Gerda added. "But you're welcome to come along."

Steven wrinkled his nose. "I'm gonna go play with my friends." He pointed to the group of boys chasing each other around for no apparent reason.

Kent waved his acknowledgment of everyone's whereabouts without missing a beat of the friendly conversation with his best buddy. Those guys seemed to really enjoy each other.

Traveling all her life had meant good friendships were hard to make, and that had always bothered Desi. What would it be like to have a special friend to share all of your thoughts with? Anytime she'd started to get to know a kid her own age, her mother would get a new hotel assignment in another city. Heck, Desi had always felt more like a mascot to the hotel housekeeping staff around the country than a friend to anyone.

Gerda guided Desi by several booths, making a stop in front of each one and introducing her. "Hey, everyone, this is my granddaughter, Desdemona." She couldn't seem prouder, and it gave Desi pause. If her mother had only given things a chance…

At the jewelry booths, she saw beautiful examples of the necklaces many of the parade participants wore and also brooches. Her eyes lit up at the meticulously knitted sweaters and hats at another booth two doors down.

"Oh, I love that red-and-white one," she blurted out.

"Try it on. Let me buy it for you," Gerda said.

"I can't let you do that."

"I've missed a lot of birthdays and Christmases. Please let me buy you a gift."

Feelings she wasn't prepared for folded into her heart. She reached out and for the first time hugged her grandmother. "Thank you."

"We'll take this," Gerda said midhug to the little lady behind the counter.

As they pulled back, Desi offered a sympathetic smile tinged with long-lost family ties. The tears in her own eyes were reflected back at her in Gerda's kind expression. They'd missed out on so much together. "That's so sweet of you. Thank you."

"You're welcome." Gerda gripped Desi's shoulders, letting her know how important this was to her.

Kent strolled up, stopping briefly when he realized he'd invaded a private moment. "Oh, sorry."

Desi and Gerda opened their hug but remained arm over arm. "Grandma just bought me the most beautiful sweater." The lady behind the counter had finished wrapping it in tissue paper and putting it inside a bag with all five of the Scandinavian flags on it, then handed it to Desi.

"That's great. You'll have to model it for me sometime." His genuine smile rolled over her, doubling the unfamiliar feelings she harbored in her heart right then, until caution stepped in. *Don't get too chummy with anyone because you won't be around that long.* At the warning, her arm slipped from her grandmother's back.

"I've got to get back to the booth," Gerda said. "Why don't you show Desi around all of the displays?"

"Glad to. That is, if Steven doesn't get his nose bent out of shape."

"I think he's forgotten me for that group of boys over there."

Gerda pointed at Kent. "I remember this one when he was Steven's age. I could tell he had a crush on Ester, and I warned her to be extra nice to him when she baby-sat. Do you remember that?"

"I do. Truth was, Ester was my first big heartbreak."

Kent went quiet as Gerda shut down before Desi's eyes. Pain replaced the tender glances from earlier, and after a goodbye nod, Gerda make a quick departure for the bakery booth.

Desi and Kent exchanged puzzled glances. How should she process what had just happened? Kent had accidentally brought up the taboo topic. No wonder it seemed so hard to ask about her mother, when her grandmother had never gotten over her running away.

Kent flattened his lips into a straight line. "I put my foot in it, didn't I?"

"It's so many years. Who would think it could still be so painful?"

"Losing a kid. I don't know how I'd survive," he said.

Desi couldn't begin to imagine the hurt her mother had caused when she'd set out on her own, barely eighteen and pregnant. Seemed as though there were always two sides to every story. Times like these, Desi wished with all of her heart her mother was alive and she could ask her the tough questions.

Kent glanced at his watch. "Well, it's after noon. The kid's distracted. Would you like a taste of schnapps in some cocoa? I know just the place."

"Sounds good." Anything to replace the heartsick feeling for her mother and grandmother that had suddenly come over her. How different would her life have been if her mother and grandparents could have worked things out?

Off they went, down the street toward a booth decorated in swaths the colors of the Swedish flag. On the way, without asking, Kent took her hand with a gentle, comforting touch, setting off a tingly domino effect all the way to her toes.

Chapter Three

Kent let rip a piercing whistle as he set the three co-coas on the outdoor table. After Desi nearly jumped from her chair, she saw Steven making a beeline for them. The kid must know his dad's call.

"That's yours." Kent handed Desi a thick mug filled with rich, hot chocolate with a strong peppermint aroma.

"Thanks." Seated beside a small round table, she blew over the top of her mug and inhaled more of the delicious scents. "You always call your kid like a dog?"

Kent winked at her. "Works every time."

The quick, subtle wink sent a comet up her spine, and she sat infinitesimally straighter.

Steven arrived, took one quick sip and put the non-spiked cocoa down. "Thanks, Dad! Gotta go."

"Wai...wai...wait a minute." Desi grabbed the boy's sleeve and pulled him back. "I thought I was your guest today. Stick around and finish your cocoa. Talk to us a little bit before you run off with your friends again, or I'll get my feelings hurt."

The boy sat on the edge of the chair, too antsy to sit still. "We're playing tag." He slurped another drink. "I'm it."

"Sounds fun, but they get to see you every day at school." Once she had Steven's attention, she took a long drink of the warm, spiked cocoa and let it go down slow.

"Have you ever been in the parade?" she asked.

Steven tried to be polite, feet fidgeting, eyes darting to the side from time to time. "Not yet. But next year the fourth-grade class gets to make a float and wear costumes."

Desi glanced toward Kent. "Were you in the parade when you were in fourth grade?"

"You bet. One of the biggest days of my grammar school life." Kent's usual guarded style gave way to a smile, making him look younger, even a little carefree.

But Steven changed. His previous exuberance closed down and he stared at his drink. "Will I wear Swedish or Norwegian colors, Dad?"

"Both, if that's what you want to do."

Kent had grown more solemn, too, and Desi's imagination started working overtime. Swedish? Norwegian? Her eyes darted between father and son. Did it have something to do with the missing mother and wife? And what was the deal with her? But like so many other times, she left her questions unspoken.

Steven finished half of his drink and plopped the cup on the table. "Now can I go play?"

"What about me?" Desi teased, reaching to tickle his sweatshirt-covered chest, trying to lighten the mood again.

"I'll bring you some bubblegum after me and my friends go to the candy booth."

"Gee, thanks. I feel so special." She glanced at Kent. "I hope he didn't learn his dating techniques from you."

Steven's eyes lit up. "I know! I'll bring you some fruit-flavored SweeTarts."

Never in her life would she ask for SweeTarts, or for a kid to spend his money on her, but since it seemed like such a big deal to the boy, she cheered. "Yay!"

Kent got a funny look on his face and shook his head as Steven sped off.

"You are going to pay him back, right?" she asked. "I'd hate for your kid to spend all of his hard-earned allowance on me."

"Wouldn't that make it our date?"

She locked eyes with Kent, refusing to get lost in those arctic blues. "How about I pay you and make it Dutch?" She looked suspiciously around, wondering if it was okay to say *Dutch* in Heartlandia.

Tiny crinkles formed at the edges of his eyes, and Desi realized Kent was smiling again. "The other night he told me you smell like his favorite candy. That's why he's buying the SweeTarts for you."

She laughed. "SweeTarts?" She sniffed her wrists. "I guess my perfume does smell a little like candy."

She offered her wrist for Kent to try. He leaned forward and sniffed, his gaze walking from her wrist up her arm and connecting with her eyes. Zing. Heat jetted from her chest to her cheeks in record time. Feeling awkwardly aroused, she took her arm back and pretended to watch Steven run off.

"How funny he noticed," she muttered.

"He's a smart kid. A great kid."

"Agreed." She sipped more of the delicious enhanced cocoa and let the newly emerged sunshine further warm her tingling face.

Kent's fingers tapped her knuckles, setting off a second wave of shivers. "He came from a mixed marriage, you know."

She cocked her head in Kent's direction. The kid was a towhead.

He had a playful glint in his eyes. "His mother's Norwegian."

"Ah. Gee, it must have been hard with two extremely different cultures living under the same roof." She'd play along to see if he'd open up about the wife who was no longer in the picture.

Kent stretched out his long legs and crossed them at the ankles then took a long draw on his cocoa. "I can't tell you how many arguments we had whether to serve *lefse* or regular potato pancakes."

"You're kidding, right? What's *lefse?*"

"It's a very thin pancake made from potatoes. Looks kind of like a flour tortilla. Great stuff. Want to try some? There's a booth over there."

Her hand shot up. "I'm good. Thanks. Just ate half a dozen *aebleskiver,* and whatever that fishy thing you brought me was, remember? But I'll take another rain check."

He studied her face. When the man let down his guard, he could melt her with that gorgeous smile straight out of a magazine. The women in this town were probably all waiting in the shadows for him to give the high sign that he was on the market again.

Hadn't Gerda said he'd been divorced less than a year?

None of that mattered anyway, since Desi was only a tourist in town. Still, she wondered about the whole story, and the more he smiled at her, the more she wanted to know the down and dirty truth. Maybe she'd venture to ask?

Except he beat her to the punch with another topic.

"So when you're not visiting your grandmother, what do you do?"

"That's a tough question." She studied her ceramic mug, noticing fine cracks in the glaze. "I guess you could call me a jack-of-all-trades. I've waited tables and worked in bookstores. I've booked entertainment for a couple of clubs here and there, mostly acted as my mother's assistant and later as her agent." She took a sip, thinking how ditzy she must sound to a doctor. "I designed clothes for a retro girl group that was on the same circuit as my mother for a while. Being stuck in hotel rooms growing up, I got pretty good with sewing, mostly fixing my mom's costumes. She gave me a portable sewing machine for my birthday one year." She paused for a moment, remembering her excitement on that sweet-sixteen birthday, and how she'd wished there were more people to share it with. "I've done a few other la-di-da jobs, too, but I won't bore you with them. Anyway, you name it, I've probably tried it."

He didn't say anything, just sat there digesting her confession. Even though he was a doctor, she hadn't tried to embellish her eclectic résumé. Truth was, she'd never ventured beyond her high school equivalency, probably not very impressive to an M.D.

"So you're the artistic type." He rubbed his chin with his thumb and index finger, studying her as if she'd lost her clothes or something. His scrutiny made her squirm.

"I guess you could say that."

"What about that *la-di-da* part?"

She scrunched up her face, not understanding what he'd meant.

"Those other jobs—you know, 'you name it and I've probably tried it.' The ones you don't want to bore me with?"

Ahh. "I can assure you, everything I've ever done has been perfectly legal."

"Good to know." He sat back, thinking. "Where'd you go to college?"

"Uh, I didn't. My mother homeschooled me since we were always on the road, and by the time I could apply for college, I was really into the costume designing. So I skipped college that year, and the next year something else came up. I guess I just never got around to going."

He sat up straight. "Hey, we've got a great new community college right here."

"Is that right? Well, I won't be sticking around long enough to go to school here, but thanks for thinking—"

He shrugged a shoulder. "Why rule it out?"

School or sticking around? She finished her cocoa. "Why make any hard-and-fast plans? We'll see."

He didn't look satisfied with her answer, but what did she care?

Steven came barreling up to them again. "Here's your candy." He shoved it into her hands and took off again.

"Thanks," she shouted, positive the boy didn't hear her. She cocked her head. "Some date he turned out to be." When she glanced at Kent, there was that heart-melting smile again. Was it meant for her or because of Steven's antics? Or maybe because he could tell she genuinely liked his son.

"For my kid's sake, I hope you'll stick around awhile."

After all of his downright sexy smiles today, she wondered if maybe Kent wanted her to stick around, too. Or was this more about him being overprotective of his son and whoever the kid cared about not leaving?

Racking her brain, she couldn't remember anyone in her life ever asking her to stay put. Well, she had received an open-ended invitation from her grandmother to come to Heartlandia for as long as she wanted. That was one thing, but no *man* had ever seemed interested in anything long term. Not that she'd just taken an innocent comment from the gorgeous man across from her and blown it way out of proportion or anything. Talk about feeling needy. *Must be the schnapps.*

As much as she'd like to think Kent had sent a subtle message about sticking around in Heartlandia, she was savvy enough to know he was only being protective of his son. Desi looked deep into Kent's morning-sky stare and could have sworn there was a second part to that message she needed to decipher, and it all went back to his missing wife.

Kent finally got Steven to settle down and go to bed around nine o'clock. The kid had talked nonstop about *the best day of his life* after they'd dropped Desdemona back home. It gave Kent hope that Steven was coming out of his hurting place and that life would get better. For both of them.

It had been a big day, and the boy had a lot to process: his new piano teacher, who had lavished him with attention and made him blush; the civic-pride event of the year; running with his friends downtown. How free he must have felt, and it had been a long time since Kent had seen him cut loose like that.

Hell, last year they'd skipped the festival altogether, Kent making the excuse he had to work. He'd made sure he was scheduled just to avoid it.

Amazingly, even tonight, Steven's unending desire to impress Ms. Desi had led him to practice his piano lessons before taking his bath. That earnest look of concentration brought a swell of love so strong that Kent almost had to sit down. He shook his head over how a pretty woman could get a guy, even at the tender age of eight, to do things he'd never do on his own.

This wasn't good. Steven would go and get attached to her—the lady who couldn't even commit to sticking around long enough to enroll in college—and then she'd leave…just like Steven's mother had. Yet Kent couldn't bring himself to put a stop to it. He liked seeing the joy on his son's face again. He understood the lure of the new, mysterious woman. She'd gotten to him, too.

Kent loved seeing his kid smile, and he liked having a little pizzazz added back into their routine. But as with everything in life, this would come with a price. Maybe Desdemona would stick around, continue to teach piano, take some classes at the city college. It wasn't as if he had any control over it or not. But God knew Gerda would love to keep her here and could use her help, especially now that she'd agreed to fill in as mayor and the election wasn't for months yet.

Kent ventured out front to get some air, using the excuse of double-checking whether he'd locked up the truck or not. His gaze wandered to the large front window at the Rask house. The lights were bright, and inside, Desi walked back and forth, talking on a cell phone.

She'd let her hair down and wore a colorful dress that looked more like a scarf. It hung to the floor and clung to her full-proportioned body, and he couldn't help but notice when the light hit her just right, she was braless.

An almost forgotten response wound its way into his chest, down his torso and through his hips. Damn, she was good-looking. *Careful, Larson. Don't let her beauty mess with your head.* How many times today had he admired her light bronze complexion, the sprinkling of freckles across her nose and those rich dark eyes? Not to mention the lush lips begging to be— He shook his head. *Think straight. She lives hand to mouth, picks up jobs here and there, doesn't stick with any particular thing for long. She's spent her life traveling the country, never settling down. She's just passing through.*

His fists opened and closed as he did battle with the two strongest organs in his body. His brain knew without a doubt she'd break Steven's heart. More than anything Kent wanted to protect his son, but he knew life had a way of playing out in the least expected ways. Why deprive the kid of the dazzling Ms. Desi?

Why deprive himself?

It took a lot of discipline, but he broke his gaze from Desdemona and strode toward the truck.

He thought briefly about canceling Steven's next lesson if Desi was going to teach. But no way would Steven let him; hell, he'd never been more motivated or prepared. Why rob the boy of his enjoyment and reward from hard work? It had been a long time since he'd seen his son so animated and carefree. In some crazy way, maybe Desdemona could be part of the healing process instead of the purveyor of more grief.

He shoved fingers through his hair, and through the

car window he stole one last, quick look at Desi. Damn, the sight of her got to him again. Yet she was the exact opposite of what he needed in his life right now. There he went, overanalyzing. Whatever warm and sexy feelings he'd allowed to slip through just now had been successfully, surgically removed. As usual.

He strangled the handle on the truck with his grip, frustrated. *For once, Larson, can't you just go with the flow?*

He jimmied the cold metal, ensured the car was locked, made an about-face and marched back into the house without another glance next door. But the image of Desdemona was already implanted in his mind... every last detail. No bra.

The next day Kent rushed home late again, having way too many patients at the Urgent Care for the allotted time slots. He really needed to learn to stick with his appointment schedule. This was the third time in two weeks he'd had to ask his babysitter to stay an extra hour.

The sitter's car was parked out front, so he pulled the truck into the driveway, noticing Desdemona sitting on the front porch again. She wasn't looking his way or he would have waved. He rushed up the steps to the front door and let himself into the half-dark house.

Amanda sat with Steven at the kitchen table, helping him with homework.

"I'm sorry I'm late again." He didn't bother to check the mail, just went right to the kitchen. "I'll take over the homework from here."

"No need, Mr. Larson. Steven's all done."

Steven closed his book, making a loud clap.

"Hi, Dad. Can I watch some TV now?"

"A half hour. That's all. I'll have dinner ready by then." Kent started for the cupboards. What the heck did he have around to feed Steven?

"I already fed him," Amanda said, gathering her things.

"Hey, thanks."

"I was starving. She made me two hot dogs." Antsy as always, Steven acted as if he needed a bathroom, quick.

"You're always starving." He leaned against the counter.

"I should get to watch an hour of TV 'cause I already practiced piano, too."

"He did really well." Amanda seemed as surprised as Kent had been at first. Piano practice wasn't something the boy had ever been consistent about.

"I'm all ready for my lesson tomorrow." Pride puffed out his chest as he stood and headed for the TV room. "I'll play my song for you later, Dad."

"Good job, bud."

Kent walked Amanda out front, already hearing the TV loud and clear on Steven's favorite kid sitcom. The past couple of days had warmed up considerably, and he'd missed all the sunshine being stuck inside at work, and since a certain someone happened to be sitting outside earlier, he thought…

Amanda waved and drove off. Kent glanced to Gerda's porch but couldn't see Desdemona anymore. Blast it, his timing stank. He moved a little closer and searched the porch. Two wine-barrel planters stocked with summer blooms marked each end of it. A large fern hung from the arch over the railing, blocking the entire view from this vantage point.

His gaze drifted to the far corner. Boots rested on the railing and they were connected to Desi. She sat in the rocking chair, staring straight at him. Damn. Busted.

Surveillance was Gunnar's talent, not his. He waved at her in the shadows and approached with a sudden rush of excitement coursing through him.

"Nice night, huh?" he said.

"Actually feels like summer's coming. In L.A. we'd already be using air-conditioning." She held something in her hand. "Hey, now that you're off duty, maybe you'd like to join me for a wine cooler? My own secret concoction."

Surprisingly, he liked the idea. "Sounds good. Where's Gerda?"

Desi stood, and Kent got treated to an up-close view of that sexy multicolored scarf dress she seemed to like to lounge around in. Something about the clunky boots beneath made her look edgy and he liked the effect.

"She had to go to some hush-hush meeting with the city council."

Knowing Steven was set for at least the next half hour, he followed her inside. The screen door creaked and flapped behind them. Walking quickly across the large living area, they were soon in the kitchen. Desi mixed Japanese plum wine with club soda over ice, then refreshed her tall glass and handed him both of the drinks. She stopped at the couch and picked up a large, long pillow, carrying it outside and placing it on the top porch step so they could both sit on it together. Out here he could keep an eye on his house in case Steven needed him.

Desdemona sat first and patted the spot next to her. He'd never been this close to her before and didn't need to be asked twice.

He took a drink. It was bubbly, tart, yet with a sweet aftertaste. "This is very good."

"Tell me about it. Problem is, they sneak up on you." Desi seemed more relaxed than he'd ever seen her, and after his long, stressful day he had some catching up to do.

They sat in silence, enjoying the drinks, and he studied the clear starlit sky, the Columbia River sparkling in the distance. Wind rustled through the front-yard trees and breezed over his face. He could smell the pine trees all the way from the hills behind town. He took another drink and relaxed a bit more. A sudden gust of wind kicked up some leaves, lifting Desdemona's hair every which way. He turned to watch the show.

Had he ever seen such soft-looking skin before? It would be so easy to reach over and kiss her. Instead he moved a lock of windblown hair from her face and tucked it behind her ear.

Desdemona gave a bashful, endearing smile. "Thank you."

Thump. It went right to Kent's heart. He fantasized tracing his finger along her back and kissing her neck— her long, beautiful neck.

The wind stopped and the air between them went thick, expectant.

She shivered.

He looked away, afraid she might notice the sex-starved thoughts written all over his face. Just because he was intensely drawn to her, he didn't want to make her uncomfortable.

"How's Steven?"

Safe topic. *Okay, we'll keep things safe.* "Great. He's all ready for his lesson tomorrow, which is a first."

"I love it." She drank several swallows of her wine cooler. Kent almost finished his.

"Yeah, dangle a pretty lady in front of any warm-blooded male and that's what you get."

Desdemona hitched her head, pulled in her chin and studied him. There was amusement in her expression, with a raised eyebrow of disbelief tossed in to balance things out. "Was that a compliment?"

"You don't know you're hot?"

She blurted a laugh. "I didn't know *you* thought I was hot."

"Am I alive?" He finished off his drink, staring straight ahead, hoping she wouldn't notice he'd felt about as awkward as a teenager.

She tapped his shoulder. He turned to find a mischievous twinkle in her eye. "Want another?" She'd noticed.

He didn't want to break up the moment, so he shook his head, though the easy-down-the-hatch drink had already tweaked his outlook. This going-with-the-flow stuff wasn't half-bad.

"Since we talked the other day, I've really been wondering about all those other jobs you've had," he said, thinking, by habit, he'd already put a stop to the go-with-the-flow bit. Maybe she had office experience and he could get her a job at his Urgent Care.

"The odds-and-ends jobs?"

Did he really want to know or was he just making stuff up so that now he'd finished his drink he could stick around and look at her more? "Yeah, those."

"I'm a calligrapher and have some pretty good accounts. I know computers can do that stuff these days, but there's nothing like the real thing. Plenty of people still want it, and it brings in decent money." She scratched her chin. "And the last job I had before I came here was at the senior center in L.A. where my mother and I lived."

"That's nice. What did you do there?"

"I posed for the Life Art classes."

"Hmm. Did they dress you in different costumes when you posed?"

"No." She acted blasé and moved her large-eyed glance toward Kent's face in a lazy fashion. "I posed nude." She used her straw to take a long draw on her drink, eyes unwavering from his.

He almost choked. "You what?"

"Pose naked." She blew a puff of air from between her lips, pulled at the seams of the pillow and punched the fluffy filling down a tad, then relaxed into the cushion. "Hey, there isn't anyone under sixty in the class and they're mostly women. Besides, it's for art."

"Aren't you self-conscious about people staring at you naked?"

"Maybe at first, but it's artistic and I feel a little daring doing it. You know, out of the ordinary."

So she didn't do ordinary, which was all Kent and Steven were. Diana had gotten tired of ordinary, too.

Still, that daring part she'd mentioned got his full attention and he let himself look her over head to booted toes, stuttering over her chest. How had he not noticed before now that she was braless again? He quickly diverted his gaze to his hands, making a fist with one and butting it against the other palm.

"Don't go getting any weird notions about me. The

first time I posed I nearly puked, but I'm not uptight about my body."

"Good to know." Okay, he was feeling his drink but things still seemed awkward. Maybe because he'd been transported back in time to a horny teenager.

"Maybe we should keep this between us. I wouldn't want to cause my mayor grandma any scandals. She's only just getting to know me." There was a touch of sassy in her grin, and he made a snap decision that he really liked Desi's brand of sassy.

"My, my, my." Kent grinned back his own version of a sassy smile and leaned on his elbows, happy to finally find the relaxation he'd needed, compliments of the plum wine and Ms. Desdemona Rask.

She leaned back on her elbows, too. Her hair fell below her shoulders as she scanned the night sky. The curve of her throat and soft full breasts below demanded his attention. He swallowed. Damn, he should never have come over here.

On impulse he lifted the mahogany-colored hair off the shoulder closest to him, feeling the thick, wavy texture.

She closed her eyes.

Crazy vibes whizzed up his arm and across his shoulders.

He either needed to kiss her or leave. Some deep, honorable part of his subconscious put on the brakes, but the urge to test out her inviting lips, just a few inches away, overrode that hesitation.

Kent reached across her chest to her shoulder and turned her toward him. Their eyes met—hers with a knowing, warm and welcoming glance. He locked into her dark, sexy gaze until his lips made contact with hers and his lids closed.

Soft. Plump. Warm. Her lips were everything he'd thought and more. He tasted the plum wine as he deepened the kiss, and her fingers delved into his hair.

The kiss set off sensations and desires he'd buried since Diana had left. Hot-blooded desire. He wanted Desdemona, and he wasn't sure what to do about it. From the way she kissed him back, he was positive she was on board, too.

When his tongue crossed the seams of her lips and he touched the tip of hers, he quit thinking. He let his mind wander with the zero-to-ninety rush of making out with this beautiful woman.

Desdemona ended it. She pulled away and stared into his eyes. It took him a moment to focus. "That was nice." Her voice was breathy. Sexy. Oozing sincerity.

Only nice? Hell. He feigned a smile, fighting off the lance to his ego. "I can blame the plum wine if that makes things easier to explain."

"What would you blame it on otherwise?"

Tell her the truth. "Your irresistibleness."

A whispery laugh parted her lips. "Is that even a word?" Her sweet, questioning expression proved she liked his attention.

"It is if it's true."

She gazed dreamily at him, those dark topaz eyes so warm and inviting, like the night. She'd liked it. Definitely. Should he kiss her again?

Desi relaxed back on the step, staring in the direction of the river. Kent rested his elbows on his knees and gave her space.

"You know, part of the reason I came to Oregon was to find my biological father."

They'd broken the ice with the intimate kiss, and he liked how she was opening up with him. "Is he from around here?"

"No. I believe he lives in Portland. My mother only told me about him when she was dying. I feel like I've got to find him. Sort of like finding the other half of me."

Kent's jaw went tight. "What about Gerda?"

"Oh, I plan to stay long enough to get to know her. I'll keep her in my life for sure, yet…"

And there you go, Larson—the reason you shouldn't get involved with her.

"Dad?" A distant voice cut further into Kent's suddenly aborted trip to pleasantville. "Are you out here? It's time for my bath."

Kent stood. Even now, after the realization his attraction to Desi couldn't go anywhere, his natural and red-blooded reaction to that kiss proved embarrassing. Good thing it was getting dark out.

"Well, I gotta go. Kid's calling," he said, sounding husky, maybe a little frustrated, and way out of practice when it came to women.

Desi stood on the steps, watching him leave, looking like a booted, scarf-covered goddess, the kind that should pose for a painting. Light from the house outlined her figure through the thin, almost transparent material of her dress. A new gust of wind rustled the hem of her skirt as she waved good-night with a smoldering smile. The sight almost made his knees buckle.

"Dad!"

"Co—" He needed to clear his throat. "Coming."

Going to see Desdemona had been a wonderfully terrible idea. He backed away from the porch, rubbing his neck. Why did everything in life have to be so complicated?

"Hi, Ms. Desi!"

"Hey there, Steven."

With a final wave good-night, Kent made his getaway…quick.

Chapter Four

On Tuesday, Steven trotted across Gerda's lawn with his babysitter hot on his heels. Desi saw them through the front window and hopped off the piano bench, leaving her current student fumbling through a song.

"Keep playing, Dagney." She opened the door before he could knock. "You're early."

"I know!" He stood there in his summer-day-camp clothes, mud on the knees of his jeans and face grimy with sweat and dirt streaks.

"I tried to distract him by taking him to the park, but he's been chomping at the bit to get here for the last half hour," said the young woman she'd seen come and go as the babysitter.

Seeing Steven set off all kinds of thoughts, mainly about his father and their amazing kiss, but also what a sweet boy he was to get so excited about his lesson. She'd hardly been able to keep Kent out of her thoughts today and was thankful for the piano-teaching distractions. Seeing Steven set her progress in reverse.

"Why don't you wait right here on the porch—" she pointed to the wicker love seat "—and I'll get to you as soon as Dagney is finished."

The pent-up excitement leaked from his face, his expression going flat. "Okay."

"It'll only be a few more minutes." She ruffled his damp hair and closed the door then sat beside Dagney, who'd stopped playing to watch what was going on.

"Sorry about the interruption. Let's start right here." Desi pointed to the middle of the page.

Ten minutes later, Desi sent Dagney home and let Steven in. He ran for the piano bench, slipping on a braided area rug on the way, almost hitting the floor on his knees. Using quick reflexes, Desi grabbed him by the elbow before he went down. They smiled at each other and after he'd calmed down they sat side by side on the piano bench.

After the warm-ups and some theory talk, they got down to the lesson.

"Wow, you even did your theory homework," she said, thumbing through the workbook.

Pride could not adequately describe the joy on his face when she put gold stickers on all of the pages. Knowing he was practically blowing a gasket trying to be patient, she pushed ahead. "Okay, play your new song for me."

The boy sat tall, placing his fingers on the keyboard, wrists straight and slightly lifted, then began the blues song. A few notes in, Desi realized he was playing from memory, and the improvement over last week was amazing. Gerda had asked Desi to light a fire under the boy's feet for music, and she definitely felt as though that mission had been accomplished.

She called her grandmother to come and witness the miracle. Gerda clapped her hands in delight. "He deserves two candies this week," she said, before giving him a hug and retreating to the back of the house to make more work-related phone calls. It didn't go unnoticed that she'd given Desi freedom to teach in her own style.

Steven gave his all to the rest of the lesson, too, and when Desi added a few new notes and chords to his music, he paid unwavering attention. Night and day from last week. By the end of the hour, Desi had introduced another short bluesy song for him to try on his own.

"This one's even cooler than the last one," he said, after her demonstration.

"I can't wait to see how you do." After putting bright stickers on his music pages, she handed him an extra-special candy, a small bag of SweeTarts, the tropical kind. She'd had a hunch he was going to nail the lesson today and decided to be prepared. "Now that I know how much you like SweeTarts, I bought some for the really great lessons."

His bright sky-blue eyes shone with pure delight, and he hugged her, giving it his all, just like he'd given to the piano lesson. The doorbell rang and, not wanting to break up the hug by answering the door, she called out, "Come in!"

In came Kent, nearly stunning her with his classic masculine looks. He wore charcoal slacks and a yellow button-down shirt, cuffs rolled to his forearms displaying strength and sophistication. His dark blond hair was slicked back with hair product, except the slightly longer hair on his neck curled out a tiny bit. Normally she'd make a guy out to be more than he actually was in her memory, and would inevitably be disappointed the next time she saw him, but not so with Kent. Every time they came face-to-face he only got better looking. The man had to be related to the Nordic gods, and his near perfection proved it.

Don't be so superficial. He's a great father, too. And a doctor for the town.

"Hi," he said, looking tentative and withdrawn, totally different from the last time she'd seen him.

What was she supposed to make of Kent's spine-melting kiss? She'd stood on the steps watching him go home last night, hardly able to believe the guy had made a pass at her. No one should let his bland white house fool them, because the man gave smokin'-hot kisses. Yet right now he seemed reserved, maybe even unhappy. Why? Was he sorry he'd kissed her?

"Hi." She gave him a bright smile, hoping to lighten the serious look on Kent's face. "Steven had a stellar lesson."

"Good to know." He nodded and smiled at his son.

Steven shot her a look as if he couldn't wait to crow about how well he'd done. "She said I did everything perfect, Dad!"

"Fantastic." Kent's smile didn't reach anywhere near his eyes. He didn't venture beyond the doorframe, either.

Steven let go of Desi, breaking up their hug, then rushed toward his dad, music books long forgotten. Kent gave him a jock's pat on the butt as he barreled straight out the door.

"I want to try the new song all by myself. See you, Ms. Desi!" From the sound of his voice he'd already cleared the porch and was halfway across the yard.

Desi cupped her hands around her mouth. "You won't get far without your music books."

In he ran, retrieving the music primers, and he sped right back out the door again.

"Call me if you need any help," she said as he disappeared again.

That left Kent and Desi alone, quietly staring at each other. Warmth edged up her throat to her jaw. She smiled, even though her right cheek felt a little twitchy.

"Mind if I ask you a favor?" Kent said after their silence had stretched into the uncomfortable stage.

"Not at all," she said with a sudden hopeful feeling. Would he ask her out, just the two of them, maybe for that midnight supper? Hopefully, if he did, he'd be in a better mood.

One large hand pulled free from his back pocket and he scratched the corner of his eyebrow. "I was wondering if you could back off a little from Steven."

She couldn't stop herself from pulling in her chin. "But we've been getting along so great and he's made phenomenal progress in one week."

"I know. That's great and all, but his heart is fragile right now. Please try to understand."

She bit back the load of questions in her mind, choosing the most obvious. "Does this have something to do with your kissing me?"

"No. I really liked doing that." Some life had come into his pensive eyes, and she breathed a little easier. "Having to ask you to back off from my son, not so much."

"Then why do it?" Desi shook her head and studied her shoes.

"It's a long story. I shouldn't dump it on you."

Must have something to do with Steven's mother not being around. It really isn't any of my business.

"Look, Steven and I get along great, and I don't understand why you want to put a stop to that, but you're the father, and I'll try to understand."

"Thank you. And I'm not trying to put a stop to anything. It's just he's a little too eager for attention these days. Too needy. It's my job to protect him." He leaned his shoulder against the doorframe, arms folded, without offering further explanation.

"From me?"

By the set of his jaw, she could tell an answer wouldn't be forthcoming. Frustrated, she asked, "You always this way?"

"Am I being a jerk?"

"Borderline." At least he had a clue. It made her smile. "You're being all mysterious. Hot and kissing me one minute. Asking me to back off from your kid the next."

"I don't mean to be." And by his withdrawn posture, he definitely didn't want to get into a discussion.

"Well, you haven't exactly been the most sensitive guy in town, running hot one time, cold the next." She hoped she could egg him on, get him to talk.

He opened his mouth but just as quickly closed it. Whatever he'd wanted to say hadn't evidently been worth the effort. If she were standing closer, frustrated as she was, she might have kicked his shin to help him along.

"Look, I'm glad Steven loves his piano lessons. It's just…" He battled inside, his eyes darting around the room as if searching for the words he couldn't quite make himself say. "Not a good time. I've got to go."

"Well, if you're hoping Gerda will be teaching the lesson next week, I can't guarantee it. Her arthritis is still bad, some of her finger joints are swollen and she's got a whole other responsibility as mayor."

And I think she's really enjoying the break. Plus, it lets me feel like I'm paying my way staying here.

"Just try to stop making Steven think you're the greatest person he's ever met."

"Didn't realize I was doing that." Again he cast her a perplexed look. He really was confused. "Are you jealous?"

"Not at all. I think you're great, too."

"Then why do I have to be different for your kid?"

He shoved his hands into his pockets and took a slow breath. "Because I asked you to."

"You're asking me to not be me. I can't help responding to him. He's a sweet and wonderful kid."

Kent backed out the doorway. "And you're a fantastic teacher." He gave her an earnest glance, as if begging her to understand the big mysterious reason he refused to share. "I'm sure you'll think of a way to remain professional without being his best friend."

He left, and the screen door flapped closed.

She stared after him, her jaw dropping. "What the hell just happened?" Had she imagined her time on the porch with Kent last night? No way could she make up that kiss. Nope. It had been real, hot and sexy, and it had set off sparks in out-of-the-way places. She'd been positive he'd felt it, too.

Desi planted her fist on her hip, ticked off and confused, staring at the empty doorway. If everyone in

Heartlandia was as hard to figure out as Kent Larson, she couldn't wait to move on.

She strode to the back of the house to the den, where she knew Gerda would be. Through with her calls, her grandmother sat on a small classic love seat watching an antiquated, tiny TV.

"What is the deal with that Kent Larson? One minute he invites me to the parade—" she kept the kiss part to herself "—the next he tells me to keep away from his kid. How am I supposed to do that when I give Steven piano lessons?"

After hearing Desi's gripes, Gerda looked alarmed. "Oh, no. Sounds like things backfired."

"What do you mean by 'things'?"

"You've really gotten through to Steven, and I can tell how much he likes you. You've gotten through to Kent, too, if the way he looked at you the other day at the parade meant anything." Gerda went thoughtfully quiet, her kind eyes drifting from the TV to Desi. "I think he's scared."

Desi sat on the edge of the love seat, needing to get to the bottom of this mystery. "Why? What about me could scare Kent?" *I know I'm a different shade than most everyone else in Heartlandia, but he had no problem with that when he kissed me.*

Gerda turned off the TV and gave Desi all of her attention. "It's not you he's scared of. It's about Steven getting attached to you. The boy lost his mother last year."

The information, out of the blue, felt like a sucker punch. "You make it sound like she died instead of getting divorced."

Gerda grew quiet, pulled inward for a couple of seconds. "She left."

Desi caught her breath. "Left?" It wasn't often a woman left her family. How bad could being married to Kent have been?

"She was a selfish one. Always had been. And willful. Always had to have her way, and in case you haven't noticed, Kent is a domineering kind of guy. They were always banging heads. Then one day instead of working things out she up and left."

A heartsick feeling hung heavy in Desi's chest. She could understand leaving a man, but how did a woman leave her child, too?

"No visits?"

"Nothing. She severed all contact, gave Kent full custody. Nearly broke Kent in two, but he keeps going because he has to. For the boy."

"Was there…abuse?"

Gerda shook her head with confidence. "Kent is a healer, not a hurter. The woman just didn't want to be married and have those responsibilities anymore, I guess."

There had to be more to it than that.

Sadness enveloped Desi. No wonder Kent had a chip on his shoulder and didn't want Steven to get attached to her. He knew she didn't plan to stick around for long. And she hadn't been the least bit concerned letting him know it, either. He'd been feeling her out by mentioning the city college and she'd blown that suggestion right out of the water.

Oh, God, poor Steven. And Kent—big, strong, gorgeous Kent. Desi needed a serious attitude adjustment in regards to the tall, stubborn doc next door. Since she didn't have a clue how to handle the situation, she'd avoid him. Let things be. After the message he'd delivered today, it should suit him just fine.

A quick replay of their kiss gave her pause. She didn't want to avoid him; she'd hoped to know him better, see where this crazy out-of-the-blue attraction might lead. But it wouldn't be fair to get involved with the man or his son because she really did have plans to leave. And evidently, they'd both already had enough of that.

She glanced at her grandmother, patted her bony hand. "Thanks for sharing."

"Of course, dear."

How similar Kent's wife's story sounded to her mother's, running off from loved ones to find a bigger life outside of quaint Heartlandia. Did the comparison stab at the old wound? Desi suddenly needed to hug her grandmother, and Gerda was completely receptive to the gesture.

As they hugged, Desi thought of her biological father. She needed to find him to put the last pieces of her life puzzle together. Until she was whole, she wouldn't have anything to offer anyone, especially not to that big galoot and his darling kid next door.

Wednesday morning, with loads of free time on her hands, Desi ventured back into town. Thanks to the parade and her afternoon spent with Kent, she had her bearings straight. She parked on Heritage Street, smack in the middle of the downtown area. The first thing she wanted to check out was the town monument and city hall. After all, she couldn't resist seeing where Gerda had been going for all of the hush-hush meetings the past week.

After a brisk two-block walk, she circled around a grassy knoll where the magnificent granite monument took center stage. The sculpture looked like a totem pole except it was made out of rock. It depicted ships and fishermen and native peoples intertwined and working together. The top looked like the tower part of a lighthouse, complete with a lantern. The inscription read "Working together for a better life. Heartlandia, founded 1750."

She wandered down the main street where the parade had been, noticing storefront after storefront, each more adorable than the last. How could such a small town support so many bakeries, knitting shops, bookstores and memento marts?

Squinting into the bright sun, she glanced into the distance toward the huge Columbia River. Down by the docks sat a humongous cruise ship. It had entered the port late last night after one long horn blast, which woke her up about three in the morning. Ah, so the tourist trade was big in these parts.

She'd had trouble going back to sleep after the horn, so here she was, wandering around the heart of downtown Heartlandia, bright and early when most of the businesses weren't even open. She glanced up to the backdrop of the hillside covered in trees and eclectically designed houses that Gerda had said got passed from one generation to the next.

She went inside a bakery called Fika with blue-and-white awnings and curtains to match and ordered a cup of coffee and a croissant. After, sitting out front, she buttered up her breakfast and ate the delicious fluffy treat, sipping bold-tasting coffee in between and scouting out the other buildings.

Her gaze came to rest on that redbrick-fronted restaurant and bar, the place where the older African-American man had greeted her on Saturday. Once she'd finished her quickie breakfast, she headed back to Lincoln's Place for a closer look.

It was closed, which was what she'd expected at this hour, but she put her face to the window, hands blocking the sun at her temples, and peered inside for a better look. There was a white piano smack in the middle of the restaurant area, which was kitty-corner to the huge wraparound wood bar. Behind the bar on the wall, and placed where everyone could see, was a portrait of Abraham Lincoln.

Movement in her peripheral vision caught her eye. It was the man she'd seen the other day, and he was waving her in. How embarrassing getting caught snooping in his window. She couldn't very well pretend she didn't notice him, though she wanted to cut and run. She waved back, and he motioned for her to come inside.

The man met her at the door, unlocking it and inviting her inside.

"I'm Cliff Lincoln, the proprietor of this establishment. Come in. And you are?"

"Desdemona Rask, but everyone calls me Desi."

"I like Desdemona better. Mind if I call you that?"

She shook her head. "So I'm new in town, and—"

"Don't I know that. You and me kind of stand out around here."

The way he spoke, like melting butter coating his words, made her smile. By the salt-and-pepper short, tight hair, he looked to be in his fifties, but he hardly had creases on his face. Whether from a life well lived or simply good genes, she didn't know, but something had worked in his favor.

Tall with evidence around the middle of a life centered on good food, he led her toward the bar. She sat on a stool, admiring the rich dark wood with intricately carved inlays. A mishmash of bench-type tables and chairs filled the rest of the casual area, but the dining room shifted into a cleaner, upscale style with black lacquered tables and chairs, white tablecloths and fresh flowers in crystal vases. The white baby grand piano divided the two diverse areas.

Without asking, he passed her a cup of fresh coffee and a few creamer containers. It would be her second cup of the day, but she didn't want to be impolite, so she weakened the strong brew with creamer.

"What brings you to these parts?" He leaned on his forearms on the bar and joined her with a cup of coffee.

"My mother grew up here. She died last year and asked me to come here to get to know my grandmother, so here I am."

"What do you think so far?"

"It's nice. My grandmother's really sweet."

"Good. Good."

"Are you from here?"

"Nope." He glanced out the window toward the Columbia River. "I used to be a chef on one of those cruise ships you may have noticed down at the docks. This stop was my favorite of all the cities. I got to know the previous owner of this place, whose name was also Lincoln. Fifteen years ago he wanted to retire and offered this place to me for a sweet price. I've been the only black man in town ever since, and no one has ever said a peep about it."

"That's wonderful. Are you married?"

"I've got a Danish wife and a couple of beautiful daughters."

Desi figured the mixed-race young girl in the parade the other day must have been his daughter. "That's great." She also wondered what it might have been like to be that mixed-raced girl in the parade twenty years ago, when people may have peeped a lot about it. But that was all a moot point, since her mother had never intended to go home again.

"You like soul food?" His question snapped her out of her thoughts.

"I always have it on the menu," he said, "for the daring types on cruises. Plus some of my regulars have come to expect it, too. If you want I can whip up some grits and fried okra?"

"Oh, no, thanks."

"Collard greens?"

"I'm good, thanks. Just had a croissant. Bit early for lunch."

"You don't eat soul food, do you." It wasn't a question.

She shook her head again, feeling a little embarrassed. "Not really."

"Cain't say you've lived until you've had my sweet-potato pie."

She couldn't resist his raised brows and friendly dare. "That does sound good." The man was being kind and generous, and even though she'd just had a croissant she didn't want to be impolite. "I'll take a tiny sliver if you've got some on hand."

"You got it. I always come in early to bake my pies." He went back in the kitchen to get the pie and she wandered over to the white piano, lifted the lid and uncovered the keys, then tapped a few notes. The instrument had beautiful tone.

"You play?" Cliff said, holding two plates with something much bigger than a sliver of pie on each.

"Yes. My mother was an accomplished pianist. She taught me. I'm not as good as her, but not so bad, either."

"Feel free to try it out. I bought that from a pianist from the cruise ship. He said he used to hang out with Liberace. Do you even know who he is?"

She nodded. "Sure I do. So where's the candelabra?"

A rich deep laugh rolled out of his chest.

She played one of her favorite Duke Ellington songs, "Do Nothing Till You Hear From Me," and added an extra-bluesy touch for Cliff.

He grinned and ate his pie while she played. When she'd finished, he clapped and brought her pie over then sat on the piano bench with her. "You want a job? I could use some nice dinner music like that on the weekends."

Did she want to follow in her mother's footsteps? It had been a tough life for both her and her mother. "That's awfully kind of you, but I'm helping my grandma with her piano students right now, and I'm not sure how long I'll be in town…." She took a bite of his sweet potato pie and took a quick trip to pie heaven. "Mmm-mm, this is good."

"I'm tryin' to tell you."

She smiled and covered her mouth. "If I worked here, you could pay me in pie."

"You could use some meat on your bones, too."

She snorted a laugh. Then why did she always feel fuller-sized than other women? "Right." She loved how relaxed Cliff made her feel, and for an instant she honestly thought about taking him up on his offer. What if?

After the last bite, she handed him the plate and thanked him. "I've got to go, and you probably need to get ready for the lunch crowd." She'd heard a few people arrive back in the kitchen, and pots and pans started clinking and clanking behind the swinging doors. "I'll think about your offer. I promise."

He showed her to the entrance. "Don't be scarce, girl. You know where to find me."

"It was nice to meet you, Mr. Lincoln."

"You, too, Desdemona. And call me Cliff like all my friends do."

She walked back to her car feeling as though she'd just made a friend, and how working part-time for a friend could help him out as much as her. But accepting the job would mean sticking around, and she needed to find her father before she could stick around anywhere. Cliff would understand that.

On Sunday, Grandma Gerda spent the whole day preparing dinner. The *gravet laks,* salmon, had been cold-cured and ready to serve as an appetizer. The batter for the *lefse,* potato pancakes, was ready for pouring and grilling. Desi's least favorite vegetable on the planet, beets, was pickled and cold. Somehow, she would manage at least one bite so as not to insult her grandmother. But it was the thought of the main meal, roasted lamb chops with mushrooms and barley, that made her mouth water.

Her mother's older brother, Uncle Erik, and his wife, Helena, would be there. Admittedly nervous about meeting relatives she never knew she had, Desi dressed up.

She wore a gray, high-waist, straight skirt with a bright yellow top that dipped a bit too low for a family meal, so she added a white, lacy camisole. She even put on her dress-up pumps, making her a little self-conscious about her height. She'd decided to wear her hair down and, since she wanted to make a good impression, she wore a little more makeup than usual.

At four o'clock Desi set the table for six, as instructed, assuming she had a couple of cousins she'd be meeting, too, then she joined her grandmother in the kitchen to watch a master at work on the main dish.

Gerda already had the barley cooked and waiting in a grainy mountain inside a stainless-steel dish.

"Chop this for me, would you?" Gerda handed Desi a pile of green leaves.

"What's this?"

"Kale. It's good for you."

Of all of the ingredients, this large, thick-veined leaf looked the least appetizing.

Meanwhile, Gerda minced onion and garlic like a TV chef, tossing it into a huge pan to brown.

"So what does Uncle Erik do?"

"He works for a big internet company in the insurance department, and they've sent him all over the world. You would have met him before now, but he and his wife just got back from Japan."

"And my cousins?"

"Oh, they're all grown and living across the country. Anni lives in Maine. She teaches school, and Christoffer lives in Washington, near the Canadian border. He's a journalist for an online newspaper."

"Wow, and they came this far just to meet me?"

"Oh, no, sorry—Anni and Chris won't be here tonight."

"But I set the table for six."

Gerda turned back to the counter and chopped a pile of brown mushrooms as if she were being timed. "I invited Kent and Steven."

Desi's blossoming appetite vanished, her stomach tightening. Kent? How was she supposed to face him over dinner and not be reminded of their kiss? And how in the world was she supposed to honor his request to back off from Steven, when they kept being thrown together?

Why had he even accepted Gerda's offer?

She was nervous enough about meeting long-lost relatives, and now the thought of sharing a meal with family and a sexy new neighbor seemed impossible.

Before she could worry another second, the doorbell rang.

Chapter Five

From the kitchen, Desi ran her suddenly moist hands down the front of her skirt and crossed beside the dining table and through the living room to answer the door. Seeming as nervous as Desi was, Gerda followed right on her heels.

When Desi opened the door, it wasn't Kent and Steven as she'd thought, but her uncle and aunt. Immediately, her butterflies shifted into another kind of jitters.

"Erik," Gerda cooed. "It's so good to see you. Come in. Come in." The tall, thin man, with blond hair morphing into silver, ducked to hug and kiss his mother—the family resemblance unmistakable.

A heavyset brunette waited her turn to say hello, and Gerda kissed her daughter-in-law's cheek. "Helena, you look beautiful as always." The woman's red-lipstick smile made Desi grin.

"And I know you've both been eager to meet our

Desdemona." Gerda nudged Desi forward, since she'd been hanging back, feeling a little shy.

Erik and Helena both gave her polite hugs of welcome, genuine smiles on their faces. Moisture brimmed in Erik's eyes and she could tell hers were doing the same. No doubt her mother's running away had left many hearts and minds hurt and confused for years and years. Desi was probably bringing all of those feelings and memories back. Her heart was heavy from trying to understand her mother's choice to never come home.

No sooner had they taken seats in the living room than a firm triple knock drew everyone's attention. With butterflies back in full force, Desi started to stand.

Gerda jumped up first. "I'll get it."

Desi sat, crossed one leg over the other and tried to look unfazed but suspected she was doing a horrible job. When Gerda ushered in Kent and Steven, both her aunt and uncle stood to say hello, so she did, too.

There they both were, shower-fresh, dressed for Sunday dinner, Steven looking adorable and Kent looking scrumptious. How was she supposed to ignore Kent with his damp hair curling at his neck?

Once again, Desi hung back, nervous about seeing Kent again, letting her uncle and aunt get first greetings, but finally it couldn't be avoided.

Gerda turned to Desi. "And here's my Desi."

Kent dipped his head in a subtle greeting.

"Hi, Ms. Desi!" Steven shot over to her side as if he hadn't seen her in a month. "I brung these for you." Steven handed her two yellow roses surrounded by Queen Anne's lace. "Look, they match your top."

"Thank you so much." Desi bent to get eye to eye with Steven. Even with her heels on, the boy seemed to grow more every time she saw him, just like the pretty white weeds surrounding her roses. "I'll get a vase." She needed time to gather her nerves and threaten them into submission. No way did she want to let on how anxious she felt being around Kent again.

While she was in the kitchen fussing with the flowers and vase, Gerda breezed in and picked up the tray of appetizers. "Bring the iced tea when you come, please." All business, in her blue top with white lace trim and matching slacks, hair parted in the middle and pulled back into her signature loose bun. Gerda acted more like a caterer than the matriarch of the family, and she made it clear the dinner party had officially begun.

Desi composed herself and got down six glasses, filled five of them with iced tea, deciding to wait to see what Steven wanted, placed them on a tray and brought it into the living room. She handed out the drinks, and when she got to Kent, their eyes met and he didn't look away. It wasn't the iced glasses that gave her a chill.

"Thanks" was all he said, leaving her wondering if he planned to treat her like a stranger all night or the woman he'd kissed as if he'd meant it. So far he was going the *mildly acquainted* route.

She got back to business, handing out drinks. "Steven, would you like apple juice or lemonade?"

"Milk, please. I'm a growing boy."

Gerda laughed. "You certainly are."

As the others enjoyed their drinks and conversation, Gerda grilled the potato pancakes, thin enough to roll each one up, and Desi got the warm serving dish of barley, mushrooms and kale and placed the already-grilled lamb chops in a circle around the top. The rich and rangy aroma of lamb overcame her jittery stomach, and boy, was she ready to eat.

"Put some of that chopped mint on it," Gerda said just before they made their way into the dining room. "Dinner's served."

Without any official seat assignments, Steven rushed to sit next to Desi. She glanced at Kent, who sat directly across from her and next to her aunt at the head of the table. She gave him a hint of a shrug. *I can't help it if your kid loves me. Why'd you accept the invitation if you didn't want him around me?*

Then it dawned on her that maybe *he* was the one who wanted to see her, and Steven was along for the ride. She stopped short of batting her eyes at him to test out her theory.

Other than Kent's stoic silence, dinner conversation flowed easily as plates of food were passed around. She discovered she had the same birthday as one of her cousins, and Erik insisted her voice sounded just like her mother's. A plethora of questions about his long-lost sister followed. Had she ever married? Had she been a talented musician? How in the world had the two of them survived? He mentioned how being five years older, he'd always thought of her as a pest, and he offered regret that they hadn't been closer before he left for college.

Only when Helena put her hand on his arm did he get the picture and forgo his grilling.

Her uncle seemed like a kind man with sympathetic steel-blue eyes, and she wished with all of her heart that her mother hadn't cut off every last family tie. She had a vague memory of Grandma Gerda being at her fifth birthday, and maybe her tenth, but after that she hadn't seen her until her mother was dying.

Though the potato pancake was delicious, it went down like a brown paper bag when the bitter thought struck that maybe her mother had been ashamed of Desi. But her mother had always seemed so proud of her—that couldn't have been the reason for her mother's staying away. Though the meeting was strained at first due to the circumstances, Desi had felt completely accepted by her grandmother from the moment she'd shown up last year in the hospital. It only made sense that their getting reacquainted here in Heartlandia had been a bit tough at first. She'd never felt for one second it was because of her being biracial.

Once she decided to concentrate on the food instead of her insecurity, everything tasted fantastic. Her stomach, however, was still uneasy what with Kent staring at her from across the bountifully filled table. She got the distinct impression he wanted to talk to her.

For distraction, she glanced around as everyone enjoyed their meal. So this was how a family dinner went. Despite her preoccupation with Kent, Desi liked the feel of this gathering. She liked these people, even the aunt and uncle she'd only just met, and the man who'd recently shaken her world with a kiss straight from heaven, but who didn't want to be involved with her. Plus Steven, who currently rested his head on her arm—gosh, he must miss his mommy—and Gerda at the head of the table, the sweet yet stern and endearing grandmother she wished she'd gotten to know better when she'd been a kid.

Desi served Steven another lamb chop and *lefse*. "I miss my mom's cooking," he whispered for only Desi to hear.

She put her arm around him and gathered him to her

side, choosing not to follow Kent's rules because this child needed some lady love. She wanted to tell Steven he could eat with her and Gerda any night he wanted but knew Kent wouldn't like that, so she just squeezed him. Her heart melted for the pining boy, and right now she didn't care if Kent wanted her to back off or not.

"You probably get told you look like Beyoncé all the time, don't you?" Helena asked, a bite of barley halfway to her mouth.

Shocked that anyone would compare her to someone as beautiful as the popular singer, Desi's eyes went wide. "Never, but thank you." Her gaze met Kent's.

His lips twitched in a fleeting smile. "I can see the resemblance."

Not wanting to look away from him, as it was the first time this evening he'd engaged her in any kind of conversation, she paused over his gaze.

"Who's Beyoncé?" No sooner had Gerda asked than Steven filled her in.

Desi didn't want things to get awkward with Kent and shortly switched her line of vision to Helena. "All I can say is, I wish."

After dinner, Uncle Erik and Helena engaged Gerda in a heated conversation about local politics and what she should do as the acting mayor. Desi worried that everyone in town might be doing the same thing, and if so, how could the poor woman please everyone? Before she could fret further, Steven invited her outside.

After a challenging game of three-way Frisbee in the front yard between Desi, Kent and Steven, the boy got engrossed in a handheld video game and they all went back inside. Acting on her earlier hunch that Kent might want to talk to her, Desi sought him out in the living room. He was partially listening to the ongoing conversation between her uncle and grandmother when she appeared, a mug of coffee in each hand.

Her stomach fluttered before she spoke. "Would you like to go out on the porch with me?"

"Sure," he said, rising, immediately rattling Desi, and relieving her of one of the cups.

She sat on the slider love seat. He kept his distance and took the matching wicker chair beside it with the paisley-patterned pillow. Okay, so he didn't want to get close; he'd sent the message loud and clear.

"I owe you an explanation," he said, right off. "I've been bossing you around, telling you to leave my kid alone, and then he practically throws himself at you whenever he sees you. You're probably wondering why."

"You could say that." Since her conversation with her grandmother, she knew about Kent's wife leaving him, but she didn't let on. His earnest expression told her she was about to find out.

"His mother walked out a year ago as if she didn't give a damn about him." He tossed her a steely stare. "It broke his heart." He leaned forward, rested his forearms on his thighs, holding the coffee mug between his hands, and kept his voice down. "I can understand if she wanted to walk out on me, but Steven? I thought I knew her. We were married seven years and had gone steady practically since grammar school."

He stared at his coffee before taking a long drink. Desi took in his comments, sensing something special happening between them. He was opening up to her, like she had the other night with him. But Kent couldn't look more serious if he were pronouncing someone dead. If his wife's leaving had broken Steven's heart, what about Kent's?

"She wanted me to sell the Urgent Care and join this exclusive clinic in San Francisco. Said she was sick of Heartlandia, couldn't live here another day." He glanced up, an incredulous look on his face. "She didn't respect my business or me. I wasn't making enough money. Anyway, I refused to move. Who would want to buy the clinic? And how would Heartlandians get medical care if I shut it down? She gave me an ultimatum, and when I didn't budge, she left. Just like that. Like we didn't mean dirt to her."

Hurt and concern for both Kent and Steven wrapped her like a shawl. She felt compelled to say something, no matter how lame. "I can only imagine…"

"Looking back, I should have seen it coming. And now when I see how Steven's eyes light up every time he sees you, well, it scares me, you know? I can't ever let a woman break his heart like that again."

What about Kent's heart? Would he ever let a woman get close again?

Since Gerda had told her why Kent was so moody and overprotective of his son, she'd had time to think about the situation. And Grandma was right—he *was* scared.

"I can see why you'd feel that way, Kent, but sometimes we can't control everything and we have to let life play out and see. Besides, I'm not his mom, just a substitute piano teacher. It's a whole different thing."

"You're a hell of a lot more than that, Desi."

If her tongue wasn't stuck to the roof of her mouth, she'd try to say something. She was a lot more than that? To whom—Kent or Steven? Desi found the sudden need to speed up the sliding rocker but stopped herself. Kent had just blown her mind a second time, and this time it wasn't with a kiss, but words.

Get ahold of yourself. Don't make a big deal out of it. Maybe he only meant she was a hell of a lot more than a substitute piano teacher?

Kent stood and sat next to her, his long arm resting along the top of the love seat behind her. "Don't you realize how much you have to offer?"

Only her mother had ever spoken to her like that— never a man. His words landed like a sucker punch to her solar plexus. She could hardly breathe as her mother's voice sounded clear as ever in her mind. *You have so much to offer the world. Get out there. Stop sticking around for me.* Her mom's prematurely aged face during those last few months before she'd died slammed into her memory and made her cry.

Kent looked horrified.

"I'm sorry. All this talk about mothers leaving got me thinking about my mom." She wiped her nose and sipped her coffee to get a grip.

"I'm here if you want to talk about it. Hell, it's the least I can do after everything I just said."

At first, she didn't want to talk about it, but Kent seemed so genuinely interested, and he had known her mother, even if when only a young boy. She'd had precious few people to tell about everything her mom had gone through. "She suffered so much at the end, fighting to breathe. And the pain. God, nothing was strong enough to stop the pain when that damn lung cancer got into her bones. Sometimes I had to give her so much morphine, I was afraid I'd kill her. Ironic, huh?" She wiped her eyes, embarrassed she'd fallen apart so easily. "I'm sorry."

"Don't be. It hurts me to hear how she suffered, too. Anytime you want to talk about it—" Was this Kent the sensitive man or the doctor talking?

He'd opened up to her about his situation, and now she had an opportunity to share her deepest, darkest feelings. Why not give it a try? Besides, he'd asked for it.

"Sometimes I used to hope that she'd drift away after the morphine. That she wouldn't wake up. Why should she? Why suffer like that? But whenever she was conscious, she looked at me like I was the most wonderful gift in the world, and she'd tell me how she loved me and how much I had to offer. And I loved her so much I never wanted to lose her. Never." She gave an ironic shake of her head. "I was so busy taking care of her, I didn't think about what I wanted to do with my life, let alone what I had to offer. It didn't seem that important."

His arm came off the back of the love seat, settling on her shoulders, rubbing them. The hint of pine and the outdoors came from Kent's aftershave instead of the fresh night air. His touch was tender and warm, and if she wasn't crying, she would have melted into his hold.

"How can I have so much to offer when I don't even know who half of me is? You know?"

She glanced at Kent, thinking how easily they'd opened up to each other. Even his silhouetted profile was gorgeous, and being so close, she couldn't deny for another second that she had a major crush on him. He pulled her toward his chest, and she rested her head on his shoulder. She'd hardly been able to think straight since he'd sprung that amazing kiss on her, and now he was holding her again. It felt snug and heavenly.

But how was she supposed to keep the distance with his son and get closer to Kent at the same time? Besides, she'd been homeschooled by her mother and had never gone on to college. He was a doctor. She and Kent were completely mismatched on so many levels.

The man let his marriage end over refusing to move to San Francisco. He was evidently stubborn and controlling. She'd been a vagabond, yet someone who'd never had the chance to explore life on her own. As soon as she figured out where to find her father, she'd be there in a heartbeat. Finding him was the main reason she'd come back to Oregon. That and spending some time with Gerda. After a while longer here, she planned to move on.

She nestled her head between Kent's neck and shoulder, thinking how strong and comforting he felt and how she could get used to his arms around her. But the timing was way off for any possible relationship. And Kent was right—her leaving wouldn't be fair to Steven, especially since the boy thought so much of her.

Kent ran his hand up and down her arm. "You look really nice tonight."

She smiled, her head still tucked under his chin. "Thank you. You do, too." What could she possibly offer a man like Kent, who was completely out of her league? "Were those flowers from your yard?"

"Yes."

"Were they your idea?"

"Steven's."

Figures. A breathy laugh jerked her shoulders. When she felt his jaw tighten, she assumed he smiled.

After a few more quiet moments, she pulled away and glanced upward. The way he always looked at her with intensity and interest, like right now, and the way he'd kissed her, she knew in her gut their attraction was mutual. She sighed in resignation, knowing that some things, no matter how appealing, were best left alone. What lousy, lousy timing.

"Need a refill on your coffee?" she asked.

"I'm good."

Wanting nothing more than to languish in his embrace for the rest of the night, she went with her better judgment and got up to refill her cup. He'd probably felt the shift in mood, because he followed her inside the house.

"Dad, I beat it! I finally beat the Cyclops kingdom!" Steven waved the hand game like a trophy.

Kent high-fived his son, then thanked Gerda for a fantastic meal and said good-night to Erik and Helena. He glanced at Desi across the room and nodded good-night. Steven was so stoked by his win, he'd forgotten all about her and everyone else and followed his father out the door.

No sooner had the door closed than Steven burst back through, running straight for Desi. He hugged her around the waist. "I forgot to say goodbye!"

Next he hugged Gerda. "Thanks. I'm stuffed."

Then off he sprang for home, leaving Desi laughing and filled with genuine affection for the kid. And his father.

Thursday morning, Grandma acted strange. She hadn't touched her breakfast, and her ritual cup of tea sat cold on the table. She'd had another one of those special meetings Wednesday night, had come home after ten and gone straight to bed. She sat at the kitchen table in her bathrobe, hand across her mouth, staring out the window. "Look at that covey of quail," she muttered. "They're finally using that feeder I set out."

Desi gazed out the window and found the gray-and-black birds with the stylish feather hats pecking around the feeder. "Do you want me to make you another cup of tea?"

"What?" Gerda said, as if startled out of deep thought.

"More tea?" Desi pointed to her cup. Gerda glanced at it as if she'd forgotten what tea was, then shook her head. "Are you okay?"

She took a long inhalation. "I've got a lot on my mind, that's all."

Not able to pry anything else out of her grandmother, Desi went about her chores and the last of her current calligraphy job. Two years back, she'd agreed to do wedding invitations for the daughter of one of her mother's musician friends. Everyone loved them, and several of the daughter's friends had asked Desi to do their invitations, too. This was the latest and biggest job yet.

Tonight for dessert, as a thank-you for the wonderful Sunday dinner, she decided to surprise Grandma with the one Scandinavian dish her mother had taught her to make, *krumkake*. It was something like a waffle cookie, and she'd need fresh eggs and real cream to make sure they came out perfect.

When Gerda was still sequestered in her bedroom, Desi decided to borrow the car and go to the post office to mail off the completed invitations, then she'd go on to the market. Before she left, she grabbed Gerda's grocery list from the notepad on the refrigerator and headed out the door. It was almost lunchtime and she wanted to be back in time to make lunch for her grandmother and to give herself plenty of time to prepare for that afternoon's piano lessons. She allowed herself only one glance next door to Kent's house on the walk to the car. With Steven at summer day camp and Kent at the Urgent Care, it looked quiet.

For Tuesday's piano lesson, the babysitter had brought and picked Steven up, saving Desi the difficult task of facing Kent after she'd made up her mind to leave him alone. He hadn't come around their house, either, so they'd probably both come to the same conclusion. Some things were best left unexplored. In this case, it was the wisest thing to do.

Desi got home a little later than she'd meant to, and she found Gerda downstairs in her den on the phone, with no less than three notepads for reference in front of her. She hadn't bothered to put her hair in a bun today, and there was no evidence of her having yet eaten lunch.

"I'm heating some soup. Want some?" Desi asked once Gerda had hung up the phone.

"No, thank you, dear. Could you bring me some antacid?"

Desi found the bright pink medicine and headed for the den. "Aren't you feeling well?"

"Nervous stomach is all." Gerda offered a wan smile and gratefully accepted the bottle.

Four hours later, after three piano students and still no sign of Gerda leaving her makeshift office, Desi fixed a simple dinner from leftovers. She'd had a fun and messy baking session and wanted to make sure they saved room for dessert.

Gerda tried to be polite and eat, but she only picked at her food. She really didn't seem to have an appetite, so why force her to eat dessert? Maybe tonight wasn't such a great time to spring the *krumkake* on her. It could keep.

"I'm worried about you, Grandma."

"Oh, it's nothing. Nothing at all." Gerda pushed her plate away and tugged on the stringy fringe of the place mat. "Just a lot of silly city business on my mind." She stood, looking less straight and more fragile. "I think I'll read in my room for a while."

Worry trickled over Desi as she watched her grand-mother amble off. What if the woman was sick and not telling her? What if Desi lost her after only just getting to know her? Old anxieties nearly swept Desi away, but she talked herself down. Gerda was fine, just preoccupied with her city council. Knowing Heartlandia meant the world to her grandmother, she figured something big must be going on. That was all it was, and from the way it was tearing up her grandmother, that was more than enough.

A surprising tender feeling for Gerda made Desi pause while washing the dinner dishes. How quickly she'd grown to genuinely care for the woman, how at home she'd felt the past two and a half weeks, and how much Gerda's withdrawing made Desi worry.

As she put the dishes away, her mind drifted to Heart-landia, her mother's home and the town her mother had run away from. It was the place that had shaped her mom as much as Gerda and Edvard Rask had.

There was so little she knew about her mother's early years, and letting Grandma remain withdrawn and dis-tracted by city business couldn't be good for her. Desi made a snap decision to heat some water for tea and carry a plate of the *krumkake* up to Gerda's room. Truth was, she was lonely and filled with questions and finally felt ready to broach the questions to which only her grandmother knew the answers.

A few minutes later, armed with dessert on a tray, she tapped on Gerda's bedroom door.

"Come in." Her voice sounded aged and weak.

Gerda was still dressed, and she sat in an overstuffed lounger beside her bed, reading several pages from a typed letter.

"I brought some goodies, and I won't take no for an answer."

Gerda's eyes brightened when she saw the *krumkake*.

"Momma taught me how to make this. We'd have it on special occasions." Gerda's wrinkled smile warmed Desi's insides. "I made them especially for you."

"Then I will have one. To be honest, I am hungry. It's just my stomach is all knotted up."

"What's going on over there at city hall to make you so upset?"

"They promised I'd just be a figurehead when I agreed to fill in, but I can't sit back and smile about everything."

"Trouble?"

"I'm not at liberty to talk." Her index finger shot up. "Oh, though I do have a question for you. Will you teach me how to open and reply to emails? The secretary types up all of the notes from our meetings and emails them to everyone. I'm the only one she can't send them to, and I'm supposed to be the mayor." She waved the loose pages as evidence.

"Of course I can help you with that. And I have a special request for you, too." Desi poured the tea and handed her grandmother a *krumkake* with powdered sugar on top. "I have so many questions about my mother and her growing up here. Can you share some of your memories with me?"

Gerda's hand went to her heart. "Oh, my goodness, I'd love to. I should have shared with you sooner, but…"

"But I didn't ask until now."

"Yes." Gerda smiled and reached out for a hug from Desi. "I'm glad you did."

"Let's eat our *krumkake* first."

"Good plan."

Desi ate in hungry silence, and the dessert tasted just as good as it always had, but Gerda took only a few bites.

"Not good?" Desi asked.

"Delicious. It's just my nervous stomach."

Was it all city hall that made Grandma nervous, or was Desi adding to it by probing into the past?

Gerda took one more bite, then put her plate on the bedside table. "Now, you'll have to help me get the box down where I keep all of her yearbooks and special school things."

After she'd finished her tea and Desi licked every last remnant of powdered sugar from her fingertips, she followed her grandmother down the hall to an out-of-the-way closet.

"Your mother was very temperamental, like her father, and I'm ashamed to report we fought a lot. If I said red she'd say blue. Used to drive Edvard crazy. Maybe I was too protective of her, but I just wanted the best."

Desi pulled a chain and a dim lightbulb offered a glimpse of several stacked boxes, some marked with Ester's name. Way in the back was one with "High School" written in black permanent marker.

"Let's start with that one," Gerda said, "and we can work our way back from there."

Desi retrieved the box and hoisted it onto her shoulder, then they started back down the hall to her grandmother's bedroom.

"When your mother was a little tot, she used to run down this hall every morning and jump onto the bed with Edvard and me. She was an early bird, that one was, better than an alarm clock."

Desi heard the affection in Gerda's voice and tried to imagine her mother as a little girl.

"She had the most beautiful white-blond hair, and her eyes were brighter than the sun. I'd snuggle her close between her daddy and me, and it felt perfect." Gerda's step faltered. Desi backed up and put her arm around her waist and walked her back to the bedroom, worrying that maybe all the memories might be too much for her grandmother.

"Your grandfather was hard to please and very old-fashioned. Your mother ran away rather than tell him she was pregnant." She shook her head as if all the horrible memories had come rushing back. "The whole town had been looking for her when she'd gone missing, and months later when we found out she was in the hospital in St. Louis, Edvard and I flew out to bring her home."

Now tears formed in Gerda's eyes, washing over the look that could only be described as *regret*. "She'd just given birth to you." Gerda took and squeezed Desi's free hand. "Edvard was so old-fashioned. He was upset, and Ester told him to get out of her life." She shook her head. "What could I do?"

A moment passed as Gerda drew herself together.

"Ester let me hold you." A tiny smile creased her wrinkled lips. "What should I have done, Desi? Go with my husband or stay with my daughter and grandchild?"

Desi's chest grew tight with emotion—love, hurt, anger, sadness—as she put the box on the bed and took her grandmother into her arms and held on tight.

Mother had taught her when a woman entered into a relationship with a man it should always be on equal footing, but grandmother's generation hadn't necessarily gotten that message.

Now Gerda wept. "We came home and told everyone we'd found our Ester, that she was fine and had a job in Missouri, and Edvard never spoke about her again."

"But, Grandma, I feel like I remember you at a couple of my birthdays."

She nodded her head on Desi's shoulder. "Yes. I begged Edvard to come with me, but he was so stubborn, and your mother was just as bad, saying she never wanted to see him again, either. I came for your fifth and tenth birthdays. But when you turned fifteen, well, Edvard had gotten sick and I couldn't leave him alone."

"I wish I could have known you better."

"Me, too. You have no idea." Gerda squeezed Desi's shoulders.

After a long hug, Gerda sat down on her bedside lounger. As if stalling, she took another bite of her half-finished dessert. "Hmm, this really is delicious. I couldn't make them any better myself."

Having her grandmother's approval meant the world to Desi, and she knew her mother would be proud. Gerda and Desi shared a heartfelt smile. The truth had finally come out—her grandfather hadn't been able to accept a biracial baby—and now they were about to embark on a very special journey together. "Shall we?" Desi reached for the box lid.

Something about the pyramid of creases on her grand-mother's forehead gave Desi pause. Waltzing down memory lane wouldn't be easy for either of them.

"Once, Ester wanted to go to a concert in Portland. Edvard put his foot down and said no. We thought she'd taken it pretty well, until the night of the concert, when she climbed out her window and snuck out to go anyway."

Desi's hand flew to her mouth. *From the second floor?* Hearing about this other side of her mother made her wonder how many other things she'd never shared. "What did you do?" Desi wiped away some dust from the box on the bedspread and sat.

"We didn't even realize she'd gone until we heard someone coming through the front door at one in the morning." Gerda's hand went to her cheek. "I thought Edvard would have a stroke right then and there. Her brother had never given us trouble. She was only six-teen!"

Her mother had never talked much about high school. Or anything else. Desi wished with all of her heart she could ask her how her life had been growing up. She glanced at Gerda, who was looking pale and withdrawn. She'd just admitted her husband had been ashamed of his daughter having a baby out of wedlock—a baby of color, no less—and she'd stayed by his side until his death. Was the pained expression regret?

Because that was exactly how Desi felt. How would everyone's lives have been if Edvard had reacted differently?

Desi refocused in order to drop the negative feelings

for her grandfather and opened the box then lifted out several school annuals. "Which one first?"

Gerda checked out the years and chose the bright red yearbook. "This one is from Ester's senior year. Let's start with this one."

Desi snuggled next to Gerda on the lounger, where the light was best, and opened the book to the first page.

"Your mother was involved in everything—cheerleading, music, drama, even the school newspaper. Oh, look, here's her senior picture."

Desi first glanced at her grandmother, whose eyes welled with moisture again, then at the typical senior portrait of a beautiful girl with clear blue eyes and straight blond hair. There was confidence in her smile and maybe a hint of mischief in her expression. Desi remembered seeing that spirited look whenever her mother felt challenged.

Gerda turned the page. "Oh, and look at that pose." She laughed. "Ester took cheerleading very seriously. Nearly broke her arm once doing that silly human-pyramid thing."

Desi smiled with pride at the picture of her mother holding pom-poms in the air while doing a split. She could practically hear her call out *Go, fight, win!*

It occurred to Desi that her mother had only rarely talked about her cheerleading. Desi had always thought it was because she was homeschooling her, and a home-schooled girl couldn't exactly be involved in a school sports program. Not when they moved around so much, anyway.

"She was all set to go off to college that summer… then she was gone." Gerda's hand went to her chest again; she clutched her blouse. "Oh, dear. Oh, dear."

"Is this too much for you, Grandma?"

"Oh!" Her pained expression sent a chill through Desi.

"Are you okay?"

Gerda held her breath for a second, then let up on the death clutch to her blouse. "I got a sharp gas pain, that's all. It's better now."

Leery of her excuse, Desi watched and worried. "Maybe a sip of tea will help?"

"That would be good."

Desi poured her more tea. Gerda reached for the teacup and took a sip, quickly putting the cup down and grabbing her chest again. "Oh!"

Chapter Six

Desi sat in the waiting room of the Urgent Care after the nurse whisked Gerda in to be examined. She'd wanted to go in with her grandmother, but Gerda had waved her off, and the no-nonsense silver-haired nurse didn't seem too thrilled about the possibility of Desi getting in the way, either.

"I'll be fine," Gerda said. "Kent will take care of me."

Knowing that Kent would be in charge helped a little, but her nerves were still ruling the day. There she sat on a hard bench, wringing her hands in her lap, worried sick. She'd felt this way before—every time her mother had needed to be rushed to the hospital. She'd never get used to it. Hated it.

The clinic was typical with sterile gray walls and subtle printed linoleum floors. The only decorations were some fake ficus trees in large colorful pots. Nurses bustled in and out of rooms, calling out requests or giving directions to each other. The term *controlled chaos* came to mind, and she'd seen it all before. This was the way the medical system worked. There was no way to predict on any given day or hour how many patients would show up for care.

The waiting room had been packed when they'd arrived, but the instant Desi had mentioned chest pain, they were brought straight in.

A half hour later, Desi was on her way back from making a bathroom stop when the silver-haired nurse who'd taken Gerda away stopped her in the hall.

"Would you like to see your grandmother?"

"Yes. Is she all right?"

"She's fine and in the procedure room. Follow me."

Desi found Kent standing beside Gerda's gurney, talking quietly to her and writing on his prescription pad. He looked casual but entirely in control and in total concentration, with one foot propped on a stool, his powerful shoulders sloped just enough to write with the pad balancing on his thigh.

"Hi, Grandma. How do you feel?"

All of the worry lines Gerda had worn into the Urgent Care had smoothed. She smiled at Desi. "I'm fine. It wasn't my heart after all, as it turns out."

Kent turned and found Desi's questioning gaze. "Hey," he said. His greeting sounded anything but professional.

"What's the word?" she asked.

"Your grandmother is suffering from stress. We did an EKG, which was fine, and some blood tests. Though it will take a few hours for all of them to come back, the initial cardiac enzyme test looks good. But Gerda's vital signs are elevated."

"I never have high blood pressure," Gerda broke in.

"Except for today," Kent replied.

Gerda nodded in agreement. Kent glanced at Desi as if making a point that it also wasn't every day a long-lost granddaughter worked her way back into her life.

Point taken.

Kent looked like a TV doctor in his white jacket with a stethoscope hanging around his neck. He tore off a tiny paper from his pad and handed it to Gerda. "I'm sending you home with a better antacid than that over-the-counter stuff and some sedatives. I want you to take one of both as soon as you get home, and for the next couple of days keep taking the sedative until you relax and your blood pressure is back to normal. I'll write out the instructions." He shifted his attention from Gerda to Desi. "Make sure she doesn't exert herself for a couple of days. No mayor duties. And no driving." He looked back to Gerda. "Did you hear me? Don't exert yourself, okay?"

"I'm old, Kent, but I'm not hard of hearing."

He gave an exaggerated nod. "This is true."

Sure, he'd known Gerda all his life, but his bedside manner was easygoing and reassuring, and Desi would bet her classic-jazz record collection that he was like that with all of his patients.

"We're going to wait until the IV finishes before we let her go home. On top of everything else, she was a little dehydrated."

"Makes sense since she didn't eat and hardly drank all day."

Kent took the prescription back from Gerda and handed it to Desi. "You may want to fill this while you're waiting, to speed things up." He walked with her and guided her out the door.

"I'll be right back, Grandma," Desi said, relieved that her grandmother was okay, but completely aware of the warm pressure from Kent's hold on her arm.

He stopped just outside the examination room, out of Gerda's line of vision. "She's totally upset about something, and it has driven her blood pressure way up. She needs to relax or she might develop palpitations."

"I'll make sure she calms down."

"Anything going on between you two?"

"Us? No. We're good. We were looking at some of my mother's things earlier, and…"

"This condition doesn't strike me as anything that came on suddenly."

"No. She's been preoccupied with some meetings at city hall, but that's all."

"Well, make sure she relaxes for the next few days."

"Will do, Doc."

They walked the long clinic corridor, which was cluttered with stray equipment and metal tables. This place didn't quite have the medicinal smell of a hospital, but it came close.

"The pharmacy's just across the street. Shouldn't take more than fifteen minutes to fill it, and I promise we'll have Gerda out of here within the half hour."

"I can't thank you enough."

"This is what I do, you know. It's my job."

"Right. I know, but I mean, I'm just glad it wasn't her heart, and I'm glad you were the one to tell her." *And to take care of her.*

"No problem there. Her EKG was fine."

"And I'm glad you didn't move to San Francisco and sell this clinic."

He sent her a thoughtful glance, hopefully taking her comments as they were meant: a compliment.

"Dr. Larson?" A tall, thin nurse rushed toward him with a handful of paperwork. "We've got a patient with severe abdominal pain in room ten."

Kent took the sheets of paper. "I'll be right there." He turned back to Desi and took her hand, gave it a quick squeeze then let go. "This is a crazy place to meet up, but it was good to see you again." His gaze did a quick survey of her, head to toe. She hoped he didn't do that with all of his patients or family members. Something about that sexy gaze told her he didn't. "Don't hesitate to call if you need me." And he was off.

Basking in the sweet and warm sensations enveloping her, she watched him stride down the hall, larger-than-life, confident and professional as all hell. Wow. Grandma was in excellent hands. She rubbed where he'd held her arm then turned and headed for the pharmacy, fingers crossed she might see Kent one more time before she took her grandmother home.

While waiting for the medicine, it occurred to Desi how important her grandmother had become. Gerda had opened her home and arms the instant Desi had mentioned she'd wanted to come to Heartlandia. As if she'd been waiting all of Desi's life to have her there. She'd been kind and encouraging ever since Desi had arrived, and Desi felt something more from Grandma, too. She felt loved. Unconditionally.

Desi blinked back the sudden rush of moisture in her eyes, realizing she loved her grandmother, too. Now that they'd been through an emergency together, they were true family.

With a heart filled with a sense of belonging—something she'd missed since her mother had died—Desi retrieved the medicine when her grandmother's name was called. She smiled all the way back to the Urgent Care, ready to take her long-lost grammy home.

Two hours later, Desi had tucked Gerda into bed. It was eleven o'clock. Her silver-and-white hair lay thinly over her shoulders on top of an old-fashioned nightgown, complete with lace trim along the neck and shoulders. The sedative made her softly etched skin look saggy, and her normal healthy glow dimmed. She seemed vulnerable and Desi worried about her. What could be eating at her enough to cause chest pain?

A sudden urge made Desi crawl onto the bed beside her and lie on top of the blanket to cuddle near her grandmother. "Mind if I stay with you for a while, Grandma? Just until you fall asleep?"

Gerda smiled and welcomed her with open arms. "I'd love it."

They snuggled in silence for a few moments, lights on, old-house noises creaking and cracking around them. Desi detected the clean scent of cold cream and loved how at home she felt.

Gerda inhaled long and slow. "I've got a lot on my mind these days, and it feels like this huge weight on my chest."

"I hope it's not because of me."

"No. No. You're the best part these days."

"Sometimes it helps to share worries."

Gerda played with and patted Desi's hair. Desi glanced up at her face.

"But I've been sworn to silence." She bit her lip, knitting her fair brows. "There's something crazy happening in our town, and I'm half-sick about it."

Desi sat up. "This is the most peaceful and ideal town I've ever been in. What could possibly change that? Zombies?" she teased. "Are there werewolves roaming the pine forest?"

Gerda huffed and rolled her dull blue eyes. "You wouldn't believe it if I told you."

She had Desi's full curiosity. "Want to try me?"

Gerda sat up and smoothed the creases in the sheets. "I'm not supposed to talk about it to anyone outside of the city council. I gave them my word."

"And your word nearly had you admitted to the hospital tonight. Sometimes sharing a burden makes it lighter."

"I feel like they set me up. Made it sound so easy to step in as mayor. 'Just until we can have an election,' they said. 'You'll only be a figurehead.' Now I feel set up, like they were saving this for—how do they say it on TV?—for my watch."

A battle ensued inside Gerda, and her conflicted expression made Desi understand the importance of Grandma's word. If she said she'd keep a secret, well, she'd keep it even if it made her sick.

"All the more reason to share."

"Oh, Desi, I…"

Feeling guilty for putting more pressure on her grandmother, Desi backed off. "You don't have to tell me, Grandma. I understand. You made a promise."

Another deep breath lifted Gerda's chest. "The thing

is—I want to. I know I can trust you, and no one will ever find out, will they?"

"You have my solemn vow." Desi raised her right hand and made her most trustworthy face, then crossed her heart for good measure.

Gerda laughed. "That's exactly what I said my first day on the job as mayor."

They chuckled together, holding hands and smiling at each other, enjoying the few lighter moments.

Gerda made a playful expression. "This sedative is making me feel all swimmy-headed and a little loose-lipped."

Desi winked. "You do look awfully relaxed." She didn't think she could feel any fonder of her grand-mother at that moment.

"Secrets are hard to keep when you feel all loosey-goosey."

Desi kept grinning, sensing the vault was about to crack. She lay back down beside Gerda, so as not to stare at her. Gerda grabbed her hand and squeezed.

"Heartlandia doesn't have a lot of natural resources anymore. The fishing industry has moved north and we aren't rich in anything but trees, and we want to keep them, not cut them down. What small textile fac-tories we once had have all closed over the last twenty years or so.

"A hundred years ago, our astute mayor Bjarnesen set out to make us the best little tourist town in Or-egon. He opened our port to cruise ships, made sure the trains took extra-long stops here and campaigned for better roads and highways out this way. More and more families turned their big old houses into bed-and-breakfasts or rentals. Everyone took extra-good care of their property and homes. The town focused on all the things that would bring people here for vacations. Novelty shops, Scandinavian goods, excellent yet inexpensive restaurants. The mayor even built the Heritage Theater and brought in talented musicians and singers from all over the country."

Gerda took a sip of the water from the glass on the bedside table that Desi had left for her. "This medicine makes my mouth dry." She took another sip and wiped a drop that slipped out. "He put us on the map and we've been living a modest but contented life as a tourist attraction ever since. We've built our reputation as a place where people work together for a better life. Fishermen and Native Americans, Scandinavian and American. Heartlandians. We boast how the Chinook people nursed shipwrecked sailors back to health and taught them the secrets of hunting and fishing our oftentimes-treacherous river waters."

Gerda yawned and cast a quick glance Desi's way, finding her undivided attention, then laid her head back on her pillow.

"You probably haven't been there yet, but we have a two-mile-long brick wall called the Ringmiren that the first Scandinavian settlers helped the Chinook people build. It circles the farthest limits of our city and it delineates the sacred Chinook burial ground. It's said that thousands of souls lie in rest there, and it is a sacred place."

"I didn't know any of this, Grandma. It's fascinating. Will you take me there?"

Gerda nodded, looking very sleepy. "It took ten years of preparation, and two years to build, but last year we finally finished our own city college." Her voice grew

weaker. "I chaired the board for the city-college project. We thought it would bring more opportunity for
employment for residents and also draw students from
surrounding cities to attend. We hired our wealthiest
businessman and contractor, Leif Andersen, to build
the college from our designs, and it is beautiful, too.
He did a fantastic job." Gerda lifted her head again and
took another drink of water, and Desi thought soon she'd
need to refill the glass.

Worry changed her expression. "During the process
of building, Leif's construction crew dug up some old
trunks filled with antique sea navigation instruments
and a captain's journals."

Desi had been enthralled before, but the new twist
riveted her attention. "Are you serious? Wow."

Gerda wiped her brow, pushing a few errant strands
of hair aside. "'Wow' is right." Her eyes blinked open
and closed as if she fought off sleep. "We've brought
in a history expert who teaches at the college, Elke
Norling. She's the sister of one of our police sergeants
who's on this special council with me. You met him at
the festival. Kent's friend Gunnar?"

Desi nodded, remembering the solidly built police officer with flashing green eyes and a cautious demeanor.

Gerda yawned again. "Anyway, as you can imagine,
we've been going through these journals with a fine-
tooth comb and they tell an earlier and very different
history for our town."

"What do you mean?"

"We've just scratched the surface, but if we can au-
thenticate these journals, which is what we're working
on, we will have to face the fact that our beautiful little

history of Heartlandia is only partly true. And the big question is what we should do about it."

"But isn't it better to know the whole story? The complete history?"

"Not when our livelihood depends on our selling ourselves as a peaceful storybook town catering to tourists." Gerda sought out Desi's eyes and held her gaze. "Not when these captain's journals tell dark, dismal horror stories about our past. Not when we have to face up to the possibility that Hjartalanda was discovered by a scurrilous ship captain. A pirate." She'd spit out the word as if it had tasted horrible.

Desi's mouth dropped. "A pirate?"

Gerda, who looked more and more haggard as she unwound her tale, nodded. "A pirate."

Chapter Seven

Desi watched her grandmother drift off to sleep just after getting to the meaty part of her tale. Amazing. A pirate had first discovered Heartlandia. Captain Jack Sparrow, perhaps? Desi snickered and fought the urge to wake her grandmother to get the rest of the story out of her, but instead she gently covered her to her chin, then turned off the light and tiptoed out of the room.

No wonder the acting mayor of perfect little Heartlandia was having chest pain.

How in the world was Desi supposed to process this crazy information? Of course she would keep it to herself as she'd promised, but, wow, what a wickedly fun twist for a town known as paradise.

She went downstairs to shut off the rest of the lights and made sure the front door was locked. Just before she turned off the dining room light, she saw Kent's truck pull to the curb. It was half past midnight.

Guiltily she stood like a voyeur and watched his tall yet graceful frame exit the car and smoothly stride to his front door, the walk of a confident man who'd worked hard and done a lot of good for his community that night. There was much to like and respect about him. The fact that he was gorgeous was icing on the cake.

She allowed herself to entertain a quick fantasy about how it would feel to be waiting up for him and fall into his arms as soon as he came through the door. She'd never waited up for any man. Clicking back into reality, she made a right turn and walked toward the dining room switch plate. No point in dreaming about something that would never happen.

A quiet tapping on the front door snagged her attention before she reached her mark. Making her way back to the door, she looked through the peephole. It was too dark to see anything but a shadow.

"Desi?"

Her pulse nearly leaped in her chest. "Kent?" Hadn't she just watched him head for his house? With leftover habits from L.A., she left the chain latched and opened the door, first making sure it really *was* Kent. "Hey," she said through the crack. With nervous fingers she quickly unlatched the chain and opened the door wider.

"How's she doing?" His huge and sturdy silhouette loomed so near, she fought the urge to run her hands across his chest to make sure he wasn't a ghost.

"She's asleep now. Doing well." Seeing him in the dark sent all kinds of reactions buzzing through her body.

The white of his teeth as he smiled made a chill bubble burst in her chest and ripple across her shoulders. "Good. Don't let her—"

"Exert herself," she finished for him, returning his grin. "I won't." For the second time that night she raised her hand in an oath. "I promise."

He lingered, taunting her with his gorgeousness. "Good. I'll check back tomorrow."

On the verge of saying the requisite "You don't have to," she stopped herself. Even though she had things under control, she didn't want to ruin her chance of seeing him again. "Thanks."

They stood watching each other for a few more heartbeats. Desi felt kind of goofy, and her cheeks were on the verge of cramping from all the grinning, but she did not want to be the first to say good-night and close the door. This crush really did have to stop.

He nodded, uncomfortably. "Well, I better let my sitter go. Good night."

"Good night." She still couldn't bring herself to close the door, and instead she stood like a silly teenager, smitten with the mysterious man next door, watching him walk away.

With Kent the last person she'd see for the night, she predicted she'd have extra sweet, and sexy, dreams.

The next morning Desi helped Gerda brush her hair and twist it into a bun.

"How do people take medicine all the time?" Gerda said. "All I want to do is sleep."

"That's why it's called a sedative, Grandma. And you're not supposed to live on them, only take them when you need to. Like now."

Gerda reached behind for Desi's forearm and squeezed.

"I love it when you call me Grandma." She wasn't sure when the term had entered her vocabulary, but now that Gerda had pointed it out, it did feel good.

Desi bent forward and hugged her around the shoulders. "Ready for breakfast?"

Making sure Gerda was steady enough on her feet to take the stairs down to the kitchen, Desi held her by the waist and hand. "Oatmeal? Eggs? What's it going to be?"

"How about some tea and toast."

"Ah, the breakfast of champions, I see." Not a very hardy way to start the day, but considering Gerda had barely eaten at all yesterday, this was progress, and Desi wasn't about to push the point.

Zipping around the kitchen in old stretched-out sweats and a hoodie, Desi made them both breakfast then washed the dishes and set up Gerda in the screened back porch, the room Gerda called the sunroom, to rest and read some magazines. She opted not to bring up the mind-blowing topic of conversation from last night, wondering if Gerda even remembered it. Maybe she thought she'd dreamed it, but one thing was sure: this morning Gerda hadn't uttered another word about the role of Captain Jack in Heartlandia.

Finally ready to head upstairs to shower, Desi hustled toward the living room, her hand on the banister, ready to swing around the bend, when the doorbell rang. She checked the grandfather clock across the entryway. It was only eight-fifteen. With her hair a straggly mess, feet bare, and wearing seriously old gray sweats, she swung the door open.

There stood Kent, fresh as a cover model, in a pale blue tailored button-down shirt, patterned tie and navy slacks that fit those narrow hips perfectly. She wanted to purr and scream at the same time. She gulped instead. "Hi!"

"Hey. Just dropped Steven off at summer day camp and thought I'd check on Gerda before I head off to the clinic."

She also wanted to run for cover, pull the hood over her head and hunch over so he couldn't see her unwashed face. But she did the right thing and led him down the hall to the sunny porch.

Gerda's expression brightened the instant Kent stepped outside. Whose wouldn't? The guy was a dream machine with that square jaw and naturally hooded set of bedroom eyes.

"How're you doing today?" He went directly to Gerda, pulling out his stethoscope and a small machine from his briefcase.

"Is this a house call? For me?"

"Just checking up on my favorite neighbor."

Gerda smiled and let him listen to her heart then take her blood pressure.

"Much better. One-thirty over eighty-five."

"I'm usually less than that."

Desi enjoyed the view of his back and broad shoulders as he leaned over Gerda. The view of his backside in those perfectly fitted slacks nearly made Desi's mouth drop.

"We're working our way down, but keep taking the sedative today. Be sure to eat and drink lots of fluids. Okay?" He stood up, affording Desi the vision of those amazing buns at work. "I'll check in again when I get home today."

He turned and smiled at Desi, and comparing his

gorgeousness with her morning frumpiness, she wanted to dissolve into the antique braided oval rug.

"Take good care of her."

"She has been," Gerda broke in. "I'm getting spoiled."

"Thanks, Grandma."

"When I was a kid and got sick, Gerda always brought over homemade soup." Kent smiled at his patient, then looked toward Desi, making her bare toes curl with embarrassment.

"You were such a healthy kid, I always worried when you actually got sick."

"That's exactly how I feel about you, Gerda. Hey, I know a chef who makes great chicken gumbo soup. I'll bring some by for your dinner. How's that?"

"My mother always taught me to never argue with a handsome man." Gerda's candid reply made Desi know for a fact the morning's sedative had kicked in.

Kent actually seemed flustered, as if he wasn't prepared to hear that from Gerda. He must have been told how good-looking he was, probably by gazillions of women, but maybe never from a seventysomething matriarch of Heartlandia before. Hey, the woman might be under stress, but she was far from dead.

Hard to believe he didn't have a clue about his effect on women.

Desi smiled inside as she let Kent see himself out. She'd endured enough humiliation over her appearance today. Why add another fifteen or twenty seconds walking him to the door? Instead, she stood at the sunroom entrance and followed him with her stare, a straight shot down the hall. There really was something special about a man whose good looks hadn't gone to his head.

Desi scrubbed her face with her hands. What the heck

was she doing letting her crush get bigger? It couldn't turn into anything. Neither of them was in the right place, and who was she to think he'd give her the time of day if she proclaimed her crush anyway?

Well, there was that amazing kiss…that *he'd* instigated…

This line of thinking was entirely too heavy for eight-thirty in the morning, and she barreled up the stairs to shower and dress. No way would Kent find her a mess when he returned with dinner tonight.

Back with dinner as he'd promised, Kent showed up at six-thirty. Only problem was, taking care of a sedated Gerda had been a really huge job. Along with canceling all of her mayoral appointments for the day, Desi had cleared her calendar for Monday, too.

Desi had wound up taking a second shower when she'd helped her grandmother bathe. During lunch she'd managed to spill more than eat. Desi had to spoon-feed her tea that afternoon since she could barely keep her eyes open.

Maybe it was time to cut her off those sedatives.

When Desi opened the door for Kent, he held a large carton that smelled heavenly. She knew she looked frazzled and her hair was askew with tiny curls overpowering waves, and she'd forgotten to put a speck of makeup on. What a mess.

He smiled anyway. "Cliff Lincoln said to say hello. He made a special batch of chicken gumbo for Gerda, too."

Desi reminded herself what a small town Heartlandia was. "Thanks. You staying?"

"Nope. Friday night is pizza-and-video night with Steven. *Transformers* awaits."

"Well, it certainly was sweet of you to look after Gerda like this."

"She's been the one solid person in my life during all its changes. First my sister moved away from home. Then my parents moved to Bend." He got sullen as he handed her the bag of food, but only briefly. "And you know the rest of the story. Anyway, through it all your grandmother was always there for me. This is the least I can do."

"It smells great. I'll be sure to let Cliff know how much we enjoyed it."

"He threw in some of his cheddar cheese biscuits and fried okra, too." Kent cracked a smile that nearly made Desi drop the soup. "He said the okra was for you."

She sputtered a laugh, getting the inside joke. Cliff was a big tease, but awfully sweet. "He knows I'm out of touch on the soul-food train."

Her mouth watered, but not for the okra. There was that smile lingering on those handsomely formed lips. Right now she imagined what it would be like to kiss Kent Larson again. The thought ran through her body like warm gumbo sliding down the throat.

A pizza truck pulled to the curb in front of Kent's house.

"Gotta go," he said, breaking the lingering look, rushing down the porch steps and across the yard.

Saturday morning, again before nine, Kent showed up on the doorstep. This time Desi was ready for him. She'd gotten up extra early, showered and put on her newest jeans and favorite red top. She was barefoot again but had given herself a pedicure after putting Gerda to bed last night. She'd also spent plenty of time with her trusty curling iron to make sure her hair was styled into submission.

She opened the door with a flourish, the way she imagined Clair Huxtable might. Yes, she'd watched *The Cosby Show* reruns while polishing her toes last night. When she was a kid she used to pretend she was part of their family. "Hi!" She smiled with all of her heart, knowing her red lip gloss sparkled.

She immediately noticed his favorable response, the glint in his eyes and the slow and thorough scan from her toes up to her head. Oh, yeah, he liked what he saw. "Hey."

Unlike his usual, he wore casual clothes—gray athletic shorts, loose white T-shirt and sports trainers—and he looked fit and fantastic with muscular legs and arms lightly dusted in blond hair.

"She's in the kitchen. Come in." Desi turned and took off, knowing how perfectly her jeans fit and giving Kent some of his own medicine. And yes, she wasn't above exaggerating her walk. Just a little.

Kent pulled his stethoscope and the small automatic blood-pressure monitor from his backpack and did his thing again. Desi looked on, noticing his long fingers and the size of his palms. The guy was a giant. Yet he couldn't have been gentler with her grandmother.

"You can cut back on the sedatives today. Just take half a dose. Then tomorrow, if your blood pressure is still normal, I'll let you stop taking them altogether."

"I like your plan, my good man," Gerda said. Desi had gotten used to her grandmother being more loose-lipped the past two days, but Kent's amused expression reminded her this was a different Gerda Rask. "By the way, that was the most delicious soup."

"She had two bowls," Desi said. "I nearly had to fight her to get my share."

"That's great. So your stomach is doing better, too, huh?"

Gerda nodded. "I got a lot off my chest the other night. My stomach is better for it."

Desi knew exactly what Gerda referred to. They hadn't broached the subject of her mother or grandfather, or pirates and city-council promises since Thursday night. Still, she was glad to have helped relieve some of the stress by being a good listener when her grandmother needed her.

"Okay, but you still need to take the stomach meds until it runs out. Gastritis takes a while to heal."

"Aye, aye, captain." Gerda snickered.

Oh, yeah, she remembered their talk.

As Desi walked with Kent to the door, besides thinking what a good man he was, she treated herself to a second long look at his muscular legs and well-developed calves. She could only imagine what the rest of him looked like. A thorough vision sprang up and the thought sent a hot rush to her face. She'd let her imagination take her too far.

"Where're you headed?" she asked, quickly getting her breathing under control.

"Steven's in a basketball league. He's got two games today." The more Desi found out about Kent, the more she liked. He was a totally engaged parent, which probably explained why Steven was such a great kid despite the runaway mother. "If Gerda didn't need you, I'd invite you along."

"That's sweet, but I thought I was supposed to avoid Steven."

Kent stopped halfway out the front door. "I've been thinking about what you said. How it was different with you being his piano teacher." He took her hand, surprising her—but in a good way—as impulses as warm as melted butter on pancakes worked their way up her wrist and arm. "The kid deserves to have fun, and if you're the one who makes him happy, that's all the better. I overreacted. I apologize."

Would surprises ever cease! Maybe she wouldn't have to be on guard every time she was around Steven, and maybe, just maybe, Kent was warming to her company, too?

She didn't want to draw too much attention to his apology and put him on the spot, so she went the flippant route. "Does that mean I can date your son again?" She blinked repeatedly for emphasis, desperately needing to lighten the sexy feelings overtaking her from the mere fact that he held her hand.

He laughed. *Yes, it worked!* "That's taking the cougar thing way too far, isn't it?" He squeezed her hand then let go.

Maybe she'd gone a little too far and should make things completely clear. "So I can give your son a hug without getting dagger eyes from you now, right?"

"I never gave you—"

She imitated the way he'd looked at her, and he got her point.

"Right."

"Thanks." Making progress with Kent and Steven gave her spirits a boost.

"And maybe he isn't the only one you can hug."

With her breath suddenly stolen, she looked into his eyes. That überblue stare nearly undid her as she took in the significance of what he'd said. She could hug Kent, too.

And he hugged her, briefly, but long enough to wake up any lazy nerve endings throughout her body.

Not knowing where to take the conversation next, and thinking it might be best to leave well enough alone, she went for the mundane. "Well, have fun and I hope your team wins."

"Thanks. It'd be even more fun if you could come," he said halfway down the front steps.

That definitely sounded as if he'd had a change of heart. First she was no longer banished from Steven, then she could give both father and son hugs as needed, and now an invitation. "Next time?" *Fingers crossed.*

He kept going. Maybe he was already too far away and hadn't heard her?

Or maybe she'd taken his coming around to her way of thinking beyond his meaning and he conveniently didn't hear her. There was nothing like a dose of reality from being ignored by a proud man walking to his car to put things back into perspective. A man who also happened to be the king of mixed messages.

Kent hung up the phone with Amanda Sunday afternoon. She'd gotten a stomach bug and wouldn't be able to watch Steven. He had the four-to-ten shift tonight, and the last thing he needed was sitter trouble.

He thought about calling Gunnar, in case he was free, but first he needed to go check on Gerda.

It had been hard to see Desi every day, when, if he knew what was good for him, he should put her out of his mind. What was that lame invitation to Steven's basketball game about? He'd been ping-ponging back and forth on Desi ever since he'd met her. His gut told him to go for it, but his brain kept putting on the brakes.

He felt a little like that cartoon character with the devil on one shoulder and an angel on the other. Bottom line, he really needed to figure out what he wanted for Steven and himself first, and then he'd know how to handle adding a woman back into the mix. He was a father now, not a carefree bachelor like Gunnar, who could chase any woman he wanted. Kent was a package deal.

But hadn't Desi said something the other night about having to roll with things sometimes? He couldn't begin to wrap his brain around that concept. It was so not him.

Yet every single time he'd encountered her the past few days, no matter how dressed up or messed up she'd been, she'd taken his breath away. Not good for a man trying to stay on the straight and narrow. A man trying with everything he had to make a normal life for Steven. Family had to come before pleasure.

He tapped on the front door and was surprised and disappointed when Gerda opened it. But considering his mixed-up, messed-up thoughts about Desi, he could use a break.

"Kent! Come in."

"You look great, Gerda." He glanced up when Desi was halfway down the stairs. The July sun had warmed up the temperature, and the sight of her smooth, mocha-colored legs beneath olive-green shorts almost made him drop his stethoscope. "Hey."

"Hey, yourself." She had that playful glint in her eyes that made him wonder if she could read his mind.

He tore away his gaze and escorted Gerda to the couch. "Let's check your blood pressure, okay?"

While he did so, Desi sat on the arm of the couch. Her legs had looked great from across the room, but up close? Man, it took all his willpower to keep his hands to himself.

"You're back to normal," he told Gerda. "Feeling better?"

"Yes. All better. Thank you so much."

His cell phone rang. It was Amanda. "Excuse me. I've got to take this." Unfortunately, she hadn't come through with a substitute babysitter. "Okay, well, thanks for trying. We'll see you Tuesday afternoon."

What was he going to do? He grew serious as he bundled up the blood-pressure machine.

"You look bothered about something," Gerda said.

"I've got sitter problems, and I'm due to work from four to ten tonight."

"I'd be glad to watch Steven for you." Desi spoke right up.

No, he couldn't do that…but exactly why not?

"Now that I'm better, there's no reason Desi can't watch him. Hey, he can have dinner here with us, then she can take him home for his bath and bedtime."

"And I'll make sure he practices his scales. What do you say?"

This wasn't at all what he'd expected to happen when he came over. His smarter self wanted to wait and put a call in to Gunnar before he committed. Truth was, he knew Steven would have a much better time hanging out with Desi and Gerda than at that old bachelor pad of Gunnar's. If he wasn't working, Gunnar probably had a hot date tonight, since his whole world seemed to revolve around his main mistress, his job, and all the other women in town after that.

Kent made a snap decision. "You know what? That would be great. I really appreciate it."

"It's sort of like paying you back for all of these house calls," Desi said, tucking some hair behind her ear, making Kent want to do the same to the other side just for the excuse to touch her.

The payback reasoning was one way to look at it, but he still worried about his son falling too hard for the lovely piano teacher with great legs.

"I'll let him know and send him over when I leave. Thanks."

On his way out the door, thinking about those lovely long legs of Desi's, it occurred to him he should be more concerned about himself, not Steven, falling for her.

Chapter Eight

Kent pulled to the curb just before ten-thirty. In the otherwise dark neighborhood, a few lights were on inside his house, and the anticipation of seeing Desi rushed his pulse. He'd been looking forward to coming home ever since the nine-o'clock lull, when he'd finally had time to think about something other than medicine and sick patients.

He sat an extra few seconds in his car, giving himself a stern talking-to. *Don't make more out of this than it is.* Desi was only doing Steven a favor because she liked him so much. *Whatever you do, don't make a fool of yourself by kissing her again.*

He got out of the car and headed for the front door. Before he could push his key into the lock, it swung open. "Hey," he said, seeing Desi and trying his best to sound nonchalant.

"Hi! I saw you pull up." Desi turned, heading past

the living room toward the kitchen. He'd left the extra house key with Gerda and Desi before he'd left for work.

Desi wore her hair in a high swaying ponytail, and it took only a nanosecond to notice she'd worn his favorite jeans, the ones with little rhinestones in the shape of hearts over each back pocket. A soft-looking loose yellow sweater that slipped off one shoulder—the one she'd worn the first night he'd seen her—rounded out the comfortable but sexy look. She'd kicked off her shoes and those bright red toenails nearly twinkled in the dim light.

She'd made herself at home. Excellent.

Damn, he'd forgotten how great it felt to come home to somebody besides Steven.

"I put Steven to bed at eight-thirty, on the dot." She pointed to her wristwatch with a peach-colored nail.

He put his briefcase on the entry table, reminding himself it wouldn't be appropriate to hug her hello. "Thanks. You saved my life tonight. Don't think my kid would've enjoyed another night in the doctors' lounge watching Sunday-night baseball. And he'd never let me hear the end of it."

"Has that really happened?"

"A couple of times. Sometimes you gotta do what you've gotta do."

"Then I'm especially glad I could help." Desi's eyes sparkled in the hallway light as she walked backward toward the kitchen wearing her signature playful grin. "I baked some cookies. Steven helped. Hope you don't mind."

"They smell great. How many did Steven put away?"

She wrinkled her nose, and now that they were in the bright light of the kitchen, he got close enough to notice those cute tiny freckles across the bridge again. "Half a dozen?"

Kent laughed and shook his head. "And he went to bed without bouncing off the walls?"

She shrugged her shoulders imperceptibly. "Well… he did get up a couple times, but I had him back in bed for good by nine. I hope you don't mind. I've never been in charge of an eight-year-old before."

Kent picked up an oatmeal chocolate chip cookie and took a bite. "Man, these are great. No wonder he ate half a dozen."

Desi turned to the kitchen counter and finished drying the baking items in the dish rack, affording Kent the chance to take in her gorgeous backside again without her noticing. The bling on those pockets, and especially what was beneath, nearly made him drool. He took another cookie and popped it whole into his mouth. The woman could bake, too.

"So how did your night go?" she asked.

How long had it been since he'd been asked that when he'd gotten home? He and Amanda had a total business relationship, very little chitchat. The college student took day classes and needed extra funds, and he desperately needed someone to watch his son after school during the year and summer day camp, five nights a week. That was the extent of their association.

He swallowed the cookie. "Busy but manageable. How about yours?"

"Amusing. He whipped me at Go Fish, and don't even get me started on his computer games. I think he took pity and let me win once. Have I mentioned what a kick I get out of Steven?"

Kent smiled, grateful that his son and the new lady

in town had seemed to click from the start. "He is a great kid."

Evidently Desi liked something about his smile because she stared at him, her eyes lingering on his lips. The cookie was great, but he suddenly wanted to taste *her,* and watching her in his kitchen, acting all domestic, heated up his insides.

Man, oh, man, he couldn't ignore that wide-eyed and welcoming gaze another instant, because those twinkly dark eyes looked as inviting as the semisweet melted chips in the cookies. The question was, what was he going to do about it?

Sure, she was here in Heartlandia only temporarily. Also true, his wife had left him—a crushing blow to his manhood—making him feel more vulnerable where women were concerned than he'd felt in his entire life. The big question was, how did A relate to B?

And what was he going to do about it?

It was hard to think logically with a beautiful, receptive woman such as Desi within reach.

She stood in his kitchen looking superfine with an easygoing expression that practically said, *Well, are you going to kiss me or what?*

What would Gunnar do?

Hands down, he'd go for it.

Kent might be completely out of practice when it came to kissing, but this moment screamed out to be seized, like the other night when he'd kissed her, and he couldn't let this second chance slip away.

Kent put the uneaten portion of his third cookie on the counter and stepped forward. By the lift of her brows, he could tell she suspected what he had in mind. Hell, she'd probably been reading his mind the whole time.

He took Desi by the shoulders, studied her warm and inviting eyes, already getting lost with desire, then planted a quick test kiss smack on her mouth. Probably too abrupt, he chastised himself. What the hell—he wasn't exactly Johnny Depp. Damn, the kiss was great, though, all warm and soft, and the sensations from her lips touching his slowed him down. He inhaled through his nose. In a kitchen filled with fresh-baked cookies, he zeroed in on the fragrance of Polynesian flowers with a hint of apricot that permeated her hair.

She didn't pull away. So far, so good.

He kissed her again.

The first thing to strike him was how soft and full her lips were and how freaking fantastic it was to kiss her. It may have been a little rocky at first, but once they reached their common ground, her soft, persistent kiss nearly melted his belt buckle. As forgotten sensations jetted below his waist, his arms encircled her, and they fit together perfectly. She stretched her fingers around his neck and pulled him closer. Now they were getting somewhere. He deepened the kiss, tasting her sweetness, her tongue testing his.

She was tall and he didn't have to hunch over to kiss her, which was a good thing, and she draped her arms over his shoulders. He also liked that she let him kiss as if he meant it, no matter how rusty he might be. She kissed smooth and natural as breathing, and he followed her guidance, relaxing into the rhythm of making out with her.

Maybe now would be a good time to find and explore those pretty little shiny hearts on each of her cheeks.

He swept his hold downward, skimming over her ribs and waist, admiring the round swells of her plentiful hips, pulling her tight to him. The friction ignited his firewall that carefully guarded his control.

He hadn't wanted a woman like this since long before Diana had left. All the wonder of love and sex seemed to have run its course those last couple of years. Diana had made him feel like a total failure as she withdrew more and more until she'd left. After she'd gone, the subject of making love had been so devastating he couldn't go there. With anyone.

Until now. With Desi.

Heat rolled from his lips in combustible waves all the way down to his toes. He definitely wanted more of this. With her.

"I still owe you that midnight dinner," he said over her mouth.

"I'd like that. Anytime."

Feeling the heat of her body next to his, her warm breath over his chin, his mind went blank for more conversation and he went back to kissing.

Kissing Desi ushered in an overpowering desire to have what a man was meant to share with his woman. Sex. This time, from the way Desi responded to every kiss and touch, it would be with someone new, not Diana, but if he was reading her signals right, it would be with a woman who wanted him as much as he wanted her.

Brakes skidded into gear in his brain, nearly yanking Kent away from another amazing kiss. Did he really want to go there? But he fought off the doubt. Not now. It wasn't as if he was falling in love or anything.

Love meant trusting, and he knew well where trusting a woman led—down a deep hole of pain and regret. But this tornado rolling through his body wasn't love; it was lust, pure and simple, and sex meant only sex. *Right?*

Desi must have sensed his hesitation. She sighed over his lips, snuggled her breasts a little tighter against his chest. His hands gripped her bottom as if hanging on for dear life. *Do not let this moment slip by.*

He hungered for her mouth and body as he dragged his lips along her throat to the quickly beating pulse in her neck. She whimpered a welcoming response.

A guttural sound slipped out of his mouth as his damn brain broke through the firewall again and drew him away from her neck and the shoulder he'd wanted to sample next. He inhaled her scent again then looked into her eyes, seeing concern, but above all confusion.

"Is something wrong?"

He could barely focus on her words for wanting her so much. Need sparked through his body and desire overpowered everything else. He gritted his teeth and inhaled long and hard.

"Is this because of your ex-wife?"

He held on tight, not wanting her to slip from his hold, and silently cussed at the ceiling. No. He shook his head. He'd quit missing his wife half a year ago. But starting up with someone new rattled the hell out of him.

Grow a pair, Larson!

"You'll be leaving at some point, too," he said, choosing the *honesty is the best policy* route.

Desi went up on her tiptoes to capture his lips for a few more seconds of bliss. She pulled back and played with the collar of his shirt. Her thick-lashed lids fluttered up and down. "That may be true, but I'm not running away tonight."

He'd never had a fling. He was the guy who went steady all his life and married the girl right out of college. This was completely out of his realm of understanding, except his body was sending an entirely different message than his overactive and protective brain.

WWGD? What would Gunnar do? Go for it, idiot! You're allowed to have sex with a beautiful and willing partner.

Kent pulled her back to his chest, his mouth seeking the fine skin of her cheeks and ears, inhaling the fresh tropical-and-apricot scent in her hair again. His wandering hands couldn't feel her everywhere fast enough. He pressed his erection against her waist, sending a shock of lust all the way to his spine. She moaned and moved closer against him.

When he looked into her eyes, he saw all the want, heat and need he felt mirrored there, and the decision was made. "Let's go. That is, if you want—"

"Definitely." Desi smiled, taking his hand, and, now that he'd gotten her consent, they practically jogged toward his bedroom. Before they hit the stairs, she tugged back, stopping him. "What's wrong with the couch?"

Maybe she worried about Steven's bedroom being so close upstairs? She couldn't possibly know the boy was a notoriously sound sleeper.

"Great." Giving thanks for the Victorian-style house with the French doors closing off the living room, he instantly changed course. Why waste another moment away from her body?

Her sweater slipped easily over her shoulders and through the matching yellow bra he could make out her nipples. He swallowed in deep appreciation, parched from wanting her so damn much. He couldn't yank off his shirt fast enough. There was longing in her eyes when she stared at his bare chest, her tongue wetting her bottom lip.

Within seconds they'd peeled off the rest of their clothes and hit the cushions in a heated skin-to-skin tangle. Her soft curves and his tight angles came together in a rush of desire so strong they practically bumped heads and knees, but nothing would stop them from their mission. She'd landed on top and he caressed and sampled her lush breasts, savoring their weight and feel, teasing the velvety dark tips with his tongue until they peaked even tighter.

She was beyond beautiful, the kitchen light silhouetting her body like solar flares. A tropical-scented goddess. Her hands were as eager as his and they explored his chest and stomach, and the building sensations beneath her fingers begged for more of her touches. More. And more.

His erection stood tall, fully engorged, pulsing at her center. She straddled his waist and he found her entrance with his fingers, coaxing her open, amazed at how ready she felt for him. His hands were on each side of her hips, on the verge of lifting her high enough to take him inside, when his brain called out for sanity.

"Condom. Damn it." Did he even have them anymore?

Desi wrapped her hand around him and squeezed gently. Sparklers went off behind his lids. "Hurry back."

He'd find one of those suckers if he had to dig through a trash can.

He moved her aside and stood. "Do. Not. Move." With one last wet kiss, he left her grinning behind closed doors. She was naked on the couch, her hair wild, making her look like an astral queen. He could imagine the senior Life Art class busting at the seams with students when word got out she'd posed for them, and he laughed inwardly as he threw on his slacks and headed for the second floor.

His good fortune at meeting her, having her waiting for him, propelled him up the stairs to his medicine cabinet. Nada. Damn it all to hell. Just his luck to have the most exotically beautiful woman he'd ever seen waiting and...

Hold on! His briefcase. He always kept samples of medicine from the drug companies on hand to give to patients who couldn't afford to pay for prescriptions. He also kept a batch of condoms to give out for the same reason. Tiptoeing past Steven's room just in case the cookies messed with his usual sleeping pattern, he rushed back down the stairs. He made a beeline for his briefcase and, thanking the aligning stars in heaven, found a few stragglers. He chose a neon yellow one, thinking about her discarded sweater and bra. The wrapper said "extra lubrication." From the way she'd felt, it wasn't necessary, but on second thought he grabbed a handful.

Practically growling from desire zinging through him, he found her right where he'd left her. Dropping his pants and quickly stepping out, he held her face in his palms and kissed her soundly. She tasted silky and sweet, delicious like those cookies. Her body melded to his, warming him through and through. Hot humming pulsated inside every cell in his body as he kissed his way down to her waist. He inhaled her woman scent and kissed her between her soft folds, enjoying her special taste as she writhed beneath his touch. Her throaty response made him wild with the need to satisfy her. He glanced up. She muffled the escalating moans by biting her lip and turning her head into the couch cushion until she came, her fingers digging into his scalp as she did.

Good thing a cruise ship could blast the horn for an hour yet never disturb the super-sound-sleeper Steven.

Kent couldn't stand another second without being buried inside her, and from the way she pawed at him, pulling and dragging him over her, she needed him, too. Her hands guided him to her entrance, then straight on to heaven on earth. She was tight and warm and slick and...

He couldn't think anymore. Every pent-up feeling he'd stockpiled over the past year fought to break free. All that existed was the feel of her, the dive and roll of their bodies and the building feral sensations. Single-minded in his quest, he thrust and pulled back, again and again, faster and faster, sensations building toward atomic fusion. Time disappeared. It was just them. Their bodies.

Crying out, she spasmed around him as the rhythmic, tightening aftershocks launched him on toward bliss. And he was gone.

But he kept thrusting with a guttural groan, their bodies tight, nuclear hot and wet against each other, and she came again, sweetening the final throes of the most amazing orgasm he'd ever had.

Desi couldn't believe what had just happened. The man who never wanted her near his son had just gifted her with a triple-header! Her body, still wide-awake to Kent's every touch, still pulsing with leftover sensations, had never felt more alive. She dug her fingers into her hair and stretched like a cat, savoring the feel. He sat and smiled down at her.

Even from this angle he was gorgeous. His wide smile stretched nearly from ear to ear, and those smoldering *I just did you good* eyes stoked a new round of tingles. He was a complete package of near perfection with broad shoulders, developed pecs dusted in light hair, muscular arms and abs that belonged on a magazine cover. How had she gotten so lucky?

"You okay?" he asked.

She inhaled through her nose, taking her time to respond. "I've never been better. You?"

He sputtered a laugh. "Damn, woman, you're hot." He cupped her hip and patted.

She went up on her elbows so she could reach his lips and gave him a peck. "Thank you."

They kissed as if they hadn't seen each other in months, eager to lock lips again and get lost in each other. His hands worked wonders on her skin, conjuring gooseflesh everywhere he touched. Her tightening nipples sent fleeting messages to her core, still simmering from sex. *Be on the ready.*

She could get lost in Kent, again and again.

He stretched out beside her, wrapping one arm around her waist, his thighs flush to her side. She sampled his glorious firm glutes. The man truly had to be a descendant of Vikings.

"Can I get you some water?" He stood, the last of his erection in evidence.

"Love it. I'm dying of thirst."

He smiled at her with those heavy-lidded eyes, rekindling her desire as if they'd never been together tonight. She glanced at her watch, the only thing she still wore. How long could she stay here before Grandma might get suspicious?

Still flying from their lovemaking, she was nowhere near ready to figure out what any of this meant. She watched with total fascination as he walked to the kitchen, handsomeness in motion.

While he was gone, she lay there, with one thought on her mind: Where did they go from here?

A quick minute later, when he'd obviously gone to the bathroom and cleaned up, he returned with one tall glass of water. She took it and sipped. When she offered him some, he took a drink. Their gazes met and held. There went that nuclear-fusion thing again smack-dab in the middle of her belly, and soon the water was on the coffee table and completely forgotten. Their only thirst was for each other, and they reacquainted themselves with each other's bodies, one touch at a time.

Chapter Nine

Midmorning Monday, Desi went into town specifically to talk to Cliff Lincoln. She'd bonded with him in more ways than the color of their skin and wanted his advice. She knew he'd be in the kitchen whipping up his luncheon special, so she went around to the back. The door was open and the wondrous aroma of simmering onions, garlic and green peppers made her mouth water.

"Knock, knock," she said, eyeing Cliff at the extra-large gas stove, stirring the contents in a thick iron pot.

He turned and broke into a toothy grin. "Well, well, if it isn't Desdemona Rask."

"Is it okay if I come in?"

"Sure. Put your feet up, take a load off those dogs. I'll pour us some coffee."

Cliff made Desi feel as at home in his restaurant kitchen as Gerda did at home. Combined with her hot next-door neighbor, Heartlandia was beginning to have a hold on her. The good kind. *Would it make you happy, Mom, to know I've found some peace of mind in the place you ran away from?* Somehow it didn't seem right. Could these feelings turn into a stranglehold like they had for her mother? The mixed-up thoughts confused her.

"I wanted to thank you for sending over that delicious soup the other night."

"Ms. Gerda Rask, besides being our mayor, is a fine woman of the community. She'd do the same for me and mine." He handed Desi a thick mug full to the brim, remembering and including the creamer. "That's Louisiana's finest right there."

Desi smiled, nodding her head in thanks, taking the cup with both hands and inhaling the potent coffee.

"What brings you around today?"

She scrunched up her nose, not knowing how to begin. "I've just been wondering…" She blew into her mug and took a quick sip of the strong, bitter brew. "How did you know Heartlandia was the place for you?"

Cliff stopped stirring, a wise expression consuming his face. "Ah, the sixty-four-thousand-dollar question." He nailed her with a one-eyed squint. "You thinking of moving in with your grandmother for good?"

She shrugged. "First I've got to find my father."

"Is that so?"

"I think it's important that I do. But maybe I'll come back."

"Right. Right." He turned off the gas flame and moved the pot to the side, then leaned against the counter and folded his arms. "So you want to know how I knew Heartlandia was the place for me. Here's the long answer. As soon as I turned eighteen I joined the navy, went around the world, then got hired on the cruise line. I guess you could say I'd been a vagabond my whole life." He picked up his mug and drank heartily. "There was just something special about Heartlandia right from the start. Every time that cruise ship docked and I came ashore, the people here didn't look at me like I planned to mug them like in so many other cities around the world. They didn't seem to care that I was black. I liked the Scandinavian feel, the beautiful trees, the gracious people and the river. It felt like home. I never get tired of looking at the Columbia River. It brought me here, and if I ever want to leave, it will take me away."

It felt like home. What does home feel like?

"You met your wife here, too, right?"

"Oh, yes, but not right away. She's twenty years younger." He gave the smile of a proud man who'd snagged a younger woman. "I worked this restaurant hard for five years, barely keeping afloat. Then I hired this sweet young thing right out of high school as a waitress, and she suggested I cook some soul food. Worked like a charm, got more cruise customers and word spread. *Try the gumbo at Lincoln's Place in Heartlandia. Check out his shrimp and grits.* She had a good head on her shoulders and she fell in love with me to prove it." He pursed his lips, trying to look humble but failing miserably. "Course, it took me a while to notice. Anyway, by then Heartlandia was my home, and I haven't wanted to leave, not once."

Desi envied his conviction. Sure she liked it here. Loved Gerda. Didn't know where she stood with Kent, but, man, she wasn't anywhere near ready to walk away from that sexy gift. But did it feel like home?

She'd made herself a promise to find her father, to learn about her roots. To figure out who she truly was.

"You want some pie or somethin'?"

"Nah, I'm good." Desi drank more of the coffee. "I've got some errands to run for Gerda since she has meetings all day, and I need some calligraphy supplies."

"You think any more about playin' the piano on weekends for me?"

Truth was, she had been thinking about it a lot. She'd even been practicing all of her favorite Scott Joplin rags and more Ellington, too, but wasn't ready to admit it to Cliff or commit to staying. She really needed to find her father, see where that led first. "Maybe a little."

"A little playin' or a little *thinkin'* 'bout playin'? Which one?"

"I've been thinking about whether or not I want to work for you."

"But you need to find your father first, right?"

She gave a wry smile and took another sip of coffee.

"What you expect to 'discover'?" He used air quotes. "That you're an African princess? That you've got a dozen brothers and sisters all waiting their whole lives just to meet you? To get in touch with your soulful side?"

He'd rubbed her the wrong way. "You don't have to put it that way."

"Maybe I do. Maybe I need you to understand that you're already Desdemona Rask. You already know who you are, whether you realize it or not."

She didn't look at him. Couldn't he understand there was more to it than that? She'd never met her father. She needed to learn about the rest of her heritage.

"I don't want to burst your bubble, but odds are you'd

be an intrusion into someone's complicated life. If there's a wife involved, it might really tick her off. Maybe you should be ready for that possibility."

"That may be true, but I still need to find out, Cliff."

"Yes, you do, little sister. If you say so, but I'm trying to tell you, it won't change who you already are. Don't become one of those people who're always looking for something else and forget to notice what's right in front of them. Take it from me—it's a waste of time."

Cliff gave her a dose of reality that didn't go down nearly as well as the strong coffee, but she couldn't give up until she found the man who'd changed Ester Rask's life forever. Maybe he'd change her life, too.

She stood, finished off her coffee and put the mug in the huge stainless-steel sink. "I hear what you're saying, but…"

"—but you've just got to find out. I know. I know. And I wish you well. You know I do." He turned the burner on again and went back to sautéing the vegetables. "If you decide to work for me, just let me know."

Cliff had played the devil's advocate, the voice of reason, and she needed to think about all the possible scenarios she could face when meeting her father. In his own gruff way, Cliff showed he cared. Heck, he'd offered her a job right from the start.

The notion came over her out of nowhere, but without giving it further thought, she crossed the kitchen and hugged him from behind.

"Thank you."

Surprise made his nearly black eyes open wide and his lips stretch into a large smile as he turned around and hugged her back with the non-sautéing arm. "Anytime, li'l bit. Anytime." He squeezed her close to his soft middle then set her free.

Desi left him smiling and humming to himself, a contented man who knew exactly who he was no matter where he lived. Even if he was the only black man in town. She, on the other hand, felt more restless and out of touch with herself than when she'd walked in.

She cornered the alley to his restaurant and got back on the main street. It was a beautiful sunny day and downtown Heartlandia looked like something off a book cover—clean, colorful and self-contained.

Thinking about clean and colorful, she was reminded of the interior of Kent's house, and how it definitely had a woman's touch when it came to decorating. If that was the case, his ex-wife had impeccable taste with a perfect mix of French country and small-town charm. The sage-green living room had complementary print wingback chairs on either side of a tall, modern rock fireplace. The deep red microfiber wraparound couch with the chaise-lounge end was perfect for their love-making last night. All the hardwood floors were in mint condition and extended into the buttery-yellow kitchen with brown granite counters and copper pots and pans hanging over the island. It looked right out of a magazine. The bland white exterior of the house gave the wrong impression. Kent's house was warm and homey, and she'd gotten too comfortable there too quickly.

Deep in thought, she almost didn't notice the police car drive by and slow to a stop. Out popped Kent's friend Gunnar. "How's it going?"

"Oh, hi. Good. How about you?"

"Doing well." The way he smiled at her made her wonder if he knew about her and Kent already. Did men kiss and tell like ladies did? If she had a best friend, she'd have spilled all the details about something that amazing in record time. "I guess I'm not much of a pinch-hitting friend for Kent, so thanks for stepping up with babysitting yesterday."

"Of course. That's what neighbors are for." Warmth invaded her cheeks. Did he know just how much she'd "stepped up" already?

"Uh, hey, the police station is just down the street if you ever feel like stopping by. I'll show you around."

Or was the guy hitting on her? "Thanks." She fidgeted with the strap of her shoulder bag. "Well, I don't want to hold you up or anything."

He may have tried to be subtle, but he looked her over good before getting back into the car. Just before he did, he tipped his hat with a suave smile.

Seeing Gunnar put Kent front and center in her thoughts again as she walked down the street toward The Paper Mill. She'd thought about their lovemaking all night. He'd satisfied every single cell in her body, and she'd gone home feeling like Jell-O. Her pulse went a little wacky remembering everything they'd done.

On a nonsexual note, she'd been grossly unfair to him considering his circumstances. She'd expected him to be completely well-adjusted, even after finding out his wife had left, making him a reluctant single father. She'd been impatient and put out by his overprotective ways with Steven, but wouldn't she have done the same thing in his shoes?

The last thing she could claim was being well-adjusted. Was she chasing a dream searching for her father, as Cliff had said? Her roots? If she really wanted to find him, how come she hadn't even tried to look him up yet? Hmm, maybe Gunnar could help out in that department.

Desi stepped inside The Paper Mill, heading right to the pens and special-paper section.

"Hi, Desi!" the clerk said.

What was with this town? She'd been in the store only one other time, introduced herself as the mayor's granddaughter, and the little bird-framed, blue-haired lady in a homemade knitted sweater behind the counter already remembered her. She waved and smiled.

After purchasing her items, she left hugging her bag, heading for the market with Gerda's list, wondering if it was a good or a bad thing to live in such a small town.

Monday evening, Kent tapped on the Rask screen door. Steven stood by his side, antsy. Kent copped to being nervous about seeing the woman he'd thought about all day at work, but couldn't stay away.

It was warmer today, and the inside door was open, affording him his first glimpse of Desi as a silhouette sauntering from the kitchen. Need sparked through him when she opened the screen and smiled. How many times had he thought about the way she laughed, light and breezy, how great she'd felt, how tenderly she'd kissed him? How she'd satisfied him beyond his wildest dreams.

She wore those crazy big hoop earrings today, and the lush glow of peach gloss on her smooth lips. He wanted to kiss her right there in front of Steven but fought the impulse. There was an extra charge in her gaze as she looked at him, and he hoped it was because she might want to kiss him, too.

"You wanna go have dinner with us?" Steven jumped the gun.

She tore away from their staring match, eyes darting to Steven. "Oh, I'd love to, but Gerda is feeling so much better she's teaching me how to make fish balls. You want to eat here?"

Steven screwed up his tiny nose. "No, thanks. Dad promised me a burger and milk shake."

"Aw, shoot. I wish I could go, but you know…"

"I know. Mayor Rask is old and she needs company."

Kent suppressed his laugh. "Now, Steven." The boy could blurt the most outrageous things. The twinkle in Desi's eyes proved she enjoyed his innocent faux pas, too. Her thoughtful gaze wandered up to Kent's.

He didn't want to appear too eager in front of his son. "If it's okay, I'll stop by later."

"I'd like that."

"I'm all ready for my piano lesson," Steven chimed in, oblivious to the full-out attraction arcing in the air between his father and the new piano teacher. "You're going to be proud of me."

"I'm sure I am," she said.

"So you better have an extra-special treat."

She laughed and Kent thought he'd never get enough of her generous and friendly ways where his son was concerned. Or her natural beauty, her golden-bronze skin, round curves and wide fawnlike eyes.

"Okay, we're out of here," Kent said, before his body could get out of hand.

Desi waved goodbye, and he checked his watch to see how long before he could have some time alone with her again. Every minute would seem like an hour. No doubt about it, Steven was going to bed at eight tonight, no excuses. "You can't tell your piano teacher how to reward you," he said, walking down the path to his truck.

"Why not?"

"That's not the way it works." Though the concept wasn't half-bad. Kent let a quick fantasy flicker through his brain of the many ways he'd like to tell Desi how to reward *him*.

At eight-fifteen he strode out the door, heading for the Rask place. Desi must have read his mind because she was sitting on the porch reading. The thought of having a few moments alone with her made his pulse race. A few months ago, he'd never expected anything like this could ever happen again.

She offered that picture-perfect smile of hers the whole while he walked up the porch stairs and across the distance to where she sat.

"Hey," he said.

"Hi."

He wanted her to stand up so he could hug her, make contact as soon as possible. Again, as if she read his mind, she stood. He welcomed her into his arms and let the wonder of holding a woman close again register in his body.

"You look pretty," he said, kissing her hair, remembering how that tropical scent had stuck in his mind all day at work.

"Thank you." Her hands rubbed his back, rushing his pulse even more. She looked up, those lush lips there for the taking. Wanting to devour her, he practiced self-control and dropped a quick hello kiss on her mouth instead.

Don't make her uncomfortable. Just because you

want to jump her bones doesn't mean she feels the same. She's a whole person, someone you want to do things for, someone you want to know better.

He let her go and sat on the love seat. She snuggled close, and her warmth kept his pulse thumping fast and hard.

"I ran into Gunnar today in town," she said.

"You did?"

"Yeah. He seems nice. Made me wonder if there might be some way he could help me locate my father." Her honesty about needing to find her birth father made his stomach knot. He'd let his guard down and had sex with her. So it was just sex for her, too, a little gift to help him get beyond the incredibly lousy year he'd survived, nothing more. He shouldn't be feeling this way, a little lost, empty and worried. Damn, he didn't know how to do casual.

"I don't have a clue how to start looking for him."

"Well, maybe Gunnar can point you in the right direction." It hurt to say it, especially since that direction might lead her out of town, away from him, but he wanted to help her.

"That's what I was thinking."

"You sure you don't want to stick around Heartlandia and live with Gerda?"

"I'm not sure of anything, but I made myself a promise to find that man. See where it leads."

It could lead her right out of town to never come back, and the idea gripped his gut, making it feel as if his belt buckle had tightened a notch. That was how it had started with his wife, too, one little step at a time until she was gone for good. Feeling already in over his head, he found it hard to breathe. Maybe it was a big mistake to have sex with her. Why the hell couldn't he do casual?

"Dad?" Steven's voice carried across the narrow yard from his front door.

"I'm right here."

"I had a bad dream."

"Coming." As he got up, Desi joined him. He gave her a quick kiss goodbye in the shadows so Steven couldn't see. The treat he'd been looking forward to all day had grown complicated and now got cut short. His need to control the situation fought with the way things were playing out. All he wanted was some more time with Desi, and all she wanted was to take off looking for her father. "Good night."

She didn't say it back, and he could see that sassy glint in her eyes. Maybe things were looking up. She shot up on her tippy-toes and kissed him a beat or two longer. A kiss that promised more than good-night. "I'll see you later," she whispered.

Kent's mood lifted, and he took the stairs then strode across the yard toward his house, grinning, a sexy buzz vibrating through his body. On this count he definitely liked the way Desi Rask thought.

Around ten, light tapping came from the front door. Waiting for Desi, he'd been reading a medical journal on the latest superbacteria and had lost track of time.

He opened the door. Desi stood on his doorstep bright-eyed and as refreshing as the evening breeze, and she nearly took his breath away. She rushed into his arms. Their earlier conversation about her still wanting to find her dad may have been a cold shower to his brain, but not his body. He kissed her the way he'd wanted to earlier, and her mouth welcomed him. With their bodies wrapped tight, they made out for several more minutes. He loved lifting her hair and kissing the spots on her neck and shoulders that made her purr. He couldn't get enough of that Polynesian-flower scent in her hair. It had messed with his mind all day at work.

Her hands couldn't seem to get enough of him, either, and his body went directly into conquer mode.

As things heated up, his thoughts got out of hand. Before he could censor himself, he broke from their kiss. "I just want to say one thing."

Her first answer was another mind-jumbling kiss. "Lay it on me."

"I want you to consider staying in Heartlandia."

Desi had never felt more wanted in her life. A huge and gorgeous hunk of man was hot for her and asking her to stick around. When had that ever happened before? Never. She'd promised her mother she'd go to her grandmother's, but she'd promised herself to go even further—to find her dad. She didn't have a clue if he was even still alive, but now was the time to make the journey.

Kent kissed her again, and her thoughts turned to mush. Men knew how to disconnect emotions from sex. If they could, so could she. It was probably for the best.

But Kent's comment gave the impression he wasn't any better at it than she was. *I want you to consider staying in Heartlandia.*

"Maybe you should shut up and kiss me," she said, avoiding his question and going right for his mouth. Kent didn't need coaxing. Nope, she was completely aware of his firm response and it was pressing into her belly. She'd made an extra stop in town today, at the drugstore, and came prepared with a couple of condoms of her own. She wondered when Kent's hand roamed to her bottom if he'd notice the wrappers tucked inside her jeans pocket.

"Did I mention my kid sleeps like a rock?"

With fire in those natural bedroom eyes, he took her hand and led her upstairs, straight to his king-size bed, where he slowly undressed her and laid her down, soon joining her after shedding his clothes.

It's just sex, she told herself, but Kent had a look on his face that communicated something more. His hands were slow and thoughtful as they explored, his every touch intentional. She quivered as he caressed her, as he worshipped her breasts and belly and the sweet spot between her legs.

She could get used to this.

Just sex, Desi, just casual sex.

They came together and she got the distinct impression he was offering so much more than sex this time. Or she'd distorted this perfect little setup of hooking up with the sexy doc next door, had read into it, made it out to be more than what it was. S. E. X.

He kissed her then looked deep into her eyes as he stroked in and out. The intimacy threw her. Staring into his baby blues, she knew it wasn't just sex. He'd asked her to think about sticking around, and he was making her dizzy with that intensely sexy gaze.

She closed her eyes and shut down her brain, letting their bodies do all the communicating. And as the moments clicked by, he knew exactly how to take her all the way.

At midnight, sated from making love with Kent, she gathered her clothes to head for home. The last thing she wanted was for either Steven or Gerda to find out what she and Kent had been up to.

He lay on his stomach with the sheet over his waist, his tousled blond hair sexy as hell, his jaw relaxed and eyes closed, his broad back dappled by moonlight. A gorgeous sight.

An ache planted itself behind her chest, and it had nothing to do with the stupendous sex they'd shared. Longing for something she'd never had before—a real relationship—left a bittersweet taste in her mouth. Was she one foot in or out of Heartlandia?

Their timing was off. But maybe down the road after she'd found her father and discovered the other half of herself, after she finally knew who she was, and Kent had enough time to completely move on from his divorce, maybe then they could make whatever this was work.

Wanting nothing more than to climb right back into bed and cuddle up with Kent, Desi got dressed, tip-toed out of the room and padded across the yard to her grandmother's house.

Once in bed, she savored the way it felt to be wanted for the first time in her adult life, and to help soothe her brain for sleep, she pretended things didn't have to be different.

Chapter Ten

"My arthritis seems to have settled down," Gerda said. "I think I'm ready to take over the piano students again."

Gerda and Desi shared the piano bench Tuesday morning, having just practiced a duet together for fun. Gerda had suggested it after tending to a few morning mayoral duties. Sunlight streamed through the side windows, making everything look golden. Desi wanted to imprint the moment in her mind as a special memory.

"Are you sure, Grandma?"

"I've missed them. Those students added purpose to my life long before I became mayor. Besides, I've been thinking too much about our pirate problems." She'd hushed her voice when she'd said "pirate problems," as though the walls had ears. "I need to get my mind on something else."

"How's that going?" Desi studied the thin skin of

Gerda's hands as they rested on the piano keys, the pencil-point-thin blue veins beneath.

Her hands flew to her lap and knotted. "Elke Norling is deciphering the journals, and she'll report back at the next meeting."

"Deciphering? Isn't it in English?"

"Have you ever seen Old English? It's like another language. *S* looks like *F,* and there's all kinds of extra swirliques—I don't know what to call them, but you know what I mean. His cursive is poor at best, and much of the ink has smeared or faded."

"I get it. It's nothing like we write today."

"Yes, and it's one big whopping job for someone who has a full-time position at the city college." Lines fanned from the corners of Gerda's eyes as she smiled at Desi. "Some of us still hold out hope that Captain Nathaniel Prince—" she put her hand over her mouth and spoke to the side toward Desi "—also known as the Prince of Doom, did his terrible deeds somewhere else and maybe only shipwrecked around here. Everything has to be verified. We'll see what Elke reports at the next meeting."

"Captain Nathaniel Prince. Hmm." Desi made a quick sketch of how the Prince of Doom might have looked. Not being very imaginative this morning, she figured he looked a lot like Jack Sparrow.

Gerda shook her head and sighed. "Yes, he was captain of a treacherous ship called *Neptune's Fortune,* according to the initial information we've gleaned from that chest. For all we know, it could be sunken somewhere near Heartlandia." Her hand went to her breast. "God, I hope not."

"But wouldn't it be cool if that sunken ship had buried treasure? Think of the tourists who would flock to see it."

"That's a major concern. We don't want to upset our community. We love things just the way they are. And if and when we make our decision about what to do, it will all land on my shoulders as mayor pro tem to deliver the news to the Heartlandians."

Though Desi was entirely amused by the possibility of her newfound hometown possibly being tainted by wicked pirates, she also understood the grave disappointment her grandmother felt about the historical black eye to her beloved Heartlandia. Besides, Desi had rocked her grandmother's world enough lately simply by showing up. Maybe it was time to change the subject, before Gerda started grabbing her chest again and needing sedatives.

"I was wondering," Desi said as she slipped her arm around her grandmother and drew her close. "Would it be okay if I kept on with Steven?"

"Of course. You've brought him so far along in just a few weeks. It's nothing short of amazing."

"And he is your last student today, which will give me plenty of time to prepare before his lesson."

"Are you going somewhere?"

"It's Kent's day off, and he offered to take me on a tour of the city college and the Ringmiren wall, so it really is convenient for you to take over the first lessons today."

Gerda clapped. "Oh, how wonderful. I should have taken you there myself, but…"

"You've been really busy, Grandma. Not to mention not feeling well."

"True." Gerda looked into Desi's eyes, hope shining in her own. "Are you and Kent dating?"

Could Desi call it "dating," or maybe she should say they were neighbors with benefits? She felt a blush coming on. "I'm not sure what we're doing, but he's a super-nice guy." *And, oh, he's so much more than that. He's an outrageous lover and a fabulous father, a respected doctor and...* "And he needs a break from his routine as much as anyone, don't you think? So when he suggested showing me around, I jumped at it."

"Well, I, for one, couldn't be happier."

That was what had been nagging Desi, too. She hadn't been this happy in...well, a long, long time, and she knew it wouldn't continue, not if she went searching for her father. Which she still really and truly needed to do.

After a late lunch outside at the Fika Bakery, Desi relaxed back in her chair, enjoying the sunshine and Kent's handsome face. The awning cast sharp shadows over his profile. She watched the grooves that formed on either side of his nose and mouth when he smiled, straight teeth peeking out from between his lips. The lips she'd made out with under a pine tree and leaning against the Ringmiren wall only a half hour ago.

Watching him made her heart tighten. It wasn't the usual feeling she had when dating a guy, that was for sure.

He'd started growing a beard along his jawline, which was brown in contrast to his blond hair. The finely manicured beard, mustache and soul patch curtained the edge of his jaw and lips, making him look chiseled and gorgeous. She liked how the new mustache tickled when they kissed. Combined with that dashing smile and those heavy-lidded blue eyes shining her way, one word surfaced in her brain. *Sexy.* Then two words—*scary sexy.* As she took in the full picture of the man—with a gentle smile only for her—a warm ball of want curled deep inside her.

He took her hand and squeezed. Was he thinking what she was thinking? The first signs of desire coiled tighter.

"I've got an idea," he said.

Oh, yes, they were on the same page.

"I'm up for anything." Desi went for coy and a double entendre.

"How about I take you—"

Take me, yes—exactly what I was thinking.

"—to the police station. Maybe Gunnar can help you out with your dad."

Not what I had in mind, but, what? You want to help me find my dad?

"Wow. That would be great." How could she refuse his generous offer?

The police station was larger than she expected and it was in the same building as the local newspaper. The standard concrete facade was decorated with huge columns on either side of the entrance. Marble floors in the foyer echoed as they turned left and headed for the bank of floor-to-ceiling windows under the Heartlandia Police Department banner and official emblem. She wondered, since it was a police station, if the glass was bulletproof.

It was stuffy inside, and Desi was nervous, but Kent held her hand and guided her to the desk.

"Is Sergeant Norling here?"

At the sound of his name, and before the young, narrow-necked desk clerk could answer, Gunnar's head popped around a corner. His face brightened at the sight of Kent. "Hey, I thought I recognized your voice. Come on back." He pushed something under the counter that released the lock and Kent was able to open the door at the end of the desk. They shook hands and patted each other's backs affectionately.

"You remember Desi, right?"

Gunnar nodded at Desi with a fleeting knowing glance. "Sure do. How you been?" he asked, even though they'd just seen each other yesterday. He shook her hand. His grip was firm and rough around the edges, nothing like Kent's.

"I'm good. Thanks." She let go a beat before he did, edging closer to Kent and away from the imposing figure in the *don't mess with me* uniform. Which, she noted, fit him to a tee and outlined a striking figure. Muscular guys, however, were not her type. At all.

"Hey," Kent broke in. "Desi is trying to locate her father. All she has is a name, a ballpark birth date and a last-known address."

"He was a jazz musician," she said. "Played with some biggies. Don't know if that will help at all."

"I can't use our database for something like that." Gunnar scratched his cheek, noticing Desi's obvious disappointment. "But I know a guy in Portland who's a P.I., and he specializes in this exact thing. Finding people." He strode to his desk and flipped through his Rolodex. "Yeah, here's the guy."

Desi caught his eager-to-please expression and smiled. "Do you think he'd help me? How much does he cost?"

After a surreptitious glance toward Kent, Gunnar

lifted a brow, engaging Desi again. "He owes me a favor. Tell you what—give me the information and I'll have him run a check on your father. If he finds anything, I'll get back to you."

"That'd be great," Kent said, touching Desi's heart by his generosity of spirit, arranging this meeting and helping in the search for her birth father. That unusual feeling she sometimes got when she looked at Kent swelled once again in her chest.

Desi wrote down everything she knew about her father, which struck her as so meager and sad, and handed it to Gunnar along with her cell-phone number.

Kent had made it very clear as they toured the city college that he thought Desi should stick around Heartlandia, try out some classes at the school, give them a chance to get to know each other better. The idea struck her as especially appealing.

Did he want more than great sex? Might he feel that same strange sensation about her that she always got when she thought about him? *Don't get carried away.*

Kent looked at his watch. "Oh, hey, it's almost time to pick up Steven from summer day camp. We've got to run."

After a quick goodbye, Desi followed Kent out of the station house, and taking his hand, she rushed along with his brisk pace back to the car.

How normal it felt to be with the man she had definite feelings for, rushing off to get his son. A quick snapshot of the future, a hope and dream she'd never realized she'd had before, popped into her head.

"So I guess we'll just wait and see what happens about your father," he said, shoving the key in the ignition, making a point not to look at her.

Firmly back in reality, she switched out of fantasy gears.

Maybe helping her locate her father wasn't selfless generosity after all. Maybe it was his way of trying to take control of the situation. Or maybe it was a test.

Later that night, after Gerda had gone to bed, Desi stole across the yard to Kent's, unable to stay away. It was after ten, they'd been texting, and he was waiting for her. He opened the door wearing a broad grin, shirtless on the warm night. They came together in a hot embrace and that growing desire she'd put on hold earlier in the day came back to life.

She'd decided to keep her involvement with Kent a secret from her grandmother, to let her think they were merely dating, not sleeping with each other. Desi didn't want to disappoint Gerda or change her old-style attitude toward Kent. Oh, but making love with Kent Larson seemed like so much more than secret sex. Especially now, with his mouth warm on her lips and his hands slipping up and down her sides, igniting every cell along her skin.

A little after midnight, Desi lay naked and cuddled under Kent's arm, her head resting on his chest. Each of his contented breaths lifted her head ever so gently. He played with her hair, tickling her neck with it.

"You know, you really should give some thought to enrolling in a few classes this fall." Knowing she'd protest like she had when they were on campus earlier, he covered her mouth with his free hand. She playfully bit a finger.

"You should quit telling me what to do."

"And I think playing piano for Cliff's restaurant is a great idea. You're a gifted pianist—why not share it for others to enjoy?"

She knocked her knuckles lightly on his temple, wishing she hadn't shared Cliff's job offer with Kent. "Did you hear what I just said?"

"Then you could work part-time while you're taking classes."

She let her feigned protest rest. His complete trust in her capabilities and confidence in her talent made her want to please him, want to show him she could do anything she set out to do, just like her mother had always said. She admitted his having a plan all mapped out for her was sweet to a certain extent. But it was her life, and she had every intention of making her own decisions about it.

Not having a father, and her dating life up to now being far from ideal, she'd never had a man believe in her before. The way Kent's hands roamed aimlessly across her shoulders, drawing her close for a tender hug, she believed him. Maybe he cared about her as more than a sexual partner. Maybe he wanted her in his life beyond the bedroom.

Maybe she should take a chance, stick around, let herself fall for him and settle down for good in Heartlandia. She kissed his chest, splayed her fingers across his defined pecs, wishing she could trust her growing desire to stay here.

Maybe it was too good to be true.

The hungry demons inside gnawed at her self-esteem. They insisted she was two halves of a whole and couldn't be a complete person until she found the other half. She was biracial to Kent's pure Scandinavian. She wasn't educated compared to him. She wasn't refined, didn't have a clue what she wanted to do with her life. If they took this bedroom affair into daylight, where he could get a really good look at her, she'd probably disappoint him.

Then what would she do? She couldn't very well live next door to a man who didn't accept her. A man who'd break her heart.

"Where are you?" Kent's gentle voice pulled her away from the negativity bombs crashing around her, and his arms tugged her farther up his chest.

She sighed, trying to empty her head.

He lifted her chin and brushed his lips across hers. Their eyes met. And held. The smoldering look undid her.

"Stay with me," he said, deepening the kiss. "Just a while longer."

That familiar and indescribable warm feeling coursed through her veins when she knew without a doubt he wanted her. Like now. She let all the questions and doubts about her future evaporate as their bodies interlaced perfectly, as they always did. And finally, all other thoughts faded far away.

Early Wednesday morning, Desi was surprised by a text from Gunnar. Meet me at the Hjartalanda Coffee House at 11:00 a.m.

C U there, she texted back.

She rushed to finish her latest batch of calligraphy so she could mail the seventieth-birthday invitations to her long-term customer while she was in town meeting Gunnar.

Anxiety about why he wanted to see her pecked around her edges, making her fingers quiver and the letters more in line with what she imagined Elke Norling was deciphering in that pirate journal. After she'd ruined a second invitation, she gave up on the calligraphy and jumped into the shower. She'd finish the project tonight and mail the invitations tomorrow.

After wrestling into her denim leggings and a summery fuchsia smock, she skipped downstairs. "I'm going into town. You need anything?" she called out.

"I could use more of that pink stomach medicine. Got another council meeting tonight," Gerda replied from the sunroom.

Desi smiled. "You got it!" She opted to head for the door without going down the hall to say goodbye. Since she was keeping the meeting with Gunnar secret, she didn't want to lie and wasn't ready to meet her grandmother's eyes today.

Fifteen minutes later, Desi entered the coffee shop and immediately spotted Gunnar. He was talking up the waitress, who looked happy as a high schooler with a supercrush. He glanced up and waved, and Desi made her way over to his booth for two as the waitress scurried off.

He rose. "How's it going?"

"Not bad." She sat, her throat going dry. There was already water on the table, so she took a sip.

"So you're probably wondering why I asked you here."

She hoped with all of her heart it was about her father, because she really didn't want to find out Gunnar was a two-timing friend to Kent and was hitting on her behind his back. "Yes, actually."

He smiled, his intense green eyes nearly bowling

her over. "Oh, I hope you don't mind, but I ordered us both coffees already."

"That's fine."

"You want anything else? A roll or something? I like their muffins."

"I'm good. Thanks."

"Okay, so I got ahold of my guy, the P.I., the other day and fed him your information."

Returning dryness nearly shut down her throat. She couldn't swallow or respond.

Gunnar fiddled with his water glass, turning it round and round on the condensation ring on the table. The waitress was back in record time with the coffees and Gunnar's blueberry muffin. "Thanks, darlin'." He soon got sidetracked fixing his coffee and peeling the wrapper from the muffin. "Cream?" He pushed the tiny stainless-steel pitcher at her.

Desi could hardly breathe as she waited. Did he have a clue how he tortured her? She took the creamer and poured; a conspicuous tremor had her nearly missing her mug. "And?"

His gaze drifted upward from her hands to her eyes, assessing her as if she were a suspect. "And we think we got your man."

Since his text message that morning, the bubble of anxiety that had been expanding inside her chest finally burst. He'd found her father? Her ears buzzed with heady excitement, nearly making her dizzy.

"My P.I. guy came up with a couple of hits close to the same birthday, but only one turned out to be a musician. This Victor Brown is fifty years old and plays saxophone."

"Yes. That's what my mother said. He was five or

six years older than her. That could be him." So keyed up, she knew she wouldn't be able to lift her coffee mug without spilling, so she let it sit untouched.

Gunnar took an extra-large bite of his muffin, swiped the tips of his fingers and the crumbs onto the plate then dug into his shirt pocket. He handed her a folded piece of notebook paper.

Could it be that easy? Hire a P.I.—find a long-lost father? She furrowed her eyebrows and took the paper.

He must have read her doubt. "The ballpark birth date is right on target. Course, it was a big help that he's lived in the same apartment for the last thirty years. Surprising, huh?"

She carefully unfolded the paper that held the key to her other half with no hope of hiding her quivering fingers.

"I can't legally run him without cause, so I don't know if he's had priors or not, but my P.I. guy said he checks out clean on his database. For what that's worth."

"Thank you. I appreciate it." She read her father's name, address and phone number. He still lived in Portland, two and a half hours away. Her pulse went a little haywire in her chest. Would she have the nerve to call him?

"So you do whatever you want. That's up to you," he said.

She felt like a heel, but had to ask. "Could you do me a favor and not mention this to Kent?"

Gunnar's brows lowered. "After he was the one to start the ball rolling?"

"This is very personal, Gunnar." The thought of contacting her father made her tremble inside. "I don't want Kent or Gerda to know just yet." *If I fail, if my father turns out to be a bust, I want to keep it to myself. No one else could possibly understand. Especially two people who want me to stay in Heartlandia. And since I might be falling in love with one of them...*

The last thought took her breath away. Was she in love with Kent?

Gunnar shoved the last bite of his muffin into his mouth and downed the rest of the coffee, waving for the waitress to refill his cup. "I don't like it, but it's your call." With his forearms against the edge of the table, he leaned in. "In case you haven't noticed, Kent Larson is one helluva great guy."

She nodded her agreement, not needing Sergeant Norling to point it out.

"There's nothing he won't do for the people he cares about."

She kept nodding. Gunnar was preaching to the choir about Kent. But she was more than his fan; she was his lover.

"He's been kicked in the teeth by his ex-wife, and the last thing he needs is to get kicked in the teeth again by you." He leaned even closer. She'd tried to avoid his eyes, but he wouldn't let her. His index finger shot up and poked the air. "You better not hurt him." He wadded up his napkin and tossed it on the table, then sat back against the red padded booth. "That's not a threat. It's just a friend looking out for his friend." He gave her a quick, obligatory smile that disappeared instantly.

Desi wasn't about to let Gunnar rattle her any more than she already was. "I understand. But I've got to find my father, and I don't want to upset Kent for nothing. I may not even be able to reach Victor. He may not want to see me. I just need some time to figure out how to handle this, and I don't want anyone influencing me. This was between my mother and me, and I'm not even sure she wanted me to search for him. She only told me about him because she thought it was the right thing to do. That I had a right to know who my birth father was. You know?"

Desi searched Gunnar's eyes for a kernel of understanding, and thought she'd found it. "I need to go through this by myself," she whispered.

His lips made a tight line. "Like I said. He's my best friend, and I don't like to see him lied to. He's obviously crazy about you, but you've got to do what you gotta do."

As Gunnar stood, taking charge of the meeting by ending it, Desi glanced up. "Thank you. Thank you so much." She put the paper in her shoulder bag and followed him outside.

How can he know if Kent is crazy about me? And by keeping this information about my father a secret, am I lying by omission to him?

To say Gunnar made an imposing picture in his uniform didn't come close. The guy oozed authority, and Desi knew the last thing on earth she'd ever want to incur was the wrath of Sergeant Norling. But she'd come too far to abandon her plans. Finding her father had been equally important as getting to know her grandmother. She couldn't stop now. This was her life journey, and she had to walk it.

She watched from the sidewalk as Gunnar got into his squad car, nodded a goodbye and drove off. If only he could understand.

Could anyone appreciate the huge significance of finally meeting her father, besides her?

Instead of running to a quiet place and punching in the numbers on her cell phone, Desi fought off the surge of nerves throughout her body, and she was suddenly consumed with the desire to find Cliff and tell him her news. Having the support of an understanding person was good, and she didn't have to go through this entirely alone. If she needed an ally in her quest, someone to give her the courage to follow through, Cliff, a man with nothing at stake, was the one.

She hustled down three blocks to Lincoln's Place and scooted around back to the kitchen door. Thank God, he was there.

"What's up, buttercup?" Always happy to see her, Cliff welcomed her in as he stood behind a chopping board.

"I've found him."

He stopped chopping. "Your daddy?"

She nodded, digging out the paper, waving it around. "I've got his phone number and address right here. I'm so nervous I could puke."

"Not in my kitchen, sugar." He walked toward her, and she ached for his support. He wrapped his arm around her shoulders and took the paper. "Mr. Victor Brown. Mm-mm-mm." He rubbed her arm. "I'm a big jazz fan, and I've never heard of him. But that doesn't matter. When you gonna call?"

She leaned her head against Cliff's shoulder. "Would you mind if I called him from here?"

"Course not. We're friends, aren't we?"

She sighed. "Thank you." Not only was Cliff a new friend, but he was also a mentor, and besides her mother, Desi had been short on mentors throughout her twenty-eight years.

Taking the biggest leap of faith in her life, she pressed the first four digits on her cell phone. "Oh, God, I'm so nervous."

Cliff pulled her closer. "Go on, little sister. You can do it. Give your daddy a call."

She pressed the remaining digits, and then on the third ring a gravelly voice answered, "Yeah?" sounding like the phone woke him.

"Is this Victor Brown?" She flashed a fearful glance at Cliff. He gave an encouraging nod.

"Who's this?"

"My name is Desdemona Rask, the daughter of Ester Rask. Do you remember her?"

A long pause ensued, followed by shuffling of what was probably sheets and blankets, the sound of a lighter flicking, a long, slow inhalation of a cigarette and then an exhalation. "I don't know that name."

Desi's heart, so full of hope, dropped to her stomach like a lead ball. With Cliff's physical support, she stayed standing, dug deep into her well of strength and began her story. How her mother was a huge music fan. How she sneaked off to Portland several times to hear him when he played with Trevor Jones, the late, great jazz pianist. She heard Cliff acknowledge Trevor Jones's name. "Uh-huh."

But Victor kept quiet, making her wonder if he'd fallen back to sleep.

Desi continued on. She told him how Ester got pregnant, ran away from home and how she gave Desi Victor's name just before she died. "She said you were my father. That you were the only African-American man she'd ever been with."

More silence. Desi could barely breathe, his hesitation squeezed so tight around her chest.

"So what do you want from me?" he said, matter-of-factly, taking another long draw on his cigarette.

Viselike tension made it hard to form the words. "I'd like to meet you."

Chapter Eleven

That night, slowly emerging from an intense orgasm orchestrated by Kent's mouth and tongue, Desi wanted to come clean. She wanted to tell him about finding her father and the meeting she'd arranged for Friday afternoon. But she'd promised to make that journey by herself. She couldn't possibly know what the outcome might be and didn't want to upset him for nothing.

His hands bracketed her temples as he leaned on one elbow and delved deeply into her eyes. "You know what's crazy?" he said, slaying her with a dark, sexy stare.

She shook her head, still reeling from his magic, amazed by the wealth of feeling, physical and emotional, he'd gifted her. She'd never felt this way about a man before. "What?" came her barely audible reply.

His thick ridge nudged at her entrance, and she

opened her legs for him. The tip prodded her, instantly sparking renewed desire.

He edged deeper inside, his eyes still locked onto hers. She was his. His lids slipped closed in a blissful expression for a moment as they both adjusted to the physical paradise they'd come to know and share so regularly.

"You feel so damn good, Desi."

"That's not crazy. That's just good. You and me. We're good," she said, pushing her hips against him, unable to deny the truth. He was good for her, and though she wasn't sure how loving a man felt, she thought she loved him. All the more reason to finally find out who she was. Until she met her father and found out about her African-American roots, she'd always feel a part of her was missing, and how could she give Kent all of her when she wasn't yet whole?

He brushed her mouth, and she recognized her own taste on his lips. "We're damn good," he said as he moved inside her then teased and backed out a notch. Her eyelids fluttered closed as a wave of sizzling shivers raced to her core. "What's crazy is— Desi, look at me."

It took all the final threads of willpower to stop focusing on the feelings he'd set off and open her eyes and look into his heavy-lidded gaze. When she did, she saw raw desire there. That look pushed her pulse, invading it with heat that burned southward to their sex.

"Even though it's only been a couple of weeks, I've fallen for you." His eyes scanned her face in a desperate fashion. "I think about you all the time. Can't wait to hold you like this every night." He pushed deeper inside, driving her crazy, making it impossible to take in the significance of his words. "I need you."

She'd heard him correctly. He needed her. The phrase wreaked havoc with her pulse and caused her breasts to tighten and tingle. She'd never been needed before by a man. Ever.

"I'm crazy about you, too." Desi could hardly speak, she was so overcome with Kent's confession and her own deepening feelings for him.

She wrapped her thighs around his waist and they joined as close as humanly possible, rocking and jutting, changing up the rhythm until nothing but blistering desire took hold.

"I love you," he said, his mouth over her ear as he thrust deep.

She gasped. The splintering intensity from his declaration and their lovemaking nearly stole her words. He loved her, and she loved him. "I love you, too," she said on a breath, hugging his back.

Several minutes later, as he drove her over the edge to ecstasy, she hung on tight, savoring every sensation coursing and pummeling through her, holding on to Kent as if she might lose him. Never wanting to let go.

Afterward, they clung together in sweat and twisted sheets. He nuzzled and kissed her cheek. "You know what I think?"

"What?"

"That everything is pretty much perfect the way it is. You and me. Together. Steven will love having you around all the time."

"What are you saying, Kent?"

He took a slow inhalation then let it out close to her ear. "That the three of us can make our own family."

She didn't answer right away, sensing he wanted her to drop her plans, picking up on his fear of possibly losing her to a dream, like he had his ex-wife. But wasn't that exactly what she searched for—her family? She needed to find the total picture of where she'd come from, before she'd be free to be a family with Kent and Steven.

Did Kent want to marry her? Shack up? That didn't seem his style. Where exactly were they headed? If she could only figure out what she needed versus what she wanted. Right now Kent was it. He'd said the words, and she'd finally admitted out loud that she loved him back.

The frenzied questions flew through her mind. Until she could formulate her thoughts, she didn't dare broach the subject of being a family with Kent.

Giving in to exhaustion, she yawned. "I love what you're saying, baby, but let's be fair and tackle this topic when we're both rested up, okay?"

"Stay with me." It wasn't a question.

And she did, until the break of dawn, when she kissed him on the forehead and slipped across the yard to her grandmother's house.

She wanted to be everything he deserved, but until she finally found out her entire history, she'd forever be half of her whole. How could she give the man she loved half of herself when he deserved everything?

Friday afternoon, Desi sat at a table near the windows at Milo's City Cafe on Northeast Broadway in Portland, working on her second cup of coffee. It had taken over two and a half hours to get here due to city traffic, and she'd had to park at the Lloyd Center and walk over.

She'd told Gerda she wanted to spend a day shopping at the trendy mall and would be home too late for dinner. Since her uncle Erik had invited her to dinner the night before, she hadn't seen Kent since Wednesday night. When he'd told her he loved her and mentioned about them being a family. She loved Kent—God, she loved him—and Steven had stolen her heart the first day they'd met.

While Kent was at work on Thursday, she'd followed a whim and, after mailing the finished calligraphy invitations, paid another visit to the community college. Knowing a man loved her made her do crazy things. But her visit had been twofold. Gerda had spoken about Elke Norling deciphering the pirate journals, and curiosity drove Desi to get a visitor pass to sit in on one of her history courses. History of Heartlandia 101.

The young blonde bore a strong facial resemblance to Gunnar, but where Gunnar was macho and worldly, Elke dressed beyond her years, hiding a nice figure in stereotypical bookworm fashion. Where he was built like a rugby player, she was petite and fragile looking. But Elke's love of Heartlandia and the subject of the day—the influence of the Chinook native dwellers on Heartlandia's birth—caused Desi's chest to clutch.

What must it be like to be part of a place you love with all of your heart?

Desi clicked back into the here and now at the diner and checked her watch. Ten minutes to two. Victor had said he'd meet her at one. She'd ordered a piece of homemade apple pie to kill time and had only picked at the crust.

The waitress stopped by. "Don't you like it?"

"I'm just not hungry," Desi answered lamely, suspecting she'd insulted the waitress and Milo's fresh-baked-pie reputation before the middle-aged lady in standard diner uniform swept the plate away.

Hunger was the last thing on her mind, even as her stomach rumbled in protest. There was no way she could eat. Especially now, when the man purported to be her father had stood her up. Maybe he got the time wrong. Or worse, maybe he wanted nothing to do with her.

Her insides were tighter than a knotted and coiled rope. She looked around the clean, slick version of a family diner. Throughout the midcentury modern building, everyone seemed happy and deep in conversation over their food, and here she was, staring at her watch. Waiting.

To be on the safe side, Desi had only told Gunnar she'd be at the café. Guessing Gerda would tell Kent she'd gone shopping in Portland if he asked where she was, she hoped it wouldn't spark concern. After all, Kent was the person who'd started the ball rolling on finding Victor Brown. He knew Victor's last-known address was right here in Northeast Portland. Kent would put two and two together. Desi kept her fingers crossed he'd be wrapped up with work all day, followed by Friday-night pizza and video with Steven, and he wouldn't connect the dots.

She pumped her booted foot and took another sip of lukewarm coffee. How long should she wait? She speed-dialed Victor's phone. It went directly to voice mail. Great. He wasn't the least bit interested in meeting her, just like Cliff had warned.

Damn it.

She asked for a warm-up on her coffee, and just as

the waitress poured from the fresh pot, a text message came through.

Desi's pulse nearly jumped out of her chest as she read. Gig came up. Meet another day?

Devastation grabbed her by her shoulders and shook. She fisted her hands, fighting off tears.

Talk about not being interested.

How was she supposed to respond to his text? *No problem. I like to waste time. Aren't you interested in meeting your own daughter?*

Another text came through. How about Monday? Same time.

Desi paid her bill, went to the bathroom and freshened up, feeling like nothing more than an afterthought to the man, and only then begrudgingly responded, O.K.

She stepped out onto the heavily tree-lined avenue of Northeast Broadway and nearly stumbled. Another text, this one from Kent— Where are you?

In Portland.

I'm on NE Broadway. Where is Milo's City Cafe?

He was here? In Portland? She checked up and down the street, suddenly winded, as if she'd run a mile. Kent was half a block away. He strode toward her, something simmering in him.

Anxiety rippled through Desi. Gerda had given her up without a second thought, and Gunnar had probably helped Kent zero in on his mark. Why couldn't those people mind their own business?

A tiny thought planted in her brain. *Because they care about you. They told him because they care.* Victor obviously didn't give a damn, but at least he'd re-scheduled.

Desi swallowed as Kent came within hugging distance. Up close, the determined expression resembled hurt, the same emotion she was feeling from being stood up by her father.

"You didn't have any intention of letting me know why?" Kent said.

"This is between me and my father." Her knees were wobbly, but she'd stand her ground no matter how hard it was. "I didn't want to worry you, and it's important to me that I meet him."

"Worry me?" he said with a tight jaw and searching eyes.

"I didn't want to involve you because—"

"Did you even hear what I said the other night?" His voice was low and measured.

"Yes, but…"

"When I told you I loved you?"

"Yes, of course…"

"You said it back to me. Did you mean it?" His brows shot up in doubt. "Or was it just an obligatory reply?"

Could she explain how terrified she was of admitting her feelings to Kent, because it changed everything? "It's not that I don't care, because I do. Deeply. I love you, but—"

"Don't play me, Desi." His gaze delved into hers, giving her time to take in what he'd intimated, and it felt awful. "When people love each other they don't keep secrets."

"Kent, please understand."

"I'm trying, but this doesn't make a lot of sense. You

tell me you love me, we talk about getting involved, then you sneak off."

"I've been honest with you from the start. The question is, have you been listening?"

"Yes, but for me, the big question is—" his tense voice softened in tone "—do you realize what you might be running to and leaving behind?" After searching her eyes, causing her to blink, Kent scanned the area. "Where is he?"

Now she'd have to admit her defeat in front of the man she'd only just begun to love. "Didn't show." Tiny pinpricks started behind her lids.

Kent's expression softened. "I'm sorry," he said, and she believed it as he gently grasped her upper arm. "Are you ready to come home, then?"

He wanted her to give up, just like that? Did he think she was a child? She yanked her arm from his grasp and started down the street. Couldn't he understand her lifelong need to be in touch with her father's side? "We rescheduled for Monday. I've decided to stay here for the weekend."

He followed, nearly nipping at her boot heels. She knew her plans wouldn't sit well with Kent and quickened her stride until they reached an empty lot.

"Don't treat me like I'm Steven." She spun around and nailed him with all the frustration tangling her up inside.

His pained look returned. Her selfish quest had hurt Kent—the guy who wanted to protect his son from women like her—and the man did a great job of wearing his feelings on his sleeve.

But could she blame him?

She wanted to take all the anger she felt for Victor

right this moment and throw it at Kent, but he didn't deserve it. The man had been through hell and back in the past couple of years, what with his wife taking off and leaving him to raise Steven by himself. Here she was, adding to the pile.

But she couldn't back off. "If you think you can treat me like a kid because you care about me, it won't fly."

He kept his distance, dug his hands into his back pockets. "Look, I understand your need to meet this guy."

"My father," she corrected him.

"Your birth father." He took a slow breath. "I'm just asking for some honesty and consideration. That is, if you care about me at all."

She did care about him. "You know I do."

Hell, she loved him, but right now he was playing the martyr and pushing her way out of her comfort zone. She wanted to say thank-you for giving a damn and that she was sorry but she had to do what she had to do. But her tongue had gone into hiding and her throat closed. Why did everything have to be so freaking mixed-up?

He swiped fingers through his hair. "The thing is, I can't be the second choice to some guy who rescheduled. I've been through that already, and I'm no fool. Won't go there again."

She understood his angle, but he needed to give her some consideration, too. Instead he wielded a martyred sword that sliced through her heart.

Riled again, she shot back, "Are you giving me an ultimatum?"

"I'm asking you to come home with me."

She went still and spoke softly. "I need to do this my way." She needed time to herself without pressure from the people she cared about in Heartlandia trying to influence her decision.

Their gazes knotted in a standoff.

His arms went wide, palms lifted, imploring. "Damn, I knew what you planned to do all along and I still fell for you." He looked like a defeated man, his eyes drooping, shoulders hunched. "I should never have kissed you, Desi. I should have held my ground and stayed that uptight dude telling you to stay away from my son." There was pleading and love in his eyes. "But I couldn't resist you and took it a helluva lot further than kissing." He approached, played with the curls of hair around her shoulders as if he'd never seen or touched them before. "I walked right into your beauty and charms and fell for you, and now I feel like a fool."

He'd taken a knife to her core and sliced right through, pain penetrating every nerve. She'd hurt him, the only man who'd ever really cared about her. She shook her head, her blurred vision making him into a melting hero. She could barely utter *sorry*.

"You're not a fool," she managed to get out.

"Then what am I? You tell me."

"You're a good man who I've been lucky enough to meet." One thing was clear—she didn't deserve him, not when she'd already hurt him and all he wanted was the best for her.

Kent straightened, pulling himself together. His eyes flashed with thoughts, his jaw twitched, biting them back, but he wouldn't stop. "You don't need some stranger to tell you who you are. You need to look inside to find that out. If that's not enough, look to Gerda, to your uncle and aunt, to Heartlandia." He gave a wan smile. "Here's a good one—look to Steven and me. You want to find out who you are then we've all got the answers. You don't need this guy who doesn't show up. Who hasn't ever shown up."

"Stop it. Just stop right there. Don't tell me how to think or what to say. This is my issue and we aren't going to solve it on your terms. Can't you try to understand what this means to me?"

He pinched the bridge of his nose, as if his head was ready to explode. "I'm trying, Desi. I'm trying, but I just don't get it."

"No, you're not trying. You're trying to bulldoze me into doing things your way." She glanced at him as the hint of chagrin changed his stern expression. "You don't have to get it. Just let me work things out on my own terms. Can you do that?"

More mixed-up than ever whether this was the right thing to do or not—was Victor Brown worth it?—she stood determined. There was no going back on this quest.

"Come home with me." His words were quiet and controlled as he tested her.

She dug in her heels and, full of fear and misgivings, went for it. "Please, Kent. Give me some time to discover the rest of myself." She touched his arm, engaging his stressed and weary eyes. "I do love you—please know that. And I'm not like your ex-wife." She'd played dirty, struck a chord, and his gaze faltered. "I need this. I need to meet my father." She touched his other arm and squeezed both. "That's all I'm asking, and I need you to understand that."

They shared a silent deadlock. She thought of another angle to get through to him. "If you love me, you have to trust me. Let me stay here, see this out."

His jaw tensed and his Adam's apple bobbed in a slow, silent swallow. "How long?"

Maybe she'd gotten through to him. Maybe he finally understood how this meeting went to the root of her whole being. "Until I finally know for sure who I am. Until I find out about all of me."

That could take forever. Kent shook his head in defeat. Every sinew and cell in his body ached. He'd lost her, and he'd only just fallen for her. She asked for the one thing he wasn't prepared to give. Trust. Not yet, anyway.

She'd asked him to trust her. It seemed just out of his reach, beyond any capability to ever trust a woman again. Diana had made sure of that. She'd started out the same way, little fun visits to San Francisco, soon needing her S.F. fix at least once a month, then she moved on to her monthly girls' week of shopping there. Hell, she'd even planned a week's vacation in San Francisco when she knew Kent couldn't get away from the Urgent Care. Then she dropped the bomb about them moving. Turned out she'd been seeing a real-estate agent, looking for the perfect house. Had plans to put Steven in boarding school. And when he said no, she left and never came back. Now she worked for that guy and probably lived with him, too.

If he left Desi in Portland, it might be the beginning to her never coming back. Her seeking her past could make history repeat itself for him. Talk about lousy timing. He wanted to kick himself for letting down his guard and falling in love with her. He wanted to cuss every foul word he'd ever learned. He'd known better from the start, yet, because he didn't have a clue how to do casual, he'd let it happen, fallen in love, head over heels. Like a complete fool.

He did love her, which was why right now, this instant, he had to prove it to her by taking the hardest test of his life. He had to take her at her word, risk trusting her, once again trusting a woman he loved. Would it end up the way it had with Diana, or was this the only way to prove to Desi he wasn't just saying words when he'd said "I love you"?

"I'm just two and a half hours away. It's not like I'm halfway around the world," she said.

"The way I feel right now, you may as well be."

"I won't shut you out, Kent. I promise."

She said she needed this. He saw the driven expression in her eyes pleading for his understanding. He had to believe how important this was for her. He studied her, saw a woman with tortured determination written all over her beautiful face. She wouldn't back down, and there was something else he noticed—she needed his trust as much as she needed this Victor person to show up.

If he loved her, he couldn't demand her to come home with him like he wanted with every fiber in his body. He had to be bigger than his insecurity.

He rubbed his beard. "Okay. We'll do it your way." It came out gruffer than he'd meant, but her expression brightened anyway.

"I promise, no matter what, I'll be back in Heartlandia by Monday night." Her beautiful mahogany eyes danced while she spoke.

Kent had to believe her. He couldn't let his worst fears take hold. Not right now. Yet the thought of losing

Desi gripped his core and nearly squeezed the breath out of him.

He loved her and wanted the best for her, and in his mind that meant her being with him...yet her eyes shone through the disappointment today.

She'd told him right from the start she was looking for her father. There was no guessing what might happen until she actually met him. This meeting might mean getting to know a whole different family and spending time with them, and that could change everything.

But she needed him to be on her side. The least he could do was give her hope, something he felt slipping through his grasp. Her father better not stand her up again or Kent would find him and deliver his message personally.

Because he loved her, he forced his fingers to relax and nodded, doing the toughest thing he'd ever had to do: pretend he could deal with this and trust she'd still want him. "Okay. Good luck. See you Monday."

Kent kissed Desi lightly, barely holding himself together, and turned to leave.

She'd promised to come back to Heartlandia, but when she did, depending on what went down with her father, it might be only the first step toward saying goodbye.

Chapter Twelve

Desi spent the weekend at an inexpensive motel, using the one and only credit card she kept for emergencies. She'd paid off her mother's medical bills by selling the house, had been living on the grace of her grandmother and until now had been able to meet her personal expenses with her calligraphy money and posing for the art class. She could count on being paid soon for the invitations she'd finished and mailed before leaving for Portland, which would help pay for the motel.

She'd called her grandmother Friday night, after she'd calmed down from her encounter with Kent. Then she told a little white lie about loving the city and wanting to stick around for the weekend, see more of the sights. Mostly, she stayed in her room and thought.

Thinking about Kent roiled up so many emotions that she didn't know what to do. Thoughts of her grandmother made her wish they'd devoured all of those boxes of pictures and mementos about her mother. Somehow, they'd never gotten back to walking memory lane after Gerda's medical episode and escalating mayoral duties.

As she anticipated her meeting with her father later that afternoon, jitters set in. A million questions whirled around her head. Would he even show up?

She held a hopeful fantasy that he'd greet her with the same open arms her grandma had, invite her into his life and share his relatives—her relatives—with her. Maybe he'd ask her to go on the road with him sometime, not that she would. She'd had enough of that with her mother while growing up, but being asked would be nice. Finally, she'd learn about her African-American heritage. Be a part of it. Own it. Know who she was and where she'd come from. Finally, she'd come face-to-face with her other half. If he did open up to her, she couldn't just walk away from the offer.

That was what Kent must have picked up on before—her desperate need to discover her living family and learn the culture. To finally become two halves of a whole. To understand why, no matter how much she loved her mother, she'd always felt different from her. She needed to face her other half and embrace it, and Kent somehow sensed that would take her away.

If he loved her, wouldn't he want that for her? Or was she being totally selfish?

And if she was being selfish, would he wait for her to come back? The thought of losing him sent a shudder through her.

She packed the few items she'd brought with her to Portland after putting on the same jeans and boots she'd worn for the past three days. Saturday, she'd crossed the Willamette River and gone to the Portland Art Museum. Yesterday, she'd found a flea market in the Northeast Broadway neighborhood and splurged on a new top. The zebra-patterned top had a drawstring neckline and loose, three-quarter sleeves. She'd found a clunky handmade necklace made out of huge green and turquoise buttons, with a matching bracelet to add some color. All at a great price. She parted her hair down the middle and let it go curlier than usual. How was a girl supposed to dress to meet her father for the first time in twenty-eight years?

After she checked out from the motor lodge, she drove back to Northeast Broadway and began her search for a parking spot, then wandered the trendy area on foot until it was time to meet her dad. Could she call him Dad? Wasn't that something a person would call a man they knew instead of a stranger? Maybe after today…

Milo's was packed with the lunch crowd at twelve forty-five. She put in her name for a table and waited outside on a bench with several other people. The day was clear and warm, and she closed her eyes to let the sun calm her.

Late last night she'd made her peace with the probability that this meeting, if it actually occurred, would be awkward and most likely disappointing. Just like Cliff had warned. She'd also decided that if Victor Brown didn't show up today, she'd let it be and not try to contact him again. She wasn't dense. If he didn't come today, she'd know he didn't give a rip about her. Yet she still held out hope.

"Desi?" a gravelly voice said near her.

Her eyes flew open to find a tall, thin man in jeans and a black leather jacket and gray T-shirt with Montreux

Jazz Festival 2010 splashed across his narrow chest. What did she expect—a dashiki with a kufi cap? Victor Brown stood in front of her, and she finally knew from whom she'd gotten her freckles. The man's dark bronze face was splattered with them.

"Yes. Hi," she said, fighting off the rush of tingling nerves and standing to shake his hand.

He bypassed her hand and gave her a friendly hug. He smelled of tobacco and biting cologne. He didn't hold her long, and the hug wasn't really affectionate or inviting, but more like a professional guy who knew how to greet people to make them feel welcomed. A smooth operator.

"I'm Vic. Let me have a look at you." His birth date made him fifty, and the roadmap of wrinkles on his face bore that out. Those nearly black eyes were friendly and warm. His wide smile revealed smoker's teeth. Tight black hair was kept short and clean-cut with silver strands here and there. He had a soul patch but no other facial hair, expensive-looking diamond studs in both ears and wore several huge rings on both hands. "Damn, you're a looker." He laughed and it turned into a cough.

After warding off an icky feeling from her birth father's first reaction to her, she forced a smile. "Thanks."

A moment or two of awkward silence followed. "So how you been?" he asked, all upbeat. "That's lame, isn't it? I should say, where do we begin?" His voice reminded her of the actor Samuel L. Jackson.

"I know," she said. "How *do* we start?"

The waitress saved them another uneasy moment by calling Desi's name for a table. Suddenly all business, they followed her inside and found their spot, quickly ordering coffee and focusing on the menu instead of each other.

Desi thought of ten different ways to start a conversation, but Victor beat her to the punch. "You live around here?"

"No. My mother and I last lived in the Los Angeles area." She zeroed in on him. "Do you remember my mother yet?"

His glance skipped around like a man put on the spot. Desi dug into her purse for a photo that Gerda had given her, the high school senior picture. She showed it to him, figuring it would make the most sense, being the one closest to when he'd known her. He took it and studied, and Desi watched as she imagined he recognized Ester and maybe flashed through some special memories.

But he shook his head slowly. "She's beautiful, and you'd think I'd remember a woman like that, but..."

Desi took back the picture, awash in disappointment. "It was a long time ago." How many gorgeous blondes had the guy been with? "About twenty-nine years." She waited for him to look at her. "I'm twenty-eight."

He rubbed his face, a hint of regret in his eyes. "Look, I've traveled around the world half a dozen times. I'm in different clubs every other week when I work. I get on airplanes and show up in cities in time for the gigs, play all night, sleep all day, then move on to the next job. Most of my life is a blur. You know what I'm sayin'?"

She could understand his point. Hell, maybe there were hundreds of Desis around the globe, too.

"My mother met you when you were playing with Trevor Jones right here in Portland."

He made an exaggerated nod. "Mmm. Yes. I worked

with him for a couple of years. Best money I ever made until he died in that car crash."

The waitress showed up and took their orders, giving Desi time to regroup from the letdown. *Remember, Cliff told you to expect this.*

"Mom was a pretty young blonde who loved music."

"Mmm, known a few of those, too." He evaded her eyes, pouring two packets of sugar into his coffee, started to stir then stopped. "Look, I don't mean to disappoint you, but even though your mother is a gorgeous woman and all, I don't—"

"Was."

He looked up, a question in his eyes.

"She died last year. She'd played piano in so many hotels and bars over the years, the best I can figure is she got lung cancer from secondhand smoke, because she never smoked."

"Your momma was a musician?"

"Ester Rask was known throughout the Midwest as one of the best hotel and piano-bar musicians in the country." The old, familiar pride welled up in Desi's chest as she talked about her mother, whom she loved with all of her heart, and her mother's talent. She'd had a worldwide and centuries-old songbook memorized right inside her head. Throw her a title and she'd play it with practiced perfection. "But she never caught her break. You know?"

"Tell me about it. I've scraped by barely making a living most of my life, playing sax in the background of all the greats. I'll be fifty-one this November and I'm working as hard now as when I was twenty-five."

The waitress delivered their omelets and Victor salted his heavily. "There's no money in this field unless you hit it big. I'm just a backup man." He reached for the ketchup. "Don't get me wrong, I love what I do. I just make enough for me. That's all."

He squinted one eye and trained his gaze squarely on her. "So if this is about money…"

Anger flashed through Desi. She bit back the first words she thought and the curses. No need to insult the man. "Not what I'm after."

Things went quiet and tension counted out the next minute or two as they both dived into their food. He ate with gusto, a free bird in the world of responsibilities. She mostly moved her potatoes and eggs around the plate.

"Are you married?" She wasn't ready to give up yet.

Victor pushed out his bottom lip and shook his head. "No, ma'am. Not my style. The world is my home and whatever band I'm working with, my family."

She was beginning to see a pattern here. No strings. No commitments. Just his saxophone, music and the road. He probably had women he hooked up with in every city he worked—his regulars. She stopped her bitter thoughts before they could eat away at her and ruin what little of her appetite was left. *Keep it light. Find out what you can.* Wasn't that her plan? "Do you have family here in Oregon?"

"Nah. Mom and Dad are both dead. I've got a brother somewhere back in North Carolina. Haven't seen him in years. My sister lives in Colorado. Sometimes I go to Denver for Christmas, when I'm in the country."

Truth was, his lifestyle seemed a little sad and very lonely.

"Do you have any pictures of your brother and sister?" *My aunt and uncle?* "And their kids?" *My cousins.*

He screwed up his face. "Nah. I know what they look like. Least I used to." He kept shoving food into his mouth, eating as if there were no tomorrow.

"How about your mom and dad—what did they do?"

"The old man sold cars, and my momma was a book-keeper. We got by okay." Now he started on his toast and slathered it with blackberry jam nearly half an inch thick. He'd stopped talking, obviously having no intention of sharing anything about his heritage.

She was searching for her history and he just didn't get it. Every answer revolved around him and what he did or thought. When it came to talking about his roots, he got tight-lipped. The fact that he had no clue what she needed gave her pause.

Desi abandoned that line of questioning and diverted the conversation to things Victor could brag about by asking about all the musicians he'd worked with. Pride shone through his face, and she heard it in his voice as he ran down the long list of music-related accomplishments.

She had to admit he'd played with some greats, and she was impressed with his solid star-power credentials. But now what? The man hadn't asked one question about her personally.

"Sorry I had to stand you up the other day," he said. "I take studio jobs whenever I can get them, and a commercial jingle came up." He nailed her with his penetrating dark eyes. "That's the name of the game. You pick up work, make money when you can. Can't always get another gig lined up before you finish another." He used his butter knife like a pointer stick. "I go through dry spells and have to live off what little savings I have. So, again, if this is about money…"

She let out an exasperated sigh. "I told you, I'm not after anything. I just hoped to find out about my African-American roots."

He laughed. It turned into another phlegmy cough. "Well, from what I learned in school, we came over in boats." He noticed how badly that comment had gone over. "My people moved out west from Mississippi back in the fifties. That's all I've got for you." He pushed his chair back from the table. "I need a cigarette. Be right back."

Desi watched his cool stroll toward the door. He was what he was, and there wasn't anything much he cared to share with her. She lost the last inkling of her appetite and put down her fork.

All her life she'd heard the phrase *blood is thicker than water* and took it to mean the bonds between relatives were closer, stronger than friends. She imagined how it would be to have a big family. Longed for it. She took a sip of water. The saying seemed upside down to her. Sure, the bond she and her mother had was broken only by death. But looking at the man outside sucking smoke into his lungs, the one who couldn't even remember doing the deed the night Desi was conceived, she felt...well...nothing. Absolutely nothing. Yet some of his blood ran through her veins.

Desi thought about her grandma Gerda. It was a whole different story. Relatives needed to *want* to be close, not stay connected just because they shared the same DNA. In Victor's case, their DNA meant squat. He was a complete stranger. Why would he want anything to do with a daughter at this late stage in his life? So far he hadn't offered one reason to pursue one another, and she couldn't really blame him, not with the life he led.

Now he was on his cell phone, and it reminded her about the text message Kent had sent that morning. I hope you find what you're looking for then come back to me.

It had made her cry then and thinking about it almost started her up again now. All she could think to say in return was I hope I do, too. Talk about noncommittal. Hell, she could give Victor Brown a run for his money on that one. Quickly dabbing the corners of her eyes, she hoped Victor wouldn't notice now that he was heading back inside.

Nah, that saying about blood and water was all sideways. Love was thicker than blood, and just because she shared the man's DNA didn't make him family. Hell, Cliff was closer to her than the man sitting back down across the table.

Kent's handsome face came to mind again, the man she'd fallen in love with. She made a rueful smile. Then, knowing that he loved and waited for her, the smile changed into a grin straight from her heart.

"What you so happy about?" Victor asked.

"I'm just thinking about my friends."

"That's all we've got, you know?" He sat sideways on his chair, going philosophical on her.

She nodded in agreement. He reached into his wallet, pulled out some cash. She reached for her purse.

"Let me get this," he said. "It's the least I can do." He smiled at her with his Morgan Freeman complexion and gentle eyes. "I do remember your momma. I had a cigarette and did some thinking. I remember. But it wasn't like we really knew each other or anything. You know what I mean?"

Feeling a blush come on—yes, she got the one-night stand part—Desi smiled awkwardly. "I get it. Thanks."

"If it's any consolation, I did try to look her up again, but it was like she'd disappeared."

Well, she had.

"Here's my card," he said, sliding all the information she'd probably ever know about Victor Brown across the table. "I'm leaving for a month in Japan this Friday, but maybe when I get back we can talk again."

"That would be nice. Thank you. Oh, and here's my card. Well, it's my business card for the small calligraphy side jobs I do."

He took it, looking less than impressed.

"I play the piano, too. Like my mother. In fact, I'm thinking of taking a job playing in a restaurant where I'm living now."

"That's good. Real good. Maybe I'll come out and hear you sometime."

"Sure."

She realized she didn't want to share Heartlandia with Victor. Not yet, anyway. Maybe when he got back from Japan she'd give him a call if he didn't call her. Give him one more chance to reach out to her. If he didn't, she'd cut her losses.

She stood and he joined her, the distance between them growing wider by the second. He had things to do and places to go. Thank God, so did she.

After Victor kissed her cheek, making her nose twitch with his potent cologne, and they said their tepid goodbyes, she walked back to her car. It would be a long drive home and she'd need the time to digest everything that had happened.

Home.

She thought about Heartlandia with the silly town slogan: Find Your Home in Heartlandia. It didn't seem quite so silly now, though; it suddenly had taken on a whole new meaning. It was a place where she could see herself putting down roots. Her own roots.

Her steps sped up into a jog as she thought about Kent.

Had she blown it with the man she loved? She prayed she hadn't broken his heart by refusing to go back with him Friday, though if he loved her the way he'd said, she probably had.

Maybe he'd finally understand her hell-bent need to face her father once she told him the whole story. From now on, if he'd still have her, she'd tell him everything. Everything.

She ran the last half block to her parked car and stumbled with one worrisome thought.

Would Kent forgive her?

There was only one way to find out. She had to go back and face him on his own turf and somehow make him know that her wandering days were over, because she'd found her family. Grandma. How could she begin to thank her for taking her in unconditionally? Kent. She sighed with the rush of memories connected to him like life and breath itself. And Steven, a little boy who missed and needed a mother figure…like a most excellent piano teacher.

She smiled to herself. Love *was* thicker than blood. Hands down.

After unlocking the car, she slid inside and sat straight. She'd met her other half and finally discovered something she'd kept hidden inside. Kind of like Dorothy in

The Wizard of Oz, turned out she'd known who she was all along. Just like Kent and Cliff had been telling her.

She was Ester Rask's kid from a hot one-night stand with Victor Brown, and Gerda and Edvard Rask's grand-daughter. She was every state and city she'd ever traveled through, every book she'd ever read and every crazy job she'd ever taken.

She was a homeschooled girl, a woman with potential, and what she wanted more than anything else on the earth right at this given moment was a home...with a ready-made family. Steven. And Kent. *Please take me back.*

She pulled out of the parking lot, pushed that 1992 gas pedal to the metal and put those treads to the road. Maybe she could beat the time it took to get to Portland on the way back.

Even if Kent didn't want her back today, she'd be prepared to stick around in Heartlandia until she could convince him that she was the best thing in the world for him. That she'd never leave again without him or his blessing. She'd strut around in sexy clothes and make the man drool until he caved and made love to her again.

Grinning wide, she put in her ear pods, and knowing Kent was at work, she speed-dialed Cliff to tell him the whole story about her long-lost father.

If she timed it right, she'd make it home before the administration office at the city college closed. She'd stop there first since Gerda would be at city hall.

Good thing she'd kept all of her options open before she'd left town on Friday.

Desi parked the car in the garage right before five that afternoon. She rushed inside the house to tell her grandmother how much she loved her and to get cleaned up before Kent came home from work.

Gerda wasn't home. Obviously she was still working at city hall today like every other Monday. She wandered to the kitchen and found a note on the island and next to it an empty medicine cup with dried antacid inside. Desi picked up the note, first glancing around the grand old kitchen she'd come to love, the heart of the house where she and Gerda met up each and every morning. She was glad to be home. So, so glad.

"I have some important town business to tend to. Don't wait up for me. Love, G."

Overwhelmed with fondness for her grandmother, Desi smiled as her eyes brimmed with tears. She picked up the empty medicine cup, worrying it might not be enough to deal with the burden of being a mayor with a big town secret and wondering what more they might find out about their pirate problem tonight.

She dashed upstairs and showered, then put on the colorful sundress she knew Kent liked, judging by the way he'd quickly ripped it off her one night last week. He usually got home around sixish on Mondays, but with his busy clinic she couldn't count on it. She took time to put on makeup and the sparkly pink lipstick Kent liked to stare at whenever she wore it…right before he'd kiss it off her.

There were a million things she wanted to share with Kent, but how should she approach him? She went outside and sat on the front porch on her favorite wicker seat with the purple-paisley-patterned pillow, needing time to gather her thoughts. Way off in the distance, over the homes, buildings and train station down by the docks, and under the long arching bridge to Washington, she glimpsed a section of sparkling teal-colored Columbia River. She'd never get tired of the view.

A bicycle whizzed by on the sidewalk, shaking her out of her thoughts. It was Steven, riding like the wind on his two-wheeler to God knew where. Her tummy jumped. Noticing her, he hit his brake and laid a skid mark on the sidewalk.

"Cool. Did you see that?" he asked, as if nothing had changed.

"That was something, all right. You planning on becoming a stunt man?"

"Nah. I'm gonna be a marine biologist and a famous musician. Where've you been?"

The kid always slayed her with his innocent wit. "I've been looking for my father."

"Why'd you want to do that?"

Desi shrugged.

"Steven!" From the front door, Kent's voice cut through her peace. Adrenaline fired scattershot inside her chest. He must have gotten home while she was showering.

"Coming. Desi's home!" Steven threw his leg over the bicycle seat and prepared to head back. "See ya," he said with certainty.

Desi stood even as her stomach dropped to what seemed like her toes. She hadn't a clue how to say everything she needed to tell Kent. He saw her and stepped outside, walking her way with assured steps. She fought off the urge to run and jump into his arms, and by his slowing pace, she figured she'd made the right decision in holding back. The man must need some extra time to work out all his thoughts and what he planned to say. Just like she did.

They were within three feet of each other. His cautious expression masked the handsome curves and angles of his face.

She couldn't hold her thoughts inside another second. "I love you," she blurted, diving point-blank into the heart of everything.

Those blue-as-the-Columbia-River eyes reacted to her words by widening almost imperceptibly. His mouth followed with a twitch at the corner.

"Can you forgive me for putting you through this?" She'd hit her stride now, her long list of things to tell him working their way out of her mouth through a tunnel from her heart. "Will you please trust me now when I say I intend to stay in Heartlandia?"

They were arm's length apart. She lifted her hands for him to take, but instead his hands came from beneath and merely touched the tips of her fingers as if testing if she were real. She wanted to grab him and never let go, but she understood his hesitation. She'd hurt him. Deeply.

"Did he show?"

She nodded.

"And…"

"It was okay. I'll tell you about it sometime. So do you trust me now?"

"If I trust you this time, what insurance do I have you won't leave again, later?"

Normally, she loved it when he played hard to get, but right now it irritated her. "You want proof?"

"Damn right I do." His hands had come to rest on his hips, like a pouting Nordic god.

She'd take that challenge.

"I'll be right back." Desi rushed up the walkway and the steps and into the house, knowing Kent watched her every move. "Don't move." She'd also noticed his immediate reaction to the dress when his gaze had started at her shoulders and followed all the way down to her sandaled feet. *Good call on the dress!*

"Did you get a note from your father or something?" he called out in an acerbic tone.

Just before she went inside the house, she made an exaggerated and playful turn. "Nice one, Larson. You been taking comedy lessons from Steven?"

He bit his lower lip rather than smile, then stared at her long and hard, waiting.

As she ran up the stairs to her bedroom, she marveled how his words would have hurt her if he'd said them before she'd gone to Portland, but right now his comment rolled off her back.

She'd finally figured out that she was good enough just the way she was. That she was exactly what he needed. She'd also learned who she was, imperfections and all, and who she loved and where she belonged and what she wanted to be and who she wanted to be with. And because of all those things, she could understand his hurt and anger about her leaving. His cutting remark just now came from being hurt, plain and simple. She'd walked away from him, and he'd been wiser than her, knowing everything she could possibly want or need had been right under her nose. Yet she couldn't see it. Not then.

She shuffled through the piles of papers on her desk. If she played her cards right, she and Kent would have plenty of tiffs down the road, because wasn't that part of being a couple? Working things out? She grinned. Making up would always be the fun part.

There it was. She'd thrown the printout on the desk

last Thursday, and when she'd paid today they'd given her a receipt, which she'd stapled to it. She grabbed the paper and her cell phone. She'd promised Cliff a final answer by the end of happy hour today.

Stepping outside, cell phone to her ear, she saw the look of confusion on Kent's face as she walked toward him. His brows shot together and the corner of his mouth hitched high. It made her smile even wider, and she approached Kent with the confidence of a model walking the runway. She held up a finger when Kent started to ask a question. One moment, she indicated. *Keep him waiting, but not for long.*

"Hello, Cliff? Hey, it's Desi. Okay, I'm in. I'm going to take the job at your restaurant."

"So li'l bit finally came to her senses," Cliff said in his droll manner.

"For the record, I expect to work for more than just tips."

"You got it. See you this Friday."

"See you then." She shut down her cell phone and dropped it into the large pocket on her full skirt. "See?" she said, engaging and holding Kent's gorgeous stare. "I just took that job. Can't very well go traipsing off here and there and hold down a job, too, can I?"

He stepped closer, looking much more convinced with a simmering expression taking hold and promising to soon change to smoldering. "No, you can't."

In her other hand, between her thumb and index finger, she flapped the paper printout in the air. "And I have more proof."

Now looking more relaxed by the instant, Kent played along. Without saying a word, he gestured with his fingers for her to come closer. His wish was her command. She stepped forward and tossed the paper at him.

"That's my enrollment form for twelve units at Heartlandia City College for the fall semester." He caught it with the finesse of a highly paid athlete. "I'll be majoring in art design with a minor in African-American studies. How about that?"

Kent took one glance at the list of classes and dropped the paper in order to take her into his arms. They hugged as if they hadn't seen each other in a year. Damn, he felt great. She wanted to tell him how excited she was to finally start college, but his incoming kiss stole her words.

I rest my case.

His mouth felt like a little piece of heaven on her lips. She went up on tiptoes and folded her arms around his shoulders, her hands caressing his neck. After a long and thorough welcome home, he pulled away.

"Now you'll be the one painting those nude models in the Life Art class, instead of modeling for them."

She nipped his chin and caught the corner of his mouth with a quick kiss, then, for the benefit of Steven being within earshot, she whispered into the shell of Kent's ear, "From now on, the only nude modeling I'll do is for you."

That got the exact reaction she'd hoped for. His second wave of kisses traced across her jaw and cheek, soon centering on her mouth again. She angled her head in a new direction to better capture his lips. His tongue had already shifted to *come play with me* mode.

"Wow, twelve whole units," Steven said nearby, having retrieved the paper and examined it. "What are 'units'?"

Laughter cut their escalating make-out session short.

Steven stood there waving the paper around, a perplexed look on his face.

"'Units' are what each class in college counts as. Twelve units equal four classes," Desi said. She held back on her need to explain to Kent that she'd decided to start at a reasonable pace and maybe take more classes in her second semester. Surely he'd understand.

"Does this mean you'll have lots of homework like me?"

Desi's eyes stayed trained on the man she loved as she answered Steven. "Yes, I'm going to have lots and lots of homework." She kissed Kent again, but only quickly. When she pulled back, his intense gaze let her know there would also be lots of making up to do for their lost weekend.

Warmth fanned out across her body, a response she'd have to get used to, being around Kent Larson day in and day out.

Steven grabbed her hand and then his father's. "Do you guys have to kiss so much? That's gross."

"Get used to it," Kent said as they walked together toward his house. "Stay for dinner with us?" He squeezed her hand.

"Love to. Gerda's running a council meeting. Won't be home until late." By the quick, satisfied glance he gave, he'd picked up on her hidden meaning. She offered her version of a Mona Lisa smile.

As Kent headed off toward the kitchen, and Steven ran for the keyboard, she followed the boy and helped him with his music lesson.

From the kitchen, she heard Kent call out, "Sandwiches okay?"

"Yes!" Steven said, as if having a sandwich for dinner was an extra-special treat.

"Fine with me," she chimed in. Who cared what he served? Everything tasted great when you were in love anyway.

Kent continued to bang around in the kitchen, and Steven showed Desi how he'd embellished his latest piano piece with some fancy finger work.

She took it all in, marveling how everything felt just right. Couldn't be more perfect.

Just like she'd always dreamed her first real home with her newfound family would be.

* * * * *

A sneaky peek at next month...

Cherish™

EXPERIENCE THE ULTIMATE RUSH OF FALLING IN LOVE

My wish list for next month's titles...

In stores from 18th July 2014:

❑ The Rebel and the Heiress — Michelle Douglas

& A Cowboy's Heart — Rebecca Winters

❑ Not Just a Convenient Marriage — Lucy Gordon

& The Billionaire's Nanny — Melissa McClone

In stores from 1st August 2014:

❑ A Wife for One Year — Brenda Harlen

& From Maverick to Daddy — Teresa Southwick

❑ A Groom Worth Waiting For — Sophie Pembroke

& Crown Prince, Pregnant Bride — Kate Hardy

Available at WHSmith, Tesco, Asda, Eason, Amazon and Apple

Just can't wait?

Visit us Online

You can buy our books online a month before they hit the shops! **www.millsandboon.co.uk**

0714/23

Special Offers

Every month we put together collections and longer reads written by your favourite authors.

Here are some of next month's highlights— and don't miss our fabulous discount online!

On sale 18th July

On sale 18th July

On sale 18th July

Save 20%
on all Special Releases

Find out more at
www.millsandboon.co.uk/specialreleases

Visit us Online

0814/ST/MB487

Discover more romance at

www.millsandboon.co.uk

- ❤ WIN great prizes in our exclusive competitions

- ❤ BUY new titles before they hit the shops

- ❤ BROWSE new books and REVIEW your favourites

- ❤ SAVE on new books with the Mills & Boon® Bookclub™

- ❤ DISCOVER new authors

PLUS, to chat about your favourite reads, get the latest news and find special offers:

- 🔵 Find us on facebook.com/millsandboon

- ▶ Follow us on twitter.com/millsandboonuk

- ❤ Sign up to our newsletter at millsandboon.co.uk

The World of Mills & Boon

There's a Mills & Boon® series that's perfect for you. There are ten different series to choose from and new titles every month, so whether you're looking for glamorous seduction, Regency rakes, homespun heroes or sizzling erotica, we'll give you plenty of inspiration for your next read.

By Request

Relive the romance with the best of the best
12 stories every month

Cherish™

Experience the ultimate rush of falling in love.
12 new stories every month

INTRIGUE...

A seductive combination of danger and desire...
7 new stories every month

Desire™

Passionate and dramatic love stories
6 new stories every month

nocturne™

An exhilarating underworld of dark desires
3 new stories every month

For exclusive member offers go to
millsandboon.co.uk/subscribe

Which series will you try next?

Awaken the romance
of the past...
6 new stories every month

The ultimate in romantic
medical drama
6 new stories every month

MODERN™

Power, passion and
irresistible temptation
8 new stories every month

MODERN tempted™

True love and temptation!
4 new stories every month